expel

Celestra Series
Book 6

ADDISON MOORE

EXPEL © 2012 ADDISON MOORE

Edited by: Sarah Freese
Cover Design by: Gaffey Media
Interior design and formatting by: Gaffey Media

Copyright © 2012 by Addison Moore
http://addisonmoorewrites.blogspot.com/

This novel is a work of fiction. Any resemblance to peoples either living or deceased is purely coincidental. Names, places, and characters are figments of the author's imagination. The author holds all rights to this work. It is illegal to reproduce this novel without written expressed consent from the author herself.

All Rights Reserved.

Books by Addison Moore:

New Adult Romance

Celestra Forever After (Celestra Forever After 1)
The Dragon and the Rose (Celestra Forever After 2)
The Serpentine Butterfly (Celestra Forever After 3)
Perfect Love (A Celestra Novella)

Someone to Love (Someone to Love 1)
Someone Like You (Someone to Love 2)
Someone For Me (Someone to Love 3)

3:AM Kisses (3:AM Kisses 1)
Winter Kisses (3:AM Kisses 2)
Sugar Kisses (3:AM Kisses 3)
Whiskey Kisses (3:AM Kisses 4)
Rock Candy Kisses (3:AM Kisses 5)
Velvet Kisses (3:AM Kisses 6)
Wild Kisses (3:AM Kisses 7)

Beautiful Oblivion (Beautiful Oblivion 1)
Beautiful Illusions (Beautiful Oblivion 2)
Beautiful Elixir (Beautiful Oblivion 3)
Beautiful Submission (2016)

The Solitude of Passion

Burning Through Gravity (Burning Through Gravity 1)
A Thousand Starry Nights (Burning Through Gravity 2)
Fire in an Amber Sky (Burning Through Gravity 3)

Young Adult Romance

Ethereal (Celestra Series Book 1)
Tremble (Celestra Series Book 2)
Burn (Celestra Series Book 3)
Wicked (Celestra Series Book 4)
Vex (Celestra Series Book 5)
Expel (Celestra Series Book 6)
Toxic Part One (Celestra Series Book 7)
Toxic Part Two (Celestra Series Book 8)
Elysian (Celestra Series Book 9)

Ethereal Knights (Celestra Knights)
Season of the Witch (Celestra~Ezrina's Story)

Ephemeral (The Countenance Trilogy 1)
Evanescent (The Countenance Trilogy 2)
Entropy (The Countenance Trilogy 3)

Melt With You (A Totally 80's Romance)

Preface

Suffering is the nature of this world. It is the golden standard by which all things are measured. It is not happiness that sets the bar, but agony. Even happiness cannot be fully recognized without the right measure of misery to contrast its borders. Suffering magnifies hunger—exhaustion—prods you to move when prosperity is just a dream out of reach. It is the mortal twin of eternal hope. How you respond to its touch molds you, shapes your future as it rains down oppression like fire over your shoulders.

Deception. It laid over my world like a bruise, covered it so completely I bought the lie that the shadow offered and found comfort nestled in its thorny arms. I walked the trail it dusted with breadcrumbs, walked into the slip noose it had skillfully wove and dove off the cliff without realizing—willingly, with vigor.

Heartbreak. There is no bigger void, no darker shade of soot—no ache more
    unstoppable than that of a broken heart.

A heart in pieces can very much kill you—without love's healing touch, you will
    surely die.
    They say time heals all wounds.
    They lied.

1

Death Throes

Rain falls like tears from heaven over the dirt lot behind the bowling alley.

Logan lies to my right with his eyes wide open, gaping up at the sky pouring down its wrath like it didn't even matter—Gage to my left with a blood-soaked shirt, same dead stare, no affect, no response. I crawl up on my knees and pull both their hands into my chest. I can't lose Logan and Gage—it's unimaginable—unacceptable. I look back down at the pink wash on my arms. Blood—my Celestra blood.

"Oh, God." I pat the ground for an errant piece of glass. Without hesitating I pick up a shard, give one clean slice clear up to my elbow and run the crimson seam along Gage's perfect lips. Before I can offer my lifeblood to Logan a voice calls from the outline of darkness, just shy of the forest.

"Skyla!"

I look back and see a familiar frame, the glint of blonde hair. It's Logan.

"Help me," I plead.

He speeds over and falls on his knees beside me.

"Skyla, you have to come with me," there's an urgency in Logan's voice I haven't heard before. He's wearing the same clothes from tonight. This is where he came while I was at the dance. He knew.

A series of screams erupt as the bowling alley begins to drain. Cries of, *oh my God* and *call 911* fill the field.

Logan yanks me up. I falter on my feet as he pulls me into the forest.

"Let go!" I try to head back, but he cages me in with his arms. "*Nev!*" I cry out for Nevermore.

"You have to trust me, Skyla. Everything depends on this moment."

"I can't leave! You're both dying."

"Death does come," Logan anchors me with a dark expression. "You'll be signing both our death certificates if you don't come now—you might be anyway."

"Just do it!" A female voice bleats out from behind. I catch a glimpse of her—it's like looking in a mirror—it's me.

"I have to help him. He's going to die." I look back at Gage lying in the mud—blood pooling around his body, glossy as tar.

"He does die," she shouts.

The ground trembles. An army of overgrown wolves with tails as long as leashes race into the dirt lot at bionic speeds. Green eyes that glow like lanterns light up the field. They awaken the forest with their menacing growls.

A series of unearthly screams erupt as the crowd from the bowling alley disperses.

"What's happening?" I trip over a branch, backing away from the scene. "Nev!" I cry out for Nevermore again, but he doesn't come.

Sirens cut through in the distance.

"We need to go." Logan hooks me in tight by the waist. "We need to leave right now." He grabs a hold of the girl behind him.

"We can't change anything in the past," I roar the words into his face, struggling to break free.

"Skyla," Logan pulls his lips along my neck—lines a fire of passion with his hot breath up to my ear, "we're not going to the past."

I look over at the carnage as a group of wild beasts circle the two of them. A growling lone wolf pounces onto Gage, causing blood to spurt out of his mouth three feet high.

"*Gage*," I scream, as the world begins to fade.

"Gage is staring death in the face, Skyla," Logan whispers. "And in a moment—you will, too."

🦋 🦋 🦋

There is no greater hope than that of life and life unstoppable. It is death, in all of its inordinate timing that afflicts our world, turns it into a ticking bomb ready to rock our existence whenever it feels the need. It shatters through me. All of my bones reduce to broken shards, cut me from the inside as we sail through the watery depths of time.

I have never moved forward, never seen what the twisted hands of fate have waiting for me outside the visions Marshall has imparted, the few I've had of my own, vague as they were. This is a venue I've yet to experience. Although my pedigree allows for such maneuvers, it would be impossible for me to partake without the supervising spirit Logan procured. His wanderlust, his self-proclaimed ideology of our love projected him into the future to do God knows what. Whatever it is, whatever waits for me on the other side of this curtain of darkness, I'm not sure I'm ready to see it, face it, accept it as gospel.

When traveling to the past you can rest assured you will always find a concrete truth, some stamp of reality that you can depend on, recognize. But it's the comfort of knowing our lives have long since moved on that you can wrap around, secure as a blanket. You may not like where you've landed, but you have the assurance you've made it past the event because that juncture in time has already seen and dismissed you. Even if the residue of your actions color your present, you need not fear where you've already been.

We race through a tunnel of darkness. Strong oppressive winds howl over us. A pinhole of light emerges in the distance as we speed towards its illumination, pulling us into its safe haven like gliding along a polished stone.

"Skyla," Logan breathes directly into my ear, wraps his arms around me like a very tight coil. "I love you."

I nod into him. Touch my palm to his beautiful face and try to break a smile, fighting tears that want to destroy the moment.

I don't know why I came, what good I could possibly do, while both he and Gage lie in the mud back at the bowling alley, exasperating themselves as they cling to life. That's where I need to be. Coming here was a misstep, the highest form of neglect, and now there is no undoing it.

"I need to get back," I lament.

He shakes his head, presses out a smile that blooms from grief.

"Tell her what to do!" The old me rattles Logan by the shirt in a panic.

"She'll know," Logan doesn't take his eyes off me.

His features soften, nothing but his love for me radiating from within. He touches the side of my face soft as feathers, brushes back my hair as the light expands around us, bright as sunshine, if you were standing on the surface of that great and resolute star.

His smile grows, his eyes tell me he's always loved me, always will. He leans in and grazes his lips over mine. Logan is alive under the guise of our love. It pulsates through his veins buoyant and hopeful.

He delivers a kiss that spans the markers of time, sends a pleasure filled quiver through me that annunciates the fact my feelings for him live, that my affection for him trembles inside me like a coward, afraid to own it, touch it, feel it.

A light so terribly brilliant envelops the three of us, dissolves us in its silent blaze. My eyes begin to adjust to the surroundings as I squint my way into this new reality. There's something vaguely familiar about the bleached floors, the glossy white walls, the patina of blue that drapes the vicinity.

"Skyla," Logan's voice is forced, tunnel-like with the distinct tail end of an echo.

I turn to find him ashen, vaporizing.

"Logan!" I snatch at his arms, swat at his person—swipe right through him as though he were less than air.

"What's happening?"

"Skyla," he points up behind me. "I love you." His voice trails in a whisper—his body evaporates into an anemic blue fog.

"Logan?" I spin around in a panic.

A wall of glass tubes fills the expanse—bodies suspended in a sterile blue liquid stretch out for miles. I recognize this place fully—the Transfer.

"Where are we?" The old me asks, her voice giving away the fact she's visibly shaken.

I don't answer—don't move, forget to exhale. I just stare up at the all too familiar face of a beautiful boy floating in his deathly slumber.

It's my sweet friend, my love—Logan.

2

Unimaginable Sorrow

In all honesty, I thought the primal scream that ejaculated from my vocal cords had the capability to shatter every glass coffin in the facility. In all honesty, I was trying to wake myself from this horrible nightmare, and I couldn't even do that to the doppelganger with me, who actually is, physically someplace sleeping.

I fall to my knees and take him in. Logan—my Logan, slumbering in his watery grave. I press my hand against the cool of the glass, feel the sting against my flesh. If only the glass, the keeping solution, were the only barriers that separated Logan and me, but I know the chasm runs deeper, that it's far more complex than any physical barrier.

So this is why Logan brought me down here, why he swept me away to the future, to pull him out of the Transfer, arrange a resurrection, land him on the planet one more time.

"You have to help him." Sleeping Skyla kneels beside me, rubs my shoulder as I press my face into my palms and sob for the boy I love. Everything in me aches to have him back, to speak to him as I explode with grief on a cellular level. Such an unending sorrow—and for what? His mortality nothing more than a casualty of Marshall's quick-handed punishment. And, *God*—what about Gage?

"What happened to Gage?" I snap at the startled version of myself.

"Who's Gage?" She looks genuinely perplexed.

I jump to my feet and take Logan in. Locked in a wet suit, his body entombed in the thick cobalt liquid.

"The other boy with dark hair. He was lying on the ground." I take a breath, looking across at myself. It makes me dizzy. My head fills with a strange sensation as though I have the power to knock myself out just by speaking with my twin from another dimension. "I thought you said he was dead?" I rattle her by the shoulders. "But you meant Logan," I whisper. "Dear God what if Gage is, too?"

She looks around the floor for a body.

"Not here," I squeeze my eyes shut with frustration, "back in the lot." A part of me wants to slap her a few good times—set her straight on everything she'll ever need to know, but Logan was right, I never remember my freaking dreams.

"I didn't see him." She cowers as if I were about to unleash a combative strike. "Logan's gone," her voice breaks. She leans into him, lays her face into the glass as silent tears roll down her cheek.

"Oh my, God, you love him," I whisper.

Of course, I love him. I felt such a strong connection with Logan when we first met, and now I know why. All those indescribable yearnings defused my feelings for Gage by default. It makes perfect sense. Logan is a minefield of deception. It's like he orchestrated our meeting from the beginning. But I could never really blame him when I feel so strongly in return. There are no accidents in my life, no coincidences, no blind love at first sight. Logan has been haunting my dreams, chiseling out neuro pathways into my brain by way of his extraterrestrial beauty long before I set foot on Paragon.

"I'll always love him." Her fingers strum over the tube creating a haunting rhythm. "I'm going to be with him forever."

"You're going to be with Gage," I correct. No sense in stringing along delusions.

"No, I'm not." Her eyes spring wide with defiance. "I'm not going to be with this *Gage* person. I'm going to be with Logan. I'm going to be Mrs. Logan Oliver," she knifes the words through the air to prove her point.

All that attitude—the posturing, the I'll-cut-you velocity in which she determines her speech, I remind myself a lot of Mia.

"He's been brainwashing you," I say lackluster because I know its not true. I know she believes it with all her heart because deep inside I do, too. "You'll love Gage, not straight away, but he's amazing." I wipe the tears off my face, taste the salty brine reserved just for Logan. "Come on," I take her by the hand and speed us towards the exit.

"So, like, are we stuck here?"

Shit! I hadn't even considered that horrific scenario.

"I don't know." I look around in hopes of spotting an ever-evaporating Logan—even in his partially dissolved state I'd take him, breathe him in, swallow him down just to have him with me. "Marshall?" I listen to my voice echo through the chamber in triplicate, with no answer. "Who's Logan's supervising spirit?" I cut into her with an unmerciful stare. She's my only hope in figuring out who or what that might be, and, unfortunately, I'm pretty sure she's clueless.

"The invisible one?"

"Yes, the invisible one." Hope rips through me like a flare. I pause, taking her in with her wild tangle of hair, her slightly sunburned skin, freckled from hours logged at the beach. We had a heat wave one January, an unseasonable roast. I remember that year. Dad drove us to the ocean every night to watch the colorful sunsets. God's art, he called it. He was right. I saw those bold, red, L.A. night skies behind my lids for years after he died. I clung to those fiery spectacles, those memories of the four of us huddled together in the sand as if they were the last bits of my father I would ever have. Savored them, drank them down like a divine elixir. Until, of course, I figured out how to go back and visit him.

"I don't know who it is," she pants, struggling to keep up with me. "Logan says it's not important for me to know. He says it just helps us get places, like a car."

expel

I give a wry smile. Sounds like Logan's analogy.

I wonder if sleeping Skyla knows *she* in fact was the transportation station, not the supervising spirit. The only thing the supervising spirit was capable of was launching them into the abysmal future with the apparent inability to bring us back—very not funny Logan.

"How are we going to get out of here?" Her face grows haggard with worry.

"*You* are going to wake up"—I pick up my pace and speed out into the elongated corridors of the Transfer—"and I'm going to find Ezrina."

Sleeping Skyla bobs along, continues to pepper me with annoying questions about the future, all of which I artfully avoid as I bolt down the expansive corridors of the Transfer, shouting, Ezrina and Marshall, in turn, like some demented vocal exercise.

"Who are these people? Will they save Logan?"

"One of them killed Logan." I want to add, and the other will almost kill you, but don't.

A rush of adrenaline surges through me just thinking of how violently Logan and Gage were mowed down, by of all things, the Mustang. And what about Gage? I stop abruptly, clamp my hand over my mouth paralyzed by the thought of poor sweet Gage lying in a casket.

A murky figure materializes down the hall. I recognize that permanent mischievous grin, those cuttingly handsome features that could rescue him from almost any situation, this, of course, being the exception.

"There's the devil," I say, racing towards Marshall. I know for a fact he said recompense was due to Logan, that the one who pierced his side with the spirit sword was due for a severe method of payback. Of course he's capable of killing Logan. He had me kill Kate by decapitating her with my ski. Conveniently, of course, everything looks like a freaking accident—an unfortunate act, seemingly doled out by someone else.

Just as I'm about to knock into him full force, an errant thought floats through my mind as I envision another possibility—Chloe driving the Mustang, white gloves cradling the steering wheel, escaping on her knees into the forest like the coward she is.

I don't let the bout of insanity interfere with the pressing need to strangle Marshall. Even if Chloe did run them over, Marshall had his hand in it. I'd bet my life on the fact he orchestrated the entire event—applauded as it all went down.

I give a forceful shove into his chest and send him flying back a good ten feet, staggering to regain his balance.

"Do you see this?" He addresses the old me from over my shoulder. "You, my love, will pursue me with a desolate passion that can only be satisfied with a kiss from these lips." He strides over and caresses her cheek.

Her face ignites in a silent plea for him to extend his touch—rife with disappointment when he releases.

"Don't you have school tomorrow?" I ask her, annoyed. "Do me a favor, wake up and take a deep lungful of that L.A. smog. You don't belong here." I give her a hard look hoping she'll evaporate back into her dreams.

"Skyla," Marshall reprimands. "There is a guest in our midst, and yet you treat her with such disrespect." He shakes his head, mockingly.

"You did this!" I push him hard. "You killed Logan!" It comes out childish, intermingled with tears.

"Do refrain from battery. I disdain being assaulted as much as I do having a minor organ slivered with a blade."

"So you're threatening me now?" I stab him in the chest with my finger. "I don't need you, Marshall. You are nothing but a murderer, a lowlife who kills people and laughs over their grave because you are incapable of giving a damn!"

"Watch your language," he seethes. "I am not in the mood." He gives a sharp look. "Ask the question burgeoning on your tongue. Let's move this conversation into the past along with the Pretty Oliver and his desire to procure you for himself."

A startled laugh rattles through my chest. "Why? So you can threaten me? So you can tell me you'll bring Logan back under one circumstance? Let me guess, the magic porthole to that resurrection miracle lies directly in my pants." I turn to the bewildered version of myself. "That's right, memorize his face. He steals your freedom," I roar. "He pins you against the wall and laughs when you need him most."

"Skyla," Marshall's voice spikes with shock.

"It's true," I yell into him. "I hate you for using me to kill Kate, and I hate you for killing Logan!"

"And Jock Strap? Dare you inquire about his fate?"

"Gage," I breathe his name in less than a whisper.

"What if I told you I've done away with them both? Spared you the trouble of having to choose, whittled down your options to one."

"As in the one standing before me?" A fire brews in me. He killed Logan, and he killed Gage. Holy freaking shit. Marshall is a madman. I've been duped and now they're both dead.

I close my eyes as the building sways beneath my feet. The world gyrates in time with my pulsating anger.

I hawk back a generous reserve of phlegm and cover Marshall's face with the bubbling brew.

He recoils, lets out a series of gurgling groans as he wipes himself clean with the back of his arm.

"Enough," he barks. "You have sealed your fate, Ms. Messenger. Mark my words, you will rue this day, lament it in tears. You will come to me on your knees sobbing, begging for forgiveness. But I will tell you now and I will tell you then, you are on your own, Skyla. What becomes of this mess is upon your shoulders." He spins on his heels and strides down the hall at a decent clip. He lets out a powerful roar before disappearing into a ball of fire.

A spear of terror barrels through me. I have a feeling I've just opened a Pandora's box of nightmares and I'm about to witness every vile thing fly into my life.

All unholy hell is about to unleash, and I'm sure Marshall will be quite surprised to see that I'm going to do my best to lob it all in his direction.

Although, I have the very distinct feeling it'll come back to me twice as hard.

It always does.

3

Appeal

"You really pissed him off good." This younger, simpler version of myself bounces on her feet like it's a good thing.

"Yeah, well, I don't need you reminding me." I blow out a breath. "Ezrina?"

"Who's this Ezrina chick?" she asks, examining a fistful of her long spiral curls for split ends.

"She hacks off your arm in a couple of years. She's not that bad, though," I shrug before unleashing another powerhouse blood curdling cry that rattles the Transfer like a skeleton.

"You scared the crap out of me!" The old me seizes in panic and begins to evaporate.

"No, wait, don't leave!" I try grabbing a hold of her, but my fingers flex right through. I don't care if she is annoying. I'd rather be here with my annoying self than suffer through the Transfer alone. Besides, it's not like she was going to remember any of this psychotic dream in the morning.

She evaporates completely, leaving a wall of crushing silence in her wake.

I wish it were a dream, but I know better. This disaster is concretely embedded in my life and the departed life of my dear friend Logan—I can't even stomach the thought of Gage not being here.

A wild shag of flaming hair appears before me so close I can smell the scent of something burning, a foul odor layered just beneath the smoke.

"Ezrina!" I grip her by the shoulders. A jolt sizzles through me, alive and vibrant, like the shock from an electric fence. It knocks me backwards a good couple feet, and I hold myself from the horror of her touch. Good grief, not only did the Justice Alliance disfigure her beauty, they turned her into a livewire, literally. And all because of the love she had for her people. At least that's Nevermore's version. My mother, the judge, might have a very different tale to tell.

"Ezrina, you have to help me. Logan, he's in the tube—I need him back. I...I love him." Maybe if I paint us as star-crossed lovers, maybe then she'll sympathize and give him back to me, untouched, unharmed by Marshall and his assault with a deadly weapon. Besides, I do love Logan. Here, in this cavernous den of insanity, it seems safe to confess that to myself.

Her lips pull into a line, comely as a blood let. Her eyes light up like fire.

"I need him," I pant. I can see she's beginning to cave, considering if only for a moment to do this very unlikely deed for me. "I'll do anything to have him back. I'll work for you. I'll hack through dozens of bodies, prep a thousand corpses for those watery graves," then an idea comes. "I'll reunite you with Nev."

Her entire person flickers with hope before she sags into her hellbent fury and growls into me.

She stalks off down the hall in the direction of the body farm without so much as a response.

"I beg of you," I get down on my knees and waddle forward in an effort to keep pace. "I'll sacrifice anything. Name your price. I swear I'll do it. I have to have him. I can't live without Logan." I mean every word as it wails from my lungs.

"Anything," she purrs, pausing just shy of the colossal room housing a bevy of Count corpses. "Live in my body, carry out my punishment," it speeds out of her an unearthly echo like she's rehearsed it, dreamed it a thousand times.

Crap. That is so not what I meant by anything.

When I teased Gage a few weeks back about falling in love with Ezrina, never in a million years did I even remotely think it would be a possibility.

"You are fallacy's child," she turns on her heels, disappearing into the blue room.

I jump to my feet and rush to her side. I've already given Marshall the big F.U. I can't lose Ezrina.

The air is warm, unnaturally thick. It's downright tropical in here with its sky blue reflection. It reminds me of Gage and the beautiful way I feel when he looks at me with those eyes kissed by God.

"Don't placate me with stale promises, Skyla," she gravels. "You can never give me the freedom I truly desire."

"Freedom?" It rattles out of me. "I'll give you freedom, I swear it."

"Swear?" She picks up a clipboard and looks it over with a mild amusement on my part.

"My mother—she can do this. She's on the Justice Alliance and the Decision Council and who the hell knows what other committees she's affiliated with," I spasm into her. "I'm going to win the faction war, and I'll preside over the councils. I'll veto every lousy decision while it's still a gleam in their uninformed eyes. And, believe me when I say, I'm going to right all of the fucking wrongs." My father's memory flashes through me like a hot, searing wind.

She studies me with great intensity before getting back to the frazzled hieroglyphics scrawled out on the chart in front of her.

"You have no power," she says it low, just above a whisper. "Desire without authority is futile."

"You can't just leave him in there to rot," I slap my hand over the clipboard. I will destroy every psychotic effort she's undertaken in the name of science if she doesn't comply.

"It's entirely up to the Counts. He's one of their own, of which you are not."

"No, they won't rescue him. Please, I need him now, today, whatever the hell day that is. I beg of you, Ezrina," I collapse at her feet. "Do this for me. I will give you what you desire. I promise." It departs from me desolate as a last desperate plea.

"A promise means an entirely different thing to those of us who are no longer human."

"I am so aware," I nod feverishly. "It's a covenant," I'm quick to relay Marshall's words. "I'll be entering into a covenant with you. Name your price." A lone tear jerks down the side of my face.

Her bloodshot eyes look up at the oppressive expanse of the ceiling. Ezrina has been trapped in the Transfer for hundreds of years. I know what she's about to ask, she'd be insane not to.

"Your mother," she gives a long blink as though just uttering those words disturbed her. "Arrange another hearing," she spears me with her disdain. "I want Heathcliff present."

"Heathcliff? Is he the guy with the eye patch?" Oh, wait, that was Rothello. Um, one of Marshall's lookalikes? "Oh!" It comes to me. "Nevermore?" I take in a breath. "Heathcliff," I touch my lips when I say it. "He'll be there." I nod. "You'll get your meeting with Nev—Heathcliff by your side."

"Supreme," she wrings her hands together as though this were a maniacal maneuver on her behalf. She speeds me over to the tank that holds beautiful Logan's body. It takes my breath away just being near him.

"It's going to be OK," I say it directly to him as though he could hear. "And, Ezrina?" I stand back and watch as she twists a nozzle at the base of the tube and the liquid begins to mysteriously drain.

"Speak." She doesn't look up while waiting for the fluid to fully dissipate.

"If, by the off chance, I can't get my mother to agree to another trial," I start.

"We swap bodies," she says it matter of fact, tips the glass tube on its side and slips Logan out onto a gurney before wheeling him towards the next room.

"I never agreed to that," I pant, keeping pace.

"Then your lover doesn't live, does he, Skyla?" She stops midflight, pins me with all of her evil, awaiting my approval.

My lover. I bathe in the words as though they were true, as though they could be and I wanted them to be in every single way.

I cut her a look, cold as a corpse in the mortuary.

"He lives, Ezrina. I'll move heaven and earth to get you that trial."

Her lips curl into an unnatural smile. She gazes down at Logan, his skin tinted grayish blue, his lips black with death.

"The honor is yours," she instructs.

"Kiss him?" This is fast becoming a warped fairytale.

"Breathe, Skyla. Give breath to the one you love."

I graze his face with my fingertips, cold and slippery, lips like rubber.

"Logan." I lean over, place my mouth gently over his, pinch off his nose and dive in with a lungful of all my love.

I've just made a deal with Ezrina, and I have no idea if I can keep it. But all that matters is that I have Logan back. He'll be with me again if only for a while.

I give another hard push into his lungs before I'm enraptured with his touch and give way to a desperate kiss.

I need him to win the faction war—hell, I need Logan for far more personal reasons. I hope he appreciates his newfound lease on life. The price may have cost me everything.

I think I may have just sold my soul to Ezrina.

I'm pretty sure I did—but I'm damn sure Logan was worth it.

4

Time After Time

Ezrina instructs me to race out of the Transfer towards the cliff adjacent to the haunted mansion that Marshall held me in during my quasi capture last month. Her instructions sounded perfectly sane and acceptable when she spouted them off while wheeling Logan into the chop shop. *Run at top speed into the base of the cliff*—she insisted that was the portal back into my world. Funny thing is, *my world* is a pretty broad definition of where I might land. Technically I could end up in China or the Netherlands. Two completely different and wonderful places, I'm sure, but miles away from where I belong. And, *hello*? What the hell kind of lunacy is it to run into a granite wall? Since when does charging into a solid surface ever sound like a good idea?

The dark shingled roof of the mansion glints under a pale limestone moon as I pick up speed. A cluster of freaky looking dead people in eighteen-century attire roam the streets with their eerie cackles, their strange buzzing speech. I try to ignore the fact they've amassed along the roadside as I parade my insanity. Instead, I center my focus on the ever-expanding cliff, and accelerate.

It draws near with its dark wingspan, wide as the ocean.

Crap!

This is so going to hurt really, really bad if it doesn't work.

A wild thought darts through me—what if this is all some ingenious way to kill me? What if Ezrina's resurrection efforts include yours truly, and she jumps into my broken bag of bones as her take-two entrance into the world?

God—I'm going to knock myself out and wake up as Ezrina. Or worse—never wake up again.

"Oh shit, oh shit, oh shit!" It bumps out of me. It's coming. The wall of granite swoops in like a buzzard in flight. It's going to take me down, initiate me into the afterlife, and forever I'll be forced to tell people I died by way of self-inflicted stupidity.

I let out a ferocious scream as I barrel towards destiny—connect with the God-breathed rock—and push right through it. An intense vibration—that tuning fork feeling comes over me, envelops me like a mist. My muscles struggle to move, my legs retard in their effort to run. It's futile, like trying to move underwater, slow and lethargic.

A burst of light emerges. I fly forward with the charge of gravity laying over me, heavy as lead, and do a faceplant into a nest of pea gravel.

I land on a murky shore with fog so thick the only sign of the ocean is the salty spray prickling over me. I get up and trip over a branch, try to gain my bearings as I maneuver over rocks and land face down on a bed of jagged stones. A sharp sting initiates over the side of my cheek as I pant and gasp, take in the familiar scents and sounds around me.

Paragon.

I rake the pads of my fingers soft along my jaw and glance down at the crimson stain. The sound of waves speeding in my direction catches my attention. I look up in time to see a wall of water baptize me with its glory, refresh me from my stint in the Transfer. I wish it could wash away the memory of Logan in that tube, the thought of Gage in a grave.

I look up to see a cliff side I've long since come to memorize. The impossible winding road to the top—the cypress trees that dot the path with their bare roots dangling exposed, holding on just to survive, it all feels like home. I know how those suspended roots feel. Without Logan and Gage I'm on a precipice. I can't do this life without them.

"Devil's Peak," I pant, saturated from my impromptu bath in the Pacific.

I struggle to my feet and begin the slow meandering plod uphill.

"I'm going to see Gage," I murmur as I crest the top and land in the barren parking lot.

Perfect. The one time I happen to need a ride there's not a soul around. This place is usually littered with at least a handful of people from East and West High. And for sure I would have broken my personal rule of never asking anyone from East for anything since they're assholes in general. But assholes aside, I'm broken and desperate, and I need to find Gage.

The sky morphs into one long shadow. The cool evening air gives rise as the ground clouds start rolling in from the sea.

God, what if I've landed myself so far into the future—everyone I know has long since died? That's so terrible I can't even stand to think about it. I should never have told Marshall off. Already I'm feeling the urge to beg his forgiveness—crawl all the way to his horse ranch and offer to lick the stables clean if he'll forget I ever evicted my spit in his eye.

A truck races down the highway, and I raise an arm in an effort to garner its attention. I trip over a rock and land hard on my right palm, flattening a plant in the process. A horrific pain rips through my arm, my fingers spasm and burn like I've just stoked a fire with my bare hand.

I let out a scream that glorifies the abilities of vocal cords everywhere.

I scream for Logan and for Gage in one long frustrated howl to somehow clue the universe in on the fact that I've finally had enough of the torment, enough of the pain both emotional and physical.

A monster truck zooms towards me at full throttle, stopping in haste just shy of my knees, which surprises me because I fully expected it to run me over. That's because I fully expect Marshall to turn me into road kill sooner than later. So, I'm rather pleasantly surprised when a red-faced Ellis Harrison appears beside me, that is until he begins unzipping his pants.

"Relax, I know how to treat Stinging Nettle," he shouts.

Then it hits me—what he's about to do, and it's like we're in synch, Ellis and I.

He stares down at my stretched taut skin, my purple bloated fingers and gasps.

"Shit! Hold still," he commands.

Instinctively I hold out my swollen hand and look away just as the flesh is exposed from under his boxers. I feel the warm liquid spear over my hand and actually begin to quell the pain before another bout of prickling torture runs up through my arm.

"Get in, I'll take you to the hospital." Dr. Ellis zips up his jeans after relieving himself on my person.

He helps me into his truck by way of a not so graceful push that lands me headfirst into the driver's seat. I pop back up and he buckles me in like a perfect gentleman as if he didn't just piss all over the hand I rely on to do just about everything. I catch a glimpse of myself in the reflection—bloodied face, hair frizzed out like Ezrina.

Perfect. I'm morphing already.

"Where the hell have you been?" He looks me over wild-eyed as he fishtails out of the parking lot.

"I'm happy to see you, too," I'm quick to reply. "You ever piss on me again, you're a dead man." I punctuate the threat with a wince as unreal pain shoots up my bloated flesh. "Where's Gage?" I cry out the words knowing full well they're embedded in a pain all their own.

Gage's perfect face imprints itself before me like a silent etch, a tattoo on the lens of my eyes that I could never get rid of, wouldn't want to if I were able.

"You don't know?" His brows form a sharp V.

"Tell me he's alive," I blink back tears in rapid succession.

"You've been gone for two effing weeks, Messenger. Logan's at some clinic his uncle shipped him off to, and Gage—" he pauses, squinting into the side of the road.

"Where's Gage," I breathe it out inaudible. Logan I could save, he was a Count, a Celestra before that, but Gage—he's a Levatio as susceptible to mortality as any full-blooded human.

The road elongates in front of us like a dark spool of ribbon that chases an invisible horizon. The black evergreens of Paragon anchor themselves into the side of the road, taunt me with their spear-like branches, they already know what's become of my love. I cut them a hard look. I'm so sick of the island and all of its secrets. It can all go to hell.

"Tell me, Ellis."

"I'll let you see for yourself."

5

True Love's Kiss

Paragon Hospital sits like a game piece erecting itself like an awkward protrusion against the dense woods. The shadowed pines encompass it like a garrison—wrap its arms around the infirmary, thick as a cloak. A listless night grounds itself in reality as the crickets saw through silence with their grating, monotonous song.

"So, I was thinking," Ellis switches off the radio and picks up my good hand. The sky blushes a severe shade of purple as a glimmer of stars bloom their illuminations from behind the foggy curtain. "Since Logan is in traction somewhere and Gage has temporarily, or well, let's face it, permanently left the building, I think this might not be a bad time to give you and me a shot." He nods into his ludicrous epiphany before dive-bombing my left hand with his lips.

"What do you mean left the building?" Before I can escalate over the alarming possibilities, Ellis's truck picks up speed and careens into an overgrown fountain. It knocks the top tier off its base and sends it crashing into the hood.

He flattens his palm against my chest as a protective measure. "You OK?" *Short stop technique in full effect.*

I pry his fingers off my boobs. "I heard that," I give him a dirty look before opening the door and landing with a soft thud into a foot of ice water.

The hospital glows against the night sky like a glittering queen as if her beauty held healing properties all its own.

I wade my way out of the fountain.

I'm going to see Gage.

At last.

expel

It takes forever to convince a girl about Mia's age to look him up in the database and tell me he's on the fifth floor, room 502.

I say the number over and over to myself like a hymn as I ride the elevator.

I'm going to see Gage, be with him—touch him.

The walls recede behind the glass as the floor pushes up with a soft whoosh. My thoughts revert back to Logan. Ezrina forbid me to stay, said if I witnessed the resurrection procedures it would unnecessarily endanger me. She swore he would arrive alive sooner than later before chasing me out of the Transfer herself.

A soft bell rings, and the doors pull open. I stride out into the long pale hall and read the gilded numbers along the wall. It just so happens that room 502 is directly in front of the nurse's station. Three women gawk at a giant red velvet cake, eager, with forks in hand. Looks like they'll be busy for a while.

I tiptoe inside as quiet as my sopping wet shoes will allow and find a series of sheets dividing up one giant room.

A girl emerges from the far end. She dips into me and squints.

"Skyla?"

"Brielle!" I lunge into her with a deep full-bodied hug. Her hair is different, brassier, blonder. "Where's Gage?"

"He's here." She holds out my hands and examines me in horror. "What the hell happened to you? Were you living in the woods or something? I tried to call, but they found your cell in the forest behind the bowling alley."

"Oh, right," I try to move past her.

"Chloe's back there." She darts a harsh look. "She's been here for him every single day since he was hit. How could you?"

"What?" I don't know whether to shake her or bolt. "I didn't do it, I swear. I'd never in a million years hurt Logan or Gage." Well maybe at one time Logan, but all that's different now.

"The cops are looking for you." Her eyes bug out in appreciation of my newly declared fugitive status. "You sure you don't want to go to Canada, change your name or something?"

"No," I step past her and note the unmistakable bulge in her shirt. I almost forgot all about the baby Count she's incubating, no thanks to Drake.

"I have to warn you, it's not pretty."

"Oh God," I cry, running down to the end of the depressive room. I slip in through the curtain and find Chloe coiled like a serpent on a small vinyl couch.

"Nurse!" she cries, bolting to her feet.

There he is—my dark prince with his ebony hair, perfect sharp features buried under a tangle of medical devices.

I take a breath and hold it. It's as if the universe skipped a heartbeat, time stood still and let me take him for one heavenly moment.

"Gage," I make my way over to him. An entire network of tubes fill his mouth, his nostrils—a corrugated plastic tube is inserted right through his trachea. A machine that looks like a robot lights up in brilliant reds and yellows each time he breathes, depresses an exhausting sigh as it forces him to exhale. "Oh my, God," I gently lay my lips over his face, feel the heat from his body far too hot to be safe. "He's burning up," I try and cool him with the back of my good hand.

Chloe, who I hadn't even noticed was missing, reappears from behind the curtain with a nurse who looks as if she might double as a linebacker on Sundays.

"The police are on their way," Chloe assures me.

"Ma'am," the nurse beats it out in haste, "I'll have to call security if you don't step away from the patient." Her thick lips are split on the bottom near a fading green bruise. They let me know she's not above getting physical to remove me from the premises.

"Gage," I lean in and whisper into his ear, brush my lips in a tender line along his temple. "Gage, wake up. It's me, Skyla." I push a kiss into the side of his face and linger against the stubble, taste the salt from his skin and just glory in his presence.

Voices begin to rumble outside the curtain—an entire army of footsteps draw near. The nurse yanks at the divider quick and harsh, eliciting a violent scream as she throws back the curtain.

"Skyla!" I look up to see Mom and Tad, Barron and Emma all staring back at me bewildered.

"Gage!" I urge him to open his eyes, but nothing.

"Get that girl away from my son!" Emma shouts as the four of them storm me like a wall of riot police.

"Gage, it's me," I plead. "I love you so much," my voice breaks, "please hear me."

Chloe scoffs at my efforts as she eyes the growing disgruntled crowd of friends and relations with a secret smile.

"Where in the hell have you been?" Tad, my stepfather, booms. He comes up from behind and buckles my arms around my back like a common criminal. *To hell with explanations, let's see her try and sidestep her way out of this one.*

"I swear I wasn't driving the car." I struggle to break free from the arm bar he has me in and stomp on his shoes like I'm trying to kill a spider.

"Let go of her," Mom pushes Tad hard in the shoulder.

"Not on your life!" he crows. "I suppose you'd like to take her home and coddle her, make her some nice hot cocoa, warm her jammies in the dryer, well those days are over, Lizbeth. If there's one thing I'm not doing, it's harboring a fugitive."

"I'm not a fugitive, I swear." I manage to free my arms. "I wasn't driving the car that night. I think Chloe was." It slips out of me so fast I don't have time to process the fact the accused is standing less than ten feet away.

A collective gasp rivals the decibel level on Gage's breathing machine.

All six pair of eyes settle over me with serious looks of disapproval.

"That girl," Tad pokes a finger in her direction, "has held vigil by this poor kid's bedside the entire time you've been out on the lamb. She has displayed nothing but her undying devotion to him. And, if I had to venture which one of you were his girlfriend, I would peg her a thousand times over."

I'd like to peg Chloe a thousand times over—with long rusted nails.

"Skyla," Mom leans in with apprehension as if she's about to talk me off the ledge of a building. "Let Gage be. We need to take you somewhere." The whites of her eyes sparkle like shards.

"No," I shake my head. "I won't leave." I lay my check against his burning flesh, press in another quick kiss and savor the brine of his skin. I would die before I left Gage again.

"He's in a coma, Skyla," Mom tries to coax me away with the soothing tone of her voice. That may have worked when I was three and throwing a fit over a toy in the grocery store, but she could breathe fire and I would maintain my position—burn alive just to be near Gage. "He can't hear you. He doesn't even know you're in the room."

I take in a breath and forget to let go.

Dear God.

"We need to go for a little drive." Tad steers me to the foot of the bed by the shoulders, forcing me to plow my feet as I move along.

A soft groan emits from behind.

"It's Gage!" Brielle screeches.

Gage gives a series of monosyllable moans, and the room erupts in cheers.

"It's you, Skyla," Brielle beams a smile over at me. "It was true love's kiss," she cuts a hard look to Chloe.

The room floods with doctors and nurses fiddling with the nozzles and hoses attached to his body.

"Go to him," Emma yanks me free from Tad's stranglehold and forces me through the tangle of bodies. "Kiss him again, Skyla. Tell him you're home."

And I do.

6

Love Song

I hold Gage by the hand—comb his hair with my fingers, just the two of us alone in the peaceful quiet of his room.

The doctor surmised it was beneficial for Gage to spend time with me, said I was medicine for his ailing soul.

Gage is severely injured, and I am the panacea. I give a dry smile at the horrific beauty of it all.

A large window sits behind him backlit by the stadium lights coming off the parking structure. The precipitation illuminates as it presses its fingers against the window as if the fog itself were checking to see if he were OK.

Skyla. His voice comes through low and resonant in my mind.

"Gage!" I whisper with an aching elation I had never known before. "I'm right here, sweetie. I love you so much. I swear it wasn't me driving," I sniff hard at the prospect of the idea even infiltrating his mind. Who knows what the hell Chloe's been loading his subconscious with the past fourteen days? It's freaking *February* according to the wall calendar.

I know.

"Oh good—you mean the I didn't hit you part, right? Because I was standing right there with you. Of course, you know, I love you."

He gives a slight nod and winces at the effort.

Logan?

"He's," I don't have it in me to tell him the truth—that Logan died and that he's at Ezrina's mercy, "on the mend. He's going to be OK."

He gives my hand a slight squeeze.

And you?

"I'm right here. I won't leave. I promise."

Mom comes back in with a forlorn expression. "Sorry, Skyla." Her russet hair looks a darker shade of crimson than I remember. "I'm afraid the police were notified you're back. They're waiting to talk to you down at the precinct."

"I won't leave." I tighten my grip around his fingers and settle my face next to his.

Go, he encourages. *Come back when you're able. I'm not going anywhere. It'll give me something to look forward to.*

"I'll be with him," Emma peers in and heads on over. She eases me off the side of the bed and replaces my hand with hers.

"I could hear him," I whisper.

Her eyes widen with delight.

"Ride with Barron," she insists before looking up at my mother. "Barron would like to drive Skyla over if you don't mind."

"It's probably best," Mom sweeps her hand out the door, "my husband is spiraling out of control."

I wait until Mom clears the curtain before resting my fingers along the underbelly of his arm.

Tell my Mom I'm getting stronger—that I love her but I need you here with me, too.

I relay the message to an exhausted Emma. She relaxes her arms over me in a full encompassing hug.

I'm so glad you're back, Skyla, she says.

"Thank you—so am I."

🦋 🦋 🦋

I had never been in Dr. Oliver's car before. Sedan, blue, it holds the scent of lemon polish, and the leather seat is slippery as oil. The head of a toy clown dangles from the rearview mirror by a silver thread hooked onto its hat. It's creepy—weird, even.

A light rain peppers us as we drive the dark streets of Paragon. Somehow Ellis has managed to remove his truck from the fountain, probably took off without reporting the incident.

"Skyla, tell me everything from the beginning." Dr. Oliver adjusts himself in the seat as we maneuver out onto the main highway. "You were at the bowling alley," he motions for me to continue.

"We were behind the bowling alley, we were having an argument," God, I hate reliving that night.

"Who was having an argument?" His hair flashes a brilliant pearl color as a streetlight combs over him.

"Gage and Logan, then I stepped in. Logan's been doing some shady stuff on his light drives." I really don't want to get into the fact I had Logan's Celestra powers revoked by way of my otherworldly familial connections which, in turn, caused Logan to retrieve me from my dreams to help him move from one dimension to another. And, I'm not entirely sure if Dr. O is aware of the fact Logan has a supervising spirit on payroll. "So, this car started up and charged us. Logan pushed me out of the way, and he and Gage were struck several times."

"That much I know." He depresses into a frown. "Who was driving?"

"Nobody was driving, at least not from what I can tell. But anyway—I totally think it was Chloe. So, then, as I'm freaking out over the two of them lying on the ground I hear this voice, and it's Logan," I tell him about the old me and the Transfer and how Ezrina said she'd take care of the rest.

"Thank heavens. I had no idea what would become of him after Arson Kragger retrieved his body from the morgue."

"Arson Kragger?" He's the wicked father of the Kragger crew, two of which are no longer with us.

"It's nothing unusual. He picks up Count corpses quite regularly. I've been dealing with him since I started the mortuary. But back to Logan, how are we going to find him?" He looks visibly upset, well, mostly angry in a bizarre relieved sort of way.

"I don't know," I rack my brain for some kind of temporal answer, "but I ended up at the base of Devil's Peak when I came back."

"Devil's Peak," he abruptly pulls to the side of the road and brings the car to a forceful stop. A pair of headlights pull in from behind—I recognize the minivan as belonging to Mom and Tad.

"Thank you, Skyla." He pats my knee. "Thank you for saving my brother and for saving my son."

"I didn't save Gage," I sweep the floor with remorse. He's still unable to open his eyes—move or breathe on his own.

"You woke him. If we can get Logan today, we'll have the three of you back in the span of twenty-four hours. Now that would be a miracle." He offers a repressed smile. "I'm headed to look for Logan. Don't worry about the police. Emma and I won't be pressing charges. I'm sure Gage will give a statement when he's able, should the state decide to proceed."

I open the door and step out into the saline night baptized with fresh mist from the ocean.

"If you find him, please call me."

"Of course." He looks down and his eyes widen with horror. "Good Lord, what happened to your hand?" He leans over and examines it.

"Stinging Nettle."

"I'll be by later to bring you something for that."

"Thank you." I shut the door and hop into the minivan with Mom and Tad.

"What the hell was that about?" Tad erupts as I secure my seatbelt.

"There was some news of Logan, and he needed to tend to it." It's true.

"Judas Priest," Tad throws a hand into the air as he glides back onto the road. "You hear that, Lizbeth? That trauma center they shipped him off to probably phoned to let him know that the poor guy kicked the bucket."

"*Tad.*" Mom spikes in agitation.

"He just dropped your kid off on the side of the road. He practically booted her out of a moving vehicle. Read between the lines, Lizbeth. This is an e-mer-gency." He turns in his seat, momentarily swerving into oncoming traffic. "And you," he pokes a finger in my direction. "Never, ever, leave the scene of a crime. You got that? You don't clip a bunch of people on a night you aren't even supposed to be out of the house and then go off on a two-week vacay with God knows who." He resettles his grip over the wheel before turning to my mother. "She's probably got another boy-toy tucked away someplace she keeps handy for these breaks from reality she's prone to taking."

"Skyla was not on a vacation, and there is no one for her but Gage," Mom defends me with a tone I'm not used to hearing her invoke in Tad's presence—for sure not aimed at him. "Skyla, explain yourself. I want the truth."

Yeah right, the truth. "Um, so, I was stuck in some whitewashed prison with a witch, and I couldn't get out for two weeks." Almost the truth, nevertheless it was all I could come up with since I'm emotionally spent.

"See that?" Tad slashes the air with his hand. "Fairytales. Witches and warlocks, ooh, I'm scared," he wiggles his fingers. "Is it working on you yet, Lizbeth? Have you crapped your pants with worry? Because she sure spins a good yarn, I'll give her that." He pounds the dash to annunciate his point.

Mom sags into her seat as we pull into the station.

I'm betting there's a certain detective Edinger just waiting to interrogate me.

The only one crapping her pants around here is me.

expel

"Skyla," Demetri Edinger, the Fem who killed my father gives a sideways smile that looks evil in every way. "So nice to see you're safe." He pulls his lips further into an unconvincing smile. "I hear you have a tendency to run away, but I want to assure you that there is nothing to be afraid of."

"I'm not afraid," I openly glare at him. "I'll never fear you, Demetri."

"Skyla *Laurel* Messenger," Mom's eyes bulge the size of eggs.

When the time comes to name my children I'll have to remember that the middle name is only to be invoked as a curse—a moniker-inspired expletive, if you will. I'll be sure to search high and low for a power name with maximum I'm-so-pissed-off-at-you-right-now impact. For sure nothing pansy like Laurel. The soft syllables alone betray the injustice in Mom's tone. I never take that name seriously. It sounds like a song, makes me want to play with unicorns and bake cupcakes.

"Forgive her, detective. She has no regard for authority whatsoever," Tad is quick to kiss the ass of the man who's trying to steal his wife. "She's a loose cannon. Odd things fly out of her mouth without warning. It's an aftereffect from the recreational pharmaceuticals she dabbles in from time to time." He says it with authority as if there were medical evidence to support his theory.

The only thing that could possibly be an aftereffect of recreational pharmaceuticals is my mother's marriage to him. That would explain everything. One day Mom is going to sober up and start using again from the sheer horror of what she's managed to legally chain herself to.

Demetri leads us to a back room. He sits before me like a shadowed wall and asks an endless list of questions which

I answer to the best of my ability without ever actually eluding to the truth. Sometimes you have to tell people what you want them to believe and nothing more. I'm sure the word lying would fit nicely in there somewhere, but I'm more interested in making my way back to Gage sans an extended stay in the psychiatric unit than gab on about time travel and Ezrina, although, ironically, Demetri would believe me.

"Where did you sleep, Skyla?" Demetri sounds bored, fatigued from dispensing the inquisition.

"I slept in the woods and ate berries." I thrash him with all of the hatred I can muster. I've already killed him in my mind at least six different times while I've been seated. I imagine his head exploding over the walls like a giant pumpkin—detonating like a powerhouse—nothing but orange, stringy guts dangling from the ceiling.

"You don't look malnourished." He blinks a dull smile.

"I found a goat by a large flat stone in the middle of a clearing, you know the one," I say, accusingly. I watch as he flinches, enjoy the rhythm of his irritation. "I sacrificed it for my hunger. Stripped it of its flesh and put it over a fire," I envision myself doing that to Demetri. "It satisfied me." Come to think of it, his head is the size of a pumpkin. If he was my father, I'd clearly be malformed. Sometimes nature knows best and doesn't allow people like him to procreate. But, then again, it has its genetic hiccups—look what happened with Tad. And obviously Mom's incessant drug abuse has confused her into procreating with him.

"Skyla, that's disgusting," Mom shivers from the goat visual, but secretly I think she picked up on the fact I accidentally imagined her procreating with her nuptial mishap.

"Relax, Lizbeth, she's lying," Tad informs. "It's her favorite hobby."

expel

A strangled tension crops up between the two of them. You could light a match, and the room would explode from the animosity between Tad and my mother.

Demetri reaches over and picks up my mother's hand. "You know, Lizbeth." He bears into her eyes with those dishonest orbs. "Under these kinds of circumstances being there for your child emotionally is the most important thing and that's what you're doing. That's what you always do because *you* are an exceptional mother."

And *he* is exceptional bullshitter.

I look over to Tad who's busy staring down Demetri.

This isn't going to end well.

This Fem is going to steal my mother right from under Tad's nose if he doesn't step up his game.

And, for once, I think I'm rooting for Tad—just barely.

"See you soon, Skyla," Demetri rises.

"For what?"

"Community service," he inhales, expanding his chest wide as a brick house.

Oh that's right, the pot bust consequence.

He nods. "We're going to restore my grandfather's estate to its former glory."

I stare into him curiously. How can a Fem have any sort of family history?

I wonder.

7

Family Time

The windows of the Landon house are adorned with pink and red hearts. I burst through the door, leaving Mom and Tad to finish the *little talk* they started after we left the station and continue in a heated manner as they walk up the driveway. It was like a broken record with Mom defending my behavior, Tad condemning me, and the two of them ignoring the fact I was right there in the vehicle able bodied and listening.

As if the fighting behind me weren't bad enough, I can hear Mia and Melissa going at it full steam in the family room.

"What is going on?" I spring up on them just as they move into each other's faces.

"Stay out of this, Skyla," Melissa snaps.

OK, so really, I sort of expected to be tackled with hugs and perhaps for them to tell me how much they missed me like they did the last time I disappeared. Heck, I'd even settle for a *where the hell have you been*, but nothing.

"The next time I catch you with anything that belongs to me, I will slingshot your ass across the Pacific!" Melissa stabs a finger into Mia's chest.

What the heck is this about? Just as I'm about to ask, Holden waltzes in the room and jars me into vocal paralysis—only it's not Holden, it's Ethan. I hope.

"Hello," I say, following him into the kitchen.

He grunts while retrieving a soda from the fridge.

"You the runaway?" He cracks it open and takes a swig.

God, he even acts like Holden.

"I guess that would be me." I lean in secretively, "I know what happened to you."

expel

He sets the can down hard onto the counter and drills into me with those strange Holden eyes. Funny because I never knew Holden before when he was actually himself, and now that Ethan is back in his right body, I still see Holden.

"We'll talk later." His voice is softer, his shoulders not stretched back taut like a jackass looking for a fight. Maybe this new incarnation of Ethan really is the new and improved version.

"For sure," I say.

"Let go," Melissa snaps. I turn in time to catch my sisters in a tug of war over a silver purse. Mom steps in and snatches it from both their clutches.

"That's enough," she shouts. "I'm sick and tired of all this fighting. I've had it with the two of you."

I've never seen Mom so dislodged from her sanity before.

Melissa snatches the bag from Mom's fingers.

"I believe this is mine, Liz*bitch*," she barks the malformed moniker in my mother's face.

"Take it back!" Mia screams.

Tad lets out a whistle that makes Sprinkles the rat dog run for cover beneath the dining room table. He claps his hands over his head three times and calls for Drake.

"Family meeting," he makes a series of circles in the air with his finger before pointing over to the couch. "All of you, and I mean now!"

Mia and Melissa sit on opposing couches. Drake sails down and high fives me before sitting at the bar as if I had merely stepped out for a shift at the bowling alley.

"I said here," Tad barks, and Drake comes over between Ethan and me. "A lot of stuff has happened to this family as of late. Ethan, you've proved yourself a changed young man, I appreciate the effort. Drake, you and Brielle..." He throws his hand into the air without finishing the thought. "Mia and Melissa, for God's sake, you used to get along better than sisters, and now look at you! Fighting over boys? Who cares about boys?" Tad chokes out the words.

It's about that stupid Armistead kid, I can smell him a mile away. If he's anything like his sister, he's a bad freaking seed.

"Skyla's back," he continues, "and before she's formally charged with yet another homicide, a few things are going to change around here. For one, your mother and I will be around the house a little more often because we no longer have to babysit that linebacker your sister tried to force feed her Michelins."

"Skyla did not run anybody over," Mom screeches out, exasperated. "And would you please stop referring to Gage as that *linebacker*? We were at the hospital to show our support for the Olivers. Thank God, *Gage* is going to be all right."

"He needs me there," I interject. "The doctor said I was like some miracle drug." It takes everything in me not to bolt out the door. I noticed that freaking Mustang is parked high on the driveway. I suppose Tad wanted the monument of Chloe's psychotic behavior for the cash value after all.

"Oh, you've got a side effect on people." Tad glares at me. "I think what this family needs is some serious alone time together."

Alone?

"Your mother and I propose we take some time just the," Tad conducts a not so silent headcount, "seven of us."

"We should go to New York," Mia beams.

"We should go to Paris," Melissa glowers over at her. "You always think so small."

"You're right," Mia snipes. "I was thinking really small when I took on your dumb last name. Mom, I'm changing my name back."

"Whoa," Mom fans her arms out like a referee. "Nobody is going to New York or Paris, or changing their names. We are all keeping our own identities and staying put. You can't just flip it on and off like a light switch. You're a Landon, Mia."

I knew she'd regret it.

"So, are we going to Seattle?" I ask. Honestly, I just need for them to pinpoint a venue so I can properly plan my escape. There is no way in hell I'm leaving Gage even for a minute. No locale on the planet is lucrative enough to drag me away.

"Nope," Tad twists. "We're staying right here on Paragon."

"It's a stay-cation," Mom offers a placid smile that springs up as quick as it dies down.

"Great." This is so freaking stupid, but I don't dare call them out on it. I think in all of their absurdity they actually stumbled onto something that borders on brilliant.

"That's right," Tad nods, rather proud of the not so big reveal. "We'll be enjoying the great outdoors right here on the island."

"Camping?" Mia crawls up on the couch as though Tad just unleashed a venomous snake into the room. "I don't do camping."

"You do now," Tad informs her. "Next weekend."

"That's Valentine's Day," Melissa is quick to snip. "The school has a dance."

"OK, we'll fit it in the following weekend. Consider yourselves warned," Tad squawks.

There's a knock at the door that rattles through the house, abrasive as gunfire.

"We're a damn family, and it's about time we start acting like one," Tad storms off towards the entry. "Skyla, it's for you."

8

Arrive Alive

I prattle down the hall expecting to see Brielle, Dr. Oliver, or even Chloe's menacing mug, but this—Logan's beautiful face is unimaginably the best thing I could have ever hoped for.

"Logan!" I jump into his arms and let him twirl me as he takes in my scent, kisses my neck, my cheeks, the spontaneous shower of tears on my face. The misty night air dusts a circle of approval over our shoulders, cool as a damp towel. His blonde hair glints under the silver dollar moon. His sharp features trap light and shadow with their perfection, spelling out the fact he's a modern day Adonis. "You're back, you're really back."

"Come in," Mom urges, pulling us inside by the elbow.

"My dad wanted me to give you this." Logan hands me a tube of white ointment.

"Perfect, thank you." I give him a puzzled look. Dr. Oliver is Logan's uncle, well, technically his brother, but for practical purposes he's not.

"I was thinking about taking Skyla out," he nods into Mom. "You know, hang out, catch up."

Mom and Tad just stand there stupefied by this viral-alert, and very much alive-looking Logan.

"So what happened?" Tad washes over him with suspicion. "I thought you were at death's door, you look perfectly fine." His voice drags as though he were somehow implying that the Olivers had purposefully deceived him about Logan's condition.

"Ship shape." Logan taps his chest. "Just needed a tune up. Hey, they ever catch the bastard that ran me over?" He needles into Tad trying to maintain his sarcasm.

Shit.

Logan must have really hit his head in the wrong place.

"You know what?" I take up his hand and jump in front of him. "I would love to go out with you. Maybe get a bite? And we can see Gage after."

Logan gives a reluctant smile.

"Don't stay out late. Tomorrow is school." Mom hands me one of Mia's jackets before I speed down the porch with Logan.

I have Logan and Gage back, real and in person. I was so afraid that I would lose them both—that everything we built together would be reduced to memories, useless as pressed flowers.

I pause just shy of his truck and wrap my arms around him, brush my lips against his beating chest.

The world has righted itself. I can see and feel everything, and everything around me spells love.

🦋 🦋 🦋

Logan barrels us down the road at breakneck speeds.

"Slow down. I'm pretty sure Ezrina's not in the mood for another restoration project tonight." I don't bother telling him about my deal with the hostess with the mostess corpses. Or, how she'll be wearing my body like the latest fashion in just a little while if I don't arrange a do-over with the fab four that comprise the Justice Alliance.

"So, where do I normally take you?" He tweaks my knee and gives a little wink.

"What's wrong?" I'm almost afraid to ask.

"My head's all clouded over. I can't hold a thought more than two seconds." He glowers into the long blank silence of the road. "I'll need you to fill in a few blanks for me."

"Let's go see Gage. We can both fill in the blanks for you."

"We'll see him right after, but for now, lets do something just you and me."

"You wanna go to the bowling alley? We can probably see Brielle."

"I was thinking somewhere a little more private. Black Forest?" He hums along to the radio, turning up the volume.

"No, way. I hate that place. Let's go to the bowling alley. You know, revisit the scene of the crime." And, really, I wouldn't mind seeing Bree.

"Suit yourself." He drives us down the highway until we hit the dilapidating rectangle that is the bowling alley.

"Watch this," he skips over the easement that leads into the parking lot and bumps over a series of small boulders that act as landscaping.

"Hey!" I shout, jostling about, snatching away at the dashboard, trying to keep from knocking into the window. He speeds us around the building to the dirt lot where the Mustang knocked the life out of him and comes just shy of hitting the trunk of an evergreen. "Shit!" I pant. "You almost smacked into that thing. And, by the way, the tree would have totally won. Don't joke around like that." The last thing I need is a head injury. A metal halo drilled into my skull isn't exactly a girl's accessory of choice for Valentine's Day.

"Who says I'm joking?" He sobers quickly, killing the ignition. "I'm going to start living life to the fullest. No more of this ambling around not enjoying myself, bullshit." He gives a dry laugh. "Come here," he says, swiveling his arms up my sweater. "I believe I owe you a proper thank you."

"I believe you do," I push his hands back down. "But not like that."

He pulls me in by the back of my neck and indulges in an unwelcome kiss by way of his meandering tongue.

Before I can push him away, the radio ignites in one loud blast, and I snatch my hands up over my ears to stop the noise.

"Crap," Logan switches it off. "Must have hit it with my knee."

"I think we should go see Gage." For sure being alone with Logan is not a good idea. I believe his thrill to live campaign is being solely run by his penis. "So, we should drive to the hospital, like now."

"He's still in there, huh?" He shakes his head at the thought. "You should wake him up with some of that Celestra magic, perk him right up."

"I didn't even think of that. You're a genius." I push him gently in the shoulder. "I'm sorry about having your powers revoked." I say it so low I'm not even sure he heard.

He stares off in a daze as though he were just remembering this reality himself.

"Shit," he mutters. "No, it's OK." He takes in a hard breath. "There are so many other things that make life worth living."

He starts up the truck, dazed by the revelation, and heads back out onto the black expanse of highway that drifts unknowably in both directions.

"What happened when you died Logan? What did you see?"

He swallows hard, still lost, gazing at the road ahead.

Logan looks fatigued, worn out underneath this jubilant demeanor. Death has discolored the world for him. I hope he gets his bearings, retrieves whatever it is he might have lost. I hope death didn't come in and rob him of who he truly is deep down inside.

"It wasn't good, Skyla," his voice wobbles. "Nothing good waits for you. We need to live it up right now. This is all it's ever going to be for us."

"Did you end up in the transport?" Marshall took me there once. A Jasper cave with angels ready to send you up or down, no in-between.

He nods. "Pushed me back down to earth. And believe you me I'm glad to be here. I really owe you one."

I give a little laugh as we pull into the parking lot of the hospital.

"You don't owe me anything. I'm just glad you're back." I lean over and hug him for a very long time, take in his scent, and feel his body rise and fall with each breath he takes.

Having Logan back is a beautiful, beautiful thing.

9

Just One Taste

At the hospital, the ornery nurses let me know by way of their aggressive snarls, their barking reprimands, that it's past visiting hours—that I can't see Gage. I wait until they distract themselves by way of a newly discovered box of chocolate I bought at the gift shop and covertly landed on their desk before sneaking in.

Logan volunteered to wait in the truck to give Gage and me some much-needed privacy, which I totally appreciate. I let him know I wouldn't have minded if he went in and said hello, hung out, but he insisted.

"Hi," I whisper. A thin vanilla blanket conforms perfectly over his body giving the illusion he's a marble statue from the chest down.

Gage smiles, his eyes are open just barely, exposing bloodshot bruises with blue sirens dotting the middle. He leans up looking very much like his old self.

I round out the bed and crawl beside him.

Gage takes a breath, sans the tubes. He lowers the volume on the basketball game and pats me over. He looks sleepy, but radiates his love for me, expresses it with every cell of his body.

"Throat hurts," he rasps out the words, brushing his lips over my cheek with a minty kiss. His skin holds the sharp scent of soap, his hair still wet from the shower. God, I hope it was a shower, not some buxom bombshell of a nurse helping him with a sponge bath.

"I won't stay long." I scoot in tight next to him.

Please, stay long—all night in fact. He kneads into my bare arm with his fingers, traces a line up to my shoulder before letting his hand fall back onto the bed from fatigue. *I can't speak.*

"Lucky for you, you don't have to," I press out a soft smile. "Logan is back."

My dad told me. Said he's real happy to be here.

"Yeah, well, I guess death does that to a person. He's all hopped up on life now."

Thank you.

"Don't thank me yet." I glance over at a pair of small metal scissors next to the comb and toothbrush on the end table. I pick them up and slit a small line up the side of my wrist, a safe distance from the blue veins that protrude from my skin like roadways on a map. A fragile seam of blood rises to the surface, cresting until it forms a wave of crimson over my pale flesh.

"Skyla," his voice breaks my name in two equal parts. *No*, he protests, closing his lids as if holding back tears.

"Yes. I want you home, healed and healthy. I want to go to Rockaway Point with you, roll around on the black sand and log some serious time under that coral tree."

You remember? His dimples go off like sirens.

"Are you kidding? I've grafted every one of the memories we've created over my heart. I remember everything about you and me." I trace out his features with the pad of my finger. "And I want to go snorkeling with you again, watch as you make the butterfly room light up—find a hotel room that we can call our own."

His brows twitch in amusement. He sears me with a seductive look without trying.

"So, if you want to get cracking on any of those good things you're going to need to get better, fast." I hold my wrist up to him like an offering.

He takes my hand and gently pushes my flesh up against his mouth, seals his lips over the wound and kisses it. Gage closes his eyes and indulges in a few good drags. It feels sensual, sexual in nature—desire coupled with pain.

"I thought you were dead," I whisper, my voice warbling on the verge of tears. "Logan took me away to the Transfer then he disappeared. I thought I'd never get back to you."

I'm not dead. A shadow digs into his left cheek. *I must have dreamed a thousand dreams about you these past two weeks.* The curve of a naughty smile brims on his lips.

"All things delicious, I suspect."

I dreamed of a future with you. We were in school, private college, on a neighboring island. It was just you and me. He strokes the side of my face with the back of his hand, washes his eyes over me with a mixture of sadness and anticipation.

"You think it was a vision?" I soak in his sad earnest gaze. I love the way he makes me feel when he absorbs me through those powerful lenses, like he's appreciating an exotic painting from afar wondering what it would be like to crawl inside the canvas— a starving man hovering over a hot meal and all he's allowed to do is take in the aroma.

I know some of them were. We are magic, Skyla. We have everything to live for. His features harden, his mind draws a wall of concrete so high and thick, I could never penetrate into that deep abyss.

"You saw something else?"

Nothing new. Just affirmations of things I've seen before.

"Anything you'd like to share?" I take a slow drawn breath—already I know the answer.

I'm tired, Skyla.

"I can cut my finger," I offer.

He shakes his head, picks up my finger and kisses it before replacing it into the safety of his own warm hand.

I'd split my entire body in half if I thought it would make Gage better.

He looks up at me with surprise, breaks out into a slow spreading smile.

I know you would, Skyla. That's why I love you.

           ✺ ✺ ✺

The next morning I'm beyond exhausted. I drive the Mustang to school—the Mustang that has a distinct Gage shaped dent in the fender from trying to snuff the life out of both Oliver boys at once. I thought maybe I could forgive the orange chunk of metal for being a part of the malfeasance that took place that night, especially since I know for darn sure it wasn't the poor car's fault, but truthfully I hate it just a little bit for being responsible even if it was on a rudimentary level.

Just looking out the windshield forces me to see that night take place like a transparency overlaid on top of the world. Logan and Gage with their statue white faces—the look of horror on Gage that I had seen once before by way of Marshall's visionary kisses.

During second period it takes all of my effort to keep myself conscious.

"Ms. Messenger, are you here to acquire numeric knowledge or drift in a dream?" Marshall knocks on his desk to further rally my attention.

"Dream—I mean learn," I say, straightening in my seat. I stay alert long enough to observe as he cascades a repetitive cloud of numbers and letters across the board in a nonsensical sequence, try to listen as he thunders through his explanation.

"Problems one through five," he instructs the class before seating himself on the edge of his desk. Marshall watches me, his lingering gaze drifts to my right, and he closes his eyes.

Oh, Skyla, he says it full with disappointment.

I arch my brows at him before indulging in the inevitable and putting my head down onto the desk.

If he's not elaborating I'm not biting—that's the thing with Marshall, he always wants a bite. The more flesh to dig his teeth into, the better.

Long night?

I give a quick thumbs up. Actually that's not why I'm tired. I didn't stay out too late at the hospital, partially because Logan was waiting in the parking lot. I was up all night listening to Mia and Melissa lob insults at one another through our paper-thin walls. Usually I'm immune to their midnight murmurings, but once their lexicon became vitriolic—laced with bitch and asshole, then, of course, I perked up to attention. I've made a mental note that the walls are akin to tattletales for the next time Gage comes over. I bet the girls have been logging each time he sneaks into my bedroom and are holding onto that info for some supreme form of blackmail. Anyway, they hate each other now. And apparently my mother is pretty high on Melissa's shit-list because, once again, she addressed her as *Lizbitch* during breakfast and no one said squat. If that's what Mom and Tad are letting fly around Landon manner, I'd like to come up with my own version of abasement and humiliation tailor made for Taddy dearest.

Rumor has it an archeological dig at the Edinger estate is in your future. Marshall shifts. *Care to trade in soggy soil for some time at the ranch? Say the word. I'll have it arranged within the hour.*

"Price is too high," I say, lifting my head just a notch.

Crap. I just said that out-freaking-loud.

The bell drills its high-pitched wail into my skull, rattles my brain around until foaming at the mouth feels like a real possibility. People are too busy shoving books into their backpacks to properly dissect my newfound verbal insanity, and, I suppose for this, I should be thankful.

A dark figure hovers over me, shadows the world on the other side of my eyelids. I open groggily to find Chloe in all her dark splendor, sharp and beautiful as a rusted out tack. You need a Tetanus shot just to give her a hug.

"I hear Gage is well." Chloe offers her signature scowl.

The lights flicker as thunder erupts outside, corrugates the classroom with its howling roar.

"What in the hell are you doing here?" For a moment I consider the fact I'm having a bad dream, some kind of hallucination that you're rewarded with after not enough sleep. I'm shocked to see her standing on West Paragon's soil as though she were never kicked out in the first place.

"The sword wasn't mine. I was able to prove there was no way I lugged that thing to school, nor did I plan on stabbing you in the gut with it. I've been back for a solid week." She glances up at Marshall and gives the slight curve of a smile.

No sulking, Marshall reprimands, pretending to clear the clutter off his desk. *You know full well you didn't fulfill your end of the agreement.*

Sometimes I really hate Marshall. I should teach them both a lesson and do my best rendition of a batshit ape—lob furniture around and accidently fracture Chloe's spinal cord, rip her vertebrae out one by one just for the fun of it. I could always plead insanity. I've practically got Dr. Booth in my back pocket. I think.

"Yeah, well, Gage is better." I pull my stuff together and stand. "You were driving the car that night, weren't you?"

Her smile dissipates. "You think I would do that to my dear friend Gage? What kind of monster do you think I am?"

"The kind that killed my father, killed Ethan, killed Emerson." I pull back a finger as I log each name. "Yes, Chloe, I do think you're that kind of monster. A murderous monster who happens to be lost in a perpetual jealous rage over the fact the boy you love doesn't love you back. Get over it." I cinch my backpack over my shoulder. "But then you're incapable of getting over it, aren't you?"

Her features contort as I speed out the door.

Logan holds up a hand and high fives me in the hall on my way towards the stairwell. I should tell Logan that Gage wants to see him, tell him how much better Gage is after just one taste of my Celestra fortified goodness. I pivot on my heels and catch Logan pulling Chloe off into an alcove. My stomach does a hard roll, burns hot with its own version of a jealous rage.

I bet that's Chloe's new game. Knife me in the back by dating Logan.

If Logan ever gets back together with Chloe, I would totally die.

I suppose that's how Chloe feels about Gage.

10

Never

"Hey!" Brielle shrieks during nutrition. "Look at you! I saw Logan this morning. Did you see him?" She clutches onto me with a rocking hug.

"Look at *you*," I take in a sharp breath trying not to look horrified by the fact her stomach is shooting out like a torpedo in her tight knit sweater. It rises and falls dramatically with each breath she takes, smacking me in the boobs on the upswing. It's like one of those games at the amusement park where you strike the hammer and the ball spikes to hit a bell. I feel like I might be handed a giant stuffed panda at any moment.

"I know. It's funny, right? I look deformed." She brushes cookie crumbs off her newfound shelf.

"This coming from the girl who thought it was perfectly acceptable to wear a belly dress to the winter formal? You look fine." She really does, considering her condition. I'm still not sure where Brielle and I stand. She never did fess up to being a Count until I called her out on it, not to mention the fact she thought it was cute when I showed up to the sacrificial stone as the promised lamb herself. And don't get me started on the fact Chloe paid her a solid grand to be my bestie. At the least I think she owes me some serious cold hard cash for pretending to be hers, well, I am her friend but that's beside the point.

"Please—I'll be in a tent by prom." She looks dejected just thinking of the idea. "So, I've totally taken over at the bowling alley. I don't have you down for hours yet. Let me know when you're ready. Hope you don't mind but I've been having Chloe pinch hit."

"What?" Chloe is like a virus that hits you coming and going. I'd rather eat dinner out of a public urinal than brush elbows with Chloe at work.

"I needed someone. There were three shifts to cover, and desperate times call for hiring desperate people. Besides, she was way mellow while you were gone."

"That's because I was gone and the fact she was able to hold a private candlelight vigil next to Gage every night." She was probably kissing him, licking his face like a cat—groping him inappropriately.

"True, she went before and after work."

"Well, someone call the Vatican. We've got a real freaking saint on our hands."

"I don't want to upset you or anything, but she's totally opened up to me. You know, we used be good friends before she ditched me for the bitch squad. I mean it's not like we're BFF's now or anything, but she's talking to me again like a real person. Who knew Chloe Bishop had a heart?"

"If she's got a heart, it's because she ate one for breakfast. Don't let her fool you. She's a heartless, soulless bitch that will annihilate anything and anyone who gets in her way."

She gives a slow nod. "She may have mentioned the fact, she lives to take you down."

"I can't really take it personally. She lives to take down anything that stands in her way of Gage." In fact, if I had to guess what she was doing on all those questionable light drives with Ellis, I'd venture to say she was working on rearranging Gage's genetic code to somehow include falling in love with her. It wouldn't surprise me one bit to find out she accidentally dismantled the universe in her impotent efforts at procuring his affection. One day Chloe is going to screw up gravity and turn us all into space debris trying to crack the code to Gage Oliver's heart. "Besides, I nailed her to a wall." An image of Logan's film playing at the bowling alley runs through my tired brain. "There is no way she's going to get in the way of my relationship with Gage ever again."

"I don't know," Brielle circles over me with a look of apprehension. "I'd watch my back if I were you."

"Chloe's the one who'd better watch her back. If I get proof she took down Logan and Gage, she's going back to hell, and I'll make sure to lock the door behind her this time."

"Fighting words," Ellis slings his arm around my shoulder. "Who's going? And how's your hand?"

"Never mind. I'm going to see Gage after school, and my hand is one hundred percent." I wiggle my urine free fingers.

The sky peels open. A flood of rain collapses over the awning we're huddled beneath. A violent spray of lightning bathes the world around us with its unusual brand of daylight.

"Party Saturday at my house," Ellis leans in as though this were a breaking news update. "I might need to take a quick trip with my *love honey* Friday night just to ensure a good time is had by all." He bumps into me when he says love honey, our new light driving safe word.

"Saturday is Valentine's Day!" Brielle hops when she says it. "I have this whole romantic thing planned for me and Drake. We're going to the falls to build a fire, if the weather doesn't ruin things."

"You can't go to the falls," Ellis scoffs. "You have to come to my house. I'm having a special event."

"Brownie bake off?" I ask. That would explain the light drive. "Oh, and no to Friday night." I'm tiring of that whole routine of me taking him back and losing my boyfriend in the process while all Ellis ever seems to lose is a few lousy brain cells.

"Better than a brownie bake off," he assures. "You'll have to come over and find out for yourselves. Trust me, no one is going to want to miss this."

expel

"You're hanging Chloe from a tree, and we're all going to take turns beating her with a baseball bat?" I ask, hopeful. The visual alone is enough to brighten my day.

"Yeah," his eyes bulge at the thought. "Something like that. Only there won't be any candy spilling out when she finally cracks open, more like snakes and rats." He snarls into me. "Just be there. Don't blow this one off or you'll be sorry," he warns. And with that, he treks off into the storm.

※ ※ ※

The week goes on with its peculiar rhythm of school and my daily visits to the hospital. I let Gage siphon off my fingers, feel his passion grow as he indulges on the salty brine of my affection. His face glows a rosy pink, his hair shines anew, black as the glossy feathers on Nevermore's back. He looks all together splendid, nothing like the near corpse he was that first day I found him intubated and attached to the animatronic robot that assisted with his breathing. I plan on satisfying him with a lot more than what my bone marrow could ever offer once they release him.

Thursday night after they evict me from the hospital, I nestle up on my window seat and stare up at the hazy night sky. The storm has blown over, and the white pristine breath of God once again finds a home on Paragon, cradling us like a child with a flower before it mercilessly plucks off the petals. Something malignant is brewing, there's a sinister rush of excitement in the air. The evergreens attest to this as they gloat in the wind. An unsettling feeling has plagued me ever since I left the Transfer that day.

A gentle peck erupts on the other side of the glass. I jump back startled to find Nevermore grazing at the window with the necrotic tip of his beak. I roll out the casement and let him crouch inside.

"Hey, you." I say, sealing out the roving fog. "I absolutely hate that you have to live out there like some kind of animal." I land my warm palm over his back, stroke his feathers soft as a dream. He stands tall, regal. Nevermore is an exceptional size even for a raven.

I am an animal. He twitches and shudders beneath me.

"Maybe," I twirl my thumb over the top of his head. "But you were very much human once upon a time. Isn't that right—*Heathcliff*?"

He lets out an unexpected caw and sends me pressing my finger over my lips in an effort to reprimand him.

"Tad will snap your neck and prep you for the frying pan if he finds you in here." Ironic because he didn't bother doing that to Gage when he caught us in bed together. My father would have sawed him in half at the waist for committing such a carnal crime even if it were totally chaste. "I think Tad's afraid of you."

He should be. I'll peck his eye out if he tries imprisoning me again. Now, back to subject at hand, Skyla—my name. Who dispensed such worthless information?

"Your lady love," I hold my breath a moment before filling him in on the dirty terms of my agreement with Ezrina.

Skyla, it expels from him with great sadness, *she's resorted to trickery in order to procure a body for herself. She's desperate to break out of that prison cell of a carcass—the sentence she's been handed is too much for her to bear. Don't you see? She realizes she's asked the impossible. The Justice Alliance is in no manner going to entertain a retrial.*

"Are you sure?" I guess Ezrina lying to me to get what she wants isn't entirely outside the realm of possibility. God, she really is like me. "Anyway, lest you forget, my mother practically runs the judicial circus in the sky. This is a no-brainer. Of course she's gonna help me out and get you guys a new trial. That's what nepotism is all about."

Oh, so you think we've suffered out our punishments for the simple fact we didn't have the right familial relations? Oh, dear girl, don't you know by now that there are rules to comply with and that those rules are set in stone?

"Let me guess—the word covenant is involved," I sigh, annoyed. That's all Marshall ever gripes about is covenants and promises. You'd think the infrastructure of the universe would come unhinged if people didn't do what they promised.

It is a covenant. There is no way to undo what the Justice Alliance has deemed a worthy punishment. This is an eternal grievance, and we must live to accept that. I myself realize those terms and Ezrina does as well. It looks to me like she took full advantage of the fact one person in particular didn't, my dear, and that person would be you.

I swallow hard at the thought.

I'd better find a way to beat Ezrina at her own crooked game, or I'll be hacking up corpses for a good long while.

Marshall blinks through my mind, and I push back the thought. He said I was on my own, and judging by the pissed off expression on his face while he was wiping my spit out of his eye, I'd say he meant it.

I'll have to get Ezrina a new trial myself.

And I don't have a ray of hope to cling to.

11

Sweet Release

Friday, everything feels gloriously normal again.

After school, a thick layer of snowy vapors swallow up Paragon before spitting us back out into the carnal reserve of daylight with harsh biting rain. Marshall completely ignored me during class. He acts as if he's relegated himself to simply being my math teacher. I secretly hate the non-attention. I desperately miss the hypersexual bantering albeit one-sided, but I'll never let on. I'll just get my community service moved to the ranch ASAP and let him molest me with his eyes and suggestive verbal assaults once I get there. It's win-win.

Chloe runs us ragged during cheer while prepping us for the almighty All State competition coming up in April. It's at the end of spring break, and the school is invited to the Cain River campsite, all expenses paid, in exchange for fixing up their dilapidated facilities. Which is great because that means I'll be spending an entire week with Gage, and, well, technically Chloe, but she's beside the point per usual. Plus, we can nix all of the cupcake drives and bikini carwashes Chloe had mapped out to raise funds for our misadventure and focus on what really matters, spending time with Gage in a hotel room.

Logan struts over in a pair of saggy jeans that hang far below the waist and threaten to fall off his person as he debuts his new swagger. He's unforgivably paired it with a skin tight shirt with the effigy of a dragon imprinted on the front—red sequins sewn on as eyes.

Holy crap. He looks like a complete douchebag, but I'm not going to say anything. Or maybe I am.

"What's with the scum wear?" I ask, stepping out of formation while the bitch squad continues to gyrate around me. That's all that's left of the team now, the bitch squad and me—another reason for me to resent Drake for knocking up Brielle.

"You like?" He taps his chest, gorilla style.

"No, I don't like. Nobody likes." Logan is really making it easy for me to get over him, and I'm not sure I like that either.

"You busy after this?"

"Yes, with Gage." I'm surprised he even has to ask.

"Can I have a ride? My car sort of ran out of gas, had to hitch a ride with Brielle this morning."

"Messenger," Chloe barks and motions for Logan to get the hell off the field, "back in line."

"Yeah, I'll give you a ride." He crimps a frown. The slight look of hurt lingers in his eyes.

Chloe yanks me into the team huddle.

"We need to start up Saturday practice. I'll need everyone here by seven."

"It's Valentine's Day," I protest. "Some of us have places to go tomorrow night." I suppose all of us, since we'll most likely all be at Ellis's, but more specifically I'm talking about me and Gage.

"In the *morning*, Messenger. Seven in the morning," she screams it in my face.

"Nice," I say, wiping the saliva she just assaulted me with, off my cheek.

"One more time!" She claps.

We start in on the routine for the All State competition. I kick and jump and put one thousand percent of my concentrated energy into the effort. At the end of the routine I take leave of my senses long enough to let Emily, Michelle, and Lexy hoist me into the air, hopeful that I might land back into the safety of their arms the way I'm supposed to and not impress myself into West Paragon's field the way I envision. Surprisingly, they swaddle me like a baby before ejecting me to the ground in one piece. I look over to Logan for approval, a thumbs up, a nod—but he's too busy texting to notice.

A light drizzle starts in. The sky dims to pitch in an instant. Strangely it feels and looks like midnight. The days on Paragon are often cut short with a boil of black clouds—daylight seems something of a myth in general. But just knowing I get to see Gage sets my heart on fire, fills me with an unquenchable light brighter than a nuclear blast on the inside.

"If the weather's crappy we'll meet in the gym." Chloe claps, officiating the fact practice is over, still not sure why Ms. Richards lets her run the show. "Good job, Messenger."

Everything stops around me. Even Michelle looks up from her sleep deprived stupor to gawk at Chloe in shock over her slip of the tongue.

"Thank you," I reply. Chloe is trying to lure me into quicksand. I can see the snarl tugging at her lip, the tightrope she had to walk just to get the words out in a level manner.

"Replicate the moves you somehow managed to pull off here today, come April, and I won't be compelled to twist your head off for ruining the championship."

There's the verbal venom I've grown accustomed to.

Emily steps into Lexy. "I'm doing couples' pages tomorrow night at Ellis's. You remember—mapping out your love life for the year and crap." It seems to be a private exchange, but I can't help but overhear. I would wash Emily's underwear by hand if she wanted me to, just to listen to the wacky shit capable of coming from her mouth. I'm that obsessed with her secret ability to draw out the future like a comic strip.

"Oh, so Gage and I can get one, right?" I ask, inviting myself into the conversation.

"You don't need to be a real couple to do it, so sure." She shrugs.

Chloe still has everyone brainwashed into believing she and Gage are the real deal. I hope Gage is able to attend Ellis's party, even if it's a five-minute stint. I want to pull him into the center of the room with all of West and East surrounding us and give him a big fat welcome home kiss. Well, technically I'm going to give him his welcome home kiss tonight. It's the *F off Chloe kiss* I'll be giving him tomorrow night and basically every other time I kiss him again in public. I still can't believe we're finally free from her evil clutches. The wicked witch of East may be back on campus from whence she came, but she's forever barred from forcing Gage to spend time with her again.

"I want one," Michelle insists. She pinches at the black unholy rose of horrors Marshall gave her as a token of his strange affection.

"Sure," Emily plucks at her short dark curls. It slithers around her finger like a thin black snake. "I'll do yours first, I really don't care."

Emily has a warm way about her. She could easily be arranging our lineup for the firing squad.

Lexy cuts her gaze across the field at Logan. "I want mine to be a little more exciting than the one you gave me last year. I'd like to see more Oliver this time, turn in my lonely-hearts club membership for a real relationship, or a one-night stand. I'd definitely settle for a one-night stand."

"Me, too," Michelle chimes in. She cocks her head over at Logan, who motions for me to hurry. "I guess I wouldn't mind more Oliver either." She lets go of the rose and licks her lips like a promise.

Looks like her infatuation with Marshall might be waning after all. I can't wait to share the news with him, but something tells me I should stay away. Bruising Marshall's ego is never a good idea. Neither is discharging bodily fluids into his ocular region, but I've already done that.

"See you in the morning," I turn to walk off but Chloe catches me by the elbow.

"Please tell Gage I'm glad he's doing better." There's a hard glint in her eye, a shard of her broken heart catches the reserve light of day and signals me with her pain. And for the first time, my own heart breaks just a little for Chloe.

"I will," I say.

"Oh, and, Skyla?" Her lips turn up at the edges. "I hope you enjoy your evening tomorrow night—as Logan and I have both learned the hard way, you never know when it will be your last."

12

Home Sweet Home

Logan gives a NASCAR worthy performance all the way to the Oliver house, jackknifing into the driveway—laughing like fiend while doing so.

"Holy crap," I scream. "Are you serious?" I stare at his hauntingly beautiful face that has always been rivaled by his inner beauty—which by the way he's managed to destroy faster than a brushfire with all this *live for the now* junk he's fielding. "And what is up with you having a pow-wow with Chloe? She fed me all this bull about how the two of you really know how to appreciate life because it can end at any moment, crap."

"It's not crap, Skyla," he says it disgruntled while killing the ignition. "It's true. And by the way," he jostles his head side to side full with sarcasm, "you can't pick my friends." His gaze floats out the windshield just beyond the forest. "Is that what you've been doing? Bossing me the hell around?" He scoffs like it's the last time that'll ever happen.

"No, I never boss you around. You broke up with *me* remember? You were the one who suggested I date Gage to protect our relationship from the Counts. You were the one who consistently kept quiet about important things I should have known from the beginning like the fact you were a Count yourself. It could be further deduced, that *you* my friend, bossed *me* the hell around."

"Wow," his chin pushes back a notch. "I, Logan Oliver, really am an ass."

I give a little laugh. I might actually grow to like this self-abasing version of him.

"I agree," I take up his hand. "I'll help you figure out who you are and what's going on. I'll carve some time out just for the two of us. You can come up to the butterfly room or something."

"Sounds like a plan." He presses his lips to the back of my hand quickly working his way up my arm with a string of aggressive pecks.

"Right," I say, plucking myself free. "Let's hurry and get those clothes Gage needs because I'm dying to bring him home."

"Yeah." He relaxes his forearm over the top of his head completely disinterested. As of last night he hasn't even seen Gage yet. "Go on, get out," he instructs. "Have my dad take you. I gotta run a quick errand."

It's pouring outside—an entire waterfall heaves itself from heaven. By the time I hit the front door, I'm more thoroughly saturated than I would have been if I jumped in the swimming pool.

The door swings open and I expect to find Emma or Dr. Oliver, but I don't—I find beautiful, glorious Gage.

"You're home," I say, stunned.

Gage glows. His smile shines, draws me in with those deep-welled dimples, makes me want to dive inside of one and never come out.

I wrap my arms around him careful as if he were made from eggshells. I'm deathly afraid I'm going to crush him, send him back to the hospital by way of my intense affection for him.

You can't crush me. I'm more than fine.

"You heard me." I bite down on a smile. I haven't given any blood to Gage since Wednesday, and I thought for sure the effect would have worn off by now. Not that I was miserly with my plasma, I offered—God, I *begged* him to drink me down like a platelet slurpee but he refused to suck me dry. He's altruistic that way, and plus, he prefers me alive unlike Pierce Kragger, Holden's evil twin, who would suck the marrow from my bones if I let him.

"And, you're soaking." He pulls me in and gives a brief look of irritation over my shoulder. "What's up with Logan?"

"Said he had a quick errand to run."

"Skyla!" Emma comes in and offers me a hug. "I'll get you a towel."

"I'll lend her a pair of sweats," Gage is quick to offer.

"Thank you," I mouth, still entranced by his ability to look so alarmingly healthy and normal which for Gage translates into unstoppably gorgeous.

"I hope you don't mind," Dr. Oliver pats me on the back. "Gage insisted on surprising you. Where's Logan?"

"He said he had something to take care of," I say.

Dr. Oliver purses his lips. You can tell he wants to say something, but he's holding back.

"Gage," he starts in stern, "you're not to overexert yourself. Your teachers have supplied a small amount of homework, but other than that, I want you resting in bed until Monday. I've had you transferred back to West." He gives a devilish grin.

"You did?" I lunge at him with a hug. "Oh, Dr. Oliver, I love you! How in the world did you pull that one off?"

"Chloe mentioned her parents petitioned the school and had her expulsion revoked," He looks to Gage. "Soon as I heard that, I marched right down to principal Rice's office and demanded they let you in as well. Considering you were nowhere near the incident when it occurred she agreed. No more weaponry at school," he holds a stiff a finger in the air.

Gage holds his hand up like a boy scout. "Never, I swear."

"And, for God's sake, you mustn't put yourself in a stressful situation. You had severe pneumonia for the last eleven days. Your lungs are still weak. It can exacerbate at any given time." He turns to me fully. "Skyla," he says, with a seed of disappointment, "I trust you to leave Gage out of any potentially stressful situations." He presses his chin to his chest, awaiting an answer.

"God, no. I would never do that. I mean I will, you know, leave him out." I think everyone in the room knows full well stressful situations and I seem to go hand in hand. This is going to be a challenge of an apocalyptic order.

Emma returns with a towel still holding the heat from the dryer and wraps it around my shoulder, warm as L.A. sunshine.

Dr. Oliver's phone goes off and he casually inspects it.

"It's Logan. He's dropping his truck off at the shop—he'll need a ride." He looks up perplexed. "Second time this week."

"I'll go with you," Emma offers. "I have something at the cleaners that needs to be picked up."

"Let's get you into some nice dry clothes," Gage pulls me upstairs by the hand.

It's just going to be Gage and I, alone, for the first time in weeks.

13

Put Your Hands on Me

Gage Oliver's bedroom is spacious as a ballroom—immaculate enough to perform surgery in. Two of my bedrooms could easily fit inside, if not three, and I could never be as organized as Gage.

The lights flicker—a violent rattle tests the durability of the glass as the windows tremble.

"Wild weather," I say as he kicks the door shut gently with his heel. He pulls me in, fresh from the shower, his breath cool from toothpaste.

"I don't want to talk about the weather," his eyes darken with lust, and he indulges in a kiss that stretches past eternity.

"I missed you so bad," I shake my head, before pressing in another round of searing kisses.

"Let's get these wet clothes off before *you* end up with pneumonia." He lifts my sweater off and it falls to the floor with a heavy splat. My skin tingles as his hands glide up over my back in an effort to warm me.

A hard thrash of branches whip against the glass—sounds like a beating is taking place, like some horrific creature with exceptionally long nails is trying to claw its way inside.

"I like hearing your thoughts," he gives a dull smile, his eyes still glazed over with passion as he unbuttons my jeans.

"Then you need more of my blood." I would gladly give Gage an infusion nightly if he wanted. Siphon off a pint and let him keep it in the fridge for reserves.

"No," he whispers, pulling down my zipper. "I'm happy just being with you. I would never take advantage of you like that. Like this maybe," he rides the zipper up playfully, "but not like that."

"You wouldn't be taking advantage of me," I say, covering his hand and riding my zipper back down. "I want you to have it. It's a gift."

"Nope, won't take it." He kisses the tip of my nose.

"You could get yourself up," I smile at the inflection, "to one hundred percent. Fortify yourself in everyway—and as much as you try to hide it, I noticed you had a limp."

"That's because I have a slight fracture on my pelvis." His dimples invert with the admission. "It's nothing. Not bad enough for surgery." He nods over to a crutch in the corner. "I just need to keep the pressure off or they threatened to re-break it."

"What? That's barbaric!"

"That's how they fix it. Sometimes you need to break something to fix it, let it heal the right way."

I blink into him stupefied by the profound wisdom he's just imparted. But, still, not loving the analogy. I don't like the idea of anyone breaking Gage even if it is to fix him.

"Sometimes I feel that way," it comes out far more maudlin than I want it to. "Like Paragon is breaking me in order to heal me in all the right places." I think of my father and wonder if healing is ever possible when death is involved. Even if I can go back and see him, it's not quite the same.

"Hope I'm not breaking you," he gives a tender kiss to the base of my neck.

"You could never break me. You're rebuilding me from the inside out. You heal me in every way."

"And you quite literally healed me." He holds my gaze intently as he says thank you with every parcel of his being.

Gage peels off my jeans. I step out of them cold and wet as he runs his warm hands over my thighs.

"Let me start the shower for you—you're freezing," he heads into the bathroom and the pipes squeak. "Sweats are in the first drawer to your right if you want them." He emerges, drips his gaze over me slow as molasses. His face flushes with heat, burns the apples of his cheeks as he gives the glimmer of a wicked smile.

I pull open the drawer by the window and the branch of an evergreen gives a spastic wave as though it were trying to get my attention. I peer outside for signs of Nevermore, Ezrina, or anything sinister, but all I see is Logan's letterman jacket, pooling with water in the dirt. Something tells me Logan won't mind. He's officially traded in his jock wear for cock wear. I'm not even bringing up the topic of Logan around Gage because that for sure is a stressful situation, not to mention the fact Logan hasn't even seen Gage this past week. It's clear they have very real issues even if Gage doesn't seem to be aware of them. And the last thing I want to do is put a damper on the moment because of Logan's inability to maintain his manners.

"Shower's ready," Gage folds his arms across his chest and watches me walk across the room, scantily clad. I try to maneuver my way over seductively, instead my foot slips out to the side causing an unnatural and, might I add, unattractive gyration as I try to right myself. Gage lets out a little laugh before reeling me in like a fish.

"I'll never be sexy. I'm nothing but an accident prone goofball."

"You're the hottest accident prone goofball I've ever met. And, I think you're damn sexy without even trying." He rips a molten kiss off my lips and walks me backwards into the bathroom. He hikes me up on the sink and wraps my legs on either side of his hips. We lose ourselves in a wild sea of kisses that inspire the lights to flicker like a seizure until they finally give under the strain and go out all together.

Outside lightning sizzles its radical fluorescent blaze, thunder growls its complaints. It's as if a war rages on the other side of these walls.

"The faction war," I pull back, forcing Gage to trail kisses down my neck. "When you and Logan were hit, I was shipped off to the ethereal plane," I pant.

"What?" He comes up for air, perplexed.

"I had one of the discs Marshall gave me, and I forfeited the region to the Counts."

"Why?"

"I needed to be with you. You were bleeding and Logan was dying. There was no way I was going to fight without you."

"Time would have froze," he says it almost as an afterthought, then shakes his head. "I would have done the same." His cheek slides up on the side. "It's OK. We just need to be really careful with those other two discs. You have one with you?"

"My jeans," I motion back to his room.

"Hop in the shower, I'll hold onto it until you get out. I have a feeling we should never be without it again."

I lean in—indulge in one last explorative kiss as though I were a cartographer mapping out the landscape of his mouth for the very first time. If there's one thing I never want to be without, it's Gage.

He pushes me in by the small of my back, rounds out his hands as low as the sink will allow. He picks me up and I anchor myself around him as he gives a gentle spin. It's bliss like this kissing Gage like a carnival ride. I never want this moment to end.

A loud clap of thunder detonates, rattling the windows, the house, every infrastructure on the island, and I leap off Gage in a panic.

I may never have wanted that moment to end but it sure felt like Mother Nature did.

More thunder, another fit of violent lightning.

I tremble into Gage.

I'm pretty certain it means something.

I'm just not sure what.

14

The Marriage Mirage

In the morning, rain continues to pummel our world like a tidal wave of grief. I don't remember it ever raining like this back in L.A. If it did it would be a newsworthy event with apocalyptic implications, but here on Paragon nobody bats a lash. A river could form in the middle of town, and the residents would simply take up pontoons.

Downstairs, Tad whistles away like he's on top of the world, scrolling over paperwork from Althorpe, the marketing firm he works for—volunteers at, whichever.

"Look at you," my mother beams. "Early bird gets the worm." It's weird to see the two of them happy for a change. I'm not sure I like her happy with Tad, but I suppose it beats waking up and finding her coffee klatching with Demetri, any day.

"I have cheer," I swing open the fridge and pull out the OJ.

"Outside? In this weather?" Mom leaves her mouth open to punctuate her disbelief.

"In the gym. Chloe's a real drill sergeant about things like this. She's serious about bringing the All State trophy back to West. Spring break is just around the corner."

"Oh no," Tad shakes his head. "No more school outings where you have the potential to boot someone into kingdom come."

"But it's going to be amazing! Archery swimming, horseback riding—" It's a real tampon commercial.

"No," he flat lines.

"*Tad*," Mom swipes the smile she greeted me with just moments before completely off her face, "I thought we decided we weren't going there just yet."

"What do you mean just yet?" Not that I want to revisit the fact I killed Kate, like ever, even if it was an accident.

"Dr. Booth is coming next Tuesday," Tad gets back to his musings. "He'll detail it out for you then."

"Great." I like Dr. Booth. He's Levatio like Gage. I'd let him detail out just about anything for me. In fact, if he weren't happily married, I'd totally love to see him detail out a relationship with my mother.

The window behind Mom looks as if it's melting from the early morning downpour. Mom reaches up, snatches the calendar off the wall, tosses it across the room at Tad like a Frisbee, grazing him in the temple.

Geez. She's pissed, and she's not even hiding the fact. I don't know whether to be amused or frightened at the sorry state of their relationship.

"See anything familiar slated for the near future?" She snaps.

Oh, I so know what this is about. Their first anniversary is coming up. I'll never forget that day because I officially declared it I Hate Tad Landon day.

"New moon tonight," he says it banal as though he were merely reading off a grocery list, not at all like one Count informing another of the next big sacrificial shindig to brighten up their weekend. I wonder who the next altar meal will be? Sprinkles?

"Not that," she gives an audible huff of disappointment.

"Valentine's Day?" His chin tucks back an inch. "What, are we teenagers? I already said I was taking you out to that Italian restaurant Ethan bankrupt us at a few months back. I even got you one of those candy hearts with the frilly lace thing glued around the box."

Boy, I've met Fems that were more romantic just before they intended to rip my flesh off and eat it.

"Well, I'll be looking forward to that glued box o' goodies," Mom doesn't bother hiding the fact she's miffed.

"I've gotta go get ready. I'm meeting Demetri for coffee. He wants my opinion on a box of antique jewels that belonged to his grandparents. Skyla, he wanted me to relay that you can start your community service whenever you feel emotionally ready. He's very understanding of the fact things haven't been easy for you lately." She runs the cool of her hand over my cheek.

Things would have been a whole lot easier on me if he hadn't killed my father to begin with.

"Great." I dig into my reserve of fake enthusiasm. "I'll start, like—" never. "Whenever I feel up to it." Again—never.

"Oh, and," she turns with a finger in the air, "Mr. Dudley is putting together a community garage sale to benefit a new nonprofit organization he's started called Army of Angels. All of the funds go straight into the Community Center. Isn't that terrific?"

"He's an angel all right," I can't help but avert my eyes.

"You can be sarcastic all you want," she starts, "but he showered us with concern while you were away. He went as far as saying he felt a fondness for you that he didn't share with other students. He really likes you, Skyla."

"Oh, he does," I affirm. He proves it every time he indulges in one of his lust-driven kisses.

Mom exits the room to spiffy up for her rendezvous with Demetri I-killed-your-father Edinger. I speed over to Tad and flip the calendar over to the end of April and dart my finger on the death date of the Messenger family.

"Your anniversary," I refrain from punctuating the fact with the word, moron.

"That's the event coming up?" He swipes the calendar from me and flips backwards. "That's three full months away."

"It's two, and she probably wants a real vacation out of it, not some jaunt in the woods that requires an umbrella and a bear trap." Crap. That's really what it's going to be like if he hauls us off to the backwoods of Paragon. And no TV or

Wi-Fi? I'll be *lucky* if the Fems come out to play. I'll need them for basic entertainment.

"Vacations are overrated," he gurgles out his protest.

"Some people think marriage is, too." I didn't want to go there, but he forced me.

"And you think your mother is one of those people." He gives a nod of disapproval.

I shrug. "We'll see how much attention she puts into her appearance for her meeting with Detective Edinger. Will she wear four-inch heels, and a hot little dress in the middle of a category five hurricane? Or downshift into who the hell cares what I look like mode because I'm happily married to the man I love wardrobe? Her accouterments will reveal it all." God, I hope Tad is picking up on my verbal cues because I'm pretty sure this is the last time I'm going to do him a solid and give ample relationship advice where he and my mother are concerned.

"Your mother loves me. She would marry me again in an instant."

"Prove it."

15

Affair in the Air

By late afternoon the sky above Paragon had been scoured clean, wiped in a thin slate of vanilla, nothing but a bevy of ghosts hovering around Brielle and I as we make our way through the fog-laden mall.

Logan actually gave me money right out of the safe at the bowling alley when I was done with my shift so I could, *put gas in that damn car he gave me.*

"You notice anything funny about Logan lately?" I ask, fondling lacy underwear from a bargain bin at the lingerie store. Brielle specifically came in looking for maternity lingerie which sounds a lot like an oxymoron but I don't acknowledge that fact, just nod as she holds up a strange knit creation that technically you don't even a need a stomach, boobs, or crotch to wear.

"He's still hurting," she says. "You know, from when you dumped him."

"For the record I didn't do the dumping." I rattle a pair of black panties in the air for no good reason.

"'Tis true my blonde love," she dusts my face off with a pair of skivvies so pink and innocent they can hardly justify their existence in this hotbed of immorality. "He told me himself yesterday. He took a wad of cash and said he was going to make himself feel better."

"Mmm," still not buying it. "Anyway, I'm glad he's back. But whoever ran him over is still out there." I bite down on my lip. There has to be a way to find out who did this. I bet I could get Marshall to fess up to it for less than a kiss—not that I would. But I'd love to see Chloe do jail time even if Marshall did use her as a pawn.

I spot Mom across the way, looking in a window at a men's store. She's probably just getting back from Demetri's.

"I'll be right back," I say to Bree before whizzing out the door.

Mom adjusts herself in the reflection of the glass, wearing none other than heels and a baby doll dress that exposes her long thin legs. Ha! I so knew it. I bet Tad gagged on his oatmeal once she debuted her Lolita costume. Heck, he might be sprawled out over the dining room floor dead from a heart attack after he figured out that I was right for a change.

Just as I'm about to shout over to her, she picks up her phone and laughs into it.

"Did I leave something behind? Oh...of course I'll see you—anytime, anywhere," her voice carries across the vicinity.

God, she's probably talking to Demetri. She's way too jubilant to be talking to Tad. Come to think of it. I don't think Tad has ever made her that happy.

"It'll have to be quick," she continues, "I have dinner at seven. How do I get there?"

Gross. He's probably giving her directions to some seedy motel.

"I'm leaving right now," she purrs and heads towards the parking lot.

I rush back to the lingerie store.

"I have to go," I hiss over at Brielle who holds a teddy over her bulging midsection that screams wishful thinking.

"Go ahead. I just saw Michelle. I'll catch a ride with her." She snatches up a bra comprised of two giant pink hearts and grins.

"Oh, it's you alright. I'll see you at Ellis's. And not in that, please."

"Skyla?" she calls after me. "Michelle mentioned she wanted to talk to you."

"I'll catch her later."

What the hell does Michelle I-hate-your-guts Miller want to talk to me about on Valentine's Day?

Thankfully my mother doesn't get far. I'm able to follow the metallic blue minivan down miles of Paragon highway, and I'm careful to keep six degrees of separation at all times. Of all the colors of the rainbow Logan's dad could have chosen for the Mustang, he chose an unsettling orange that's about as subtle as a traffic cone even in Paragon's heavily misted environment. Maybe that's why he chose it because it was a safety issue. God knows every time I see a fender bender on the side of the road there's at least one silver vehicle involved. So, I guess the justification is there, but still, it doesn't allow for blending into the scenery while pursuing your mother on a slow speed chase to prove to yourself she's having an affair with your father's killer.

Obviously, I need to take her back in time to see Dad again. Obviously, the two of us need to sit her down and fill her in on a few facts about the man who has my father's blood on his hands, who isn't even human by the way. Marrying Demetri would be a far greater offense than marrying Tad could ever be. There must be some familial violation involved when it comes to befriending your dead husband's killer.

Who knew Mom's affair with Demetri would be the deciding factor that makes me land square on Tad's side of the fence—odd how life works that way—finds enemies that make your adversaries feel like old friends.

She takes a turn and goes down an unincorporated road that leads past the falls. I pull over and let her disappear beyond the horizon before I tail her. There's nothing out here, certainly not any hotel. What if she wasn't on the phone with Demetri after all? What if she's got *another* client who finds Lizbeth Landon too hot to handle? God, what if he's a serial killer, and I'm about to rescue Mom from death's clutches? I speed up a little only to find her car already abandoned on the side of the road.

The sky darkens, dusting the island with a lavender patina. I park and get out, following the trail of tiny holes she's plowed in the dirt with her heels all the way to an all-familiar clearing.

"Oh my, God," I breathe the words. In the distance, I see a group of people in long dark robes. The large flat stone of sacrifice in the middle of the field shines like a dulled out coin.

Mom laughs while a tall shadow of a man hands her a robe. She shakes it out, examines it for a good long while. The man turns, darts a quick look in my direction revealing his hooknose, coal black eyes.

There he is. Demetri the brainwasher.

She throws the cloak over her dress, invoking a long hug from him as a reward. I watch as her pale arms ride up and down his back like a pair of withering lilies.

Mom pulls back and listens to whatever bullshit it is he's feeding her and laughs. Her voice echoes through the woods, the fattened clouds that hover above aren't enough to contain my mother's newfound elation. Her echoing laughter bypasses the sky, enters into the stratosphere before shooting off into dark abysmal space.

She takes up his hand and dutifully falls in line at the unholy altar.

I wonder how much longer before he convinces her that I should be lying on the stone in front of them.

I wonder how much longer before he convinces my mother I should disappear from their lives forever.

16

Down in Flames

Later in the evening, I get dressed and head over to the Oliver's house without even trying to break up a raucous knock 'em down drag out fight between Mia and Melissa. Instead, I let Tad deal with the fallout and don't even bother offering up information when he asks a million times if any of us knows, *where the hell our mother is because they've got reservations, and he'll be damned if he misses out on dinner tonight.*

I pull in next to Gage's truck and kill the ignition, glancing at the raging bash across the street. Ellis's party is already in full swing with bodies milling around nine deep around the circumference of the house—odd because usually people are in it.

I make my way through the cool of night, up to the Oliver's house, shivering because I forgot my jacket just as Gage opens the door.

"Hey beautiful," the words swim from his lips.

A pair of headlights pull into the driveway at an alarming speed. I jump into Gage afraid there might be some reprisal of what happened behind the bowling alley, only it's not the haunted Mustang heading in our direction, it's a giant white truck.

"Looks like Logan is home," I say before diving into an I'm-so-happy-you're-alive slash Happy Valentine's Day kiss with Gage. I love his mind-numbing kisses. I could easily spend an eternity in a lip lock with him.

A branch falls from the roof and hits him square on the head.

"Whoa," Gage backs up, plucking leaves out his hair.

"Perfect timing," I laugh, picking the stick up and waving it over our heads like mistletoe.

"Happy Valentine's Day," he murmurs through a series of soft pecks.

"I was about to say the same."

"Enough with the love fest," Logan shouts from the driveway. "Come check out my wheels."

Logan stands admiring his truck from a good ten feet away so we join him. My mouth falls open at the atrocity.

"What in the hell possessed you to do that?" Gage groans. Just looking at the vandalism that's taken place causes him physical pain, I can tell.

Giant red and yellow flames expand across the breadth of Logan's truck. They look cartoonish, silly and vulgar all at the same time.

"I'll second that," I say. "What the hell got into you?"

A hurt look crosses Logan's face before morphing back into the pissed off expression he's been sporting like a mask as of late.

"I mean it's different," I try to rectify the situation.

"Oh, it's different," Gage takes another step back. "Is this a joke? This is a joke, right? These are stickers, or magnets." He goes over and starts picking at the paint.

"The only joke I see around here is you," he presses out a dry smile and heads across the street to the party.

"He didn't mean it," I say.

"Of course, he meant it. Logan doesn't say things he doesn't mean. He just plays it off that way."

ʋ 𝓨 ʋ

We follow Logan across the street where Ellis's house thumps into the powder white night. Bodies swirl, disembodied laughter fills the air, and there are enough cars parked haphazard on the property to fill a dealership.

expel

I'm secretly looking forward to having a couple's page done for Gage and me.

We find Emily at the breakfast nook where she has already set up shop. Her dark head is lowered, speaking with Brielle and Drake as she dutifully goes over paperwork with them as if she were explaining a life insurance policy.

An aqua glow electrifies the backyard. I can see the pool outside the window. A thick seam of vapors rise off the water, and people are actually jumping in, so I guess that means it's heated.

Ellis walks by and I snatch him up by the elbow.

"Is that the big surprise? You heated the pool?"

"It's Valentine's Day," he nods as if it's a given. As if pool heaters the world over were traditionally fired up for just this occasion. "I thought it'd be a nice surprise."

"It would have been a nicer surprise if you would have warned us. We could have brought our bathing suits," I say. Not that I would have. Well, maybe I would have.

"That's half the fun, Messenger. No bathing suits. I've got three topless girls from East winning the water-wrestling competition. Now are you just going to stand there and let them take down our school like that? Or are you going to get out there and do something about it?" His serious demeanor makes me want to smack him.

"She's not saving the school with her body, Ellis," Gage interjects.

"Relax, I've got you covered my ailing friend. I have one more slot opened for judging— I was just on my way to offer you the position. Just wait until the synchronized swimming portion of the evening."

"No thanks," Gage adjusts himself on his crutch. "I'm not into synchronized swimming."

"Neither am I," Ellis assures, "But again, three girls from east, *topless*."

"Geez," I smack him hard in the gut. "You're a pervert and so is anyone watching."

"Logan happily volunteered. In fact, he's out there now holding down the fort," Ellis ticks his head towards the back. "It's nice to have him back. He's always so uptight. It's like he's finally loosening up."

"Yeah, like, a lot," I marvel. Like unraveling at the seams, but I leave that part out. I have a feeling discussing Logan and his bizarre behavior will set Gage back weeks in his recovery—hell his wardrobe alone is enough to send the both of us into a fashion induced coma.

"Never mind that," Gage points over at Brielle who's balling.

I speed over to her. "What's wrong?"

"It's not working out like I thought."

"What's not working out?" I ask, taking the paper out of her hands. It's a million little pictures of babies and furniture and a crooked looking house, much like Emily's own creepy family abode, and a bunch of other crap that's too difficult to decipher in this defused lighting.

"We're headed for trouble," she whines. "Our couple days could be numbered."

"That's bullshit," I say, trying to refute whatever Emily may have told her. Although deep down inside we both know it's not. Emily bats a thousand with those pictures she hammers out. They have an uncanny way of predicting the future. "I guess the good news is that there's still a chance."

Emily catches my eye sitting there alone with no new customer filling the void so I pat Brielle on the back and push her off towards an agitated looking Drake.

Just before I can pull Gage over to the breakfast nook, Chloe swoops in and takes a seat. She doesn't even acknowledge Gage. Who knew Chloe would fall into submission so easily? And here I thought you couldn't keep a good bitch down.

Emily draws something up at dizzying speeds, turns over the paper and continues her sketching spree—double-sided no less. Chloe has a saga worthy love life in store for her this year. I wonder if this means anything? If it falls in line with the duplicity my mother is pulling, a.k.a. seeing men that don't belong to you, or if it simply means Chloe will go through an entire line of suitors she blackmails into being with her, probably the latter.

"This is Ethan," Emily starts.

Should we be listening? Gage asks, plucking at my hand.

Very much so, I assure.

"Remember," Emily reprimands, "this is only for this year." She pulls a pencil from a plastic cup blooming with markers and uses it as a pointer. "Your relationship goes somewhere with him. You have something real here. It's funny because I didn't think you were that into him." She shrugs it off. "This is Logan."

Shit.

"You are so going to piss off Michelle and Lexy, but not too much because he was on theirs, too."

What?

He is a free agent, Gage is quick to remind me.

"He's hot and heavy with you for a while then it's cold turkey right around here." She points off to some timeline I'm not privy to. "Same with Lex and Michelle. It looks like he gets pretty serious with someone else and shuts the rest of you down, but you continue with Ethan, and I see this for the rest of the school year."

Chloe gives a heavy look in our direction. She leans into Em and whispers. Emily nods and whispers back, bringing a smile to Chloe's face.

Obviously it's about Gage.

Gage is the soil in which she buried her heart. Chloe waits for springtime, for the sun to warm over it, for a good shower of my bloodshed to fertilize her efforts. She's insane if she thinks anything is ever going to bloom out of that rancid maggot pit that lies buried in her chest. Devastation, maybe, but that's all that will ever come from there.

You better not make Chloe's year, I say, yanking Gage by the fingers.

"I'll be too busy making yours," he leans on his crutch and kisses me full on the mouth, causing the room and all of its interruptions to melt away.

"Next," Emily beeps it out, obtrusive as an air horn.

I scoot in next to her, and Gage takes a load off his aching leg in the seat across from us. Emily stares at me banally as though she were reading a newspaper printed across my forehead.

"You sure you want him here for this?" She flicks a finger towards Gage.

"Yes." I fully expect to see an entire page cluttered up with nothing but our love—hearts and rainbows, a unicorn or two with our names tattooed on its rear in a giant frilly heart. Gage, on the other hand, looks like he's ready for a nap, like just walking across the street has proven to be too big of a physical challenge.

Emily zigzags her way at top speed across the front and back of the thick parchment set in front of her.

"So you can interpret the things you draw?" I'll have to beg her to tell me in detail what that freaky body art she scribbled over me this last winter meant.

"Sometimes," she says it bored as if she was fine with it either way. If it were me, I'd totally want to know what the hell my haunted drawings were trying to say.

Emily continues to spit out microscopic scenes across the page before coming abruptly to a halt.

See? Easy as pie. Gage and I are so utterly predictable in our happily ever after, it took less than ten seconds for her to whip it out.

She reaches over and grabs another sheet.

"What the heck are you doing?" I spit it out in a panic.

"Ran out of room." She darts around the page before flipping that too, over. To my horror she picks up another sheet and continues without missing a freaking beat.

"Looks like a lot of loving going on," my toes curl when I say it. Truthfully, I'm regretting this big time. The last thing in the world I want to see is that I, in any way, veer from Gage in the next year.

"Um, you know, I think we'll get going now." I try to stand, but she yanks me back down.

"You have Gage, you can relax. But these other two, they're not," she shakes her head, "something's different about them. This one's not human, you're not like into some freaky shit, like dogs, right?"

She pegged it—dogs of the celestial variety.

I shake my head, quick and nervous.

"I don't know what's up with these two. I'm not even sure this one's human," she says before looking up at Gage. "You've got some serious competition from a lion and a, well, I don't know what the hell that is, some prehistoric velociraptor with wings."

"Great," Gage arches his brows like he knows exactly who they are.

Obviously Logan is the lion and Marshall is the prehistoric demon-looking creature. Gage gets up to make room for the next boyfriend awaiting the relational guillotine. Not that our session with Em was punctuated with a blade to the neck. Gage and I are impervious to failing. He has nothing in the world to worry about.

"Thanks Emily," I whisper. "Can you save these for me?"

She gives a knowing nod before flicking me away.

Well, that didn't go so bad. Didn't go so great, either.

A shoulder bumps me from behind. I twist to get through the merging crowd only to find myself face to face with my second least favorite Kragger, Holden's not so long lost fraternal twin.

Crap.

"Guess who's got regular scheduled visits with a social worker?" Pierce leans his face into mine. His hot beer breath rakes against my cheek. "And a lawyer who tells me things don't look too damn good for me." He spits as he grates the words out.

Nat steps between us, all beady eyed and pissed like she might kick my ass if the situation warrants it. Her curls are embalmed in dried out hair gel, her eyes outlined like an obscene raccoon.

"I'm not in control of the state," I say. "I don't decide who they go after." Or apparently take down. Personally I'm rooting for the state. Even if Pierce didn't knock a dozen people unconscious, or spin Nat in the air like a pizza that day last fall, doesn't mean he should have gnawed on my neck in the cemetery or any other venue he chose to suck my body dry. Besides, if he's not incarcerated soon, I might have to do something drastic the next time he tries siphoning the lifeblood from my veins, like kill him.

Pierce leans over Nat. The two of them glower at me as if I had just set their children on fire.

"I'm in control of *me*." Pierce blasts his ethanol in my direction as he continues his verbal badgering. "I decide who I go after." He thrusts a piece of paper at me, and knocks me off balance.

Gage pushes him back a good ten feet without hesitating.

Nat runs over to help scoop Pierce off the floor as the crowd filters between us.

I unfurl the note. *Cease and desist*. Legal action against my parents? This is horrible.

I stuff the letter into my purse.

"Let's go outside," I spin us towards the exit in the event Pierce feels obligated to return the favor, only, for Gage, a shove like that might actually crack his hip in half and give him pneumonia. I might have to adjust my to-do list and move killing Pierce up to a priority position. There is no way in hell I'm going to let Gage end up in the hospital again.

I can see Logan from the patio helping some girl take off her sweater before pushing her into the pool. He's no lion—he's human all right.

A hot roll of nausea explodes in my stomach.

"I can't stand this," I say, ushering us into the yard.

I'm going to end Logan's hunger for attention. Smack some sense into him, make him aware of the fashion felonies he's been committing, not to mention the ones he's about to perpetrate with his flesh.

"You should probably let Logan do his thing," Gage says, pulling me back. The words escape from him slow, like a tire losing air. "Let him go."

"You're right." I place my hands on my hips, but really I don't want Gage to hear me admit that I could never let go of Logan, let alone watch him do his ludicrous *thing* especially when that *thing* involves publicly ogling topless girls from East.

The damp cool of night blows against me as I watch Logan's hands race around the bare waist of Carson Armistead, her hips sway seductively in rhythm to the music.

Jealousy rips through me like a fire line.

How the hell am I ever going to cut Logan Oliver out of my heart if my heart keeps breaking at the thought of him with someone else?

17

Strike Three

Chloe stops me cold on my way to push Logan into the pool. "I bet it guts you like a rusted knife knowing that Logan has recovered from his severe case of Skyla fever," she hacks out each word with glee.

I choose to ignore her, a tactic I should employ more often when dealing with Chloe in general.

Heated or not, he needs to log some serious time away from the push up bra brigade storming in his direction. Obviously his brain is in malfunction mode. That blue toxin Ezrina dipped him in eroded all of his good character, his sound judgment, and, yes, his slight obsession for me seems to have dissipated as well.

Logan jumps up on an ice chest and cups his hands around his mouth. "The line starts here!" He jumps down and twirls the next recipient of his attention like a ballerina.

My mouth falls open as he gyrates his hips over hers inspiring her to do the same. An entire row of girls magically crop up to have their clothes peeled from their bodies by Logan himself. It's sickening.

"This isn't Logan. This isn't what he's about." I say, trying to push my way around Chloe. It's high time someone remind him he doesn't need to assert himself as the head of the stripping committee.

"Face it," she seethes, "the green eyed monster has you by the balls Messenger. You can't stand the fact he's moved on—that the Skyla-shaped scales have fallen from his eyes, and he can see you for the loser you really are."

"I've got a license to thrill," Logan pushes into a scantily clad Carson, and holy freaking shit—they are totally rutting. Logan's douchebag jeans are about ready to slide right off his person. I can't stand to look so I bury my face in Gage's chest.

"Some people's kids," he says, not even flinching at Logan's poor impersonation of an *officer of the law*, which is proof positive he's boarded a train for imbecile-ville.

"He's gone insane," I say, shaking. "Do something."

"This is exactly what he was like before you came to Paragon. Nothing's changed." Gage assures me.

"He's over you," Chloe laughs. "Hurt much?"

I look past her shoulder as he gets on his knees and unbuckles Carson's pants. He pulls them down with one swift tug and bites into the panties riding high on her hip.

"That's it." I push past Chloe, muddle my way through a throng of overeager girls filling the interim and finally break through the crowd.

I yank him off his knees by the back of his shirt.

"Whoa," Logan throws his hands in the air, "looks like Skyla, here, wants her turn right now."

He reaches for my waist and peels off my sweater quick as a magician. Before I know it, I'm standing there in my black lace bra in front of East and West, a gloating Chloe, and a very pissed off Gage.

"Stop," I scream like a siren before snatching back my top.

Gage knocks him backwards a few good feet. "What the hell has gotten into you?"

I like this side of Gage—kick some ass first, ask questions later.

"You trying to start a war, dude?" Logan glares at him, gone is the spirited playboy who's been arousing girls poolside for the past half hour.

"I'm trying to figure out what the hell to do with you," Gage counters.

Logan steps into Gage, digs a finger in his chest. "You can start by getting the fuck out of my way."

"You know," Gage winces into his annoyance, "you haven't even bothered with a hello since you've been back."

"Oh, I haven't?" Logan makes light of the fact. "You poor, fragile thing. Have you been spurned by my lack of attention? Please, allow me to give you a physical token of my undying devotion." Logan backs up his arm and wallops Gage right in the stomach, sends him skidding across the sopping wet cement.

I let out a viral scream. "He had internal injuries!" I shout into Logan's face.

I use all of my Celestra induced anger and send him sailing into the deep end of the pool. Logan lies at the bottom of the plaster like a crime scene cutout before resurfacing with a roar.

"Gage!" I push Chloe off his person. "Are you OK? You want me to get your dad? Take you to the hospital?"

"I'm fine," he squints as he rises. "Let's get out of here."

I hand Gage his crutch, and we head out the side gate.

"That's it. He's done. No more Logan in my life," I announce as we hobble down the driveway. "First he dresses like he's auditioning for the part of doofus on a reality show, not to mention the graffiti he's inflicted on his poor truck—then he *hits* you? Obviously, he's undergone a serious head injury. You can't tell me Logan was always a grade A asshole."

Gage pauses to catch his breath before we cross the street.

"No, not usually. But, then again, he's been pretty messed up after breaking up with you. You're his first serious heartache." Gage holds his sympathy out like a chalice. He swills it around, beckoning me to take just one sip. "Sometimes heartbreak really screws with your head. Imagine if we were with different people, wouldn't you hate that?"

Chloe rips through my mind. "God, yes." Truth is, I'd more than wig out. "Actually that's an unbearable thought." I hold my breath until I can effectively chase the idea out of my head. It's too painful to consider a world without Gage. But, then again, a world with this new version of Logan isn't so fantastic either.

"You'll get used to it." Gage squeezes my hand and dispenses a shy smile. "Time will heal that ache, Skyla, but you have to set him free. Let him do what he has to do," he depresses a sigh. "Who knows? You might even want him to see other girls—root for him."

My blood boils at the thought. It's seriously doubtful I'll be rooting for Logan to get in another girl's pants, although Gage does paint a rosy picture of this fictitious future.

"I guess anything's possible," I placate him with a short-lived smile.

"You wanna go inside and watch a movie?" There's a natural seduction about him. I'd watch him brush his teeth if he asked me to. "I sorta gotta lay down."

"I'd love to lay down with you."

"Lamest Valentine's ever, right?" His dimples ignite without a smile.

"Lying next to my boyfriend and watching a movie, and said boyfriend happens to be you?" I slip my arm around his waist. "Best Valentine's ever, I swear."

I pull him into a kiss as fierce and wide as the ocean.

Everything in me aches for Gage.

"Let's go inside," I bite down on the implications.

"Let's."

🦋 🦋 🦋

It took over an hour for us to break into the house. His key broke off in the lock and I had to climb through the laundry room window that was half as narrow as it needed to be, getting myself securely lodged in the opening. Finally Emma and Barron came home and used their key to the backdoor to get inside. They helped pluck me free after rubbing my hips down with lard from a red box Emma found lurking in the back of the fridge. *Lard.*

I change into a pair of his sweats and gingerly crawl up next to him, nestled in the center of the bed. The movie begins. A soft grey flicker ignites the room as I twirl my fingers through his slick, glossy hair. Gage is exhausted, already sleeping gently at my side. The movie plays on but I watch Gage, so beautifully alive. I couldn't breathe when I thought he might have died. I can't imagine life without him. And here he is. I place my head over his chest, relax over him and pretend ten years have passed, that we're long married and Gage is my husband.

I wake to find another hour has slipped by. I lean in and give a careful kiss to his cheek and tiptoe out quietly.

Across the street, the party is still pumping. A pink glow illuminates unnaturally from the back of Ellis's house and it prompts me to head straight over to see what in the hell is up now. Logan has probably ruptured a dozen implants fondling all the mammary glands that flung themselves at him. I bet that's liquid oozing out of at least a dozen silicone prosthetics, clouding up the water.

I bump into Michelle who's on her way out with some boy, and to my horror the boy in question is the breast man himself, Logan.

"Where are you two going?" I ask curt.

"I've been meaning to tell you," Michelle points up at her bare neck, "took your advice."

Marshall's rose—it's missing. I give a private smile.

"Feel better?"

"Tons," she leans in. "Best part—I've got Logan back," she marvels.

expel

"Yeah, well, about that," I snatch him forward. "I've got to finish something first."

18

Right Here, Right Now

OK—so, pissing off Michelle Miller on the first day of our questionable road to friendship probably wasn't the brightest idea given her sanity is in the process of being restored. But, nevertheless, I'm with Logan and we're driving off into the blank of night so I can fill him in on all sorts of facts about himself, such as, contrary to his behavior, he really is not an ass.

"Where should we go?" I ask. I've been driving for a half hour solid, and he looks as though he's about to nod off.

Who would have guessed that I'd put both Oliver boys to sleep on Valentine's Day?

"Falls." He points over to the backlit sign, so I pull into the dirt lot overlooking the lake.

A smattering of rowboats are strewn about the glittering pool of black. An entire constellation of stars speckle the water with their hazy reflection, quelling the sound of the falls with an auspicious calm. Couples sit knee to knee, others with arms and legs lassoed around one another, lips pulled together as one. The entire setting is undeniably romantic.

"Let's go." He ejects himself from the car before I can properly protest. It was going to be one thing to sit in the car and discuss Logan's prick-like behavior, it's entirely another hopping in a boat with him, depending on the warmth of his body to keep me from freezing to death.

I'm guessing Gage will be less than impressed to learn where his girlfriend has managed to land herself on this night in particular and with the perpetrator who assaulted him just hours before.

expel

I chase after him in the virginal night, a puff of fog dances over the moist ground as my feet disrupt the mist that hugs the soil. My shoes snag on crushed reeds, my ankles turn on the unsteady landscape, retarding my ability to keep up with him. It's too dark to navigate the terrain. It feels as though I'm about to fall down a very steep staircase with every move I make.

"Wait!" I shout. My voice echoes off the embankment, disrupting the sentimental atmosphere people are busy etching into their memories. Girls are like that—cataloging holidays, anniversaries, birthdays—all relationship milestones deep into our memory bank. We could tell you exactly how we spent most of those occasions down to what we were wearing. We stain our conscious with the vivid details of sight and sound and scent, even what the goofball with us had on and whether or not he looked like a moron.

The sound of rushing water intensifies as I draw closer to the lake. It blankets over my voice and tempers my anxious shouts for Logan to slow down.

"Logan!" I catch up to him at the waterline, panting from the sprint.

He plucks a boat from out of a marsh and slips it onto shore. Rust rises up on the paltry vessel's side, a thick blanket of algae covers the bottom. Makes it look like a living thing, the leaf of some exotic plant you could crawl inside and float in.

"Come on, I'll row us out."

I don't think twice, just hop in like a trained circus poodle. I'm exhausted, and at this point, the thought of taking a seat sounds far too inviting to pass up. I'd sit on a Fem's lap if the situation presented itself.

The stars shine in all their glory through an ethereal haze that illuminates a rich shade of blue, and I wonder if this has anything to do with the Counts but shrug it off because it's Valentine's and magical things abound on this celebratory commercialized span of twenty-four hours.

Logan rows us off to the quiet end of the lake, away from the other couples seeking privacy behind the falls. Brielle and Drake are somewhere out there, or Drake and Emily, either way, Drake's car is in the lot.

"You really saved my ass." He expels a sigh, and an entire smoky-river emits from his nostrils.

"About that—" I start.

He pulls me forward until I'm sitting on his lap.

"Um, excuse me?" I try to rise, but he warms my arms with his hands, tempers my shivers by leaning me close to his chest.

The romantic implications of it all hit me, and suddenly I feel a tremendous amount of guilt for boarding this vessel. Of course, I'll have to confess all this to Gage come morning. I'm sure that won't be stress inducing in any way to hear his girlfriend spent ode-to-couples day sitting in her ex-boyfriend's lap.

I hop off his knees and land next to him, trying to hide the fact I can't control my shiver. I'm here to help him, not help myself to him.

I should feel heroic over the fact I'm saving Logan from an impending, and rather permanent, douchebag status that he's bravely frontiering. This is high school after all, once you determine your social standing, it sticks with you for life. Ten years from now when everyone's waxing nostalgic for all things West Paragon I'd hate for people to think of Logan, and the next thing that rolls off their tongue to be, *he was such a douchebag*. It's like a prison sentence he'd wear for life.

"OK," I roll my head back onto his shoulder and he lands a soft kiss on each of my eyelids. "What was that for?" I panic.

Confession—the fact Logan peppered my face with kisses is going to guarantee a setback for both Gage's health and the health of our relationship.

"I'm showing you my appreciation," Logan tries seducing me with his citrine bedroom eyes. "I'm alive—breathing right now, all because of you. I hate dead. Being dead sucks."

"Yeah, we've already determined that, and, by the way, you're welcome. Don't feel like you owe me anything because you've done so much for me with the Mustang, the insurance, the job—*bail*. Let's call it even." OK, so I should probably offer to pay him back, but that's not an acute issue at the moment.

Logan maneuvers the boat between a thicket of reeds tall as a person. The strong scent of rosemary perfumes the air with a fragrant howl as a choir of crickets destroy the silence with its chirping symphony. I close my eyes a moment—let the world vanish to cinders beneath my newly christened lids.

"I don't think we're even," he whispers, dragging a fire line down the side of my neck with his lips.

"Whoa," I straighten in an effort to stave him off, causing the tiny craft to wobble. "You know," I push my shoulder into his face to deflect his unwanted affections, "you've been acting more than a little strange since you've come back. I know you mentioned the live for today stuff and you're really stoked about having a new lease on life, but let's call a spade a spade—you're about to go down in the history of West as a total jackass supreme."

"Probably," he says, slinking his hands up the back of my sweater and offering a spontaneous massage.

Sadly, I delay in deflecting those particular efforts because, for one, his hands are oven hot, and two, the massage feels rather necessary at this point.

I give a few involuntary moans as I point over the tops of my shoulders, and Logan is quick to accommodate.

"Recognizing the fact you're an asshole is a great start," I pluck his arms free from under my sweater since he accidentally on purpose just unhooked my bra, but I don't call him on it. "So, the *old* you was kind and courteous, and would never in a million years juggle the breasts of three girls at once."

A quick bout of laughter escapes him.

"I'm here to live, Skyla. I'm a guy. We were born to juggle, snuggle—you name it. Besides, what fun is being Logan Oliver if I can't enjoy a breast or two?" His hand crawls up my front like a tarantula.

"Logan!" I bat him away.

"Come on, Skyla." In one swift move he knocks me back and lands on top of me with his full weight, "Let me give you a proper thank you. Show you how well all the essential parts are functioning."

"Again, no need for a thank you or a demonstration," I try to wrestle his hands from gliding back up my sweater, but it's proving to be a futile effort. And judging by the rock hard bulge in his jeans, everything's in full working order, that, or he's smuggled a root beer bottle on board.

Logan pushes his lips over mine, crushes me with his chest as he fiddles with the buckle on his jeans.

"Stop! I can't breathe." God—I'm going to have to use my Celestra strength just to get out of this mass tangle of flesh. The strange part is, he hasn't had one single thought. He's either put a moratorium on thinking, or the Mustang caused a mass exodus of brain cells. Chloe's power-mower skills have turned Logan into a classic jock airhead rife with hypersexual tendencies.

Logan doesn't stop. He reaches up my sweater, lands himself on second base without the proper invitation.

"Let go right now," I seethe, "or I will go ninja all over your ass."

But he doesn't listen. He's all hot and bothered, twisting and writhing over me, too busy suctioning his lips to my flesh to hear me. I try to slap him out of his lust-inspired stupor, but nothing.

Logan squeezes and gropes like he's testing produce at the grocery store. I hone in all of my pissed off glory and knee him hard in the balls. I think I've just successfully reduced the odds of him procreating with his newfound asshole genes, down to nil.

Logan rolls off into a fetal position, choking on his pain.

I yank an oar off the side mount, spike it into the water in an effort to get back to dry land, and the boat starts on a sideways spin.

"I'm sorry, Skyla." He thrusts himself on top of me.

In an effort to scoot the hell away, I accidentally launch my upper torso into the water. I manage to hook my knees over the side of the aluminum structure to halt myself from falling in completely. Water rushes in, fills my ears with the soft sound of effervescence. Giant bubbles prick my face as I let out an underwater scream from the icy shock.

My arms flail as I try to surface for a breath. Logan reaches down and grabs a hold of my hair at the base of my neck. My left leg ejects into the water as the boat gyrates wildly. Logan locks his hand over the back of my head. My arms flail in histrionics, my legs kick out—can't breathe.

My nostrils burn from taking in a blast of frozen liquid.

"Stupid bitch," he grunts, pushing my other leg over the side.

It occurs to me as I sputter and twirl my way to the surface that just maybe Logan wasn't helping me up—just maybe he was holding me down, throwing me overboard.

I come up and pinch my nose, spit several times as I continue to gasp for air. Logan thrusts the oar in my direction with a violent swing, and I manage to duck before he decapitates me with the effort.

"Stop pissing around, Skyla," he disrupts the night with an unnatural aggression.

I swim over to shore, climb over moss-covered rocks turning my ankle in the process.

"Skyla?" He calls, but I don't answer.

I run like hell to the Mustang and give a NASCAR worthy performance the hell away from Logan Oliver.

19

Love Hurts

I'm so thankful Mom and Tad are still not back from their Valentine's misadventure. I loathed the thought of having to render an explanation as to why I'm sopping wet, not to mention the fact my face is red and swollen from sobbing over the idea Logan Oliver really is a jackass. I'll just have to learn to live with the fact he's morally bankrupt and virtually irredeemable.

I catch a glimpse of the horror that is me in the hallway mirror. I have the lake's equivalent of seaweed woven throughout my hair, and I'm ten times more pathetic looking than previously imagined. A nice hot shower is in order before I map out my revenge on said jackass, but as I'm about to head upstairs, the steady rhythm of hiccups captures my attention.

I spy Mia crumpled on the couch in the family room pumping some serious heartache into a pillow, and I race on over.

"What happened?" I ask lower than a whisper, ignoring the fact she might parrot the question in my direction.

"Gabriel danced with Melissa all night."

"That's because he's an ass," I say it sweetly, pushing the perspiration-soaked hair from off her forehead.

I just want to run to the freezer and grab a pint of chocolate peanut butter ice cream and spend the rest of the night watching chick flicks with my sister, but I have to wash the bodily fluids of Logan the predator off my person first.

"Look," I wag her by the chin. "I'll run up, take a quick shower, then maybe we can watch a movie and eat ice cream."

"You mean it?"

"Of course, I mean it."

"Tad says all you ever do is lie, that we shouldn't trust you." Her features soften with disappointment. Mia accepts every word from Tad's lips as gospel. That's what the hell is wrong with this family—they keep listening to Tad.

"Tad is just another ass like Gabriel Armistead." And Logan Oliver.

Really I should educate both her and Melissa on Chloe's faux maxim she espoused at winter formal, *chicks before dicks and all that good stuff*. Plus they're sisters, there must be some deeper code of ethics when dating and relations are involved. Logan and Gage dart through my mind. That ended badly.

I give her a heartfelt hug, feel her hot cheek rub up alongside mine and savor the moment. When Mia was little she used to inundate me with hugs, beg for them like they were candy. Once Melissa came along, the only body part she wanted to shower me with was her middle finger. This is the Mia I miss—sweet, achingly sweet and vulnerable, Mia.

"I love you, Mia," I whisper. "I'll be right back. I promise."

※ ※ ※

I can't get into a scalding hot shower fast enough. I lock my door and push the dresser over a notch out of habit, pull out a pair of sweats that happen to be my own for a change. Soon I'm going to have an entire pile of laundry that belongs to Gage. Of course, I'll wash it for him, fold it—spray it down with my perfume before I give it back.

How am I ever going to tell Gage about what happened tonight without stressing him out into a coma? Of course he's going to get pneumonia—*double* pneumonia along with a triple coronary. It'll be a miracle if I don't finish him off before prom.

Logan is on a determined path toward assault charges, or worse—manslaughter, judging by the way he held my head underwater. I shudder recalling the words that flew from his lips. He's become unrecognizable, a beast, a monster. Maybe that's why you should never bring people back from the dead. Look at Chloe? And Holden? Both your textbook assholes and probably Ethan, too, I just haven't had time to analyze him properly.

On my way to the bathroom, a strange arrangement of jewelry catches my attention. Two of my necklaces form a large silver heart, set over my laptop.

Great.

Mia and Melissa must have been fishing around in my jewelry box again. I flip up the magazine that hides the third disc Marshall gave me. Clearly I'll have to put this in a location Mia and Melissa would never think to look, lest I wake up one morning and find it strapped around one of their necks. I flip the coin in the air and catch it. The wall safe in the butterfly room is the best place for this.

I head into the shower. I don't even wait for the water to heat up before jumping in and lathering up with enough soap to remove the lake slime off my body.

Logan and his misguided behavior run through my mind. Obviously serious brain damage has occurred. How can I be mad at him? He could never be so cruel or heartless. This is devastating. Maybe I can talk to Ezrina? I bet she has some elixir somewhere that can repair the damage, and he'll be back to his sweet self in no time. Although—if I continue to let him act like a monkey with his balls on fire, it might be a great way for me to finally get over him. It might be the only way.

I let the water run over my shoulders, a little too hot, for a little too long. Unexpected tears mix into the fold. For some reason these four smoky walls are the only place it feels safe to admit that I still have very strong feelings for old Logan. I don't care what Chloe or even Gage try to feed me about him, I know sweet sensitive Logan wasn't a figment of my imagination. I cherished the way he would drink me in with those glowing amber eyes, the way he soothed me with his calm, even tone—his vibrant kisses, each with a life of its own. Was I truly so blind in love that I couldn't see him for the person he really was? There is no way he could have always been so horrible. It's just not possible.

Our short time together runs through my mind like a silent movie. The first moment we met, our first time at the falls, battling Fems, him taking me under his wing and training me—how he let me go to protect me. An entire wall of tears gush from me, warm and salty rivaling the water pouring over my shoulders for attention. I give in and mourn Logan, the old version that I would die to have back. I miss his easy ways, the constant assurance of his love.

I miss it. I miss the way Logan Oliver loved me.

I turn off the water and wrap the towel around my damp flesh, get out and stare at my soft impression in the foggy mirror. I'm too numb to move, too warped from the heartache of losing the lover of my heart, to face a moment—an entire future without him.

A letter begins to form on the glass. The letter S, then K, then, Y- L - A.

"Go to hell, Holden." Holden Kragger is going to try to officiate this as the worse Valentine's ever, but I won't let him.

Another set of letters form beneath my name. L -O – G – A - N.

Logan? Was I mumbling Logan's name in the shower? God—what if Holden, the not so friendly ghost, has harvested the power to read minds?

Just as I'm about to smear his efforts, a heart emerges, enwreathing both our names.

expel

"Skyla," a soft voice whispers, "I love you more than the heavens love the sun and the moon."

A soft blue light illuminates the bathroom from behind.

I turn around and find a familiar lovely face staring back at me.

Logan.

20

Logan

"Oh my, God," I breathe.

Logan and his pale perfection, his transparent blue features staring back at me with a clear look of wonder and agony rolled into one.

"If you're here, then who—" I take in a quick breath, not willing to volunteer the information myself.

"Holden," his voice emits a ghostly whisper.

I let out a little whimper. I've screwed up before, turned perfectly good things into a pile of shit quicker than a vapor can mingle with the atmosphere, but this, this was of a scope and magnitude that left little room for anything but the unhinging of my jaw. This would permanently reside as the innermost deepest mistake I have ever made.

Marshall blinks through my mind. He said I was on my own. He could have averted this tragedy from the beginning if I had only restrained myself from blinding him with sputum.

"That wasn't you on the boat tonight," I huff a small laugh, full with relief.

He shakes his head.

"When Giselle comes—" I don't want to imply he's not good enough in his transparent state, but, "well, she looks in every way human."

His cheeks fill with color, flesh converges over his velum features, and he appears fully formed in jeans and t-shirt.

"Logan," I jump up and hug him, losing my towel in the process. I knead my hands into the hard flesh of his arms, pat him down like a criminal, run my fingers over his face, trace the outline of his smile, before kissing him full on the mouth soft and lingering—so sad—so happy.

He pulls back and takes me in, holding my gaze with his hypnotic sense of being.

"Um," he points down never letting his gaze wander south of my chin.

"Oh, right," I reach over and grab my robe, wrap it tight around my body, and lead him out to the bedroom. "I can't believe you're here. I mean I didn't know you weren't *here*, here. Oh my, God." I cup my hand over my mouth. "He's destroying you."

A loud rattle on the other side of the wall inspires me to drag Logan up to the butterfly room for privacy.

Logan pulls me in next to him as we settle on the black glittering floor, the galaxy at our feet. He drops a long forlorn kiss on top of my head and sighs.

"I knew something was wrong," I say it low, ashamed that I wasn't aware from the beginning.

"I've missed you with an indescribable ache, Skyla." He bears into me with those resolute eyes that testify to his words. "You and me," he swallows hard, "we're right together. I see it clearer now than ever before."

A spark ignites in me. Deep inside I know this to be true. I don't understand it, I'm not sure I want to. This never-ending anguish, this never-ending misery, it carries on its sad refrain deep in my soul, haunts me. But now he's dead and still nothing seems simple.

"What are we going to do about this?" I cradle his perfectly warm hands—hold them carefully as if they had morphed into a newborn.

"You can't let on that you know its Holden."

"Why? I hate Holden."

"You need to kill him," it comes out sharp. "If you confront him, you'll ruin the element of surprise."

"Kill?" It comes out weak. "I can't kill you. Let Gage kill you, or better yet— your uncle." I find the prospect of me snuffing the life out of Logan Oliver in any incarnation highly improbable.

"We'll figure it out. Speaking of Gage." He takes in a deep breath as if Gage's own state of being were almost as challenging as his.

"Dr. Oliver doesn't want me to stress him out." I bite down on my lip.

"I know. He needs to finish healing." Logan stares at our conjoined fingers, picks up my hand and bumps his lips over my knuckles. "What happened at the lake?" His voice trembles with anger.

"Were you there?"

"There was a binding spirit around the vicinity. I could only get as far as the parking lot."

"He was rounding out second base when I kneed him in the balls."

"Good girl," he tugs at my hand. "Sorry about that," it depresses out of him. The line on his cheek where I cut him sags, and I reach over and trace the hard ridge of flesh with my finger.

"You're here. You feel so real. This isn't fake. Why can't you live like this? We can have Holden shipped off to prison for impersonating you."

"It doesn't work like that. This is a temporal form. I can't live my life like this, and I won't stand for Holden tearing down my existence just to satisfy his every itch."

More like satisfy every bitch.

"Can others see you?" I squeeze his hand.

"Only if I allow them."

"Maybe you should show yourself to Holden. He can drop dead of a heart attack, and you can have your body back." I'm only half-kidding.

"I have a feeling he doesn't scare so easy." Logan's jaw goes rigid. "He's already drained the bowling alley of three night drops."

"Probably sponsoring that lousy wardrobe of his. Did you see what he did to your truck?"

Logan gives a slow blink of dissatisfaction. "I'm more concerned with what he plans on doing with every girl on the island, starting with you."

Holden scoffed at being Ethan, no wonder he was kissing my feet with gratitude when he turned up in Logan's body. It's like graduating from a paddleboat to a cruise ship. He was probably trying to do me a *favor* by sleeping with me first, before hitting the bevy of bathing beauties waiting for him back at Ellis's. I've got to stop him from defiling Logan's body.

"Skyla," Logan gives a devilish smile, "we're holding hands. I can hear you."

"Did you get your powers back?" I'm hopeful. Right about now I'm sorry for every lousy thing I've ever done to Logan.

"No. It comes with the territory. I've been hanging out with Giselle. She taught me a few tricks."

"Giselle—she wanted to come and spend time with the family, then you guys..."

"She told me," Logan flexes a sad smile. "I'm hoping I could come, too."

"You don't need an invitation. Besides, if we're lucky Holden will be dead by midnight." I start to rise, and he pulls me gently down, lands me back on the floor with a soft thud.

"It's not that easy. We can't have any external injuries. I don't have Celestra capabilities. It's going to be difficult explaining why I'm alive if the entire left side of my head is bashed in."

"Right, we need to do this with no one around, totally covert ops. I'll drown him or poison him, something that won't leave any marks, and when he kicks the bucket you can, you know, zoom right back in."

His lips pull into a bleak line.

"It's not that easy, is it?"

He shakes his head.

A sense of dread overtakes me. "We need Marshall, don't we?"

He gives a weak nod.

Just freaking great.

21

Only You

Clouds lay over the morning, hard like sedimentary rocks with periodic layering in every shade of grey. A waxy film douses the outside world with just enough fog to soften the hard edges of the pines, the needle-like protrusions of the still bald maples.

I sweep a quick glance at the forest outside my window for signs of Nevermore, but avail nothing in my search. Instead, I dress for church in a bright red angora sweater two sizes too small that gives the illusion my breasts are about to hulk their way out into the world—a pair of skinny jeans and heels. Really I could wear sweats and no one would bat a lash. Paragon Presbyterian tries its best to emulate the Christian casual trend that's been assaulting the religion of late. No shirt, no shoes, no problem—plus there's a makeshift Starbucks and donut buffet at the rear. Soon they'll be serving mojitos and oysters as a ploy to get people to go forth and be fruitful.

Gage sent a text saying he couldn't make it this morning. Said he was still sore from the body piercing Logan tried inflicting on him, thought he'd lay low. I'm totally going over after and hanging out with him—that is, after I pummel Marshall with pleas to help me get Logan back into the right body, thus the breasty red sweater and high heeled embellishments.

Downstairs, I find the entire family amassed in various levels of undress. Mia and Melissa are both so ripely pissed at this fragile hour it hardly seems possible.

Mia! The *movie*.

Crap.

"Mia," I go over with my arms spread wide and attempt to hug her, but she ducks, successfully evading the maneuver.

"Back off." She holds up a spatula as if she were about to cut out my liver.

"I totally fell asleep," I press my hand against my chest. I'm actually telling the truth for once. Logan stayed for a good long while, and I fell asleep in his arms. He said he'd stay the night, but babysitting Holden was his newfound responsibility. Nevertheless, I officially hold the title of worst sister ever.

"You fell asleep?" She charges me with a serious look of doubt. "I went up to your room and the door was locked," she leans accusingly, "so I picked it. Then it was jammed, so I had to *push* my way in. But guess what? You weren't in your bed. You weren't in the bathroom." She bores into me a look of concentrated revenge, or hatred, really it could go either way. "I heard voices in that secret room of yours." She walks over and flips the pancakes already singed on one side. I swear I think I see Marshall's effigy on one, but I'm quick to glance away and not stray from the emotional trauma at hand. "I got the message," she hisses. "Plus it was Valentine's Day, so I would have done the same." She bats me away with the kitchen tool in her hand.

"So you're really not mad at me?" I find this doubtful.

She shakes her head while breaking off a piece of pancake and popping it in her mouth.

"Thank you!" I go over and hug her by the shoulders. "I'll take you to the mall or something."

"Movies. I plan on having a date in the near future," she whispers, eyeing Melissa at the table from over my shoulder. "Maybe next Tuesday if I'm lucky."

"That's a school night."

"It's five dollar Tuesday, plus this isn't serious enough yet for a Friday or a Saturday." She shakes her head annoyed like I should be aware of the hierarchy of date nights.

"So who's the date with?" Now that Melissa has saddled herself with the demonic Armistead spawn, I don't really mind the idea of Mia seeing a boy, or two or twelve.

"Gabriel Armistead," she whispers, licking the syrup off her finger.

"*What?*" I hiss. "I thought you were balling your eyes out over him last night because he was such a jerk?"

"Who's a jerk?" Mom comes in wafting of expensive perfume, already dressed in a long navy skirt and white ruffled blouse. Her feet are pressed into heels that rival my own, both of which could double as circus stilts.

"Skyla," Mia doesn't miss a beat before walking off with a plate of flapjacks.

"Looks like the gang's all here," Tad howls.

If Tad would emote just a smidge of sarcasm when he says stupid stuff like that it might make me respect him just a little bit more.

"Alrighty then." Mom dons an over-processed smile as she heads to the kitchen table, motioning for the rest of us to do the same.

"Your mother and I have news." Tad invokes an authoritative baritone, exclusive to imbeciles and stepfathers, as he hovers over the lot of us.

I, for one, hope this has nothing to do with either procreation or recreation. Two concepts that I'm loathe to entertain with the Landon bunch.

I take a seat in between Ethan and Drake at the bar, in not-so-eager anticipation of the announcement.

"You're finally having a baby!" Mia shouts it out like they've been depriving us of the honor of knowing for months.

"Not yet sweetie," Mom corrects. "Last night, Tad and I came to a very serious decision that will affect all of you in the near future."

Dear God, they're getting a divorce.

Tad really fucked up good this time.

"Let it be known, that only a mere twelve hours ago," Tad pauses, threading his arm through my mother's, "I asked this beautiful woman to once again become my blushing bride—and she said yes."

Nothing but dead silence from the peanut gallery. None of us are all that thrilled with this rather dramatic bit of non-news.

"That's it?" Melissa barks. I think they've actually managed to offend her. "You're already married."

"I know, sweetie." Mom uses her sugarcoated tone to reconcile the fact she's capable of making the same mistake twice. "And you're all going to be in the wedding— again."

Actually, this is pseudo great news. As long as Tad is still in the picture that means whatever the hell was going on with Demetri is long over. Unless, of course, it's all some elaborate effort to throw us off track. That would be a strange cover for an affair—remarrying your husband—it reeks of ingenious Fem inspired deception.

"Our one year wedding anniversary is coming up, and we thought what better way to celebrate than to renew our vows?" Tad nods into the idea.

"Of course, we'll keep it simple, just family in the backyard," Mom beams like this is going to make her year.

"Brielle will have to come," Drake says.

"Oh, and Gage," I add.

"I'm bringing Gabriel," Melissa raises a brow in Mia's direction.

"Who's Gabriel?" Tad straightens. "Look, this is already getting out of hand."

"It's just a few extra people." Mom is sharp in her rebuttal.

"You're right," Tad loses a little color. "We'll just throw a few more hot dogs on the grill."

Hot dogs?

And planning a wedding? Is Tad truly so clueless that he doesn't realize a wedding is one of the most stressful events in a girl's life? He's insane if he thinks they'll survive this couples catastrophe. He might as well have handed her divorce papers last night, signed and sealed—traded his wedding band in for cash at the pawn shop on the way home.

Nobody says a word to fill in Tad's moronic void. Instead, Mom pushes out a feeble attempt at a smile and ends up with an uncertain look on her face.

I have a feeling that will be one of the nicer sentiments she shares with him in the upcoming weeks.

I have a feeling Tad and Lizbeth Landon are about to go down in flames.

22

Church on Time

I drive the Mustang out onto the strangled stretch of highway that knifes through Paragon proper. Between the dark shadows of the pines I can see the pounding surf, the hard white spray of the sea sift through the fog.

Mia insists on riding along. I've already warned her she needs to hitch a ride back with Mom and Tad. She doesn't say a word about last night or her plans to do a relationship takedown with Gabriel Armistead. Instead, as soon as we hit the church foyer, she bolts into a group of kids her own age—more precisely over to a golden haired boy with a perpetual smile, who stands a head above the rest a.k.a. the perpetrator in question who's messing with my sisters.

"A little young for you, wouldn't you agree?" Demetri hovers over my shoulder wearing a black hat, trench coat to match. He plucks the fedora off his head and offers a hideous grin.

Before I can answer, Mom pops up beside me.

"Fancy meeting you here," she tips her chest in as she says it.

"I was just about to invite Skyla to my grandfather's estate. Why don't you accompany her, Lizbeth? I'm afraid I may not have made the best impression. She seems to be having some hesitancy regarding her community service."

"I would love to see your grandfather's estate!" Her eyes spring wide like twin lanterns. "Name the time and day." She wiggles with delight as if he just asked her to prom.

"Any day this week that you're available. I'm subject to your schedule. You have my number. Just give me a call when you're in the neighborhood." He redirects his attention to me at a lethargic pace. He's relishing this, I can tell. "Skyla, I have a feeling you and I are going to get along just fine."

That's funny—I have the distinct feeling we're not.

I give a courteous nod before ducking into the sanctuary.

Faux Logan is sitting in our usual spot, leaning into Chloe as she whispers toxic sweet nothings into his ear.

Figures. She's probably been coaching him on all things Logan since day one.

Brielle comes in and we take a seat together.

"Hey," she scoots in until our shoulders touch. "Heads up, my mom is super pissed at your mom."

"What?" I look over to where Mom is carrying on a deep and meaningful conversation with Demetri and her breasts.

Darla, Brielle's mom, joins in on the fun. It looks natural, not at all catty or aggressive.

"What's she pissed about?"

"She says all your mom cares about is you," she huffs as though this were an outrage.

"So?"

"So? I'm the one having her grandchild. My mom wants me to go to that special clinic you went to when everyone thought you were knocked up. My mom said your family couldn't care less if I gave birth out in a field with the help of a drunk ranch hand and a rusted out hoe."

"That's not true," I swivel around in search of Drake. He's the one who should be putting out this hormonal fire, not me. I spy him near the back, where both he and Ethan vie for Emily's attention. I turn to look back at mom. "She's really happy about the baby." In all honesty, I don't think I've heard her mention it once.

"Oh, good. I'll let my mom know. She can call off the lawyer."

"The what?" The last thing Mom and Tad need is some serious legal drama playing out. That's precisely why I haven't presented them with the cease and desist letter Pierce inflicted me with.

I look back over at the three of them. Both Mom and Darla glare in our direction. If I didn't know better I'd swear they were both honing their hate-filled laser stares right at me.

"Looks like your Mom is really ticked," I whisper.

"Yeah, well, she's not your biggest fan right now. She thinks your parents favor you over Drake, but I'll set her straight."

Ironic, how the only one not scowling in my direction is Demetri—only I don't find it ironic at all.

He offers a maniacal smile exclusive to villains and heinous Fems the world over.

He's screwing with Mom, and he's screwing with Darla.

I bet if he has his way, he'll burn the whole lot of us to the ground, the way he did my father.

After church I make a beeline over to Marshall's quaint ten thousand foot abode.

A strange wind picks up, jostles the branches of the Juniper trees, makes them wave their branches quick and spasmodic. It's unnatural, unearthly...

"Logan?" I whisper to myself. I bet that was him, scratching against the window that night in Gage's bedroom, he probably set out his letterman jacket for me to see, broke the key off in the lock when Gage and I wanted to be alone, christened us with a fallen branch in the middle of a kiss.

I huff a laugh.

expel

Ellis and the fountain, Holden kissing me in the truck and the music exploding in our ears that first night he came back—that was all Logan trying his hardest to preserve his love for me.

I return my focus to the road as I pull into Marshall's expansive driveway. I thought for sure I'd see him at church this morning. I just assumed there was some law that stipulated he, rise and shine, and give God his glory, glory each and every Sunday.

I give three solid knocks at the door and wait before jiggling the knob trying to let myself in. It's cold outside, the kind of chill that knifes through each layer of clothing easy as butter.

The door swings open and I gasp at the sight of him.

"Marshall?"

"Ms. Messenger." His skin is illuminated bright as a glow stick, as if he overslept in a radioactive tanning bed.

If he can't control the bizarre condition then I completely understand the reason he sequestered himself from public view. A florescent facade would certainly be fodder for gossip amongst the congregation.

He escorts us deep into his living room.

"I didn't see you at church today," I say, in lieu of firing off a half a dozen sarcastic remarks about his phosphorescent skin condition.

"Feeling high and mighty are we? I gave accounting at the throne," he growls, "thus the unearthly brilliance. I dare say I've trumped you in all matters spiritual, this day and every other. What can I help you with?"

"I think you know," a marked irritation spikes in me. I don't appreciate the never-ending supply of head games Marshall indulges in.

"Clue me in, Love. I'm rather irritated at the moment." His hair gleams like gold floss, his chiseled features blush a burnished bronze. Marshall could kill with his razor sharp looks—only he decided to use a car.

"You did this to Logan." I go to push him in the chest, and he catches me by the wrist.

"Enough with the childish antics," he reprimands, tossing my hand back. "I've spent the last interim of my existence defending you."

"Defending me? To who?"

"The Sector alliance, your mother—*God himself*," he seethes.

My heart lurches.

I thought *I* was the pissed off one in this conversation, obviously I'm sadly mistaken.

Marshall launches his fist into the piano, causing a magnificent explosion of sound. The entire framework splinters and lands the piano in pieces on the ground as if a bomb went off.

"Hey! I liked that thing," I shout, trying to inject a little semblance of sanity into the moment.

Marshall glares at the damaged instrument, and, as if in obedience, it magically rights itself and returns to its black lacquered splendor.

OK—if that was a show of prowess to make me aware of who exactly it is I'm messing with, he's got my undivided attention.

"Why were you defending me?" My entire demeanor softens. I touch his cheek, marveling at his radiance, and he storms off in the other direction.

"You surrendered region one in less than five minutes!" His voice booms in a fit of rage. "It's obvious we're going to have to conduct a strict level of combat training. I'll start by drilling into you something you seem to be lacking—a commitment for the cause."

"Logan and Gage—"

He cuts me off, "Your hormonal overdrive has placed us in jeopardy."

"They were *dying*!" I roar.

"Precisely why they weren't brought into the offensive." He gives a long blink. "Skyla, out of love I gave you the discs—to your mother's protest I gave you those life saving sensors. She wanted you caged in each battle like a corporeal beast. Do you understand what I'm telling you?"

"No," I take a step back, alarmed at his anger-induced passion. "I really don't."

"Skyla, you were in no mortal danger. No matter how long the battle would have waged you would have been returned to the exact time in the evening from which you were taken. There was no point in squandering the disc let alone handing the Fems victory on a platter." He glares. "They're beyond recognition, what with all of the spiritual high fives—ego's the size of small planets." He spears me with his copper eyes. "To say there is rampant disappointment in the celestial sphere over your actions, would be modest. Of course, the blame has been pinned square on my shoulders." He straightens, looking out the window at the corral in the distance.

"Why you?"

"I afforded you the opportunity," he whispers it in shame. "If it weren't for me you would have fought like the warrior you were born to be. I've taken what could have been your greatest moment and reduced it to nothing short of an act of cowardice."

"It wasn't cowardice. It was love," I correct. "I *love* Logan and Gage. I'd give up the entire universe for them."

"Congratulations, Skyla," Marshall pins me with a glacial stare. "You just may have."

23

Out of My Head

I head straight over to Gage after Marshall's spectacular meltdown. I've never seen him so livid. A storm has moved in. The rain outside falls in long teardrop spears, pressing themselves against the foggy window of Gage's bedroom.

I snuggle into Gage as we watch an old movie that I actually saw in the theatre with my father a bazillion years ago. I miss my father with an irrepressible sadness. It's his unjust murder that drives me to win the faction war, to put the Counts and Fems and any other demonic form of being in its place for what they've done to him.

Gage dips a kiss down over my eyebrow as he pulls me closer to him.

"We need to plan a serious Valentine's do-over," he punctuates the idea by circling his thumb on the inside of my palm.

"You're on." I flatten my lips against his and just lay there, listening to the sound of his breathing, taking in his clean scent.

"So where did you leave things with Dudley?" He looks at me with great intensity from one eye to the other. The slight veil of fear and jealousy lurks in his question.

"That was it," I say, looking around the room for signs of Logan. I told Gage all about my visit to Marshall's. So much happened that I forgot to bring up Logan's bodily debacle—the reason I went there to begin with. "How are you feeling?"

"Exhausted," he lets out a breath. "Looks like I would have been better off dying and letting the Counts resurrect me," he finishes it off with a deep guttural cough.

expel

"Don't you ever say that," I run my hand up his sweatshirt and lay my palm against his hot stomach. Not only do I not want to hear about Gage's death wish, he wouldn't qualify in terms of a resurrection.

I make lazy figure eights on his skin and feel his muscles contract and spasm as I trickle over them. "I can't believe we're free of you know who." I don't dare say Chloe's name out loud in the event she's got Fem operatives on patrol in the vicinity.

"You and me both. We can finally focus on one another and nothing else." Gage gives a searing kiss, branded by his love. "By the way," he pulls back and examines me with a placid smile, "she called today."

"Oh?" I push up on my elbow. Something tells me Chloe is about to inject her pointy shoe right into my rear in a big way. Trying to keep Chloe out of our lives is like trying to put out a fire with gasoline, sooner or later our world is going to blow. I can feel it deep in my bones. In fact, Chloe Bishop would make a gasoline fire seem like a welcome reprieve from her wrath. There is really no comparing her wickedness.

"I guess she's been working at the bowling alley while we've been disposed." He bites down as if he's keeping something from me.

"Brielle mentioned it." Crap, I bet she's done some amazing business move like tying the pizza kitchen to every lunch program on the island, and now the bowling alley is going to make millions all thanks to her stroke of genius.

"Yeah," he gives a soft cough, sounds like pennies rattling away at the bottom of his lungs. "Did Brielle happen to mention Logan's been helping himself to the safe and that payroll and bills haven't been paid this month?"

I pluck my hand out of his shirt.

"Oh my, God." Logan is going to lose the bowling alley no thanks to Holden and his dumbass buffoonery. "We need to sit him down and have an intervention. I mean, I'm all for living life to the fullest, but he's got this whole live it up thing ass backwards. He's going to end up in such major debt, the next death wish around here will be his." Although, knowing Holden, somehow I find this doubtful. I'm sure he has no problem running both his new business and new body into the ground. Forget debt, he'll have the clap by the time prom rolls around—flesh eating clap. "Did Chloe mention anything else?"

He shakes his head.

She's such a kiss up. I could have told Gage those things, but I didn't want to stress him out. It looks like I'm going to have a one on one with my least favorite nemesis, clue her in on the fact she's going to land Gage in the hospital. If she cares anything at all about him, she'll stay the hell away. Like that would ever happen. Chloe's going to keep up the good little snitch routine as long as she thinks it'll score some major brownie points with my future husband.

I take in a breath and look up at Gage.

"You're quiet," he eyes me with suspicion. "I'm sorry I brought her up."

"No, it's OK. I'm glad you did. It made me realize something important."

"What's that?" His dimples depress in a smile all their own. He coils a lock of my hair around his finger with great care as he awaits my answer.

"How special you are to me. How we're going to spend the rest of our lives together." I draw him a map with my kisses rather than expend any more energy on words that could never do what lies ahead for us, justice. Gage runs his hands up the back of my sweater, swivels around to the front with one long hot stroke. He lifts his shirt and lays his bare stomach over mine. A sharp bite of heat bisects my insides and I moan from the pleasure of his touch.

Gage is my future and Chloe's past. It's about time I clued her in on those two facts.

expel

🦋 🦋 🦋

Later, as I get into the Mustang to head home, I text Chloe to arrange a tête-à-tête and lo and behold, horror of all horrors, she texts back that she's at my freaking house. Probably crop dusting my bedroom with strychnine at this very moment.

I race down the solvent streets of Paragon, through the beginnings of a major downpour and bolt into the house, out of breath and soaking wet.

"Skyla!" My mother pauses at the kitchen counter and gasps at my appearance. Her fingers freeze midflight with a slice of pizza in her hands.

I find Chloe seated beside Ethan at the island. Next to them, Brielle and Drake wolf down their lunch, as if all is well in Landon manner. Looks like the queen of all bitches is conquering new territory.

"What's going on?" I speed over to the four of them.

"You'll have to excuse Skyla," Tad shouts over to Chloe. "She's prone to rude spontaneous outbursts."

"Oh, I'm well aware." Chloe doesn't miss a beat.

"Get your own," Ethan shields his pizza as if I were about to swipe it right out of his mouth. I bet it's a kneejerk reaction to the lifestyle he indulged in while living on the streets. Little does he know, the monster that knifed him sits dutifully by his side, and she'd be happy to steal more than the artery blocker he's about to inhale.

"Can I talk to you for a minute?" I yank him up by the elbow and drag him out to the hall.

"What?" He shakes me loose, genuinely perturbed. "Make it quick. I'm starved."

"Why is Chloe here?" God, I hope he says something logical that might officially warrant her presence, like an unforeseen yet, oh so necessary, assassination.

"She's hanging out. I kind of like her." He looks past my shoulder back into the family room.

I pull him deeper into the hall by force.

"Are you out of your mind? She disemboweled you to further her own personal agenda. She thinks of everything and everyone as an object to get what she wants. Nothing good is going to come of this. Chloe is nothing more than a parasite," I say that last part a little louder than intended.

"I have a plan." He darts into me deliberately with his beady Landon eyes, and for a split second he looks like Drake's evil twin.

"To do what? Blackmail her? Drink her blood? I've heard it all before none of it works. She's an unstoppable force of destruction."

"I'm going to date her," he blinks into his admission.

"What?" I screech. Ethan Landon is proving to be an entire stack of stupid.

"She's totally into me." He shrugs, clearly flattered by Chloe's sobering lies. For one, Ethan looks nothing like Gage, and for two, still not Gage.

"What about Emily?" I ask, grasping for straws.

"She's OK. But she doesn't quite dovetail into my agenda the way Chloe does."

"What agenda?"

He walks back into the kitchen, leaving me hanging.

I follow him back and grab a plate, slap a piece of pizza on it with the cheese sliding off.

"How's Gage feeling?" Mom asks while shouldering into Tad as though she didn't log time with Demetri at the barbaric stone of sacrifice.

Chloe twitches when she says his name. She might get thrown into a full-blown seizure if we actually conduct an entire conversation about him. On second thought...

"Gage is fine. He's feeling better. We're going to get together later this week and have a Valentine's do-over." I watch Chloe as I take a seat at the table, a safe distance away. She lowers her lids before glinting back up at me with those torches of fire. Messing with Chloe like this is like soaring too close to the sun. It might feel good for a moment but before you realize it you've reduced yourself to ashes.

"That's nice," Chloe chokes the words out. "I was thinking," she clears her throat. The protective hedge glimmers prideful around her neck. It conforms to the hills and valleys of her throat as if it were contemplating strangulation. Now that would be an irony I could appreciate. "I think we should have a get together this Saturday, at my house." She says that last part as though she were setting out a trap. "You know, just couples." She lowers her lids seductively over at Ethan when she says it.

Gag me.

Hang me.

Send me to Ezrina's so she can detach me limb by limb rather than watch this monstrosity unfold. Clearly the one with an evil agenda here is Chloe, not Ethan. If his idea of taking out revenge on someone is *dating* them, clearly he is Tad's begotten, yet slightly forgotten, seed. Hey, maybe that's why Tad married my mother? Revenge.

"That's great!" Brielle beams. "I so need a do-over Valentine's, too. I ended up puking all night and leaving early while Drake here, saw a late movie with Emily," she says her name with an acidic tongue.

"Drake?" I gape at him. How could he? But I thought I saw his car at the falls? But that would mean...

"What?" He over dramatizes a shrug. "It was a coincidence. We were at the theatre at the same time, that's all."

Drake seems to suffer from the same dumbass disorder that his father and brother before him, do.

I look over Tad and Mom making googly eyes at each other and try not to hurl my cheeseless pizza at them.

"What about our camping trip?" I look to the two of them to save Ethan from the atrocity of date night with Chloe. There's no way in hell Gage and I are going.

"Canceled." Mom shivers when she says it as if she herself had just staved off some grievous horror, which she totally did. "Besides, I have an appointment at the clinic, and if the weather is this nasty, we might have to pull an overnighter," she coos into Tad.

OK. I've had enough repulsion to suppress my appetite for the rest of my natural life.

An ebony lacquered bracelet dangles from Mom's wrist. It harnesses my attention with a gold symbol emblazoned on the side.

"Nice bracelet," I say, full with suspicion.

"You like it?" She runs her fingers over it, twists it repetitively. Her cheeks brighten a lively shade of crimson. "I picked it up at the mall."

"You said you found it in a parking lot." Tad postures himself away from her with a serious look of doubt.

"Yes," Mom straightens in her seat. "I found it in the parking lot at the mall, so technically I picked it up there." She squints into the infinity symbol gleaming under the light.

Tad presses out a look of relief just knowing his hard earned dollars weren't spent on something foolish like bejeweling his wife.

I have a feeling she picked it up all right, right out Demetri's evil paws.

The infinity symbol gleams, the gold floss is lit up like fire from the lights above.

Infinity. I bet Demetri really does want to live and rule forever, crush Marshall and the rest of the Sectors with the heel of his cloven hoof for an *infinity*.

Something surges in me, and I feel protective towards Marshall, the entire human race.

To hell with Demetri and his fantasies.

expel

The only infinite thing he'll have to look forward to, is my wrath.

24

Forever

After school on Monday, under a smooth charcoal sky, Gage announces he has a surprise for me.

I climb into his truck and watch Paragon glide by in a whirl of viridian and sage, an entire kaleidoscope of dark green glory parades past us at dizzying speeds. That's what it felt like traveling into the future, the push of the world exploding in one dark blur, wrapped safe in Logan's arms as we waited with bated breath for some new revelation. That's what it's like right now with Gage, although miles safer, and without the prospect of death staring me in the face once we arrive to our destination. At least I hope.

Nevermore glides over us as though he were leading the way. I wonder if Nev could protect me from Ezrina? If he would want to?

I take Gage up by the hand. Going anywhere with him is heaven.

Gage picked me up for school for the first time in ages this morning. Everything feels normal again, right—everything except for the fact that Logan is really dead, but I push that away for now. It's far too painful to contend with.

"So where we going?" I admire him from an arms' length. He's got on a leather jacket, the scarf his mother knit for Christmas sits nestled around his neck. The stubble on his cheeks has filled in, giving him that outdoorsy appeal which I find dangerously hot. I'm not sure I like him looking like he could start a forest fire, especially not with Chloe haunting the corridors of West, even if she is spraying Ethan openly with her venomous pheromones.

"Consider yourself officially kidnapped," it rumbles out of him in one husky growl. His lips turn up as he steals a quick glance.

"It sounds like you're being a very bad boy." I reach over and run my fingers through his hair, touch the freshly shorn bristle against the back of his neck, smooth in one direction, sharp as a cats tongue in the other.

He gives an impish grin and points over the steering wheel before making the turn.

"Rockaway!" I bounce in my seat. I've been dying to come back ever since we shared a special moment here, and I officially declared it our place. The beauty of the landscape alone takes my breath away.

We park close to the succulent covered path that spreads its swollen leaves towards shore. I jump out of the truck, pluck my shoes off and race into the midnight colored sand. "This is amazing!" I shout up over the deafening waves, my feet sinking in the cold grit beneath me.

Gage tweaks his brows. A seductive smile plays on his lips as he tosses a thick blanket over his shoulder. He swoops in on me like an eagle darting for prey, scoops me up in his arms and sinks a kiss on my lips before breaking out into his signature killer grin.

"Put me down," I protest. "You're going to hurt yourself." God forbid *I'm* the reason Gage ends up supine in a hospital bed.

"No way," he trots us down the beach towards an ancient coral tree with a wingspan that stretches out for what feels like miles. Its bright red trumpets dance against the ashen sky, taunting it with the blush of a sunset that Paragon may never know or see.

Gage lands me soft on the ground before laying out the blanket.

"For you." He pats a seat beside him, and I hop dutifully across from him.

Gage leans in and indulges me on the pleasure of his mouth, drowns out the waves, the wind, the rattle of leaves up above until all I hear is his erratic breathing, his heart racing over mine.

"Boy," I whisper, "I think you're setting the record for best Valentine's do-over, ever." Chloe errantly wafts through my mind. She's become the tick feeding off the blood supply of our love.

"I try," he huffs a little laugh. "Actually," he picks up both my hands, "you make it very easy." He drills into me with his iridescent gaze and everything in me surrenders.

I love you, madly, I smile into him as I say it.

Gage tilts his head, doesn't respond. He twists his lips as though he were about to say something.

"You didn't hear me." I can't hide my disappointment.

"I can't hear you," he confesses it soft as an apology.

"I'll give you more blood. You'll heal faster—you'll be Celestra for a time, like me." Being Celestra has been mostly a curse, but the benefit of going back and seeing my father makes every heartache tolerable. I'd walk a burning tightrope each day just to see my father's smiling face, some days I have.

"No," he shakes his head, taking me in with his unwavering heavy gaze. "I would never hurt you or take advantage of you that way. I'm healing fine, I promise. I'm OK."

Gage gets on his knees and digs around his pocket.

"Protection?" I ask playfully. As much as I'd love to give myself fully to Gage, the idea still scares the hell out of me. Ironic, since I can battle Fems, work side by side with Ezrina, and live under Tad's tyranny, and yet I freeze solid as a statue at the thought of lying naked under the covers with my boyfriend. It's what comes after that has me afraid. What will become of the old us, and who will this new us be. I'm sure Gage will be more than happy to walk me through it when the time is right.

expel

"You're close. It starts with P." His dimples twitch. "Present," he says, pulling his hand out of his jeans in a closed fist. "Close your eyes."

I do as I'm told—giddy at the thought of what it might be. Gage gives the best gifts. He gave me his class ring, which I still wear faithfully on a chain, never, ever taking it off. He gave me the sweetest bracelet for Christmas. I love it so much I don't even care that I've snagged just about every sweater I own with it. I'd gladly trade my entire wardrobe for any token of Gage's affection.

"OK, open." He exudes a serene grin as he holds his hand out.

A simple silver band sits nestled in his palm. There's a blue heart set in the middle of the ring the exact same hue as his eyes, and I'm instantly in love.

"Gage," I gasp. "It's beautiful!"

"Skyla," he breathes my name in a broken whisper.

Oh my, God.

I think Gage is about to propose. This is *huge*, monumental even. I should totally get my phone out and record this or something.

A gust of wind kicks up the sand, slapping it against our flesh like a thousand pressing pins.

Gage nudges the blanket out from underneath us and hooks it onto a pair of adjacent tree limbs, building a cozy fort for the two of us. Just enough light filters in, creating the perfect romantic environment. Mother nature may have wanted us to abdicate the throne of our love, but we overcame the obstacle just the way we always do.

"I love this ring," I say, crawling into his lap.

"I had it engraved." He glints it into the light.

"What does it say?" I'm dying to snatch it from him and squeeze it with all my affection, but he holds it between the two of us like an offering.

"It says," he whispers, pulling me in by the waist, "Gage loves Skyla, Forever."

My heart melts when he says it.

He slips it over the ring finger of my left hand, smiles down at me with heartfelt affection—a poem written on his lips.

"Is this a promise ring?" I pet it soft with my fingers. It's so beautiful it glows, just like Gage and his love for me.

"It's, an, I'm-going-to-love-you-forever ring." He bears into me intently, lets me know he means it from the deepest part of him.

I take in a breath and hold it.

Gage is going to love me forever. Tears filter to the surface, and I blink them away, unaware of their origin, not wanting to delve too far into my emotions to figure it out.

"I'm going to love you, forever, Gage," I say it like a promise. I pull him in and offer a kiss that resonates my feelings exactly. This is one commitment I never intend on breaking.

Gage lies me down in the sand, lands over me gently without crushing me with his full weight. I giggle into him, happy to be here, be anywhere with Gage—our tongues intertwine in one lusty exchange. I reach up under his shirt and run my hands over his firm body. I can feel his heart race as his love pulsates in and out of his chest for me.

It's going to be like this always—unfettered emotions, unbridled, passion. Something in this moment solidifies us, magically transforms the two of us into one spiritual entity. I can feel the bonding of our souls, our destinies converging onto the same narrow path. We have our entire lives to look forward to.

We linger in soft easy kisses that go on—forever.

25

The Psycho and Me

That evening, long after Gage drops me off at home, Tad cages me in the family room and paces the floors like an expectant father, waiting for Dr. Booth to arrive.

"Relax, will you?" My mother scolds, losing herself in her knitting. She circles yarn around her finger aggressively, plucking miles off the skein as she observes his odd behavior from the couch.

Melissa postures herself in defiance. "He's just excited that the shrink is on his way over to finally figure out what the hell's wrong with Skyla," she scoffs, bypassing us on the way to the kitchen.

Mia openly glares at me as if I represented everything that was defective with this family when we both know damn well it's Melissa she's pissed off at.

"Melissa," my mother tries to disguise the disdain in her voice. I can tell Mom has just about had it with the entire Landon lot. Although, if the alternative is having us shack up with Demetri and trying to make me call him *daddy*, I'll cling to the Philistines of this household like a life raft.

A bold knock explodes over the door, and moments later, Tad shepherds Dr. Booth into the room.

"Skyla!" He comes over and shakes my hand. *This will be interesting*, he nods into me as he says it.

"Please, sit," Tad pulls a chair from the dining room table and speeds it over. Obviously he has his hopes pinned on a speedy incarceration. Bastard.

"Thank you," Dr. Booth takes a seat across from me while Tad lingers by his side like his own personal caddy.

"Can I get you a drink?" Tad bows slightly. "Some warm tea, perhaps?"

God, I hate it when Tad gets all overly nice. It oozes of fake affection. Dr. Booth should incarcerate *him* for the sole purpose of trying to impersonate a human.

"No, no, thank you." Dr. Booth gives an uncomfortable smile before redirecting his gaze. "Skyla, your family requested we have an informal meeting to discuss the direction of your treatment."

"Direction?" As in game over, I want to add, but don't.

Mia and Melissa cower next to the refrigerator in hopes Mom and Tad will forget they're in the vicinity, thereby eavesdropping with greater efficiency. I don't care. I don't have a single thing to hide.

"It's been brought to my attention, via your parents," his gaze cuts over to Tad, totally ratting out the parent in question. Ha! I love Dr. Booth. He's so on my side. "That you have been blurting things out that don't necessarily lend themselves to the conversation." He nods as though I should acknowledge this on some level.

"Only because, sometimes it's necessary," I give a curt nod back, knowing full well he can decode the meaning. As a Celestra, part of the deal is having lopsided conversations. It's practically an occupational hazard.

Dr. Booth frowns. "I'm afraid in this society, it's inevitable. We all have a mishap or two."

"Mishap or two?" Tad balks. He repositions himself to better fit in Dr. Booth's visual field. "She has outright lost her mind. The girl speaks and answers people without the proper initiation. She's fried her brains out on all those illegal substances she's been peddling. And, don't deny it, Lizbeth. You can't deny the fact she was the center of a drug bust a few weeks back and you and I are both lucky all they wanted was a little community service. We could have lost our shirts if that gravy train of hers didn't step up and offer to post bail."

expel

I huff a laugh at the thought of Logan as my gravy train. And it so wasn't my pot, well, technically it was on my person, but still.

"This is not a laughing matter, young lady," Mom's voice is sharp as an arrow.

An angry growl of thunder goes off overhead and the lights blink on and off.

"I'm sorry," I apologize. "I wasn't trying to laugh. I'm nervous—and I thought of something funny that happened at school today." I don't know why I didn't just tell them the truth—that I was laughing at Logan as my gravy train. I suppose because it's my kneejerk reaction to run away from the truth whenever my mother is involved. Unfortunately, I think I've rewired my brain into believing it's OK to feed her a steady stream of bullshit whenever possible. "I'm sorry that I spoke out of turn," I glare at Tad when I say it. "And I'm sorry about the pot bust." The only thing I'm really sorry about is my mother's serious misfortune of hooking up with Tad.

Another crackle of thunder rattles the house, shakes the windows within an inch of their fortitude.

Tad waves off my apology. "It's getting late. Perhaps this would be a good time to introduce the new avenue of treatment."

Good God they're going to strap me to a metal gurney and blitz me with electrodes. I'll be set on fire from the *inside*. I bet this has been Tad's evil plan all along.

"We would like to introduce a low dose of medication," Dr. Booth intercedes. "Something to take the edge off of everyday life—something that might help you relax."

"Like how relaxed?" I envision myself as a zombie, complete with fried hair and missing teeth.

Dr. Booth shakes his head with a defeated look on his face as though Tad strong-armed him into this.

"It's a tranquilizer, Skyla," Tad bellows. "It'll make you feel high as a kite. I'm sure you'll be clamoring for more the minute you feel the fabulous side effects. And don't get any big ideas like pushing the stuff for profit. I'm picking up the ticket on this one with my own cold hard cash."

Funny how fast his wallet flies open when it comes to doping me with antipsychotics.

"Your mother and I will be dispensing the medication ourselves." Tad folds his arms across his chest.

Perfect. I foresee an accidental overdose in my near future.

"Mom, are you OK with this?" I'm shocked that she's just sitting there maneuvering those knitting needles as though she were training to place for speed and agility in the knitting Olympics. I'd like to pluck one of those slender spikes from her hands and impale Tad in the eye.

"You gave us no choice." She ceases all movement abruptly, scowling when she loses her place. She loops yarn around her finger in swift hostile movements before continuing with the knitting offensive taking place in her lap. If she keeps this up, she'll disembowel herself without the aid of Paragon's own corpse practitioner—Chloe.

Dr. Booth hands Tad a prescription before rising to his feet.

"Can I have a word with you in private?" I ask, ushering the good doctor to the entry.

I open the door and we step out into the icy night air, the awning just barely covering us from the downpour that's unleashed itself over the island.

"I'm sorry, Skyla. He left me no choice. He threatened to have my practice overrun with state regulators. It was the least I could do to get him off my back."

"What about the zombie pills?" I bounce on my toes in a panic.

"I'll call tomorrow and ask your mother to bring the bottle down to my office for inspection. I'm a stickler for accuracy." He winks. "I'll replace the medication with a placebo, they'll be none the wiser."

expel

"You're a genius!" I jump up and hug him.

"No more one-sided conversations young lady. And stay away from illegal substances." He flicks his wrist and his umbrella blooms in one giant burst.

"I have a perfectly good explanation for that," I say.

"You always do," he gives a sly smile before disappearing behind a curtain of water.

Thank God I've got Dr. Booth on my side. If he were really the staunch asshole Tad wishes he were, zombie state or not—I'd be locked up for good.

Skyla.

A voice echoes through the rain, carries unnaturally like the long chord of cymbal with its perpetual steady sizzle.

I don't need a face, an effigy or even a shadow to place the voice. I know exactly who that is.

I jump into the house and lock the door.

It's the last person in the world I want to see tonight—Ezrina.

26

Hells Bells

Who knew Tad would run out to an all night pharmacy and get the prescription filled? Who knew that he and my mother would stand guard and watch as I ingest the tiny white disaster?

The next morning, I sit in Marshall's class nodding off intermittently. I stare off into space while batting away the army of bugs crawling over my skin, which come to think of it, may not actually exist.

The bell finally rings, dismissing me from my misery. Marshall calls me to the front with his voice reverberating in an unnatural echo. I assure Gage it's fine, and he kindly waits outside the door.

"What?" The word pulls like cotton from my lips.

"I have a bone to pick with you." He tosses the stack of homework he's just collected onto his desk and half of the papers fall into the hungry mouth of the trashcan below. I want to giggle at his impotent effort, but all I can afford is a moan that gets stuck in my throat.

"What?" I ask lazily. It seems to be the only word left in my lexicon thanks to Tad and his eat-your-brain-cells-for-breakfast stupid idea of a pill.

"I ran into a certain someone at the Transfer who gave me the most curious bit of news." He folds his arms in disappointment.

"Ezrina?" Normally I wouldn't accommodate him with the truth.

God! What if one of the side effects of this horse tranquilizer is losing the ability to bend the truth? Bending the truth is my specialty. This pill is like Kryptonite to me.

expel

He gives a curt nod. "She informed me that you entered into a—"

"Covenant," I cut him off.

"And you gave your—"

"Word," it comes out lethargic, and I give a slow and refractive nod like all those stoners at Ellis's parties.

"And now you're going to have to—" he generously motions for me to finish.

"Learn my lesson," I say, rather proud of my spontaneous confessional.

"You haven't learned a thing from dealing with Holden the first time. You don't make promises to just any creature that happens to be the vicinity. Remember, Skyla, you are a little higher than a human, nothing more. You certainly lack the ability to gift Ezrina with what you've promised."

"My mother does," I say, fully aware of the fact I've screwed up royally.

"In the event you haven't noted, your mother isn't synonymous in any way with mercy. It's not her specialty. You, my friend, are digging your own grave. The only tragedy being, you won't have the privilege of curling up and dying. You'll live forever in the body of a misshapen hag. Does this please you?"

I shake my head.

"And I suppose the Pretty Oliver has already exposed you to the fact you'll be needing my services to procure a new body."

"He doesn't want a new body. He wants the old one." I gasp at the thought of another metaphysical mix-up.

"You, my love, are in what they like to call, here on earth, a hole," he reprimands. "I suppose it won't take you long to make yet another idle promise concerning your flesh."

"I guess you know me." My words fall to the floor and crash around my feet in shame.

"There's only one problem." He lifts my chin with the tip of his finger.

"What?" It fires off like an echo.

"I'm no longer accepting the offer as payment." He picks up his coffee and begins to head out of the room. "Enjoy the afternoon, Ms. Messenger."

※ ※ ※

After another bliss-filled day at school with Gage, my mother informs me we're headed to Demetri's to acquaint ourselves with the premises before I officiate my community service.

All of the euphoria I felt hours earlier has dissipated at the thought of exploring the Fem frontier with my mother and the evil pinhead trying to lure her into his lair.

"He's giving us the grand tour." My mother beams as we round out the long roads of Paragon Estates that stretch out like a yawn.

This is much farther down in the Estates than I've ever been before.

"He must be loaded," I muse.

As the property lines expand, so do the habitats of the rich and infamous. Giant, sprawling estates that make Marshall's multilevel expanse feel impossibly humble, the acreage itself altogether restrictive for a horse ranch.

"Here it is," her voice escalates with glee as she pulls onto a paver stone path that travels through a small forest hedging up on either side.

"Have you been here before?" Really it's an innocent question. But the fact my mother neither has an address or directions sprawled out in front of her is an alarming indication of what that answer might be.

"Never." Her eyes cut out the driver's side window. "He said it was the second driveway on the left once we passed the crossroads, and this would be it."

A giant wooden sign arches over the opening of the forest that reads *Edinger Estate* with an infinity symbol cradled between the words. I glance over to Mom's arm where the glossy bangle happily hops as she steers us into a circular driveway.

"Oh my, God!" Mom gasps when she sees the enormous structure.

"Holy shit!" I spike up in my seat not nearly as mesmerized as my mother, but equally taken aback.

It's the freaking Transfer! The haunted mansion Marshall held me hostage in. A replica. An original—who the hell knows?

It takes everything in me not to knock my mother unconscious and speed us back down the driveway.

Demetri steps out, dark and greedy for my mother's affections. He wears a carnal grin, nothing but lewd intentions written all over him. Mom bolts from the car and into his arms like he was my father incarnate.

Look at her.

She's not even hiding the fact she's into him. And what exactly is it she sees in him? He's like the second coming of Rasputin if not the first.

"Hello, Skyla, welcome," Demetri greets me as I stretch my legs.

It feels more like some dysfunctional family reunion, definitely not like the beginning of any public restitution that's supposed to be taking place. I rove my eyes over the structure, the entry, the balcony above. The giant white dwelling is identical to the one in the Transfer, and for a brief moment I'm not entirely convinced we're on Paragon anymore.

"I am in *love* with this place!" My mother radiates with pleasure. Demetri's arm remains slung low around her waist as she twists and turns, drinking it all in.

"It could have been yours," he offers.

I choke at the thought of him trying to suck my mother in with real estate. Sure, Tad may be currency deficient, but at least he...he's...oh, crap.

"She's happily married," I snipe. "Aren't you, Mom?"

"Of course, I am." Mom offers an incensed look that ensures a verbal assault once we get back in the car.

"I apologize, Skyla," Demetri drops his arm to his side. "Your mother and I are simply old friends, nothing more."

"I just thought I'd throw out the obvious," I shrug. "She's very much in love. In fact, she's getting married to my stepfather again." How she could possibly stomach saying yes twice, I will never know.

"Another wedding on the horizon?" He feigns enthusiasm as he motions for Mom to guide us up the stairs.

"Oh, it's just our first anniversary is coming up, and we thought it might be fun to renew the vows." She brushes it off as if the idea were childish to begin with.

"Where's the venue?" He stops shy of opening the door.

"It's just a little thing we're doing in the backyard. You know, with a weenie roast afterwards. No big deal. Of course, you're invited."

"Backyard? Sausages?" He scoffs, holding back a laugh. "I won't hear of it. Have it at the estate. I implore you to at least consider it."

Perfect. Tad can never compete with Demetri now.

"Are you sure? I could never impose," she bats away the thought.

He picks up her hand and presses his lips to the back, looks up at her with those dark mysterious eyes that killed my father.

expel

"You deserve all of the splendor and majesty life could afford on your wedding day, Lizbeth. And I'm here to make sure you have it all."

Splendor—majesty? I'm here to make sure you have it all?

Yeah, right.

Just friends my ass.

27

Smooth Operator

Demetri leads us inside. Surprisingly, it looks a lot less Transfer, and a lot homier in an opulent museum, art gallery—safe house for Fems, sort of way. Creamy marble floors, expansive ceilings, a double grand staircase that sweeps up with intricate ironwork. An enormous chandelier sparkles overhead, dripping with crystal formed into long pointed spears. Not one sign of the dearly departed, expending dated fashions the way they do down under or wherever the hell the Transfer really is.

Demetri leads us through one giant expanse after another until we hit a wall of windows that expose the glory of his paradise-like backyard. An oversized pool sits adorned with fountains that splash heavenly blue waters into oversized bowls made of stone.

Foliage and flowers I have never seen before crawl along either side of the walk. A wall of roses leads into a maze of flora and fauna with hedges twice as tall as a man. It's all, right out of a storybook, and knowing Demetri, it might, quite literally, be. He's a freaking mentalist. He's probably been inventorying my mother's brain for her idea of the perfect abode and produced it on command in an attempt to further lure her into his chamber.

"Would you look at this?" My mother groans with an ache I've never heard her dispense before. Desire springs for all the things she can grasp with her eyes. It's doubtful she isn't having remorse over marrying Tad at this very moment. The covetous hunger in her suggests she'd flag down the first divorce lawyer that crosses our path and have that wedding with *Demetri* come April.

"Shall we?" He holds the door open to the back for us.

expel

A heavenly scent of exotic blossoms greets us—so sickly sweet is the aroma of their nectar, I swear, there must be calories involved. A spray of pink open-faced flowers I've never seen before dots the delicate black ivy—an entire gazebo covered with lavender wisteria demands our attention off the back. This is nothing short of spectacular, a breathtaking horticulture wonder.

Forget my mother's wedding—I want to marry Gage right here in this perfect paradise. I play with the ring he gave me that symbolizes our forever brand of love and wander away from my mother and Demetri who have become embroiled in their own conversation regarding lobster, filet mignon and other things that will most likely take Tad out of the wedding equation rather swiftly and permanently.

I had never even thought of what my wedding to Gage might be like, outside of that courthouse vision he had. It would seem that part already came true after my court hearing when the judge stared Gage in the face and told him to kiss his bride, a.k.a. me, but I know for a fact, deep in my heart, that I'll be marrying Gage one day.

I hate that this is Demetri's grandfather's estate but it doesn't stop me from getting lost in the fantasy of walking down a petal-strewn path and straight into...

"Logan?" I squint into the bushes and see a blue velum form in his likeness before he fills in completely. He's leaning against a boxwood hedge, and gives a quiet smile, so I go over. "Hey!" I wrap my arms around him and press into a deep warm hug. "You feel so, real."

He inhales sharply into my neck as his chest rumbles with laughter.

"So do you," he pulls back and smiles with his eyes bearing into mine. "After the accident, the first time I saw you—it felt like a dream, like *you* were the ghost."

I take in a breath at the idea. "What's it like?" I lean in and relax against his chest, wanting to hear all of the details about what lies beyond.

"I'm not sure. I opted out of paradise. It's not my time, so I don't have to go."

"Are you in the Soulennium?" I'm completely fascinated by whatever Logan has to say. I've never been dead but I have been to the Soulennium, once with Marshall, and once with Giselle and my mother.

"That's exactly where I am." His brows crease. "Never mind, I don't want to know how you know about the Soulennium. What's going on?" He twitches his head towards Demetri, so I fill him in.

"Also, I want to tell Gage about you." I look down at my ring and sniff.

Logan picks up my hand and rubs his thumb over the sparkling sapphire. His lips twist with mournful agony. You could fill every black hole in the universe with the sadness exuding from the two of us.

"Why do I love you?" I catch his gaze and hold it. If I could only have the answer to just one question, this might be the one.

"Do you love me?" Logan's face is stone. He doesn't bother to show me his cards, just holds them, waits for me to purge my emotions so he can pick and choose the ones he wants to keep.

"You know I do," it comes out depleted as I lead us deeper into the labyrinth the shrubbery provides.

Try not to sound so enthused, he says, picking up my hand. A wall of silence springs up between us, a serenity so threatening it looks to topple right over our heads.

What I really mean is why didn't I fall in love with Gage first. Is it because you met me in my dreams? I fell in love with you then. I could tell by the look in my eyes I loved you. I'm specifically talking about the old me back in

L.A., the one Logan thought it was a good idea to use as a mode of inter-dimensional transportation.

I don't know why, he stares into the ground as we slow to a meandering pace. *But I'm not sorry you do.*

You said you knew something, I stop to look into his eyes. *You said you knew the end and that I should save something for you in here.* I place my fingers over my chest.

Logan carefully plucks my hand off, rounds his gaze over my features as though he were absorbing me into his cellular structure.

I only know one thing. It's amazing, Skyla. He buries a smile into the side of his cheek. *But it doesn't tell me whether or not we'll be together—if we'll be happy.*

Tell me.

Logan doesn't answer, just gives a long blink as if wishing he could.

I stare down at the ring Gage gave me—caress it from the underbelly with my thumb. How could I be so careless to fall in love with two people?

You weren't careless. Logan squeezes my hand.

I always forget you're listening and say the stupidest things. I fight off the tears that want to come.

Logan presses out an easy grin, causing the line in the side of his face to invert.

There is a purpose, Skyla. If it's one thing I've learned while I've been away from my body, it's that everything happens for a reason. I know you love Gage, he tips his forehead into me, *but*, he gives a depressed sigh, *I'm sorry, Skyla. After the faction war, I'm not going to stand around with my hands in my pockets. A new war is going to begin. And I won't give in until I win. That's the only war I care about—the one for your heart.*

"Skyla!" My mother calls. "Time to go inside."

"Come with me," I whisper.

He shakes his head. *I can't get in. There's a binding spirit. I've already tried. I'd better go see what Holden is up to*, he whispers, pulling me into a soft kiss on the cheek. *Be safe.* And with that he evaporates, makes me wonder if he were simply a delusion all along.

I see my mother up ahead with her neck bent in laughter over something moronic that expelled from Demetri.

How can I judge my mother so harshly when my own heart lies in two distinct places?

28

Mirror, Mirror

Under the watchful eye of my mother, I enter into the gothic estate. Demetri carries on ceaseless chatter with his *Lizbeth* as though I were never born, as though Tad and the rest of the universe no longer existed under the timber of this colossal roof.

We had entered into a world which was governed by Demetri's special ruling, and I have the distinct feeling he's slowly amputating Tad from my mother's life until he finally chooses to dispose of him. It's simply a detail that has yet to work itself out.

"Skyla," Demetri waves his hand in the air like an illusionist, and for a moment I'm convinced I'll evaporate just the way Logan did. "Feel free to explore. Upstairs, the attic, the basement, nothing's off limits. I'd love for you to familiarize yourself with the premises." He grazes out a toothless grin. "Go ahead, I've nothing to hide."

His last sentence spurs me upstairs fast and furious without even thinking through the possibilities. There could be an entire herd of Fems relaxing, watching a ball game up there—enjoying a rousing game of foosball. Ezrina could be wielding her battleaxe waiting to do a flesh swap, or an entirely new batch of freaky things I've yet to learn about, nevertheless, off I traipse to the second story.

A series of elongated halls quarter the top of the estate. I choose the one with a soft blue light glowing in the distance. I bet he's got his very own glass casket, complete with Ezrina's homemade keeping solution that juices the Counts into existence each time one of them pops off unexpectedly. This I've gotta see.

I speed down the hall and approach a huge archway, pausing just shy of the entry and peer inside.

It's a...library?

A giant overgrown lava lamp sits in the corner. It stretches from floor to ceiling with three blobs of aquamarine goo lethargically oozing towards the surface.

That's it? That's the big unearthly reveal?

I step inside and peruse Demetri's reading selections, old classics, probably first print runs worth millions. Leather-bound spines gleam with gilded lettering, line an entire third of the room. Another series of clothbound books run the distance around the lower circumference. They show their age, faded and disintegrating along the hard lined seams. Their lowbrow consumable status, cowers in the recesses of the heavily shelved unit. If you hadn't seen them dancing around the periphery you might never know they were present and accounted for.

I make my way deeper into the room. A leather-tufted sectional complete with animal print throw pillows adorn the lower portion of the room.

I have to admit, that as far as home libraries go, this one's a stunner, a praiseworthy relic of literary recognition that would set any scholar agog with affection for the infinity of resources. I run my fingers against the spines at random in the event the wall decides to spin and expose a secret room, but nothing. I reach the end of the aisle and a glimmer of light catches my attention.

"Crap," I whisper.

At the base of the long wall of bookshelves is a narrow entry about a foot wide leading to yet another room. An entire corner of the wall is missing leaving a gaping hole in its absence. It's brightly lit inside. It looks rather unassuming from what I can tell with yet another sectional, a circular glass coffee table, so I turn sideways and squeeze my way inside without hesitation.

expel

I look up and startle at the horrific sight above me. Instinctually I close my eyes and let out a scream that sears my throat with its invasive barb.

Each wall is lined with mounted creatures, lions with distinctly humanlike faces, oversized cat's with tourmaline stones set as eyes, a bearlike animal with ivory fangs that drip down to his throat.

I've seen these things before, not in my nightmares but in my waking hours, during my flesh-bearing tournament with Fems. It's a catalog of all the otherworldly creatures I've seen and some I've yet to encounter. I bolt for the exit and smash into a wall.

It's gone!

I pat the stone lined corner from where I entered only to find it sealed over.

"Shit!" A part of me isn't that worried. My mother is here after all, and there's no way she'd leave without me. Unless, of course, she thought I ran away again, or worse, she's in on this horror.

I spin on my heels and walk along the border of the room, nothing but shelves upon shelves of strange collectables. Pewter beasts that I'm unable to classify sit in various poses with ruby cut eyes, an entire section of glass orbs with what looks like real fire burning on the inside. They're fascinating. I want to pick one up, but I know better. They probably have the capability to launch me clear into another dimension, into a *real* fire. Or who knows? I might spontaneously combust. I bypass the temptation and meander from shelf to shelf inspecting an odd collection of prehistoric toys, long metal-pronged objects that look as if they might double as barbaric torture devices.

Pictures. An entire shelf devoted to candid shots of people doing mundane things, walking, brushing their hair, a crowd lost in conversation. Odd. It's as though none of them were aware they were the subject of the photographer's interest. It feels like an invasion of privacy just glancing at the gilded frames that encapsulate them. One in the back captures my attention. It's a girl with an all too familiar profile—*me*. I reach over and extricate it, careful not to knock down any of the frames in the process.

It was taken of me at school. I can see the effigy of Cerberus painted on the wall in the distance. I have a look of wonder on my face, my right hand hitched up on my shoulder securing my backpack.

Oh God.

I remember this day.

I place the picture down as though it were a snake.

That was the night the clown Fem chased me through the dirt lot and the forest exploded into a ball of fire. These pictures—they must be taken right before a Fem attack.

"What in the hell?" I back away not wanting to inspect them any further.

I move along until I'm greeted by a long oval mirror, perched high on the metal leg of a bird. I catch a glimpse of myself. I look exhausted, my hair frizzing, ballooning up in the back from the weather. My face twitches unnaturally in the reflection, winces and blinks unexpectedly.

I know damn well I didn't just do that.

There's something about this mirror—I reach forward to press against the glass and my fingers never cool to the touch, just push right through. I pull out reflexively before indulging one more time and gliding my entire arm into the strange expanse. It feels warm in there, moist.

"Must we learn each lesson the hard way?" A male voice booms from behind.

I extract my arm and jump around in one fell swoop, totally expecting to see a lion faced Fem, or an over grown cat, but I don't.

"Marshall!" I speed over and wrap my arms tight around him. My heart pounds fierce as a prison riot while I bury my head into his chest. I hadn't realized how afraid I

expel

was until this very moment. "Get me out of here. This place is horrible."

"Shh." He digs his hand into the back of my hair, patting my back in an effort to quell my fear.

"What is this place?" I look up at him. One thing is for sure, Marshall has the ability to make me feel safe even in a room full of mounted Fems.

"It's a trophy room, Skyla." He pulls a bleak smile. "Might I suggest you forget you've ever set foot in here, and please, for the love of all things holy, stay away from that thing," he nods in the direction of the mirror.

"What is it?" I pull him with me towards our deceiving reflections. "It's like us, only it's not." I point up at myself. "Look my face is twitching, so is yours, and I can—" I attempt to stick my hand in it, and Marshall snatches it back.

"I'm apprised of all it is capable of." Marshall stands behind me and wraps his arms around my waist securing me from doing anything foolish like dipping myself into the mirror again.

"Tell me, I want to know all about it." I stare at it in wonder as our reflections move in snatches. We warp and pop as though we were watching images of ourselves on old depreciated film.

"I gifted this to him," he sighs. "It was a peace offering after the last revolution—an olive branch of sorts. I thought we might forge a brotherhood with the Fems."

"I thought they were your subordinates?"

"They very much are for the time being. I wanted them to know I would make an effort to step over the old boundaries they found dissatisfying and treat them as equals. It didn't work." He glowers into his reflection as though he were scolding himself.

"Where does the mirror lead? What kinds of powers does it have?"

"That, dear Skyla," Marshall nods into his reflection while increasing his grip on me. It feels as if I'm a child, and Marshall is trying to stop me from peering over a very steep cliff. "That, my love, is the Realm of Possibilities."

"The Realm of Possibilities," I let the words roll off my tongue. "What happens there?"

"Everything." He breathes it into my ear like a temptation. Marshall is the serpent, and I am Eve, hungry for the gift of knowledge.

"It is good," his breath dances across my cheek. "And, it is evil."

"What happens if I go inside?"

"Ask them," Marshall wands his hand over the multitude of dead Fems mounted up above.

I think I have my answer.

29

Time of our Lives

The next morning something stirs in our world. Misery wafts on the horizon like a bitter perfume. Its scent precludes the lot of us but nature gives rise to the caveat.

A scarlet sky—the dense bushy evergreens pressing into one another fighting for space on the island's rocky shore. It was as if alarms were going off all around us. Our world was infiltrated with warning bells, one sounding off after another. But all I could comprehend was the joy of holding Gage freely throughout the halls and sprawling lawns at West. The fact my boyfriend was able to shower me with kisses before and after class, in front of the student body at large without having to fear that my life would be swept from under me was unadulterated bliss.

At school, Gage sits behind me, protective and faithful during second period, as Marshall goes off on a tangent about the revolution of mathematics. He espouses its glorious riches dating back since the beginning of the time, the mathematical wonders of nature, the golden spiral ratio.

He passes around a nautilus shell. It's soft, smooth inside, glows a beautiful iridescent, it contrasts the gnarled outer layer that's been exposed to the harsh elements of the sea. I pass it back to Gage, bite down a smile because he eclipses the glory of the nautilus shell as it vies for attention as one of God's greatest creations.

I spin back around and my mind drifts back to Demetri's hall of horrors, rife with celestial based felonies. I just can't excavate from my mind the things I saw at Demetri's haunted estate. The strange carcasses staged all over the secret room. Marshall had to walk me through a wall just to return me to the library from where I came. I wonder what my mother would think of Demetri if she knew what those framed pictures meant—how far out of her skin she would freak out if she ever laid eyes on the atrocities hanging just below his ceiling?

It turns out Demetri wants me to help him catalogue his grandfather's belongings. There was talk of a donation to a local museum that helps preserve the history of Paragon. It was my mother's suggestion and Demetri flinched when she said it. I suppose it's doubtful he'll be parting with his haunted devices anytime soon.

"Take Ms. Messenger for example," Marshall's voice penetrates me, it comes at me unnaturally invasive as though something perverse just happened, and I was only mildly aware of it. "Algebra is a wonderful tool that helps display the relationship between objects—even people."

I shake my head slightly in an effort to thwart the oncoming assault.

If Marshall thinks turning Gage and I into some kind of twisted allegory will help my classmates master the art of relational studies, he can forget it. Things are going too damn well with Gage to ruin them with Marshall's lewd and crude illustrations.

"Mr. Harrison sits in front of Skyla, and Mr. Oliver charitably holds up the rear, therefore the three of them have a relational value. Of course, if you added Ms. Bishop to the mix who sits unprotected by such robust bookends you would devalue the relationship of the subjects involved."

I cut my gaze over to Chloe without daring to move my head.

Note to self, accost Marshall for inciting the cheer bot Pit Bull in my direction. Of course, her wrath should be centered on the culprit in question, but Chloe's instincts are skewed. It's me she's after. A storm could rage, flood all of the roads, cut all power to the island for days, and yet Chloe would have no problem laying the blame at my feet.

expel

"Therefore, Ms. Bishop is the weaker unit in the relationship," he continues to propagate, "altogether unfit for the calling and should be removed from practice. I revert back to the original unit of three. They have the proper connection that empowers them to do all things."

The bell rings. The entire class stares up at Marshall with blank faces unaware of the contextual meaning of his parable. I get it. Chloe needs to be removed. Then Gage, Ellis, and I will prosper in the faction war—we have been empowered to do all things.

"Mr. Oliver, may I see you a moment?" Marshall calls out while busying himself at the desk.

I walk over with Gage, still adjusting my backpack, my heart beating erratic over what irresponsible verbiage Marshall might decide to spout off next.

"Yes?" Gage flexes his dimples without trying.

"The dimwit, with whom you reside, has decided to abandon his scholastic efforts." Marshall doesn't bother decoding his speech. "I'm informing you of this grievance so you can knock some sense into him before I review the matter with your parents. I'm afraid academic probation is a real possibility. Are you aware of the implications?"

"No football," Gage nods into him. "Got it. Appreciate you letting me know."

We head for the door. Leave it to Holden to so consummately screw everything up. Logan will be lucky to be on the sidelines let alone on the field come next fall.

"Ms. Messenger?" Marshall flicks a finger for me to return.

I backtrack sans Gage who is wise to Marshall's private conversational schemes by now.

"What?" I hiss. I'm still completely perturbed at the idea of having to deal with a stabby *Ms. Bishop* for the rest of the day—if only it were a day. I have a feeling this punishment is going to transcend the rest of my life.

"I've had a vision." He doesn't bother to look up from adjusting his briefcase.

"No thank you," I say. I've sworn off Marshall's lips for an eternity. I spin Gage's forever ring on my finger, feel the pleasurable pull as it warms over my skin.

"You're attending a gathering Saturday night." He looks up and smiles. "I'll be home that evening should you need my services."

"Why would I need your services?" I seal my mouth shut because I'm not going to fall for his lip trickery anymore. "What kind of trouble am I getting into?"

"Past tense, Skyla." He straightens a stack of papers. "I've no clue what trouble awaits you, but I've been informed you've already done everything you'll be drawn and quartered for." He spears me with great intensity. "I'll be up late should you desire my company."

"No, thank you. I'll be with Gage."

I walk out the door.

I'm going to do everything in my power not to run to Marshall Saturday night.

I glide my arm around Gage, and we walk down the hall like a couple.

It's heaven like this.

Skyla and Gage, forever.

※ ※ ※

At lunch, Gage and I watch with our mouths on the floor as faux Logan embeds himself in a group of girls while doing his best Ellis impersonation. Only he's not acting like Ellis, he's acting like Holden—exactly who I wish he wasn't.

"He's really back to his old self," Gage muses resting his head against mine. He keeps alluding to the fact Logan was a real ass-wipe prior to his relationship with me.

"What are you talking about?" And what is Holden doing out of class? Logan doesn't have lunch this hour. He has A lunch and Gage and I have B.

"He's back in the game, on the hunt, the prowl. It's his element. He thrives in estrogen laced environments."

"What?" If Logan were really here, there would be no way he would act like that. I look around the vicinity because I'm willing to bet he is in fact here, dying of embarrassment. No pun intended.

"Hey, guys." Brielle plops a tray laden with the cafeteria's interpretation of edible fare out on the table. There is no way Brielle is going to be able to consume all that food. It hardly seems possible anyone is capable of such an excessive digestive feat.

"Hard left," Gage whispers in my ear.

I look over and see Drake extricating a stream of stupid from his lips, lobbing his nonsensical words in Emily's direction. What in the hell is wrong with him?

Ethan and Chloe stride by, and she comes to an abrupt stop at the sight of us.

"I know we got off on the wrong foot, Skyla," she gives a shy smile.

Yeah, like killing my father, wrong foot.

"But it would really mean a lot to me if you guys came to my house tomorrow night. My parents are out of town and I'm calling in a pizza." She reaches back and touches Ethan's cheek like a habit, "we're picking up a movie and just hanging out—no big deal."

Ethan swoops his hands around her waist, draws her in before kissing her soft on the temple.

"I don't know," I say, backing further into Gage. "We sort of have plans." Not really but we can manufacture them from thin air if we had to.

"If you change your mind, the fun starts at seven," she shrugs. "You know where to find me." Chloe doesn't look at Gage once.

"They'll be there," Ethan assures. "I'll make sure of it." He winks over at me as they take off.

"Yeah, right." I spin around and let Gage drape his arms over me. Let him wash my lips with his magical kisses.

Tomorrow night is just for the two of us. We have finally hit our stride.

Gage and I are together, open and free right here at West. We have both Chloe and Logan's blessing, well, Logan's for a time, and Chloe's as long as there's a prison sentence dangling over her head. But this priceless moment, these sacred hours—they are just the beginning.

This is the time of our lives.

30

The List

Saturday morning, long shards of darting rain fall slantways against the window. It creates a sad drumming in our corner of the world. Something about the rhythm, the unrelenting heartache embedded in its Morse code makes me miss my father.

I head down to the kitchen, still dizzy from waking up too early and bump into a body.

Gah—it's Chloe!

Her rumpled hair rises in the back, she's wearing sweats and a flimsy t-shirt that might as well be wet because, freaking shit, I can see right through it. I know for a fact she's not wearing a bra.

"Your pencil erasers are showing," I hiss.

"Is that anyway to speak to our guest?" Tad says, rather dismissively while going over paperwork with Mom. In all honesty, I didn't see them there hovering over the table.

"Guest?" I balk. I had to sign a contract that I'll never breathe the same air as a boy, and Chloe is here at this ungodly hour of the morning with her breasts making an eye-popping debut as our *guest*?

Ethan wanders in with a severe case of bed head. He wraps an arm around her waist offering a sloppy kiss before heading to the fridge.

Brielle and Drake amble down looking equally disheveled and outright skank from a wild night's romp.

"What the hell?" It comes out just above a whisper.

"That reminds me," Mom hops up and dispenses a fat white placebo courtesy of Dr. Booth. "It's just a trial, Skyla. I think I'm seeing an improvement already," she says, winking in secret.

I'm still suffering from my fatigue hangover coupled with the shock and awe campaign launched by the Landon brothers, so I can't even begin to decode that wink she just gave.

"What's that on your finger?" Mom's mouth opens with surprise. "Is that an engagement ring?"

"Actually it's—" I note the fact Chloe has stopped all movement and is scuttling in my direction.

"It's a forever ring." The words swim from my lips like a dream.

"She's lying, Lizbeth." Tad takes a sip from his coffee, doesn't even bother looking up while delivering the barb.

"Why would I lie?" Tad's idiocracy has finally stymied me.

"Why wouldn't you," Chloe says it low while picking up my finger and inspecting the silver band, the blue eye of Gage staring right back at her in the shape of a heart.

"I'll tell you why." Tad holds up a yellow legal pad and waves it in the air. "Found this hidden beneath a stack of magazines on the coffee table."

Still no clue what the moron in question is railing about.

Am I in the right house? The right time zone? Because something is way the hay off this morning in this corner of the universe.

"Listen to this, Lizbeth," he begins. "It appears your daughter finds it perfectly acceptable to one-up our wedding and plans to jockey herself into the Paragon social limelight with a lavish affair just one *week* before our humble but meaningful event." His face turns a strange shade of pomegranate. I'm shocked at how genuinely pissed he seems. Either, A, Chloe planted that stack of bullshit or B—

expel

"Those are my notes," Mom snatches the legal pad from his stubby little fingers. "I moved the wedding up, and I may have changed the location."

Or that.

"What?" Tad stands as if it were an outcry that my mother didn't find his backyard barbeque adequate enough to fulfill her romantic desires. "We were going to get a new TV, and the whole family was going to watch a baseball game." He holds out his hands perplexed.

Doesn't every girl dream of renewing her vows during the seventh inning stretch?

"I know," Mom shakes her head, "I know we said that, but Demetri offered his estate, and I couldn't say no. It's amazing. It's going to be like a fairytale." She bites down on her lip, and her eyes avert heavenward as if she were watching the event unfold on the ceiling.

"Fairytale is right." Tad takes back the legal pad and riffles through its sunny pages. "Lobster? A seven tiered marzipan cake? Imported cheeses from around the world?" Tad's head swivels like it might actually become detached.

"It's my wish list," she snipes.

Tad looks to Ethan and Drake for help. I don't know why he doesn't buck up and give Mom a decent wedding. She wasn't asking for the Waldorf Astoria. In the least, he could have offered her a church and taken us to an all you can eat buffet afterwards.

"We can't afford this," he spits it out forced like a geyser. "Have you forgotten the all expenses paid vacation we're giving these two next weekend?" He points hard at Drake and Brielle. I'm sure he means a visit to the obstetrics clinic Brielle strong-armed them into taking her to. I shudder at the memory of my own trip there.

"Oh, Hon," Mom's voice reduces thick as molasses, "We don't have to pay for any of this. Demetri insisted. It's his gift to the family." She goes over and wraps her arms around his waist, pecks a kiss on his cheek. "This is going to be the thrill of a lifetime."

"As long as I get to be the groom," Tad sneers over her shoulder.

He won't if Demetri gets his way.

❦ ❦ ❦

Chloe traps me in the hall before ushering me backwards into Ethan's room. I'd shout for Brielle to rescue me, but she's entertaining everyone with the tiny feet prodding from her bulbous stomach.

The bed is unmade. The air is stale, smells of old socks and questionable his and hers body odor.

"Listen," she says, sealing the door shut behind her. "I know we've gotten off to a rocky start."

"Criminal offenses were committed," I'm quick to remind her. "You're the sole reason my mother is in there planning to reenact the second worst day of my life." The first being my father's death, but I'm so melancholy this morning I might cry at the mention of him.

"No, I'm not responsible," she shakes her head defiantly. "I've been thinking about what you said, about the Sectors and the Fems pitting us against each other, and it all became crystal clear. They wanted you here. They used me. I was nothing but a pawn in a game of high stakes manipulation. I swear it. I'm not shitting you. They need us both for different reasons. I know the rules to the game," she fingers the protective hedge around her neck absentmindedly before dropping her hand back to her side. "They need us to fight the war because they're not allowed."

"What?" It does make sense. I drop my gaze to the underwear strewn around the floor. "I'll see what I can find out." From Marshall, from my mother, but I don't tell Chloe that. "I think you might be right. Why else couldn't the

expel

Sectors and the Fems duke it out themselves? Why would they need an army of half-breeds unless they weren't allowed to play the game?" I hate calling the faction war a game. Logan has hinged our future upon it, so have I in a way.

"You notice anything strange about Logan?" She tilts her head into me like we're suddenly besties.

She knows.

"He's not himself," I whisper to see if she'll bite.

"That's because he's Holden Kragger."

She went there.

"Now what?" I can't believe I'm talking to Chloe of all people about the precious soul I've managed to displace.

Chloe lunges into me with her deathly black smile, her eyes reduced to slits.

There's something dangerous happening here and I can't put my finger on it.

"I've assigned Michelle to him," she confides.

"What?"

"Relax, she's too into Dudley to do something stupid. That way Logan keeps his flesh clean and free from all the hoes lined up to take advantage of the situation. Holden had a very specific thing for Michelle. He about died when he told me they were going out. It's all going as planned."

"How are we going to get Logan back?" *We*? Mother F—I've just drifted past sanities horizon.

"I'll let you handle that. I've got enough blood on my hands." She drops a remorseful gaze to the floor before darting back into me with those hard steely lasers. "Skyla, I don't want you to say anything in return, but I do want you to know I'm really sorry about everything. I'm going to hate myself until the day I die over the role I played in your father's death. And, I feel pretty terrible about keeping you and Gage apart, too." A single tear rolls over her cheek. "I think deep down inside I wished Gage would have felt the same way about me. I thought given enough time—enough of everything, that he would have loved me." She swallows hard, shaking her head. "But, I have that with Ethan now. He worships me." She presses her lips together.

The fact that all Chloe Bishop ever wanted was to be worshiped doesn't surprise me, but I doubt Ethan is the congregation she's looking for. A greedy deity like her wants love from a pure and holy being, one that would qualify as a god himself and that just so happens to be my boyfriend.

I nod into her.

"I begged Ethan's forgiveness," she continues. "He's going to help us with the faction war. He's as pissed as I am."

"Whose side are you on?" I know damn well, where her allegiance lies.

She reaches over, picks up my hand and closes her eyes a moment.

I'm with the Sectors. There's a hard glint in her eyes. *We're going to get those bastards who are screwing with our lives for sport. I always defeat my enemies, Skyla. Nobody has the last laugh at my expense. God pity the poor souls who try and mess with me. They will never see me coming.* She wraps her arms around me tight. *Truce?*

I gaze down at her an undetermined length of time unable to appraise the situation for what it really might be. I'm not sure what I have to lose. I still have Gage.

Truce, I say.

I'm hugging Chloe Bishop, and I've just agreed to a truce.

Clearly, I've meandered into an alternate universe.

31

Full Disclosure

Gage and I drive over to Chloe's house after pulling a shift at the bowling alley together. I love working with Gage—stealing a kiss in the office, the crazy noise infused kisses in the dark arcade, the cool lingering of his lips in the walk-in freezer.

"Are you sure this is how you want to spend Saturday night?" He kills the engine, observing Chloe's house through slotted lids as if it were a looming threat.

Rain beats upon the windshield like a thousand tiny hands imploring me to reconsider.

"I'm sure," I whisper. "Besides, Ethan begged me to come so did Brielle. Ethan's got something up his sleeve. He's not as quick to forgive as Chloe believes."

"And why are you?" Gage smoothes his thumb over my hand, lowers his head until his brows sit low on his forehead like two ebony birds.

"I'm not," I sigh. "I just," I shrug. "I think deep down inside I want to believe her. Everyone's redeemable right? We all make mistakes, huge, horrible mistakes and in the end when we wake up to what we've done—most of us are sorry."

"Chloe doesn't have a heart, Skyla," he presses into me with a kiss. "And the fact yours is too big is the reason I love you most."

Gage and I consume ourselves in a sea of endless kisses. Time stretches out, loses its grip on us, ushers us into something eternal that we were designed for right from the beginning.

"I love you so much," I whisper soft in his ear. "I don't think I could breathe without you."

Inside, the Bishop home holds the scent of fresh baked cookies. The dim lighting and consistent spasm of cackles give the night that Ellis-esque feel.

It feels quasi-safe with Brielle and Drake here. Emily, Lexy, Michelle and faux Logan add a certain air of comfort to the environment. The roll call of bitchiness is complete with Nat as the honorary member, and Pierce, who has become as his namesake suggests, the constant thorn in my side.

Michelle is joined at the hip with Logan which weirds me out because despite being Holden, in nature, he's still staunchly locked in Logan's congenial framework. I know deep inside that in no way what Holden does with Michelle reflects on Logan, but I can't help but feel a stab of jealousy at the same time. It looks like Chloe was right. Holden is a lust slave to Michelle. He follows her around like a Golden Retriever, happy to fetch her every need.

Pierce glares at me from across the room.

I've been carrying that stupid cease and desist letter around in my purse to circumvent it from accidently landing in Mom and Tad's hands. Of course Pierce doesn't want to go to juvy over the stupid shit I accidentally did while hopped up on Michelle's rose of terror, but then, really, neither do I.

Holden pats him on the back as he makes his way into the kitchen. I'm sure Pierce has been apprised of the fact his brother incarnate is in the vicinity.

I think the entire Kragger clan owes me big time, and I don't mean by way of threatening legal action at every turn. Pierce should cease and desist his presence from my life as a thank you even if Holden's state of being is temporal.

I pull Gage deeper into the family room, wrap my arms around his waist and swoon into him dreamily. We're here

expel

together at Chloe Bishop's house of all places. It all worked out on its own. I didn't have to sleep with Marshall to get Chloe off our backs.

Of course, we could have done without the Mustang turning his insides to pulp and killing Logan. I'm still convinced Chloe was behind the scene of that crime. Speaking of which, I haven't heard Gage cough all night. I bet he's plenty recuperated for me to fill him in on the bizarre turn of events regarding his dearly departed uncle slash cousin. I hate keeping secrets from Gage.

"Guess what?" I whisper into his ear.

He moans into me while massaging my back. It feels so good I can melt into a puddle right here at his feet.

"I want to talk to you later about something super important," I breathe it hot in his ear.

"Does this super important topic require a hotel and protection?" A devilish smile plays on his lips.

"No, but we could talk about that, too." I tweak my brows.

I press a heated kiss into Gage right here in Chloe Bishop's living room and miracle of all miracles I don't end up with a knife in my back.

"All right," Ethan begins corralling everyone into the family room. "Let's get this movie going before it gets too late."

God—he even sounds like Tad.

"Brace yourselves girls," Chloe warns as she makes her way over to the entertainment unit. "It's three glorious hours of battleships and tanks—Ethan's pick. He won the wrestling match." An image of the two of them going at it bounces through my mind. "Next time, I assure you," she continues, "the cover will be pink, and there will be hot shirtless man-candy to drool over for two hours straight."

"I'll give you some man-candy to drool over," Ethan bumps her with his hip.

Ethan and Chloe really do look and act like a couple. They shared a soda at dinner, and she ate his pizza crust. Now they're nauseating us with an awkward display of questionable kissing.

"I think he's chewing on her," Gage whispers.

"He is. But in his defense, one doesn't get a whole lot of practice kissing when they're dead."

"Let's do this," Pierce barks, wrapping an arm around Nat.

I feel Kate's absence most when Nat's around. It infuriates me that Marshall used me to do his dirty work. Chloe is right. We're nothing more than pawns on some giant celestial chessboard.

Gage and I sit on the loveseat, squeezing in next to Brielle and Drake while Chloe dims the lights.

The television in Chloe's family room eats up an entire wall.

I have to say I'm impressed with this rather odd gathering. It's sort of a nice break from Ellis's rambunctious affair with nary a red Solo cup in sight, which most likely implies there won't be any puking later with the exception of maybe Brielle.

The TV blinks, and my smiling face pops up on the screen. A sappy country song aggregates through the speakers and offensively begins twanging in our ears.

"What the—" Before I can get the words out, Marshall ignites the screen with his lips secured over mine.

Chloe glares in my direction. "This one's for you, Gage."

An entire montage of me kissing Marshall—kissing Logan enfolds. Even Ellis is thrown into the mix with his pants down, me kneeling before him. Never mind the fact he was putting out the fire on my hand, it looks entirely lewd from the angle the video was taken.

I'm frozen.

expel

A stale breath is caught in my lungs that I may never let go. Gage sinks limp into the seat beside me. I'm too afraid to look at him, to look at anyone.

It goes on for an eternity.

Marshall and me, rolling around on the bed at the Pine Pole Lodge—me in my corset, his hands caressing my bare waist. Logan loving me at the bowling alley, the house, the school—everywhere a lip-lock. The lust written over the two of us could combust the room into flames.

The music comes to a roaring crescendo, the Mustang gyrates overlooking Devil's Peak.

Time feels as though it's picking up speed. My stomach does a hot revolution because I know what's coming.

The camera pans in a tight clear shot of Logan writhing over me, the haunted dress Marshall gave me for the winter formal, bunched in a mess around my hips. The passion on my face is undeniable. My lust for Logan burns a hole through the air, electrifies the atmosphere until the universe sizzles from our searing affection.

A stone sinks in my chest, obliterates my heart to nothing.

It's over between Gage and me. What I've done is unforgivable.

I glance over at Chloe in disbelief. My sins recanted for everyone to see. This was her plan, her pleasure.

She hid the blade in her tongue—in her deceit to lure me over.

I was the enemy, the feast, the sport—the entertainment.

And I never saw it coming.

32

The Heart of the Matter

A stony silence fills the room. The image of Logan covering my body with his, burns bright for everyone to see. The color on the screen melts to the hue of coffee grounds before a loud pop explodes, and smoke rises from the back of the unit.

Logan.

He's a little late, not to mention culpable for all this misery just as much as Chloe. Of course, I'm the biggest perpetrator of all. Chloe may have built the gallows, but it was me who provided the rope with which to hang myself. All of my most personal misgivings splayed naked for Gage to see.

My heart tries to pummel its way out of my chest—my flesh completely numb as if it no longer wanted the job of covering such a whore of a carcass. A Mack truck could run me over and I wouldn't feel a thing—hell, I might welcome it. I'd run in its path if given the opportunity.

A horrible sting radiates through me, the laceration to my heart, too much to bear.

Gage gets up, walks calmly out of the room as if he were going to the kitchen, the bathroom. He hits the front porch so fast I can't keep up with him.

"Gage!" I scream through the roaring downpour as I tap down the stairs.

He turns to face me, all of the color has bleached from his skin. His eyes are wide from the aftereffects of witnessing my indiscretions, witnessing the manner in which I had been grinding our love down to powder all along.

expel

Chloe set up a minefield and walked our love right into it, but they were my sins. I should have fought Marshall—held Logan at arm's length.

"It's not what it looks like," it comes out inaudible, unbelievable.

Rain falls like acid, dissolves the meaning out of any sorry word I could ever hope to utter. Even if those kisses from Marshall meant nothing, why wasn't I reporting the offense? And Logan? How do I classify those kisses? As undesirable? Unwanted?

"I swear to you—I didn't initiate any of that." It pulses from me as a desperate cry.

"You didn't stop it." The words spike into me like rusted hooks.

"Can we go somewhere? I—"

"No," it speeds out of him without reservation, filled with an underlying rage.

My fingers drift to the ring he gave me, the one engraved with our special brand of forever love.

"I don't deserve this," I say, twirling it without the fortitude to take it off.

He spears me with his injured eyes, bears into me with a palpable heartbreak that shatters the infrastructure of everything we stood on.

"Keep it." His gaze lingers, heavy-laden with grief. The world wobbles around us as we succumb to this unimaginable pain.

Gage makes his way over to his truck, takes off so quick a wall of water ten feet high showers the road in his wake.

"Gage," I fall to my knees. It's hard to tell where the rain ends and the tears begin. My chest heaves in spasms—loud guttural cries escape from my throat. I cry—hard, bitter tears that I haven't shed in such abundance since I was a child—since the time of my father. This was a new brand of heartache, the penalty for my sins too high a price that I could ever hope to rectify.

I lie down in the middle of the street, let the rain consume me, cut into my flesh with its punishing bites as I try to dissolve from the planet, become my own universe. I am nothing—a detestable Sodom, begging for the fire. I could only pray to burn to launder myself for Gage. Not even an inferno could purify what I had become—filth and dross. The rain could never cleanse the pain, the shame. I lost any chance of happiness I could have ever hoped to have and sold it for a few stolen kisses, visions that I never needed, never welcomed.

I broke both our hearts, forever.

With the strength of a lioness, Brielle peels me off Paragon's pavement and rolls me into her Jeep. She fills me in on the cackling that went on once I chased after Gage, lets me know they replayed it a good three times on Chloe's laptop for all to see, again and again.

"How the hell did she get all that? She's a fucking witch, that's how." Brielle shakes with anger. You would think it was her heart that was perforated with bullets. "I'm so damn sick of Chloe cock-blocking you. This is just another ploy to get Gage. It won't work." The jeep picks up speed. "Chloe is the human equivalent of a Dingo, only instead of stealing your baby, she's trying to steal your soul."

Something tells me she would steal my baby if she had the chance.

Brielle is panting with hatred for Chloe. Drake stayed behind. He chose to stay with Emily. Perhaps that's the true offense here, the reason for her white-knuckle grip over the wheel, her death glare into the blank open road.

"Do you hate me?" I ask. It comes out childlike.

I hate me. I don't know why Brielle's answer should reflect anything different.

expel

"What?" We swerve into oncoming traffic momentarily. "*No*. Why would I hate you?"

I hiccup, sniffling back the deluge of waterworks still trying to purge themselves from my system.

"You broke up with Logan a while ago, right?" she asks.

Before I can nod or get into her line of thinking, an old woman on the side of the road garners my attention. She wields an ax over the stump of a tree, hacking at it without regard for the monsoon that's dousing her with its affections.

"You see that?" I ask, twisting my neck to get a better look as we speed by.

"See what?"

Ezrina.

"Nothing," I say, taking in a quivering breath.

"So, Mr. Dudley," she continues, "being with him is practically a graduation requirement. They don't let you out of West unless he sticks his tongue down your throat at least once. It's not like you could help yourself. He's like a drug, one hit and he's got you for life."

"Right," I say stupefied as the rain turns a putrid shade of red, douses the windshield with its crimson splendor. Oh my, God—the sky is bleeding. "Do you see *that*?"

"What?" Brielle angles into the road as if trying to make out a deer, or possum.

It's clear she's not privy to same weather phenomenon that I am.

"I need to go to Dudley's," it speeds out of me. It takes everything in me not to text Gage and beg for help, not that he'd give it—nor could I blame him.

"Totally." She lifts a hand in the air. "I swear, I get it."

"Not for that," I don't bother defending myself. I'm sure Chloe will have the entire scene emblazoned in the school newspaper by Monday.

"Oh, sure," she doesn't sound convinced.

We drive another ten minutes before pulling into his circular drive. I speed out of the car, through the salty plasma gushing from the sky and storm his porch—pound my fists against the door, ferocious like a riot.

Brielle takes off and I'm left alone, bloodied, in the dark.

A walloping thump ignites just above my head, shakes the mahogany, strong as an earthquake. I look up to find a newly embedded ax—the handle protruding over me like a promise.

The porch light comes on. Marshall swings open the door and gives a bleak smile.

The blood magically fades from my clothes, and I'm simply soaking wet, standing on his porch. Marshall plucks the ax from the door like it were a daily occurrence, common as a wreath at Christmas.

Deep down inside I know nothing will ever be normal again.

33

Heartbreak

"I knew you'd come." Marshall wraps an arm around my shoulder and leads me to the couch where two cups of steaming tea sit unsupervised.

"You knew this was going to happen, didn't you? You said so," I hiccup the last part out in anger.

"No, Skyla." His face catches the light and exposes his grief. "All I knew is that you would come to me brokenhearted."

Marshall encapsulates me in his arms and I bleat out a stream of silent tears over his shoulder until I can see his flesh illuminate from under his shirt. Not even the pleasurable impulses that course through his body are enough to quell this desperate ache. Marshall was an accomplice of Chloe's in the destruction of my forever. He could deny it with every good intention, but he was the constant in that horrific display of my affairs.

"Chloe," he breathes her name over me like a curse.

Glimpses of what unfolded on that oversized TV shutter through my mind. It's my way of telling Marshall what happened, how I stabbed Gage with a thousand deadly pixels of my own doing.

"I'm sorry, love." Marshall helps me to the sofa. He holds me for an hour solid without placating me with silly sentiments about how everything will work out, that all of this will blow over and that Chloe will die in a fiery car crash. All of the assurances I long for are null and void from his lips tonight.

"I thought we were going to be friends," I hiccup. "She's an animal."

"She should be caged," he echoes.

"Ezrina, she's after me," I clutch onto the collar of his dress shirt until the buttons threaten to give way. "I saw her on the road. I need to see my mother."

"It's not that easy."

"Then get Giselle," I take in a trembling lungful of Marshall's spiced cologne. Gage, and his perfect angelic face pumps through me and I start in on the tears again. I've plunged from a very steep cliff, and I will never recover.

I lose myself in the darkness of Marshall's chest.

This wound can never be rectified. I've killed everything we were by polluting the oxygen that desired to sustain us, choking out our love with these lips I shared so freely.

Buried deep in the black world behind my lids, thoughts dissolve, elongate, pull like taffy until sleep comes over me, welcome as a song.

I appear on a hillside, an unblemished sky, vapid and bland. Trees spike up like a fortress, raven and sable—nature throwing out all the wrong colors. I had taken everything that was right and perverted it. It was only fair that it should follow me into my dreams.

Skyla, Logan trembles as he comes upon me, offers his platonic embrace before pulling me in, wiping my tears away with the soft of his lips. *Will you forgive me?* His sincerity catches me off guard. Logan who owned me, still does, he wants to share the blame, dive into this ocean of grief with me.

I don't think fate knows what it's doing. I shake my head, convinced of this. *I should never have fallen in love with you. It was a mistake.*

There's a reason for everything, Skyla. Logan is drained, bone tired. Death has mopped the floor with him, made him drink down the dirty water, and he's had enough of it all, I can tell. *Gage will understand. Chloe portrayed you in the worst possible light.*

It didn't take much, I say.

I didn't know about Dudley. He squints a sad smile before tilting his head. *I had no idea he was playing you every chance he could.*

He was showing me—

He cuts me off. *Visions, I know. Giselle filled me in.*

There it was. My shame had spread over two dimensions, heaven and earth knew of my offenses, how abhorrent I was to have let it happen while Gage pined only for me. He loved me with everything—bore his soul on paper, dreamed of my face before he even knew me. I bet he wishes I would throw myself off Devil's Peak and break my neck.

Gage made me feel safe. And now I was alone, as good as naked in a forest full of Fems. Nothing will be right again. Gage is gone, our relationship as dead as Logan.

I struggle to wake, fight to open my eyes and when I do, I'm all alone on my bed with the storm wailing its wrath outside my window.

※ ※ ※

In the morning I awake to incessant knocking. For a fleeting moment I think Gage has come to see me and bolt up out of my restless slumber.

"You going to church?" Mom appears from the other side of the door. Her glossy hair lays over her shoulder, her lips fully outlined and colored in a dewy scarlet. I had never seen my mother pay such careful attention to her appearance as I have of late.

"I'm not feeling so good," it comes out hoarse.

She speeds over and checks my head for a fever. "You weren't drinking last night, were you?" Her anger comes out disguised as concern.

"No," I fall back on the pillow. Just drunk on sorrow, I want to say, but don't.

"The rest of us are headed out the door. If you need anything, call. I can always stop by the store and pick something up." There's a sadness in her eyes like maybe she knows. I'm sure Chloe has deposited a copy of my infernal DVD on every doorstep on the island by now—uploaded it to YouTube. Crap, I hadn't even thought of that until now.

Mom leaves and clicks the door shut behind her.

I'm going to be alone.

Ezrina stalks the outer recesses of my mind, causing me to bolt up and do a quick change. I need to see Gage. Apologize until the sun goes down if I have to. I pause in the mirror, horrified at the girl staring back at me, her face bloated with grief, eyes like bloodied tumors. Instead of giving my best to Gage, this malfeasance would be all I could offer.

I grab my purse, my keys and head out the door.

The brisk air slaps against my skin with its glacial bite, the sky washed anew from the storm. The soft glow of fog, the gentle lamp-lit grey that illuminates the island cuts into my tender eyes. It makes me wish I had sunglasses. I'd gladly dip the world in washed tones of sepia.

Nevermore lands on the hood of the Mustang.

"Nev," I groan, placing my hand over his back. The strong smell of tailpipe emissions leftover from the minivan burn my nostrils.

Word has reached the Justice Alliance over your agreement with Ezrina. He twitches his neck three times.

"Great," I lack enthusiasm but mean it nevertheless.

Not great, Skyla. They're annoyed at the prospect. Do nothing more with the situation, I implore you with my life.

"OK, Heathcliff," I whisper his name with human lips, a foreign sound to him after hundreds of years.

Enough! His wings expand with fury. *Why must you delve where you don't belong?*

"I made a covenant. I belong here now. You and Ezrina, belong. Love should always prosper. You can't tell me otherwise."

Not under these conditions, not with eternal damnation awaiting one and ceasing to exist the reward for the other. Skyla, you are about to foolishly end my days. Stand back from my life. Remove yourself before you cause any more turmoil. I demand it.

Nevermore bolts into the sky quick as a spiraling arrow. With amazing pent up fury he screams into the quiet reserve, blackens the sky with his pulsating wings.

Damn it all to hell.

It takes real talent to piss off a bird.

Soon I'll have to add blipping Nevermore out of existence to the growing list of things I'll never be able to forgive myself for.

34

Sit a Spell

I give a series of spastic knocks at the Oliver's door. God help me if Holden opens it. Logan's face or not, I'm going to clock him a good one. I'm in the mood to administer a serious beating, and the first imbecile that gets in my way will most likely reap the reward.

Emma pulls back the door with a semi-complacent smile on her face.

"Skyla," she downgrades to less than a frown.

"I need to see Gage."

"He's not well." She folds her arms tight across her chest.

A pang of embarrassment envelops me. She must know what a horror I've become to her son. How he'd rather eat dead rats for dinner than see my face ever again.

"Can I come in?"

"No," her lips droop with displeasure.

God, she really hates me now.

"Emma," Dr. Oliver appears from behind, "of course you can come in, Skyla. Join us in the living room if you don't mind. Logan has company in the kitchen."

I bypass Emma with a palpable discomfort. Michelle gives a slight wave from the breakfast table with a deck of cards in her hand. She looks bored. I like bored. The last thing I want is Holden fornicating with anything that moves while occupying Logan's mortal being, not that I want him fornicating with Michelle. I'd strap a male version of a chastity belt on him if I could.

Then, like some anomaly, I see Logan standing over Holden, and he stretches back a smile.

I jump a little at the odd sight.

"Skyla?" Barron calls for me, concerned.

"I'm right behind you." I give a quick wave to the hologram hovering in the kitchen, and he glides over to me with ease. I follow Barron and Emma to the living room, safely away from Holden and Michelle.

Emma eyes me like I'm some kind of savage. It's clear they know what I've done to Gage, or at least she suspects as much. She probably has all along. I bet you there was an *I told you so* involved when he came home and branded me as the heartless bitch who used his heart as a chew toy.

"Do you think I can go up and see him?" I ask, taking a seat on the distal end of the sectional. Logan, cloaked in his invisibility, sits beside me with his arms flexed over the sofa ready for the show.

Barron shakes his head. "He stomped upstairs last night and locked the door, says he's not feeling well and that we should leave him the hell alone."

I jerk when he says it.

"Why should we leave him the hell alone, Skyla?" Emma sits straight as a pin. Her face set in a perpetual scowl. This is not going to end well.

"I...well, Chloe...there was this film, but it was fake, part of it was real. It just looked bad."

"English," Emma snips.

"I sort of...I really didn't mean to..." Then it bleeds out of me. Marshall and his true Sector identity, the steady stream of worthless visions, Logan who surprised me with his kisses. How I never told Gage. How I would have taken it all to the grave if I could have. How I suddenly wish I were in one.

"This is what you did to him?" Emma exasperates herself just getting the words out. "He loved you like he's never loved anybody before." She circles me with her disappointment. "My nephew—you used him."

"No," I shake my head, "I swear, I never used anybody."

"She didn't use me," Logan's voice comes through, just barely audible.

"What was that?" Barron tilts his head in curiosity.

"She's throwing her voice," Emma narrows in on me, "like a ventriloquist. Those Celestra are capable of any number of tricks." She says *Celestra* like it's a dirty word.

"It wasn't me," I say. In a minute I'm going to knock her out of my way and go Celestra all over the door to Gage's room until I gain entry.

"It was me." Logan materializes, slowly.

A series of choking sounds emit from Emma's throat while Barron twists his lips at the curious site.

"Knew it," Barron seethes. "Who's the dim-wit taking up space in this residence?"

"Holden Kragger," I say it below a whisper. "Sorry." I mouth that last part only because I killed Holden to begin with.

"To the mortuary with him," Barron tries to stand, but Emma pulls him down by the elbow. "Hypothermia—we'll drown him to preserve the tissue. We must reverse the situation."

"You're dead?" Emma's face crumbles, contorts in a pinch of anguish so sharp I have to look away from her grief. "You did this, Skyla?" She asks breathless.

"No, I don't know who did this. I swear, I was standing next to them just before the Mustang hit." I point over at Logan who has metamorphosized into his perfect coat of flesh.

"Travel back and find out," she shouts the words at me.

God, why didn't I think of that?

"I will."

"She can't," Logan corrects. "There's a binding spirit. It was there that night—still is."

"Oh," I reflect, "that's why Nev couldn't come. And the two of you couldn't push the car out of the way. But you traveled." Just when Logan is about to redeem himself, another shady action rears its ugly head.

"I used my supervising spirit," it comes out sober. "It's of no use to me now."

"I know it was Chloe without a doubt," I offer. "Marshall would never have gone after Gage. You were the one who knifed him. It was you he was after."

"Logan!" Emma bounces in her seat.

The woman is going to have a cardiac episode if this conversation continues in this direction. She's so freaked, you'd think Ezrina was in the vicinity. Speaking of Ezrina...

"I need Giselle immediately," I say to Logan. If I don't get that meeting with my mother ASAP, I'm going to have a whole other set of problems, and for most of them, I'll be wielding an ax.

"Giselle?" Emma whispers her name.

Everything stops in the room. I thought they knew. I thought—

Emma falls into a comatose state as Barron fans her with a magazine. I leave Logan to fill them in on the details and bolt up the stairs because I'll be damned if I've come all the way to the Oliver's house to not see Gage.

※ ※ ※

I traipse through the dark halls painted a shade reminiscent of dried blood. Not a seam of light beneath his door, not one sound to give evidence of life beyond its border.

I press my cheek against the cool of the wood, pick up on the sweet scent of his cologne and ride its intoxicating wave. I listen for footsteps, the television, but nothing. The wall of silence presses into me, painful and crushing, so I give a gentle tap.

"Gage?" I love the sound of his name as it leaves my lips. Although uncertain and broken, it's a song I could listen to night after night. "Gage? Can I come in, please?"

I twist the knob, but it doesn't give. I would go in uninvited, kiss his bare feet, wash them in tears while begging forgiveness if he let me. I'd knock down every wall on Paragon just to prove my affection for him.

"I love you," I say. "I swear I do." I rub my open palm over his door as though it were his skin, press my lips in soft against the veneer. "Forever."

35

Marshall Arts

Marshall sends a text and asks me to meet him at the West Shore, says it's most important, so I drive over still reeling from the aftereffects of a newly broken heart.

Marshall waves at me from the waterline as powder white sand dusts his shins. He's sporting a pair of inky blue swim trunks and nothing else besides his immaculately chiseled body. My stomach lurches at the sight of him, even at this distance Marshall is an amazing specimen, a testament to testosterone in general. He shines in all his glory like an opulent shell, some exotic being that has washed up on shore. It's a wonder he hasn't amassed a harem by now.

The island burns with a molten red sky. It climaxes with heated rain that feels tropical in nature as it needles its aggression out over the vicinity.

"I'm getting wet!" I hold out my hands and scream as I run down the beach towards him.

"That's entirely the point," he shouts back. He darts a finger at me and a sudden blast of frigid air hits my newly exposed skin. My clothes have disappeared and I'm wearing a rather itsy bitsy, teeny weenie, yellow polka dot bikini.

"Very not funny," I say, covering my girl parts in haste.

"Very well," he says, pointing over at me again and the two-piece is replaced with a modest navy one-piece. The rain softens its harsh bites and reduces itself to a drizzle.

"Better," I pant, landing beside him. "I've got news for you. It's too cold to swim."

"Swim?" His eyes ignite in flames. "The amphibious exercises I've planned for us hardly qualify as a leisurely swim. This is work, Skyla. Intense training is about to commence and I suggest we begin by confirming our commitment with a kiss." He slides into a seductive grin as he pulls me in by the waist. He's morphed to the younger version of himself, which weird's me out, but I find it intoxicating and exciting all the same time. It's amazing to see him this way.

"No kiss, but I am committed—to the *war*. I assume that's the topic of conversation," I say, plucking his arms off my waist.

"You assume correct." He takes up my hand and walks us towards the cool damp sand. An errant wave rides high on shore and covers our feet with its bubbling reserve.

"So not going there!" I scream, running back a few good feet to get out of the glacial line of fire. "I'm going to die in there. I'm a human remember? I need to maintain a body temperature, and anything below zero takes me out of the running for this little thing called life."

"Don't idle." Marshall points next to him for me to return.

"I'm not your child. I don't have to listen to you."

The beginnings of a lewd grin twitch on his lips. "Oh, dear Skyla. I would never even venture to think of you as such." His chest expands as he takes me in. "Now, the first subject we'll cover is how to circumvent this little obstacle of heat loss you seem to be ruminating over. Simply raise your body temperature to a comfortable level."

"Oh, just like that?"

"Yes, just like that," he huffs. "You're a Celestra. You're capable of virtually anything. You have yet to tap the depth of your capabilities. Might I remind you, your mother is a Caelestis? If you can believe it, you can do it. The limit to your possibilities lie within your own lack of faith. Now," he looks down at the far end of the beach where the waves detonate over the boulders loud as a car crash. "Run to the point and back, that should get your adrenaline surging."

"Surging? For what? And I don't have any shoes."

A pair of bright orange running shoes encase my feet as soon as the sentence sails from my lips.

"Satisfactory?" He tips his head into me. Marshall is alarmingly handsome. I'm not sure I should be alone with him considering my heart is lying all over Paragon in pieces.

"Satisfactory," I breathe.

"Good," he pats me on the back. "You're going to run, Skyla. Fast—using more strength and endurance than you're used to exerting. When you think you're incapable of moving any quicker, immediately revert the thought and believe you can. You should hit the point and return to this very spot within ten seconds."

"Ten seconds? The point's, like, a mile away. It would take me an hour to run there."

"Three quarters of a mile to be exact. And I'll generously extend to you an extra second. You'll do it in eleven."

"There are rocks," I say, scanning the distal end of the point. "I can't run over those. I'll twist my ankles."

"At the speed in which you'll be traveling you'll hardly skim the surface. It's just this side of flying. Of course, if you choose not to believe and break faith in the middle of this experiment, yes, you'll twist more than your ankles."

Gah! I'll kill myself playing his ludicrous war games.

"OK, so how do I go about—"

"Run!" Marshall doesn't wait for me to finish my question. He roars like a lion, powerful and fierce and, well, let's face it—for all practical purposes I start running to get the hell away from him.

I run. It takes more than an extra large dose of delusions to tell myself I can run faster, and oddly each time I do, my legs propel at bionic speeds. The wind cuts across my face at such an accelerated rate it's impossible to inhale. I hit the point and turn back around. My feet glide over the surface of the rocks, the sand—at one point I'm gliding over water. I bubble with laughter as I knock both Marshall and myself to the ground in an effort to slow down.

"Twelve seconds," he whispers in my ear as we roll towards shore. He pulls me on top of him and steadies me, looks into my face with those twin brandy goblets he surmises the world through. "You were a vision to behold. How does it feel?"

"Exhilarating," I pant. I'd roll myself off, but I don't have an ounce of surplus strength left, and besides, Marshall strums through me with his incredible feel good vibes and initiates a well needed massage over my already vibrating muscles.

"I'm glad you think so. It's time to begin the exercise."

"What?" I slap him in the chest without meaning to. I'm sure Chloe will add this footage as a DVD extra, she'll have it playing from here to eternity in every dimensional plane possible. Just the thought racks me with guilt. My entire body aches for Gage and his kisses.

"The water, Skyla." Marshall wraps his arms around me and rolls us twice until the icy sting of the Pacific baptizes us with its precipitous fire.

A scream gets locked in my throat and I can't breathe from the shock of the arctic jolt.

"Inhale," he commands, carrying me out deeper until the water covers his shoulders. "Demand your body to accommodate you. Rile yourself up with fury, whatever it is that prompts you to initiate that Celestra reserve you seldom tap into."

Chloe and her maniacal video graphic maneuver sail through my mind—the DVD of my own undoing. My blood boils from the pure hatred I feel for her, for the situation she highlighted last night for all to see. Mostly I'm angry at me for putting myself in compromising situations with Logan and Marshall—like I am now.

"We're going under, Skyla." There is not one note of pleasure on his face. It's as if he knows it's a bad idea but he's going to do it anyway.

"No," I protest.

"Take a deep breath," he instructs.

And I do.

Marshall wastes no time plunging us below the water, swimming us out into the deep reserves, nothing but the black underbelly of the ocean waiting to greet us.

I coil my arms and legs so tight around his body, I may have accidentally fused our flesh together in an effort to *believe* I won't slip off.

I'm going to leave and you're going to swim back. Your clothes and keys are waiting on shore.

"No!" Stupidly exhale most of my reserve and latch my hands around his neck in an effort to strangle some sense into him.

Marshall pulls me in, places his lips over mine and expels a lungful of blissful air into me. I take it in, quiver as it fills me. I need Marshall to survive in this watery graveyard. It's reminiscent of the way we met and I hope to God it's not the way we say goodbye as I leave this planet. Not that I wouldn't see Marshall on the other side, but still.

Don't leave me, I beg, greedily taking the breath he offers and then some.

Very well, he says. *Swim us back. It'll be more work for you, but you're more than capable.*

I tighten my fingers around his neck in the event he decides to pull that 'just believe' crap, but he doesn't.

And I swim.

I flex my entire body like a mermaid pulling and dragging Marshall like a corpse attached for the ride.

I can't, I cry, arching my back in pain.

You can and you must, he shouts into me.

I pull his lips over to mine but all I'm capable extracting from him is a rather invasive kiss.

I need air! I drill into him. My lungs burn with fire. Inhaling my way into kingdom come seems like a very real possibility.

No, love. Swim, push yourself past your mortal abilities. Push deeper and harder. Swim as if your life depended upon it—the faction war does. Push through the pain, Skyla.

I try to free myself from his grasp and bolt to the surface, but he holds me down. In a fit of anger I tunnel us through a wall of water, an entire school of fish, and tangle of seaweed until the surface and the sand converge at an acute angle.

I yank us victoriously to the surface and inhale a blast of air that knifes through my lungs like fire.

"You did it," Marshall pants, embracing me. The glorious rhythm he exudes chimes through my body like a soothing composition.

"I did it," I say, trying to catch my breath. I rest my head on Marshall's shoulder and close my eyes.

I did it.

If I could do this then I can do anything—except get Gage back.

I'm afraid no matter how hard I believe that may never come true.

36

The Bitch is Back

The next morning Brielle offers me a ride to school but I refuse, on the grounds I have to work after, and I checked the schedule—so does Gage.

I spent all morning primping and plucking through a pile of sweaters just to find the right one that might entice Gage to offer a slow blink in my direction. It's going to be impossible for him to ignore me because he just so happens to be in all of my classes sans cheer, and, well, he has football practice, so technically we'll be on the field at the same time. I sense an accidental body slam coming on.

But Gage isn't in first. So far, he hasn't shown for second, either.

Chloe shares a laugh with Ellis before class as if she didn't just grind her heel into my heart, as if she didn't witness Gage splatter across the walls from heartbreak.

"You need to watch your back Chloe," I hiss, pulling Ellis toward our seats. "Hear the news?" I ask him as we situate ourselves.

"I *saw* the news. She hooked up the school. It's gone viral. Hey," he leans in confused, "dude, I don't even remember us being together."

"Case in point, you should lay off the street drugs."

The class filters in. I'm met with shocked expressions, judgmental stares. Chloe has everyone believing I was with Dudley among others. And, ironically, it's *Marshall* they think I cheated on.

"Morning." Marshall breezes in. *Skyla.* He glances behind me. *I see you maintain the power to attract celestial baggage. The Pretty One pines for you dead or alive, how magnificent that must make you feel. Do consider repaying his devotion—toss a flower out to sea, light a candle in the window, commit to your specialty and make irrational promises that you have little intention on keeping—a sexual favor, a body—the standard fare.*

I make a face at Marshall's factiousness. Only, I really am going to find Logan a body, and it just happens to be floating around right here on campus.

"Hey," Logan materializes in a watery form, lands in the seat behind me without inciting so much as a breeze. As far as I can tell no one else can see or hear him.

I tip my ear back to listen.

"Rumor has it the falls are beautiful this time of year," there's a slight flirtation in his tone. "I have news about your mother. Can we talk after practice?" he asks.

"I have to work," I whisper.

Ellis spins around and stares into me. Crimson explosions cover the whites of his eyes like a film.

"You need a ride or something?" Clearly I've confused Ellis.

I shake my head and motion for him to spin around again before Marshall turns this into some kind of spectator sport.

"Ms. Messenger," Marshall booms from the front. He leans against his desk and folds his arms, content to be rolling me around like a cat with a ball of yarn. Little does he know I've long since unraveled. "Do feel free to share your work schedule with the entire class. Have any discounts you'd like to offer to drum up business? Perhaps a field trip to the establishment is in order?" He doesn't look amused.

I shake my head at the offer.

"Very well, then," Marshall busies himself passing out papers.

"Gotta go," Logan whispers. "See you in the butterfly room tonight?"

I nod in anticipation. Obviously, Logan has arranged for me to see my mother. He's like the new liaison, or something. If I'm lucky, I'll get Ezrina a new trial by midnight and get her off my back for good. Then all I have to do is off Holden once again, but now since Dr. Oliver is apprised of the situation, I'll be spared that gruesome assignment as well. Everything is going perfect. I twist in my seat to smile at Gage and meet up with an empty chair.

Except that, that's not going perfect at all.

Marshall looms over my chair sorting papers. *I've been invited to dinner later this week.*

"What on earth for?" I hiss.

Do stifle your excitement. Your mother is working on an ad campaign for the humanitarian effort I'm putting out.

"A garage sale does not a humanitarian effort make," I whisper. Although in Marshall's mind, it's probably the equivalent. "What's this really about?" Voices continue to escalate all around us, steady and buzzing like a swarm of bees.

It's a primitive form of revenue retrieval. Not to mention a strategy of warfare. You do realize you could be transported at a moment's notice to the nether regions of the ethereal plane. You have a disc with you I presume.

I shrink in my seat.

Looks like I'll be making a quick pit stop to the homestead before hitting the bowling alley. Second thought, I might just sneak out after class. Who would really notice?

Marshall walks past me slow and determined, his eyes never leaving mine.

Marshall, that's who.

But he should be the last to care.

✼ 🦋 ✼

Rain beats down between classes. It's so chaotic outside, people are running up and down the walkways with backpacks flung over their heads, trying to shield themselves from the assault. No one will care that I'm speeding out towards the parking lot. I can totally be late for third. I'll just say I had to use the bathroom, for like a really long time. What teacher in their right mind is going to contest the fact that I was dealing with a faulty tampon or that I was temporarily crippled with blinding cramps?

I speed home to find the minivan tucked high up on the driveway signaling the fact Mom and Tad are on the premises. I'll have to be covert—in and out like a ghost.

There's a disc hidden under a pile of clean underwear sitting on my dresser, only the mentally disturbed would think to riffle through that.

The roof above the porch christens me with the water runoff, saturates my jacket with its harsh cold sting. Sprinkles greets me in the entry as I make my way inside. He spins in spastic circles with all of his hairless fury. His tiny nails clatter against the tile, creating a ruckus that I suspect will send Mom sailing down the hall at any moment. Figures—he's a tattletale just like Mia. I give a quick scratch behind his ears and slink upstairs.

Voices emanate from down the hall, so I scurry towards my room. God forbid I hear moaning or Mom screaming Tad's name out in contrived ecstasy. Honestly, he could be strangling her, and I wouldn't speed to her rescue on the off chance of catching them in a compromising position.

I pause just shy of my door. It almost sounds as if—freaking shit! The murmurs are coming from my room.

I flatten my back against the wall and try my best to decipher the conversation.

Mom giggles. I can hear her self-abasing tone as though she were blatantly refusing a compliment.

The deep baritone voice of a male vibrates through the walls—then laughter. That's not Tad. I peer around the wall at the risk of getting caught and spy a tall dark figure

expel

reaching his hand out to my mother's cheek. Demetri. Good God they're getting it on right there in my bedroom. He's probably infiltrated her head with some lie about it being a stupid Count ritual, when both he and I know it's nothing but a big F.U. to my father and me.

I see the large silver disc protruding from the edge of the dresser, and I reach up to try and snake it.

"You hear something?" Mom peeks behind his shoulder just as I duck out of her line of vision.

"It's just the rain," he says. "Here, let's close the window."

I reach in blindly a second time and snatch at the disc victoriously, scraping it against the dresser in the process.

I don't wait for my mother to say anything or for Demetri to feed her his steady stream of bullshit. I bolt for the Mustang as if I had just robbed a bank.

I'm halfway to West again before I can even begin to wrap my head around what just happened.

✯ 🦋 ✯

I sulk all day over the fact my mother has slid so easily into infidelity, and that, I, as her adopted offspring, am doing so well in that department myself. Case in point, the love of my life didn't bother to show up at school today because I wrung his heart out with exactly those circumstances.

Just before cheer, I have the misfortune of bearing witness to a near x-rated PDA between Chloe and my newest stepbrother. It sickens me to watch Chloe paw all over Ethan. I haven't had the initiative to confront him yet, but I have a feeling he couldn't care less about what his so-called girlfriend did to ruin my life.

The bell rings, mercifully ending their never-ending lip lock.

"OK, everyone lineup, I have a few new maneuvers I need to get across today." Chloe lets it out in one shrill cry.

I watch her like a predator. I'm sure Chloe would love for me to pummel her into the ground right here at West. Of course that would warrant a suspension, an expulsion, and I would never risk my scholastic standing to take her down. I know for a fact she's working a shift at the bowling alley tonight. I have a few maneuvers I'll be sharing with her later, too.

We run through a couple of routines for the All State competition before Ms. Richards blows the whistle and barks at us to break into groups.

God—she really looks like Ezrina today. Her sun burnt hair blows wild, stands straight up every now and again, giving her that light socket effect that I'm pretty sure no woman goes after. Maybe I could arrange a meeting between Ezrina and Ms. Richards? I mean, Ms. Richards is her super great, great, whatever, and Ezrina did lament the fact she never visits. But somehow I'm certain Ezrina would rather be united with her Heathcliff—Nevermore. I can't believe he went ballistic just because I said his name. Having both Gage and Nevermore pissed at me simultaneously feels like an apocalyptic worthy event.

"Let's go," Chloe is all business, pulling me off to the side so we can do our doubles routine.

"No freaking way," I yank my arm free.

"What's the matter, Messenger? You didn't think you were going to pull that shit on him *forever* did you? You think Gage wants someone like you? Someone who's never met a penis she didn't like?"

I strike her across the face so fast I need the sting on my palm to assure me it happened.

"Nice." She spits while rubbing her cheek. "My comfort comes from the fact he's already looking to me for consolation. Called me three times since Saturday. How about you, Skyla?" Her coal black hair enwreathes her face,

expel

makes her lips pop like cherry blossoms. "Oh, that's right. He mentioned he was never going to speak with you again."

I walk off the field—ignore Ms. Richards' reprimand to get my rear back there and hit the shower.

Getting back at Chloe is going to have to involve far more than just a beating. I might have to consult my favorite Sector to delineate the perfect path of wickedness to embark upon.

But even more than I feel the need to inflict eternal punishment on Chloe—I crave Gage.

I need Gage and our forever back, or not even Chloe's demise could bring me pleasure.

There is no pleasure and no sun, no breath worth taking without him.

37

The Boss of You

The cool crisp breeze of afternoon is replaced with air thick as tar. Long black sheets of torrential promise stretch out overhead, ready to pronounce their fury.

After school, I race over to the bowling alley, still hopped up on adrenaline after Chloe's remark. The thought of her speaking with Gage shreds my heart to ribbons. It elicits a groan wrenched from the deepest part of me just thinking about him filling her ear with his velvet voice—if it's true at all. I've learned my lesson. Trust Chloe and my entire world blows apart.

In the bowling alley I find Brielle on her phone with her feet up on the table, head back, and laughing.

I make my way into the kitchen on the lookout for Gage. My heart pumps like a horse at the gate, bucking and jumping with the anticipation of seeing him, but he's not here. Instead, an older woman, a part of Logan's regular staff approaches me.

"My check didn't clear," she grunts, her face splotched unnaturally as if she had given herself a raspberry facial. "You need to talk to your boyfriend because if this goes on another week, he's going to lose the entire crew." Her tiny eyes glisten with anger.

"I'll get right on it," I say, knowing full well I'm impotent to provide.

I find Holden in the office hunched over like a rock, pilfering the floor safe.

"What the hell are you doing?" Honest to God, everything Holden touches turns to shit. He's helping himself to Logan's stash like he's a bona fide premium access user.

expel

He hops up without securing the lid and stuffs a wad of bills in the pouch of his sweatshirt, bypasses me without so much as a hello.

I chase him out to the dining area and pull him back by the sleeve.

"I'm talking to you," I say, spinning him on his heels.

"Don't feel bad." Chloe strides over—her face alive with the thrill of watching my life spiral out of control. "She accosted me during 6th."

"What's your problem?" He shakes himself loose.

I can tell Holden is trying his best not to act like a dick since the question itself came out laced with a false sense of delicacy.

"*You*," I say, digging into his pocket and waving the cash in front of his face. "I'm taking over."

"OK." He shrugs, taking half the bills away from me and shoving them deep inside his jeans. "Have at it. See if I care."

Brielle walks over wide-eyed with her mouth agape.

"I heard the checks aren't clearing. How much are you overdrawn?" I ask.

"He's negative eighteen thousand," Brielle pipes up. "Accounting's sort of my thing. Plus, I don't mind snooping into people's finances when the opportunity arises." She shrugs into her admission. "And what the hell is wrong with you?" She barks into Logan. "It's like you're a totally different person." There's the distinct look of grief on her face.

"People change." Holden blinks a smile. Creepy the way he genuinely makes Logan, who has the face of a god, look like a total ass. Maybe this was what I was anticipating, predicting in that hallucinatory vision a few months back after gobbling down Michelle's demonic rose? "So," Holden writhes into me, "You and Gage are really over, huh?"

I don't reward his jackass behavior with an answer. Besides there's no way I'm going to admit to the fact Gage and I aren't together. I'd sooner lick Chloe's bare feet after she ran ten laps in the men's restroom than entertain that theory out loud.

"I was thinking you and me should give things another shot." He pinches my left boob.

Reflexively, I smack him in the nose with my purse. I'd consider doing some serious reproductive harm, but since he's not technically ever going to reproduce with that body, I find it a pointless endeavor.

"Touch me again and I'll lop off your balls," my chest heaves into the words.

"She will," Chloe confirms. "She's no stranger to detaching body parts."

"I am feeling stabby," I poke him in the chest, "and bitchy, and all around pissed off, so stay the hell away from that floor safe, and keep your lobster claws to yourself." Holden is proof positive that true beauty comes from within.

"That's my safe." His amber eyes glint with something familiar from a faraway dream.

"Not anymore. You're fired." I turn on my heels to face Chloe. "You, too!"

"Me?" She crooks a hand into her chest.

"Don't even ask what you did." I shake my head. "You are a liar, everything about you is a lie. It drives you insane that you can't have the only thing in this world you want. Where's Gage, Chloe? Is he by your side?"

"As long as he's not by yours, it's just as good." Her dark eyes linger over me like gunpowder.

Chloe revels in my misery, gains strength from my pain. She watched me go under like a ship taking in water. She was the storm pushing me down. She wanted to hold Gage afterwards, tell him it would all be OK as she cradled him in her poisonous embrace. Little did she know she took him down too—drowned him first.

"I don't need this job." Her lids lower as if she were trying to seduce me. "I've already got another one lined up."

expel

"I hope you're scraping gum off the street with your teeth." Of course later I'll think of something far more offensive and to the point.

"I'm in charge of cataloging crap from detective Edinger's estate. Isn't that where you'll be doing your community service?" Chloe twitches a smile. "Say hello to your new boss, Skyla." She bites the air before heading out the door.

Crap.

Just, crap.

🦋

It's a living miracle I arrive alive at Landon manor. The storm rages overhead, shags its heavy precipitation out with aggressive uneven bursts.

"Dinner is in the microwave," Mom says from the couch.

Really I just want some OJ and a nice hot shower, a chat with Logan in the butterfly room regarding bank passwords and the possibility of changing the combination to his floor safe. I plan on shutting Holden out financially, but I have no clue how I'm going to rectify his eighteen thousand dollar debt by week's end. And Gage? How long do I let him simmer down before I go bounty hunter and kidnap him for the sake of our relationship?

I'll cyber stalk him tonight—text him nonstop until six in the morning so he can see how freaking insane I am without him. He'll need a restraining order to keep me away and even then I won't listen.

I pause a moment in the cool of the refrigerator. I can't go on like this without Gage. I don't even care to appropriately devise my revenge against Chloe. I just want him back so I can breathe again. For a moment I consider dropping to my knees in prayer, doing a faceplant in the not so appetizing strange yellow pie staring back at me. And, oddly, it was baked in the tin we sometimes use as a dog dish.

"Stop fanning yourself with the fridge," Tad snarls.

I head over to the microwave and pull out the plate Mom set aside for me.

"What is this?" I don't mean to sound offensive, but really I have no clue how to categorize the mountainous glob set before me.

Drake walks by and retches for effect.

"It's an asparagus and broccoli quiche with whole wheat crust—no salt. Made it myself," Mom beams. She gives a satisfied smile into her knitting, assuring me she's content serving up the questionable nutritional offering. For Mom, cooking is more of a flaw than an attribute.

"It's pretty cold up in my room. Was my window opened today?" I ask, totally indifferent to the fact I haven't been upstairs yet.

"Oh," her eyes widen as if she were about to get caught with her hand in Demetri's cookie jar. Just the idea of her touching his anything sets me on fire. "I had to go in and, um, grab some laundry. I might have fiddled with it. Sorry about that."

Knew it!

What if she did the deed with him right there on my bed? I'm going to have to burn everything. Although I seriously doubt Lizbeth Landon did the nasty in her daughter's bedroom while her husband was floating around on the premises.

"Were you home all day?" I ask Tad for no good reason. He's already convinced I've fried my brain, so a whole slew of random questions shouldn't surprise him one bit.

"Nope." He twists his lips while glossing over the paperwork fanned out before him. "Had a meeting in town." He looks towards my mother. "Guess what, Lizbeth? We no

expel

longer need to call a cab whenever that faulty minivan acts up," he shouts. "Tomorrow afternoon a brand new company car is rolling off the ferry for yours truly."

"You're kidding!" She stops spiking the air with her needles and jumps to her feet.

"I wanted to surprise you, but Skyla, here, dragged it out of me."

I abstain from correcting him.

"Best part?" He gives a greasy smile. "It's F-R-E-E."

"That's my favorite word!" Mom rushes to his side.

"Mine, too," he says, as they engage in an awkward open-mouth kiss.

Seriously? Eww.

"Guess what else?" He continues. "Althorpe is hosting its annual company dinner right here on the island. All the big wigs and their families will be joining us in a couple weeks."

"That's great!" Mom shrieks as if we had just won the lottery. "And family is invited? Even better!"

"I'm bringing Brielle," Drake pipes up.

"I'm bringing Chloe," Ethan says, stumbling over to the fridge.

"Of course, you can bring Gage, Skyla." Mom nods as though it were a given.

I give a weak smile and turn around.

I'm not bringing Gage because he hates me, and I'm pretty sure Ethan's not bringing Chloe because I would have killed her by then.

38

Dance of the Butterfly

I shove Ethan around in the hall before trapping him in his bedroom, knocking him back on the bed like a bowling pin.

"What the hell was that video expose` on my love life about the other night?"

"I had no clue she was going to do that. She's a freaking nutcase." He leans over and combs his hair back in the mirror. "Besides, it pissed me off. Makes me want to go after her even more."

"It does?" I pause, stunned. "Like, as in go after and mate with her, or go after and get rid of her?" I'm betting it's the former. Placing my hope in a Landon family male would be both foolish and dangerous.

"Getting rid of her."

"Well, good." I'm pretty sure that the big dismissal will take place after he's physically through with her. He seems intent on rocking her world—his bed—same difference.

"You should trust me," he deadpans, because he knows I can't. Honestly, it's all starting to sound a little canned, like he's telling me whatever it is he thinks I want to hear. I don't like where this is going.

"I do," I say without conviction. Why do I feel like I'm about to get sucked into a wood chipper? "How are you going to get rid of her?"

"I'm going to exterminate." His expression darkens.

I don't know that I want Chloe *dead*. After experiencing the non-finality of it all with Holden, Logan, and Chloe herself, I'm not sure another celestial piranha is what I'm after. Not that Logan is a piranha. He's a lion—a hot lion, albeit without any fur, or skin or bones at the moment.

expel

"So what's the plan of action?" I'm tired of Ethan skirting the issue. If he's mapped out his strategy, I want in on the details. Second thought, if the end result is manslaughter, I'd hate to go away for guilt by association. People go away all the time for stupid stuff like that. "Never mind, I don't want to know. Just make sure death is not involved." That's too easy for Chloe. She needs a good life sentence of misery—one without Gage preferably. That alone is a cruel and horrific punishment much harsher than a quick trip to the transport. That alone might kill her. Come to think of it, a life without Gage would kill me, too.

🦋 🦋 🦋

I head upstairs and find Mia snooping around my drawers.

"Get out!" I shout. I don't care if she is trying to piece together the perfect ensemble to steal Melissa's boyfriend, I'm cranky and tired, and I just want Gage to crawl in through the butterfly room and make everything all right. He used to protect me from the Counts in my life, and now he's probably hoping they'll turn me into a salt-free quiche and eat me for dinner. "How did it all go so wrong?" I didn't mean to say it out loud.

I crash on the bed and bury my head in the pillow.

"Hey, what's the matter?" Mia comes over and gives one long scratch down the center of my back. Her fingernails sizzle across my flesh, and it actually feels nice.

"Gage hates me," I muffle into the foamy expanse.

"Gage?" She balks as though it were impossible.

I twist around and pull my pillow into my chest, hug it as though it were a body.

"Did you guys breakup?" Mia's face lights up at the prospect of fresh gossip.

"I guess we did, unofficially. I wouldn't know, he won't speak to me." I don't know why I'm sharing this with Mia of all people.

"What happened?"

"He caught me kissing Logan. It was an accident. I never meant to do it." My heart sags because outside of those kisses I still have very real feelings for Logan. "Do yourself a favor and fall in love with just one boy."

"I know, right?" She looks up at me with childlike innocence, reminds me a lot of the Skyla I used to be—the one Logan made to fall in love with him by simply showing up in her dreams. "Plus, it means you're a total slut if you run around kissing other boys, just saying."

"Logan, kissed *me*. I am not a slut." What my heart feels and what my body does are two different things. I tried giving everything to Gage, wanted to, but in the end I just wasn't ready. But now I'd run to him naked in the middle of this viral downpour if he wanted me to, if he let me.

"And that teacher?" She narrows in on me suspiciously.

"He means nothing." That's not entirely true. I do feel some sort of connection to Marshall, but it's spiritual in nature—at least I'm pretty sure. Nevertheless, no more vision hunting through his upper orifice. I'm done with that game.

"If I could only have Gage back," I whisper, lost in a fog of despair.

"That's how I feel, Skyla. Gabriel was mine, and Melissa stole him."

"Are they a couple?" I'm horrified by this. They're sisters. Talk about a relationship killer. Then again Logan and Gage still sort of have one, or at least they did until Holden showed up.

"He says he's still into me, but Melissa keeps inviting him to the movies, the library, and he keeps going."

"Sounds like an ass. You can do better."

expel

"I don't want to do better. I want him back."

I relax against the wall and consider this. Why shouldn't Mia fight for her man? Why should us Messenger girls sit back and let the boys we love drift into the arms of other girls?

"Then you need to fight for him," I start. "Be the first one to talk to him at school, when you see Melissa cornering him, break up the party. All's fair in love and war, right? Ask him to the mall, the beach, the falls." An image of me swimming in my bra and panties with Logan last summer zips through my mind. "Well, maybe not the falls. Oh, I know! Ask him to the Althorpe dinner. Mom says we can bring dates, and he could be yours." I shrug into my genius.

"Thank you!" She leans in and hugs me before running into my closet.

"Get out," I say.

"Oh, I am. I'm leaving through the butterfly room."

"What?"

"Gabriel's picking me up. We're going for ice cream. And, before you freak out—his sister is driving." She climbs into the secret compartment, and I follow her up.

"Mia!" I scold as she crawls into the attic and disappears. She doesn't answer. She's already halfway to stealing her boyfriend back just like I suggested.

It seems I'm only capable of somewhat competent ideas.

🦋 🦋 🦋

I curl up on the black sparkling floor of the butterfly room and wait for Logan to come.

An easy slumber wraps its arms around me and ushers me into a restful languor. Dreams of Gage and Chloe walking along the beach hand in hand devour me. They cut through me with anguish. I call out his name, but he doesn't answer. He whispers to Chloe instead, and they share a secret smile.

I startle awake as a pair of warm arms wrap themselves around me, and I take in a sharp breath.

"It's just me." Logan helps me sit up. I'm still reeling from the spectacle of imagining Gage and Chloe together as a couple. "How was your day?" He gives a tired smile.

"I fired you," I scratch at his stomach. "Chloe, too." I raise my brows rather proud of that one. "You wouldn't happen to have eighteen thousand dollars lying around would you?"

"Is that what he took?" Logan's jaw redefines pissed.

"That I know of," I add. "Will your uncle front the money?"

Logan shakes his head. "Don't ask Barron. The mortuary is hurting right now. I know for a fact he just pulled money out of the house to cover expenses. The last thing I want is for anyone to go bankrupt trying to satiate Holden's appetite for financial destruction." He exhales a lungful of air. "I guess I'll lose the bowling alley." He says it despondent as if there were no other way.

"I'll try to help." I squeeze his hand. "Don't give up hope, promise?"

"I promise." He leans in, touches his forehead to mine. "What's going on with Gage?"

"If it makes you feel better, I'm dead to him, too."

"It doesn't make me feel better." Logan's spirit is feather soft, rich with an otherworldly understanding. As if in crossing over to death, he gained a plethora of knowledge and wisdom. Logan always knew too much to begin with and now he was in an intellectual realm all his own. "I want you and Gage to be happy. I know it sounds strange," he struggles to get the words out, "but I hope there's a time for us. I think there will be."

"Does it go along with what you know?" I don't mean for it to come out as sharp as it does. Sometimes, I just wish

I could wring Logan's mind out like a dishrag over my mouth—absorb all of his insights into our future, to the future that I share with Gage, and see it from his bird's eye perspective.

"It does," dejection flexes through him. "But I care about Gage, too. I don't want him upset, or heartbroken."

My insides twist at the confirmation that I broke Gage's heart.

"Yes, he's hurting, Skyla, but he's healing, too. Just give him the time he needs."

"What if he needs forever?" How's that for irony?

"He won't," Logan looks down upon his admission. "I'm sorry for the pain you're both going through, but, in truth, I can't get past the idea that you belong with anyone else." His eyes graze over me with open heartbreak. "With everything in me, Skyla, I swear it was you and me who were meant to be together. I think of Gage, and I want to tear the planet to pieces because I pushed you into him." He drops his head back, despondent. "I swear on everything that is holy, it was supposed to be you and me." His voice ends on a threadbare whisper. Death has reduced him to less than human, and I've reduced Logan to ashes, slashed him to pieces with my incessant pining for Gage.

What do I say? How do I respond? Of course, I love Gage, but a very real part of me understands exactly what Logan just said as though the testimony had sailed from my own lips.

"Let's get you back into your body," I whisper, artfully choosing my words.

He gives a wry smile. "I talked to my uncle. He's going to research the most efficient way to off Holden and get me back without any damaging effects."

"I'll make sure Marshall gets you to where you're supposed to be."

"Not at the expense of your body, Skyla."

"No, nothing like that, I swear." I tug at his hand. "I miss you, Logan Oliver." I bring up his hand and plant a gentle kiss on his finger.

He gives a smile born of sadness. "I've been missing you for months, Skyla Laurel Messenger," Logan wraps an arm around my shoulder. "I wish it were summer and we had just met. I'd do everything different."

"You mean, Gage," I sigh.

"I don't think I could have stopped what the future holds, but, for sure, it didn't have to play out this way to get there. Yes, I mean Gage, I mean us—Chloe."

"How do you think Chloe was able to capture all of those precise moments? You know, me and you—me and Marshall."

"And Ellis," he leans in.

"That was the most innocent of all. He was peeing on my hand."

Logan squints and shakes his head as if he wants me to spare the details.

"Chloe got those pictures the same way I was able to create that film we used to frame her," he says. "Supervising spirit."

"Figures. Speaking of spirits, did you find Giselle? Did you tell her I desperately need to speak with my mother?"

"I did." Logan tips his head down. "And Giselle relayed the message."

"That's great!" I can't wait to get Ezrina off my back. "What did my mother say?"

"She said she doesn't plan on seeing you again until after the faction war. She said, no, Skyla."

39

The Good Girlfriend

The week sweeps by in a torrent.

No sun, no warmth, no Gage.

Dr. Oliver pulled him out of school temporarily so he could proceed with home study, says his cough came back and that's the best way to keep him out of the hospital for now. I have a feeling I'm more than slightly responsible for his convalescing condition, for his newfound desire to pursue scholastic knowledge from the confines of his bedroom.

I've been sending a steady stream of texts, a deluge of emails to Gage, but nothing came of it. He doesn't take my calls, doesn't respond to a single mode of communication. I'm not sure how much longer I can handle being cut out of his life like this.

I think tomorrow after my community torment at Demetri's, I'll swing by and see if I can at least get him to prove he's still filling his lungs with air, that he's still on Paragon proper.

"So you wanna go shopping and get some new gear for that dance next week?" Brielle asks, lounging on my bed. Her belly rises into the air like an anthill.

"The Althorpe dinner?" I stop combing my hair midflight.

"Yeah, your mom says it's formal. Like prom but with old people."

"Charming. I think I'll pass on the spending spree. I'm trying to scrape up everything I can to help Logan." I've managed to amass a whopping fifty-two dollars and twelve cents.

I guess it didn't suck quite enough that he was dead—he gets to watch the business his father built kick the bucket, too.

"So, you talk to Gage?" She makes the transition with the utmost care.

"No, did you?" The thought of him using Brielle as a liaison has me hopping over to the bed with excitement.

"He called and asked me to cover his shifts."

He speaks!

"Did he sound OK? Was he coughing? Did he ask about me?"

"Yes, no, and, unfortunately, no."

"Oh." I mean I'm thrilled that he's not coughing up loose change, but I'm devastated by how easy it is for him to live life without me. Having Gage out of my world is like being thrust into permanent darkness. I'm left groping around the landscape, hoping to find the smile that once lit my universe. "I can't stand that he hates me," I lament.

"He doesn't hate you," she scoffs. "Gage Oliver is incapable of such mortal feats. He's just pissed—more like devastated. You made him feel like less than nothing. He was totally into you if you hadn't noticed." It doesn't come out mean the way she says it, just a simple observation. All of it true.

"Brielle," I lean back against the wall in defeat, "what makes a good girlfriend?"

"A good girlfriend?" She contemplates this for a moment by twirling a copper lock around her finger. "Someone who bakes cookies, gives back rubs, laughs at all their stupid jokes—makes them feel like the smartest person in the world."

I had never done any of those things. I had never baked Gage cookies, and he baked me a cake for my birthday. He gave me countless shoulder massages, and I never once returned the favor. Of course, Gage never told a stupid joke, and I would never placate his genius because he

expel

just happens to be the smartest person I know on the planet. But I would laugh at the simplest thing that flew from his lips if I were ever presented with the opportunity again.

It would be pure joy.

🦋 🦋 🦋

Friday evening Marshall arrives twenty minutes early for a dinner party Mom threw together at the last minute. She had invited him so they could finish the ad for his island-wide garbage sale that spans time and distance, and, I'm pretty sure, dimensions.

I'm not certain what's driving Marshall to encourage the good people of Paragon to declutter their closets, but it's safe to say, it has supernatural consequences that might reach as far as my baby making station.

"What is that glorious aroma?" He bows into Mom with a partial hug. He's either bending the truth and reflecting on the heavenly scent of those burgers grilled atop Mount Headless during ski week, or he outright has an olfactory defect. The house happens to smell like hot crap on a sunny day.

"You like?" Mom gives a sultry wink before escorting him back to the family room. Marshall wraps an arm around my waist, and I'm quick to push away his efforts. "I'm pairing pan-fried calves liver with a nice wheatgrass salad. I'm on this new health kick to get me into ultimate prime procreating condition. You did know that Tad and I are trying, right? I'm sorry if this is too much information." She leans in feigning embarrassment.

My mother doesn't mind sharing with the free world the sorry state of her uterus. I wouldn't be surprised one bit if I were driving downtown one day and came across a picture of her and Tad's dehydrated baby making parts splayed out on a billboard like some disturbing PSA.

"No, I wasn't aware. But I wish you the best of luck in your donation to humanity." He winks playfully. "I look forward to blessing the world with my own seed one day."

Seed? Must we go there?

"Oh, you should have lots of children," she's quick with the reply. "With a face like that I'm sure women are knocking down the door trying to help you fill an entire school bus."

"One would think," he muses over at me.

"Anyway, I'm mostly vegetarian now," Mom announces. There's a prideful undertone that suggests she's embracing the anti-conformist rebellion sponsored by her journey to motherhood. Frankly, I'd prefer she wolf down a burger and fries. Normally, my mother and Tad would take turns scoffing at vegetarians. They thought the vegetable offensive was nothing more than a well-constructed ploy by foreign adversaries to destroy the cattle industry. This bovine conspiracy was further justified by Tad as yet another measure in taking down the financial structure of this great country, which evidently relies solely on sticking a cow's ass in a grinder. "But there's so much great protein in calf's liver, I thought why not?" She turns her palms out. "But I'm strictly vegetarian otherwise. I steer clear of dead animal byproducts," she goes on to defend the mutiny of perhaps the last cohesion that held her and Tad together. "The liver is amazingly rich in iron, and it's cheaper than dirt."

"If only it were dirt," I whisper. I'd rather eat dirt. Hell, I'd take it straight from the cemetery—fresh off a casket.

"So, let's see," she opens her laptop and pounds on the keyboard. "What would you like the ad to say?"

I lean in. "How about, look at all the crappy hobbies I wasn't good at?" I offer, taking a seat at the island.

"Skyla," Mom sings my name in a tone that lets me know I'm pushing it.

Marshall postures. "I'm thinking more—bring us your weary, your downtrodden, your huddled masses of clutter," he suggests.

"Hey, that's snazzy." Mom types away unwavering.

"That's plagiarism." I'm quick to discredit Marshall's undying genius. It's written on the Statue of Liberty, everybody knows that.

It's not plagiarism if I were the one to suggest it to the author in the first place, he gives a smirk.

Mom hops up from the barstool. "Excuse me while I toss the dinner rolls in the oven. They're *buckwheat*," she whispers into him as if buckwheat were code for sinfully delicious. I'm afraid the entire dinner is simply going to be sinful. If digesting infant mammal organs and a salad made of weeds is the way to fuel your body to enhance reproduction, I'm pretty sure I'm out of the running for children.

Why so forlorn? Is Jock Strap still evading your efforts at communication?

"Please don't refer to Gage as Jock Strap," I whisper. "I need an emergency appointment with my mother. Can you arrange this?"

Only if I go with you.

"Done."

Then it's a date. He gives a wicked smile.

Unfortunately, I can't swear off Marshall's efforts just yet, and this type of behavior is precisely why Gage will be eating vital organs and buckwheat with another girl someday in an effort to procreate. But with Ezrina eyeing my skin like her new favorite jacket, there's not a whole hell of a lot I can do about it.

It's a date.

40

Dinner with the Enemy

Chloe.

 She sits at the table next to Ethan as though she were the newest Landon family member. If Ethan's twisted form of revenge is chaining Chloe to himself for the rest of his natural days, I'm afraid the punishment will be his to bear. No human should put up with what Chloe has to offer. She'd release a rattlesnake into a newborn's crib if she thought it would bring Gage back to her. Ethan has it all backwards. Dating Chloe is not a part of his revenge—it's a part of *hers*.
 "So, we need to start pulling crap together for the kid," Darla, Brielle's mother, artfully leads us into sparkling dinner conversation.
 "Yes, a baby shower is definitely in order," Mom lays a platter of bovine toxin filters, evenly shriveled and singed before us.
 The doorbell rings, and Mom frees herself from a conversation comprised mostly of caskets in lieu of bassinets and human remains as rattles and teethers. Brielle has a warped sense of style when it comes to the miniature Count brewing in her belly.
 "So," Brielle starts, "I saw this thing on TV where you set up this blowup kiddie pool and you have the baby right there in your living room. How cool is that?" Her emerald eyes blink into me with amazement.
 "Totally." My stomach trembles with nervous laughter.
 "Not in my living room," Tad says it low, in an effort to keep off my mother's radar. God only knows this sounds like an idea my mother would glom onto, heck she'd jump into the kiddie pool herself in hopes of squeezing one out herself.

"Why not?" Marshall provokes. "It would be a gift to witness the miracle of life blooming in the heart of your home. Think of all the memories you've yet to impress."

I can't even imagine the thought of my mother retching in pain in some ridiculously small swimming pool while trying to expel Tad's evil spawn from her body.

"The screaming, the bodily fluids sloshing onto the carpet," Tad counters, "Why don't we initiate these memories at your place? That way I can feel all warm and fuzzy each time I drive by."

Marshall's face drains of color. "Come to think of it, the bleeding and screaming might be better fit elsewhere."

There will be bleeding and screaming at the Landon home one day, Skyla. Do you believe this? He gives a devious smile.

I reach down and touch his hand. *Does it involve Tad?*

Deliciously so. He nods into Tad and gives the impression he were acquiescing to his wisdom.

Hmm, I don't know if I like the word delicious mixing with the idea of Tad bleeding and screaming. Sounds like a kitchen accident.

"I think a home birth sounds fantastic," Chloe pipes up. There's a strange gleam in her eye as if her fantasy of giving birth in a blow up pool somehow involves Gage. "You could get shoulder rubs, and foot rubs, and be catered to by the one you love right there in your living room."

For sure it involves Gage. I could practically see the cartoon bubble over her head with my raven-haired boyfriend feeding her grapes, well, my sort of boyfriend.

I think Chloe is sadly mistaken regarding what real labor and delivery is like. Back in L.A. they made us watch the Red Asphalt version of childbirth, and it may as well have been called This Red Bloody Ass is Your Boyfriend's Fault.

It narrowed in on the true consequences of unprotected sex by way of demonstrating how mindboggling elastic the female anatomy is. And judging by the drawn out high-pitched wails, this experience was neither brief nor painless. I'm pretty sure grapes and massages were the last two things on that woman's mind.

"Look who's here?" Mom drags Demetri in by the hand.

"I was just dropping a key off for Skyla. I'm afraid I have an appointment tomorrow, and I won't be able to let her in. I've left instruction on the entry table. My secretary will be arriving around noon." He tweaks Chloe on the top of the head when he says it.

Lovely.

"Won't you join us?" Mom steers him over to her spot at the table next to Tad and scoots in another seat from the kitchen quicker than he can protest.

"I want to thank you for making my wife's dreams come true," Tad gives a curt nod. "Weddings don't come cheap you know."

Ironic. I thought everything came cheap with Tad. It was like the unexpected bonus my mother got on her wedding day—an entire lifetime of frugal living courtesy of the cheapasaurus himself.

"Not a problem." Demetri blinks a smile. "I want nothing more than to make all of your wife's dreams come true."

I bet that includes in the bedroom. I'm guessing if Tad thought he could save a buck on the wedding night by letting Mom bunk with Demetri, he'd be tolerant of the situation.

Demetri's face blooms with a grin as if he heard.

I swear that cheesy smile never leaves his face. Someone should clue him in on the fact that humans scowl once in a while—like I'm doing now.

"I'll be hosting an inter-island bargain and barter in the next few weeks," Marshall glares into Demetri. "I don't suppose you have any long abandoned artifacts floating around you might want to be rid of. You know, the odd trunk, vase—mirror," Marshall pronounces vase, *voz* and I crimp a smile at the old school drama of it all.

"I'll pilfer through the estate. I'm sure I can purge a collectable or two."

I place my fingers over Marshall's knee until he brings his hand over mine.

It's that haunted mirror you're talking about, isn't it? I ask.

Nothing irritates him more—with the exception of losing your mother of course.

I take in a sharp breath at the revelation. If Demetri is anything like Chloe, he might just fill Tad's stomach with a blade on his wedding day and save a dollar's worth of that marzipan cake.

"Are you OK?" Mom mouths over to me.

"Oh, I was just thinking the food might get cold," I whisper.

By the way, I squeeze his hand under the table. *I need about eighteen grand for the bowling alley—better make it an even twenty.*

Looks like the bargain and barter begins tonight. I'm sure there are far more interesting things you're willing to part with. We'll speak.

Tad rises and doles himself out a liberal helping, first, per his usual custom.

I'm shocked to see Chloe indulging herself with the biggest liver of the bunch and a big heap of shrubbery on the side. It looks downright offensive. The golf greens alone are enough to make me retch. All I can think of is the times I've seen Sprinkles vomit up the grass out front after realizing what the heck he just ingested.

"You know, Lizbeth," Tad grinds the food in his mouth, "I'm going to go out on a limb here—I don't think we should be serving lawn clippings as a side dish."

I hate when I agree with Tad.

"Is it that bad?" Mom has mia culpa written all over her face.

"Oh, I don't think so," Brielle douses it with ranch dressing and wolfs it down before her taste buds can properly discern the offense.

"This is grass?" Drake bounces in his seat.

"I'd rather smoke it." Ethan pushes back his plate.

"A newborn's liver always tastes fantastic," Chloe gleams her mischievous smile as she takes another bite. It's full of toxins, pesticides, poisons and yet, somehow, Chloe is enamored with its coagulated goodness.

"God!" Darla takes her plate and Brielle's, and dumps them back into the serving platter. "I don't know what the hell you eat in L.A., but here on the island we tend to stray from cannibalistic tendencies. Ya'll get your stuff," she instructs half of the table. "I've got bacon next door." She rises with Brielle, Drake, and Ethan in tow.

"Oh, no! I promise it's not human," Mom bats her hands in the air in an effort to wrangle them back into their seats. "It's newborn *calf*."

"Oh, Hon, we don't do baby legs neither," Darla knocks back the rest of her wine before moving along. "But to each his own, right? What doesn't kill you, makes you stronger, hey?"

"Right," Mom bites down on her lip as her face crumbles.

Chloe finishes up the last few bites. "Delicious," she says, leaning into Mom and Tad.

Figures. This meal was equipped with two of Chloe's favorite things, blood and poison.

"We'll get together soon to discuss details for that baby shower," Darla points over at Mom. "The little midget's gonna have the best of everything." She waves before taking off with half the party.

expel

I'd join them, but I'd be remiss if Marshall and Demetri were to provide a celestial showdown using Tad as a weapon, and I wasn't around to cheer.

"I have to make this up to everyone," Mom shakes her head. "I'm inviting all of you to the Althorpe company dinner next week. It's formal, but I promise, the culinary expertise of the chefs will make it well worth the trouble."

"I wouldn't miss it for the world." Demetri zeros in on her like some psychotic serial killer. Clearly he is coveting his neighbor's wife. Isn't there some cosmic code that calls for a stoning during such offenses?

The thought of Demetri being taken out by a comet inspires a mild sense of jubilation in me.

Tad leans in and examines him, waves his hand over Demetri's face in an effort to break the spell.

"Thank you for the invitation, Lizbeth," Marshall intercedes. "I'd be more than honored to be in the company of such wonderful people as yourselves."

"You never know," Mom tilts a smile at him, "your Mrs. Right might be lurking in the crowd that night."

Marshall gives a polite nod at the thought as he caresses my hand beneath the table. *I'm banking on it.*

41

Missing you

Long after midnight, the tiny prattle of raindrops sizzle along my window as I lie in bed tossing and turning. I pour over every memory that Gage and I ever shared like some sort of morbid eulogy to our relationship, always falling into the glaring hole of my deception. It's destitute to think there may never be another moment to add to the collection. That I had unwittingly already experienced the very last kiss he would ever give me.

I send him a quick text.

I miss you ~S

I wait an hour for a response but nothing.

There's a rattle in my closet, and I spike up in bed. It's him!

I run my fingers through my hair and sit up in anticipation as a dark shadow emerges tall and gangly, smelling profusely of something banned by the government. Its just Ellis.

"I gotta do a quick run, wanna come?" He sits at the edge of my bed and bounces three times straight to pronounce his urgency.

"Yeah. Like you don't need me," I say, taking off my covers and stepping into my shoes, albeit from two different pairs. I'd change, but I've found that PJs are perfectly acceptable attire for lurking in the bushes. "What's the code?" Ever since a demonic Fem took over my likeness, I thought we should have a password to affirm my identity.

"I'm supposed to ask you," he says.

"Oh, right. How about we say it together, and that way I know it's you?"

He holds out his fingers and counts to three.

expel

"Love honeys," we say in unison. Our voices meld in rhythm. It sounds pretty, like an old-fashioned song.

I take Ellis up by the hand and away we go.

※ ※ ※

It's cool out this night—homecoming of years past. A thicket of fog lies over the island, sealing us in its comfortable haze. Headlights trail down the road, lighting up the world for a moment with their quiet illumination before the void fills in with shadows again.

"I'll be quick," Ellis darts up the driveway high fiving a crowd of guys in the stoner circle out front.

I must have landed us later than usual. I'm probably in the forest right now hunting Chloe down with the spirit sword. A repressed smile emerges at the thought. Chloe and her masterful destruction of my relationship—she has no idea what I have planned for her—neither do I, but those discretionary details don't seem relevant at the moment.

A husky voice calls out goodnight as it fast approaches.

It's Gage!

I take in his sturdy frame, recognize that signature hop to his step that suggests he had a good time. God—I would give anything to love him again.

"Excuse me!" I call out, dashing out of the bushes in my pajamas and mismatched shoes. OK, so, if I would have thought this through I could be looking really hot right now and not like some psychotic pajama-wearing lunatic who's playing fast and loose with time in an effort to stalk my boyfriend. At least it's not the pink PJs with images of kittens in teacups wallpapered all over. I look down and, to my surprise, I'm mocked by both kittens and teacups alike. Perfect.

"I was just thinking about you." There is not one note of anger, or sarcasm in his tone as his gaze settles. Those hungry eyes burn for me, and it takes everything in me not to bow in his presence. I've already impressed myself on him in the past. "You wanna hang out?" He ends the question with a rise of curiosity as he inspects my strange attire.

"I spilt something, and this was all I had," I fan out my arms. "Yes, I would very much love to hang out." I stop just shy of attacking him with a massive hug—accosting him with my lips.

"You want to drive down to Devil's Peak?"

"No," I practically shout it at him. No driving. "I'm not in the mood for a drive." I shrug.

"OK. How about a movie? No one's awake at my house," he leans in and his dimples explode with glory.

"That sounds perfect."

I privately laude Ellis's genius all the way over to the Oliver's living room as Gage places in a DVD. I hold my breath as the movie gets started in the event Chloe's revenge spans time and space.

The movie cues up, the opening scene is peppered with a slow trickling list of credits, and I exhale my anxiety. Gage sinks into the couch beside me and lays his arm just over my shoulders. I scoot in close to his thigh, nuzzle against his neck and take in his sweet familiar scent.

"Is everything OK?" His mild sense of worry proliferates into an all out look of concern.

Tears start to build, and I fight them off with a series of hard blinks.

I reach up and trace his lips with my finger. He bites down playfully before pulling it back up to his lips and kissing it softly.

It would be so easy for me to take advantage of him like this, knowing full well he'd throw me out the door if he knew who I was, what *future Skyla* had done to him. I lay my hand over his chest and take in his features, broad and solid, every bit a god—if not more so—than Logan.

expel

I let him come to me with his lips, cover me with the hot of his mouth and indulge in a kiss that ignores the constraints of age and time—it spells out love and forever much better than any careless sentiment that I could ever utter.

We spend the next hour in a playful tug of war with our tongues, his hands hot on my waist, my thighs. I miss the pleasure of being with Gage, even now while I'm with him lost in his kisses I openly yearn for him. I didn't know it was possible to feel this way, love this deep and yet, ache with fathomless hurt at the same time.

"Would you forgive me if I made a mistake?" I whisper it soft into his ear as the movie drones on.

"Of course I would." He reaches down and sweeps his thumb over my cheek, wiping away tears I didn't know existed. A part of me wants to fill him in on who I really am or who I will be in his life one day—the mistakes that will put out the fire of our relationship and leave us choking on the smoke. "I doubt you could hurt a fly, but I'd forgive you of anything." His eyes spark with renewed lust for me.

I lean into his chest, close my eyes—rise and fall with his steady breathing.

I've hurt you, Gage—and you haven't forgiven me.

42

The Deal

The dark clouds overhead, glide steady like the shadow of a very long train, rolling over Paragon.

I let myself into Demetri's oversized McMansion and stumble into the entry with nothing but the hollow sound of my footsteps to greet me.

"Hello, beautiful," strums a soothing male voice.

I turn in fright to find an aura of blue, filling up the room with its shimmering majesty.

"Logan," I reprimand. "You gave me a freaking heart attack."

He morphs into his fleshly version and offers an apologetic smile.

"I need a hug." I wrap my arms around him. He feels real in every way, solid and alive.

"They've moved me from the Soulennium."

I pull back, trying to decode what this might mean.

"I'm a semi-permanent resident of the Transfer until I get my body back—*if* I get my body back."

"You will," I assure, picking up Demetri's twisted list of demands, glossing over it before tossing it back from whence it came. "In fact, I'm going to tell Gage about you." It's part of the big plan I concocted to manipulate Gage into committing vocal discourse with me. I'll simply blurt out *Logan is dead,* and I'll have his full attention. But, then again, Holden has him masterfully pissed. Gage might actually cheer if I told him Logan was in a cadaverous state.

"You probably shouldn't tell Gage until he's finished his round of antibiotics. My uncle said he was very close to another internment at his least favorite spa. Let him get better." He presses out a weak smile. "Can I take you somewhere later? Falls maybe?" There's an air of desperation in his voice—a hint of mourning for all we could have been.

"Sure. I heard Ethan and Chloe mention something about a party at my house tonight," I shrug. "It's the last place I want to be."

Logan blinks out of the room.

"Logan?" I step around the corner in the event he fell through the wall, or he's spontaneously decided to engage in a game of hide and seek.

"I've banished him from my presence," Marshall strides by as though it were the norm for people to pop in and out of existence—and in Demetri's house of horrors, it just might be. "I'll be making an anonymous deposit to the trolling alley nonprofit fund this Monday."

"Trolling," I parrot. Funny, and yet, so true. "Thanks! What do I owe you? And I no longer pay in flesh."

"I'll consider your time equally as delicious. I'm holding a celestial boot camp exclusively for you. We must prepare for battle, love. Bring your game as you would say. You'll need it."

I follow him down the long expansive marble floors right into the cavernous kitchen. Marshall pulls open the stainless fridge and bends into the massive steel unit inspecting the offerings.

"There's someone who wants a word with you," he muffles.

"My mother?" I spring up at the thought.

"No, love." He closes the refrigerator door and exposes a very toxically fueled Ezrina. "I'll leave you two to discuss the finer points of your agreement, carry on." And with that, he disappears.

"Trial," Ezrina's voice echoes. It vibrates through the miles of stainless appliances that line the kitchen, trembles beneath my feet, electrocuting my bones.

"Yes, I'm working on that," I round out the large island in the center of the room, slow and steady, as not to let on that I'm about to bolt.

From behind her back she produces a long handled knife the size of a small sword.

"Body," her voice quivers as she speeds in my direction.

"No!" I hold up my hands in defense, fully expecting her to slice off all ten fingers in one clean sweep. In an aerobic worthy feat I manage to jump to the back of the kitchen, caging myself in like a lumbering beast.

Shit. I'm so freaking stupid.

"I *swear*, I'll be talking to my mother real soon," I plead. "That job has her horribly bogged down." Really? That's the best I could come up with? And is reminding Ezrina what my mother does for a living really the best idea? After all, it was my mother who cursed her to a life of servitude. "But, I promise, I'll be speaking to her about your situation as soon as possible."

A silver blade rotates through the air, enlarges in diameter as it speeds in my direction. A hard thud bullets through my left shoulder. I stare down in disbelief at the protruding handle as a bloom of heat radiates from my newfound wound.

I let out a whimper while staring at the metal tongue protruding from my flesh.

"I *swear*?" Marshall manifests before me, extracting the knife with a lack of delicacy. "I *promise*?" He balks, rinsing the blade before letting it drop to the bottom of the sink. "Have you learned nothing about dealing with spiritual beings? You don't offer up a binding agreement on a whim, Skyla."

I inspect the vicinity behind him and note that Ezrina is gone.

"So *now* you tell me." I press a white dishtowel against the crimson geyser spouting from my body.

expel

Marshall removes the towel and rubs his hand hard over the puncture. It feels horrifically painful and gratifying all at the same time.

"I've sealed you. I'll leave the pain as a reminder."

There's a rattle in the entry, female voices murmur and laugh.

"Your nemesis has arrived. Do refrain from lobbing cutlery at one another. I'm afraid I've other affairs to tend to—healing the masses is low on my priority list for the day." He dissolves in a thunderclap.

I'd rather play catch with Ezrina with a quiver full of knives than hang out with Chloe any day. Too bad I don't have a choice.

Before I can hit the entry, the voices escalate into something just this side of a brawl.

Emily and Chloe both glance in my direction before continuing their tirade.

"I didn't steal anybody, tell her Skyla," Chloe demands while perusing Demetri's wish list for the day. "I don't steal people."

"No, she kills them." I'm more than happy to agree with Chloe when factual information is concerned. More so, I'm finding this whole tell the truth thing rather addictive. I'm sure Tad will label it a disorder like everything else, especially after I tag every sentence I utter to him with, *you moron*. There are some truths I'd love to espouse.

"And what about Brielle?" Chloe scoffs at Emily. "You tried digging your claws into the father of her child. That makes you a monster in my book." Her dark hair pops in contrast to her pink sweater. Chloe in pink is like dipping a cockroach in chocolate and trying to pass it off as wholesome. There's something innately wrong about the combination in general.

"Oh really?" Emily crosses her arms, unable to capture Chloe's full attention.

Emily has a butch way about her. It scares me enough to know to stay the hell away. But Chloe never shows fear, she owns it, makes it sing to her like a lullaby.

"Let's see," Emily continues, "Just around Christmas everyone thought Skyla here was having Gage's baby and that didn't stop you from becoming a level five cling on. Everyone knew he was into her. You must have had some major dirt on him to make him stand by your side like your new gung ho boyfriend. Only he wasn't so gung ho, he was sulking. Did you pay him to hang out with you? That is your specialty, right? Buying people?"

"It was Dudley's baby," Chloe's voice booms across the marble expanse, reverberates off the stone like the clatter of a rattlesnake. Chloe owns up to nothing else but the supposed error in Emily's condemnation.

Marshall appears in the adjoining room, relaxing in an armchair. I'm sure he's lapping this up with his feet on Demetri's antique furniture while visions of our lovechild dance in his head.

"Skyla was involved with *Dudley*, still is," Chloe insists. "You saw the evidence. Don't make me sick trying to throw Gage in my face. He has feelings for me." Her lips tighten as she scans the to-do list one more time. "He told me so last night."

My stomach sours.

Shit. Chloe is finally reaping the benefits of the hellion ways she's been cultivating since conception. Gage is vulnerable right now, not that I believe a single word Chloe says since every other sentence she utters takes a leap in logic. I'm pretty sure the one solid feeling Gage has for Chloe is comprised of revulsion and loathing.

expel

"The only way people have feelings for you, is if you manipulate them into having them," Emily spits the words out laced with venom.

It's like she read my mind.

"Skyla," Chloe takes in a deep cleansing breath further ignoring Emily's rant, "there's an office upstairs, first door on the right. Mr. Edinger needs an itemization of everything in his grandfather's desk. Emily you can assist her because, quite frankly, you make me want to vomit." She leans in. Her eyes glow like coals as she comes in for the kill. "And Ethan wholeheartedly agrees. He said he'd rather chew his arm off than touch you. Also," Chloe perks up, "he says you have the face of a possum." With that she traipses upstairs.

Emily speeds up after her. I'm assuming she's headed up to do the task at hand—

not slaughter Chloe like she really wants. Although, we are alone, and God knows I'd never rat Emily out if she happened to accidentally, on purpose, disembowel Chloe with a paperclip. However, with my luck, she'd pin all the blame on me, and with my long destructive history where Chloe is concerned, people would believe her.

Marshall is nowhere to be seen as I head up after Emily. First door to the right manages to produce an archaic looking office complete with marble statues of sleeping angels perched high above the bookshelves. The room itself is dark and cloying, devoid of any natural light. The desk is smooth cherry with a heavy gloss, nothing but a small globe, pieced together from gemstones, sitting on top. My fingers meander over to it, and my wrist drops from the heft.

An oversized office chair, a tufted hunter's green, beckons me. I take a seat and glide over the hardwood floor on its casters. I roll the fat globe back onto the desk, pull open the long drawer in front of me and inspect my findings—a blank note pad, about a dozen loose pens.

Cataloging, pencils, paperclips, two boxes of staples, is not the way I planned on spending my Saturday.

I used to think doing community service with Demetri would be sheer torture, that I would rather chop my feet off and walk on my hands the rest of my life but this certainly beats roadside assistance with a shovel and a trashcan. There's no orange jumpsuit involved, so already it's made of win.

I pull out my cell to see if there's a message from Gage, but nothing.

It's so deathly quiet here. I wonder what Emily is up to? Didn't the Gestapo specifically order her to shoulder up with me in office supply labor detention?

God, what if she really is trying to kill Chloe? I bolt up and take off down the hall. The same blue glow captures me, and I head over to the overgrown library to see if the secret passage is still opened—see if the Fem Hall of Fame has any West Paragon High cheerleaders doubling as visitors or decapitated wall mounts.

A cold breeze accosts me in the library, feels like ten thousand disembodied spirits all rallied to greet my presence. I speed past the stacks of ancient texts, the air sweetened with decaying parchment. The cracked and aging hardbacks hunger for my touch. They entice me with their gilt lettering, hold the promise of transferring their knowledge in exchange for rubbing their spines. These books crave love, attention, human hands to cradle them. This is what Demetri should donate to the garbage sale, the whole damn library.

A crack of light emerges at the end of the long line of mahogany bookshelves. The opening in the wall has reappeared.

Chloe is in there, milling around.

Figures.

She hovers over the haunted pictures and looks as if she's taking her aggression out on one.

What in the hell is she doing?

expel

She's shaking it like a snow globe and laughing at the effort.

Chloe glides over to the mirror, sticks her hand in just like I did. My heart picks up pace, drumming on the inside until my ears hone in on the rhythm. It takes everything in me not to run over and push her in.

I imagine her head mounted on the wall of horrors as Demetri's latest conquest and an unnatural rise of pleasure purrs within me.

Chloe doesn't move, doesn't flail for help—simply relaxes as her arm swims inside the unknown realm as if she belonged there.

Emily appears.

Shit!

I lean over and see a giant arched entry that leads in from the hall. I'm hardly impressed that the entire house can change its shape at will. It's about as dead as Demetri's so-called grandfather. Come to think of it both the house and the grandfather are probably Fems.

Emily moves in slow and stealth behind an unsuspecting Chloe, the clear look of fright contorting on her face. Her pale as plaster skin lies in stark contrast to the dark wiry curls she wears like a bad Halloween wig. Emily continues her noiseless effort and comes upon her the way you would approach wild game that has the ability to bolt before capture. Emily holds her hands out, gives Chloe one swift push in the back and sends her flying into the shimmering glass.

Emily ditches out of the room quick as an apparition. I bolt back through the library and try to catch up to her in the hall.

"You see Chloe anywhere?" I ask, not sure whether to reprimand or applaud her.

"She wasn't feeling good." A dark look of satisfaction comes over her. "I think I'm going to take off. I'll catch you later." Emily speeds down the stairs. A moment later the slam of the front door echoes like a gunshot.

I run back down the hall to the room of terrors, hesitate before walking through the newly formed entry. The grotesque faces mounted to the walls press over my shoulders with the weight of their stares—oppress me with enough fear to send me into paralysis.

"Chloe?" I say loud enough to fill the ethereal plane. I walk over to the oval crafted wonder and look inside. The aura of a rainbow surrounds my reflection. My hair sparkles iridescent blue. "Chloe?" I lean in with my face, feel a slight electrical impulse as my nose penetrates the barrier. I push in just enough to take a look inside. It's a room identical to this one, everything set in reverse order.

I pull my head out and take a giant breath.

No sign of Chloe.

And, I, for one, hope it stays that way.

43

I Ain't Missing You at All

When I arrive home, a loose number of Ethan's party guests have already meandered onto the property. I choose to ignore the rising body count and head inside. The Landon residence feels like a shanty after spending hours at Demetri's palatial estate.

I still can't believe I hung out at the haunted mansion alone after Em pushed Chloe into the other side of the looking glass. I was totally hopped up on life once Chloe was no longer an active participant, in this realm anyway, and ended up cataloging every freaking thing in that gargantuan antique desk. Nothing but boring everyday crap you would find at the bottom of your backpack, or the junk drawer in any household.

Eventually, I made my way over to an elongated sofa and fell asleep a good five hours. No matter what the circumstance, no matter how many homicide attempts Chloe suffers through, I want to log as many hours as possible at Demetri's den of horrors to rid my debt to society.

Today is turning out to be a trifecta of perfection, what with no sign of Demetri, Chloe evaporating into another realm, and soon I'll get to spend a little time with my dead ex-boyfriend, which will really clear my head. Now, if I could only get Gage into the equation, somehow, life would be just freaking grand.

"Hey," Ethan calls as I'm about to climb the stairs. "Where's Chloe?"

"No clue," I shrug. Totally not a lie. "And when is this revenge of yours supposed to kick in?" Not that it's important now. But it'll look good that I asked in the event Chloe decides to show up never.

"I'm riding this wave as it comes. Don't worry, it'll get done," he assures.

That's what I was afraid of. The non-plan, the idiotic Landon strategy, the, I'm going to trick Chloe into my pants scheme. Ethan is incapable of taking down a viper like Chloe. Even death can't keep her down. I'm betting she ditches the mirror before midnight. In fact, I bet she's already crawled back out and brought a pack of magical Fems right along with her.

Female voices escalate from my bedroom. The door sits ajar, and I can hear the distinct sound of cackling. Sounds like Mia and Melissa made up.

I swing open the door. Only it's not Mia and Melissa. Instead, I'm stunned to find Carson Armistead sitting in my chair with her leg slung casually over the side. Carly Foster is lounging on my bed, extruding a huge bubble from her lips while her bare feet push into my pillow.

"Excuse me?" I penetrate the air with my insolence. "Get the hell out." There's no point in being nice to these girls. Nice is lost on just about everyone on Paragon.

"Calm down," Carly squeaks. I think at some point in her life Carly had her vocal cords permanently scarred with helium. There is no good reason any human being should be able to mimic a rodent so perfectly. Then again around these parts, one doesn't necessarily need to be human. "We're just reliving our childhood." She shags out her straw-colored hair.

"We practically grew up in this room," Carson swivels in my chair, staring lazily at the walls. "Chloe had a slumber party like every single week."

God—I wonder if they know about the butterfly room?

"That's nice. Get out." I run my fingers through my hair before picking up the detangler and misting myself down. It ignites the room with the fresh scent of apples, eliciting a strong memory of when I first entered the haunted hotel in the Transfer with Marshall.

A gasp gets locked in my throat—Logan is there. I try to shake the thought away. He'll be *here* soon, and that's all that matters.

"Remember that time we snuck out and firebombed Brielle's house with a bag of flaming crap?" Carson laughs like she's already ripped.

Wow, real mature. No wonder Brielle can't stand Chloe—she treated her like crap, literally.

"Or that one time we snuck down the hall and made out with Brody?" Carly snorts. "Oh, wait, that was just me!" She hacks out a laugh in pieces until nothing but air cuts from her lungs.

The slight hint of Ellis's own private reserve hits my nostrils.

"Wait a minute," I head over to the open window. I hadn't even notice it was cold in here because Ethan has the front door wide open and the entire house is frigid as a meat locker. "Were you getting high in my room?" Crap. They're freaking stoned.

Now that I think of it, everything smells like Ellis in here.

"Out," I yell.

They rise in unison, stretch their limbs lethargic as kittens.

"You still seeing that teacher?" Carson tilts into me as if this were a genuine concern.

I'd say no, but the thought of Carson and Carly double-teaming Marshall sends a rise of vomit to the back of my throat.

"None of your business." I don't get it. I should be *pushing* them at Marshall, he might even gift them with demonic necklaces before the clock strikes twelve, and that would crown this as an unordinarily perfect day. But I can't help feel a twinge of jealousy when I consider him plying them with his special brand of obsessive attention. Unfortunately, his quirky evil ways have grown on me.

"That means yes," Carson bites down on her lip. "I saw the DVD. *Skyla Does Paragon.*" She grazes over me with delight. "You know what I don't get? Why would you leave Logan Oliver in the first place? He dropped everything for you, and then you go after Gage. I mean Gage is hot, but you had Logan," she says his name as if he were worth his weight in gold.

"And now Michelle's leached herself onto him," Carly opens her mouth with gaping concern as if they have a genuine dilemma on their hands.

"She's with him," I interject. "They're totally an official couple." I hope Chloe was right about Michelle's babysitting status. As much as I hate the thought of Michelle actually loving on Logan's perfect body, I'd send Holden into the transport once again a little sooner than anticipated if he hooked up with Carson or Carly—God forbid *both*.

They leave in a huddle to go over a 'solid game plan'.

I need to get Logan back in his body and fast.

❦

I set out to check in on Mia and Melissa, as I'm clearly the only responsible adult in the vicinity, but they're both suspiciously absent from their bedroom. I trot downstairs to canvas the area. A sea of bodies has filled in the nooks and crannies with arms and legs intertwined. This is quickly becoming a house of ill repute, which doesn't surprise me since most of Ellis's parties end up with half the downstairs rooms occupied for any number of carnal misdeeds. The lights are all out, as deemed mandatory per Paragon's unofficial party guide.

I wander into the darkened kitchen and find Ethan and Holden hanging out with a bunch of guys playing a drinking

expel

game with the requisite red Solos. I go over and snatch the cup out of faux Logan's hand.

"There's plenty more where that came from. Get your own, Sis." Holden's eyes widen for a second as he catches himself in the gaff.

"Where's Michelle?" No sign of Miller. I don't like this one bit.

"She went out with Lexy—said she'd be right back."

"Oh good," I breathe a sigh of relief.

"They're getting your least favorite person," he gives a greasy smile. "How did you not kill her?"

Coming from Holden it's practically a compliment. And, oh crap, now they'll never be back.

"You should text Michelle and tell her Chloe's a big girl," I suggest. "She can take care of herself. Besides, she seems pretty into you, and there are a lot of guys out on the prowl tonight. I'd keep her close if you know what I mean." I shrug when all I really want to do is shudder.

"I've always had a thing for Michelle." Holden is spellbound at the mention of her name.

"Beautiful girl." I hate having this conversation with Holden while he hides behind Logan's face. It kills me on a primal level.

"You think there's a chance for us again? You know, me and you?" The question is laced with honesty and for a moment it really does feel like Logan.

"Um," I'm pretty sure stringing Holden along is a bad idea. "I think we had what we had," I lose myself in his fiery eyes and a twinge of sadness quivers through me. "Look, I gotta go. Do me a favor—stick with Michelle. You'll lose her forever if you cheat on her."

I know.

That's exactly how I lost Gage.

44

Hot Water

I search high and low for Mia and Melissa and can't find them anywhere. I'm on the verge of an all out panic, thinking all kinds of horrible things. They could have been kidnapped, dragged into the forest by a pack of wild wolves—Marshall style, or God forbid, Ezrina hacked them to pieces in an effort to drive home the fact she's pretty damn serious about getting a new trial. Or maybe Mia did something stupid like expose the butterfly room to Melissa— and all of West Paragon Junior high is busy indulging in some serious hormonal debauchery up there.

I head out to the front yard where hoards of people are amassed in small groups. I don't have the time, or initiative, to properly eavesdrop on a single conversation, which is fast becoming one of my favorite pastimes at one of these events. Without Gage I have no life, the closest thing I get is listening to others brag about theirs'.

A seam of light escapes from under the garage door. I head around to the side and let myself in. About a dozen different faces turn in my direction at once. Mia, Melissa, and the who's who of Paragon minor sit in a circular arrangement, most of them in old lawn chairs we dragged out from L.A. where it actually made sense to own furniture specifically designed to occupy the yard. Here it works as a body buffet for the garage and, come to think of it, this all looks rather cultish, what with them all in black and hovering in a circle.

"I'm going out," I announce stupidly.

"See you later," Mia says, giving a quick wink. There's a boy holding her hand, *holding* it. Badly I want to go Ezrina on him and detach his appendage at the wrist—teach him a lesson for touching my baby sister, but don't. Really I should squash this relationship with the Armistead kid before either one of my sisters gets too fixated. The last people on the planet I want to be even *quasi* related to are the Armisteads.

I head back out and smack into Ellis.

"Love honey," he says it seductively with a wet smile on his lips, and for a minute I think I'm going to have to duck his unwanted advances.

"Are you high?" Should I be asking? I really don't see the point anymore.

"The only high I participate in is at W.P." His demeanor sharpens. "No, I'm not high."

"Oh," I laugh. "West Paragon. I get it."

"Been clean two weeks." He pushes his cheeks high into a grin.

"Ellis!" I bounce on my feet and pull him in. His sweater is still laced with the indelicate scent. I think it's time he started bathing in cologne like the rest of the male population. "I'm so proud of you."

"Yeah, well, I do what I can." He sweeps his eyes over me. "So, you and Gage really aren't together anymore?"

"It would appear." I can't stand the thought of Gage so thoroughly pissed at me, enveloped in hatred, hot as a fire. Then again, Gage is too generous to hate anyone. I've disappointed him, and that's the worse feeling of all. "Have you talked to him?"

"Nope." He catches my gaze and holds it. Ellis has soft eyes, a deep dimple on the right cheek. And, although I'd never admit it out loud, there's something about Ellis that has the power to make me melt.

"So you wanna hang out some time?" He lights up with hope. "You know, just you and me?"

This is going to get awkward quick.

"Yes, I totally want to hang out with you some time. Maybe next weekend we can catch a bite to eat?" Like at the

Althorpe dinner. I just don't want to come out and say it quite yet. The plan is to grovel to Gage, first.

"Alright," Ellis bobs into a smile.

Besides, catching a bite with Ellis is the epitome of innocence. If I've got one platonic male relationship, it's right here.

Ellis offers up a knuckle bump as he makes his way over to a girl sporting a spray tan gone awry, and I head upstairs to the butterfly room.

Time to fly to the falls with Logan.

The walls of the tiny secret room ignite and shimmer as thousands of paper butterflies come to life. Logan appears in his blue translucent state before filling in with muscle and sinew, fully formed flesh dressed in a plain t-shirt and jeans.

"Nice show," I pick up his hand and press it against my cheek. "You're a punctual little spook."

"You're a funny girl, Skyla." he looks mildly amused at the barb. "One day things won't be looking so great for you, and I'll be the one with the sense of humor." He pulls my hand over and brushes his lips over my knuckles, sweeps a fire line right up my arm. "Forgive me, but I've been thirsty for you ever since I woke up this morning."

The thought of Logan thirsting for me, wanting to be near me, presses over me with a heavy ache.

"So, are we off to the falls?"

"You have a bathing suit?" He nods with a mild level of concern. Logan wants to follow all the rules with me now. No more swimming in our underwear lest we be splayed across all six screens at the Cineplex.

expel

Logan takes up both my hands and closes his eyes. I take him in this way, he looks lonely, vulnerable, and strangely as if he's praying for me—to me.

A grey film fills the air. It's bitter cold outside. It takes several blinks for me to realize we've morphed over to the falls.

"Did we just light drive? Cause if not, I'm amazed at the mad skillz you've acquired postmortem."

"Not a stitch in time was removed," his bare chest comes into view. Logan stands before me in a pair of grey swim trunks.

"It's freezing here." My teeth chatter like castanets.

"I promise, you won't be cold." Logan reaches down into a small pool of water that sits in an alcove, tucked away at the quiet end of the lake. His hand floats over the surface, ignites a sizzle in the small circumference. The water glows an electric sky-blue before defusing to a deeper shade of sapphire, the exact color of the night sky back in L.A. "Warm as a bath," he announces, offering me his hand.

I pull off my sweater and jeans, exposing the most modest one-piece that my closet had to offer. I dip my foot in the water before committing to hypothermia, but it's warm, super warm.

"I'm without words," I say, getting into the water with him. I sink down to my chin and scoot into him on a rock that acts as a bench. "I kind of like Logan the magician."

"I'm worse than a magician. I'm an illusion, Skyla," he whispers it in secret, so the moon, the stars that hide like cowards behind a slippery veil of God's own breath won't hear. "This is temporal. If nothing happens soon, I'll be taken to paradise."

"Will I see you again?" I hold my breath, afraid that I might already know the answer.

"There is a chasm. You cannot come to me, and I can't go to you." A desperate sorrow blooms in his voice, and it devastates me to hear it.

255

"What about Giselle? She obviously knows her way around a chasm or two. She pops up all the time."

"Your mother is using her, assigning her missions. She has a free pass for now."

The thought of my mother using someone makes her out to be no different than the Sectors and Fems. If I wasn't slightly pissed at the entire lot of them, I'd be in awe of their utilitarian efforts.

"You have any luck getting her attention?" I ask hopeful.

"Nothing." He fully submerges himself before springing up and with his hair slicked back. It reflects a wash of moonlight over his head like a halo. Logan is luminescent, dead or alive his excellence thrives. I reach over and touch his baby fine hair, his cheek, his lips. It all feels so real. He couldn't possibly be an illusion.

"I never want you to go away," I whisper. It comes out broken, my voice so ready for tears. "I need you forever." My stomach explodes with heat when I insert my buzzword reserved for Gage into the equation. But it's true—no matter how much I don't want it to be, I need Logan as much as I need Gage.

He cups his hands over my face so soft, so careful and places his lips to my forehead. He pulls back and bears into me with a powerhouse gaze, drops his warm hands to my shoulders. A seductive smile plays on his lips.

"I don't plan on going away," his breath sweeps across my arm, ignites a series of goose bumps from the pleasure of his being.

"We are never going to work." The words bleed out of me hard and unwanted. "It's not fair that you made me love you." The first tear falls. I tilt my head, and the salty stream trickles into the line of my lips.

"The faction war," he whispers it with a hopeless fatigue. "Things happen," he sighs. "One thing I can tell you for sure—you have a destiny. You can make it easy on

expel

yourself and allow the Master to lead you, or struggle, rebel, land somewhere in the vicinity but never, by a long shot, experience the treasure and the glory he has in store for you."

"And the Decision Council, they play into this?"

He gives a gentle nod.

"My mother is shaping my future." I huff at the thought. "Then why won't she see me?"

"Not to offend you—or her, but, rumor has it she's..." he briefly glances upwards. "for lack of a better word, a thorny rose."

"Could have fooled me." Figures. I land this ultra amazing unearthly mother, and she turns out to be a celestial spitfire. "I need her mercy, Logan." I don't dare tell him why.

"Skyla?" His eyes ignite with worry as he holds up our conjoined hands. "Tell me everything—tell me now." There's a slight mark of irritation in Logan's tone. It's bad enough to have Gage and Nev pissed off at me, I don't plan on adding Logan's name to the ever-expanding list, so I do. I tell him everything.

He stares at me a really long time. At first I think he's trying to think up a way to get me out of the body swap with Ezrina, since we can both safely surmise that the Justice Alliance sure as hellfire isn't going to renege on their almighty covenant slash eternal punishment, but, instead, he gazes deeper into me, touching the nexus of my existence with his heartfelt sorrow. Logan leans in and bumps his forehead to mine, his nose, his lips, closes his eyes as a thin seam of tears lines his lids.

"You love me," he whispers in a long strained hiss like steam from a kettle.

"Of course, I love you," I pull him in by the waist until our bare stomachs touch, sending a wave of pleasure swimming up my spine. "I'll always love you."

Our silent, elongated tears stream into the warm inky water. Our bodies move in a macabre slow dance as a gentle whirlpool pushes us along.

I love Logan with an undying passion—one I know that may never get quenched even after the faction war.

There's a time and place for us, Skyla. Not here, not now. He doesn't open his eyes or acknowledge the thought.

My heart comes alive like a jungle drum. Somehow, for some unknown reason, my mother has threaded two very different hearts alongside mine.

His eyes open and he sinks low into the water, takes me in under the umbrella of fog like I were the most exotic pearl. "Never give up on us, Skyla," it comes out a secretive warning. "Do what you have to do with Gage, but please, don't ever stop loving me."

45

The Letter

Days slice by.

Long incisions gash into my existence created by the serrated knife of Gage's absence. It's unconscionable that the sun could rise, that time in its own selfish measurement could go on like this, move so brazenly forward without Gage gracing me with his infectious smile, the lure of his husky voice, his strong arms wrapped around me until I fall asleep. Nothing matters anymore. Color, the light, it all turns into the same shade of soot—insignificant as a melted candle, finished with its task, unimportant in every other way.

I pull a sheet of blank paper from out of my printer and stare at it a very long time. I've tried to get in touch with Gage using every modern day modality possible. The only device left to consider is the most archaic form of communication—a letter.

I start off with *Dear Gage* then quickly reach for another sheet. *Gage—My love*, *Hey*, none of it fits. I rip through a dozen pieces of paper before giving up on formalities and write from the heart.

Gage,
I'm broken.
Thoughts of you consume me. I miss how you used to hold me, love me until I thought I would explode.
This rarity—this whiplash love of ours, I want it all back.
I'm going to be at the Althorpe formal dinner Saturday night, and I wondered if maybe you would like to go with me?

I would die to see you there.
All my love,
forever,
Skyla

I seal it in an envelope and head downstairs.

"I'll be stepping out for a minute," I say to Mom who's busy bastardizing yet another recipe to fit her stringent nutritional needs. The entire family, collectively, has lost a good twenty pounds, albeit from starvation, but still, it's a win.

"Oh, I've been meaning to tell you, Tad and I want to take you and Gage out to celebrate the engagement. I would throw a party, but since Ethan's girlfriend ran away again, the mood around Paragon isn't so chipper."

Chloe has been dubbed a runaway. Ironic because that was the lie she concocted when I accidentally resurrected her with my own sheer stupidity. Now that she's busy running around in the Realm of Possibilities, trying to keep her head attached to her body, they've labeled her the same.

"Technically, it's not really an engagement ring." I spin the band over my finger, warm the flesh beneath it with Gage's affections. "In fact, we don't have to celebrate anything right now," I lower my gaze. "Or ever," I whisper.

"Is everything OK with the two of you?" She sweeps over like there's been a death in the family. In a way there has, and I'm one hundred percent responsible for the massacre.

"We're taking it slow." More like we've come to an abrupt halt, but I leave that part out.

"Slow is good," her eyes well up with tears for me, like she knows there's nothing good about this. "Are you going to see him now?"

"Just dropping something off. I promise I'll be quick."

"Come here," she wraps her arms around me, encompassing me with her warm circle of love.

expel

"I'd like to talk to you again," I say. "You know, in private." I want to get some straight answers out of her regarding the Count round table meeting she attended just a few weeks ago and what the hell her intentions are with my father's killer.

"You bet," she pulls my chin up with her finger and kisses the tip of my nose.

Something tells me if Lizbeth Landon were on the Justice Alliance I wouldn't have a thing to worry about.

But she's not.

✽ ✽ ✽

The freedom of having my own car—just months ago I craved it. I dreamed of bolting from a house full of Landons', fleeing from Tad's psychopathic rants, to hit the barren open road. Of course, on the island there are only two directions that will take you anywhere, and at any given time they could only lead me closer, or further away from Gage. I'll always head towards Gage if I can help it. I hope for the rest of my life all roads will lead to Gage.

It's in these spasms of misery that I find it most difficult to breathe. I can't fathom how much he detests me. How much he must crave that the Counts would do away with me and he could resume the life he knew before I ever set foot on this island.

I make my way past the gates and park across the street at Ellis's, high up on the driveway in the event Gage sees my car and decides to slash my tires. Not that he would. Its doubtful Gage is capable of hurting me, or anything that belongs to me, in any way.

The air is bitter cold, no clouds today, just dull oatmeal skies with ground fog that spins around my legs as I move through it.

I miss the days Gage would lay his affection over me like mist over Paragon. Everything reminds me of Gage. I see his face in the sky, the trees make up his likeness, he resides permanently behind my eyelids like a recurring dream. A serious kick of adrenaline pumps through me as I fast approach the Oliver's door. Logan's truck is gone and so are both Barron and Emma's sedans. I ring the bell, followed by a brisk knock. Charlie gives a few good barks alerting my presence to anyone who might be inside. I wait fifteen solid minutes, but Gage doesn't come.

I stare down at the envelope in my hand with his name scrawled across the front in large flowery letters. It looks far too cheerful. One look and he'll think that I don't miss him. For a minute I contemplate tearing it up, throwing the remains in the bushes, but I slip it beneath the door and hope for the best. I lean my cheek against the wood, feel the icy sting until it warms to my skin. There is no comfort for me, no oil of joy in exchange for my mourning. This is heartbreak, heartache, agony, and anguish all on a never-ending loop.

Hell on earth.

A prison made of my own doing.

✺ ✺ ✺

I plod back over to Ellis's. His monster truck is crammed up against the garage so close, I swear my fingers couldn't squeeze through the reserve of space.

I repeat the process, ring the bell, give a brisk knock. This time the door not only opens, Ellis greets me with a look of welcome surprise.

"Get in, girl," he pulls me into a hug as I cross the threshold. "Need a light drive, buddy?" He's sporting wireless glasses that I think I've only seen him wear once before. Ellis is adorable in them, and I wonder why he doesn't employ their obvious powers to retain girls by the dozens. At least with them on he might actually attract the right kind of girls.

"No light driving today. Just in the neighborhood, thought I'd drop in—see what the house looks like under all that Goth glory." It looks feeble, humble.

Everything about Ellis's home looks foreign to me with this disproportional amount of light slicing through the wooden shutters. Something in me wants to toss room-darkening blankets over the offensive orifices. They should be ashamed of the way they bleed the secrets of this unholy abode. The darkness softened the home, added a layer of mystery that the light refuses to honor.

With the lights out I could make my way around, but in broad daylight I need a map just to get to the kitchen. I've come to classify Ellis's house as a creature of the night, but now that I see it for what it is, I'm a bit disappointed in how commonplace everything really seems.

"Want some cookies?" Ellis leads me towards the kitchen as the fresh baked scent of something sweet fills the air.

"No thanks." The last time Ellis played pastry chef I became an honorary stoner by default, ended up making out with Pierce Kragger because that's where brownies enhanced with narcotics gets you.

"What? No cookies?" A female voice calls out, stilted, as if he has her locked away in the pantry.

A woman pops up from behind the counter. Her long, over-processed hair lies thick and straight, almost the exact color red as my mother's but with a touch more pumpkin, and decidedly singed. A ruffled apron covers her waist, leaving her red silk blouse precariously exposed to the sticky elements.

"I won't hear of it. You must try my cookies," her lips struggle to rise.

"Mom, this is Skyla. Skyla, Mom." Ellis scoots into a seat at the bar, and I join him.

Ellis has a Mom—a real in the flesh, drop dead gorgeous mom. Go figure.

"Hi, it's so nice to finally meet you," I extend a hand, and she greedily shakes it. She seems overtly thrilled that I'm here and yet oddly unable to convince her face to follow suit.

"Olivia," she says before the buzzer goes off and she trots away in four-inch heels.

"Botox," Ellis whispers as she scuttles to relinquish another batch from the oven.

"Amazing," I say, under my breath.

It's clear where Ellis gets his wide-set eyes, his high cheekbones from.

"You know," she strides back. Her heels click against the stone floor, creating an echo reminiscent of Ezrina. "I do believe you're the first girlfriend of Ellis's I've yet to meet." Her lips move sideways as if she were trying to throw her voice while her eyes dance in amazement.

"Oh, we're just good friends." A guilty feeling comes over me for not spontaneously offering Ellis a promotion. "I can always count on him for anything." I have serious reservations about just having used the word Count. It probably works like a bat signal. An entire coven of them will descend upon the Harrison estate. Or maybe she thinks I'm one of them now. Use it in a sentence, and you're secretly outing yourself to the crew.

"That's fantastic. Some of the longest, most satisfying marriages start out as friendships." Her eyes squint as she recalls a distant memory.

"She's a divorce lawyer," Ellis translates.

"Attorney at law," she corrects. "Paragon Legal," she throws in the advertisement. "I handle just about everything, but unfortunately it's the demise of the matrimonial dream that keeps a roof over our heads. That,

expel

and my alimony," she whispers that last part with a twinkle in her eye.

Judging by the way Demetri has my mother running to him like a magnet, I gather we'll be procuring her services sooner than later.

She opens her mouth just a crack and pushes a cookie inside, examines me with a feline intensity. She gives a little giggle and shrugs. It's as though her body has adapted to exaggerated responses since her features have lost the ability to mandate emotion. Her baby smooth flesh is unnaturally alluring, her foundation is spread thick and even around her face like a well-frosted cake. It takes everything in me not to reach up and touch her. Something about her rubbery flesh reminds me of the corpses at the morgue. Perfectly smooth skin just doesn't exist naturally in the order of things unless, of course, you're dead. That's when you truly lose the ability to worry over anything anyway. Ellis's mother is simply one step ahead of the game. Then again she is a Count. Speaking of Counts.

"Hey, I have this problem." I pull the cease and desist letter out of my purse and start in on the story with Pierce—how he really didn't take down a crowd of people and beat up his girlfriend. "But my parents will kill me if they find out I'm lying."

"So will the courts," her ears peak back. God—that was probably a full-blown scowl. "I'll look this over and see what I can do." She peruses it quickly. "Damn Kraggers," she whispers mostly to herself. "I'm going to retire to the office. Take care, you two." She gives a quick wink—more like an eyelid malfunction rather than the coy nod of approval it was meant to be.

I'm moving Botox injections to the top of my do not attempt list. Most people have a bucket list, but I'm pretty motivated to keep up my *do not attempt* list. Sadly, there are a number of things on there, and, to date, the Counts and Fems have demonstrated their ability to help me face my

265

fears. Things like, do not attempt to climb the highest tree on the island, do not run into granite walls, and do not hack off the arm of your enemy and wear it as your own, have already been officiated.

"Nice to meet you," I shout after her as she speeds down the hall.

"Stay out of the wine cabinet," she calls out. "I mark the liquor." Her voice melts into reverberations as she disappears down the complex maze of hallways.

"She marks the liquor?" I'm shocked by this. Imagine her surprise if she discovered her son's outright illegal misuse of questionable vegetation. That the supervising spirit she saw fit to gift him with on his sixteenth birthday was essentially *buying*. "I thought your parents were still together."

"That's because my dad still lives here," he shrugs. "Big house."

That would be my luck—Tad and Mom divorcing only to have Tad still neatly tucked in her bed at night because of how much financial sense it makes.

"Gage still giving you the cold shoulder?" He leans over the counter and snaps up a handful of cookies.

"It would appear."

"Weird about Chloe disappearing," Ellis locks eyes with me. His expectations of a confession are high, I can tell.

"She's a little runaway," I sing it soft like a dream and give a tiny smile of approval.

"You know something."

"I know that Gage most likely won't be joining me for the big company dinner my mother is dragging me to on Saturday. Wanna come with?" I take the smallest cookie and pop it into my mouth, the molten chocolate chips sear into my tongue.

"I'll be there." His eyes glow with pleasure. "And, about that DVD. I still can't get over what it looked like was happening between us."

An image of me on my knees in pain and Ellis unzipping his jeans ready to baptize me with a golden shower flies through my mind.

"It certainly painted a picture," I say.

"So, back to Chloe." Ellis squints into me with a tiny smile playing on his lips. "I guess you were really ticked off at her for outing you like that."

"I'm perpetually pissed at Chloe. I don't like where you're going with this."

"I'm just saying, I don't think she'd run away."

"And I'm saying I don't have one idea of where Chloe Bishop might be."

Ellis gives a dirty smile. "And I'm saying you do."

46

Sing the Blues

All week West Paragon High rides the coattails of Chloe's mysterious disappearance. You'd think we were ringing her curtain down the way the masses huddle in grief, moan like ailing canines in front of the news cameras that set up shop on campus. If any good came out of it, about three-dozen kids scored some serious airtime exploiting the travesty of not having an army of triage counselors on the ready. The entire segment led to a funding debate, and now the School Board is reviewing the matter.

Not everyone is broken up about her abrupt departure. Emily has happily embedded herself into Ethan's arms, consoling, soothing away his pain with the balm of her affection.

Gage still hasn't bothered responding to my multiple attempts to accost him verbally, either, in person, written or electronic. He holds strong to his punishment. He's cut off the oxygen supply to my world, pulled away so completely it leaves me languishing in the vacuum of his absence.

Rumor had it he was at West on Friday picking up work, but by the time I raced down to the main office he had already left. I overheard the secretary say he'd be back in class next week, that he had just received the doctor's clearance. This buoyed my mood until I realized that I was probably better off with him ignoring me behind my back rather than the prospect of him openly refusing to acknowledge my presence. I couldn't take that. It would be too much to bear.

I imagine him walking down the hall laughing with a throng of beautiful girls, looking through me as if I were

expel

made of glass. The idea of his stony silence delivered firsthand, breaks me.

On Saturday night, Ellis picks me up and we drive down to the Harbor Lights Ballroom at the Paragon Resort. West had its winter formal here, that was the night of the inadvertent Mustang romp with Logan, the night Chloe decided to relinquish Gage to me right before she drilled my fender into his intestines. I don't need a supervising spirit to light drive me back to that night. I know in my heart what she did.

Surprisingly the resort is just as raucous as the night of winter formal, only the girls filling in the evening wear sport more wrinkles, longer dresses and far less attractive men on the crook of their arms. Trolls I tell you, every one of them that works for Althorpe. I wouldn't be surprised at all to discover there's some troll underworld woven into the infrastructure of the corporation.

Mom and Tad mingle freely with Demetri and Darla by their sides.

Figures.

Demetri's manner of brainwashing my mother into loving him is strikingly similar to Chloe's—hang around long enough in hopes to wear down their defenses. Didn't work so well for Chloe, but Demetri seems to have perfected the snow job to a science. I watch as my mother freely wraps her arm around him, tweaks his shoulder as if offering a massage. She laughs far too easily at whatever comes flying out of his mouth, and I bet if given the opportunity she'd bake him a batch of whole-wheat cookies with that lame chocolate substitute which smells suspiciously like feet. It's hard to stand by and watch as Lizbeth Landon vies for girlfriend of the year award.

"I know her." Ellis lights up while looking at some girl across the room. "She's that chick from East I've been trying to hook up with for the past six months." He looks perturbed by this. "I'm gonna go over." He whips by so fast he leaves a breeze in his wake.

"Alone and beautiful." Marshall leans in shoulder to shoulder, touches my hand with the back of his. "My absolute favorite combination."

"I thought you had a thing for angel wings," I say, adjusting my red pullover dress from a couple Christmas' ago. "And by the way I'm not alone. I'm here with Ellis."

"Ah, yes, Mr. Harrison. First you burn through the Olivers, then this dolt of a demotion—my how the mighty have fallen."

Five freaking minutes and Ellis couldn't be loyal to me as his date. I've always suspected he would so make a lousy boyfriend.

"I, however, would be loyal to the grave," Marshall is quick to interject after so rudely reading my thoughts. "And seeing that I am an immortal, you would have my undying love forever."

I cringe when he says that final word.

"Yeah, well, forever's not stacking up to be such a surefire thing."

"Forgive my poor choice of words. *Eternity*—an infinite duration that human minds are incapable of fathoming." He turns into me and steps in uncomfortably close. "My love blooms in triplicate each day for you, Skyla. I've never felt so charged, so alive, for another in my entire existence."

I stare at him wild-eyed, watch as his chest pulsates with excitement as he breathes the words. It's strange having Marshall proclaim his love for me and yet somehow exhilarating. Gage has left my thirsty soul parched for affection.

I reach up and touch the hard line of his jaw.

"You are a gorgeous creature," I breathe. "Any woman would be more than pleased to have you." I let my hand sink

expel

in measure with my heart as I think of Gage sharing his future with some nameless, faceless girl.

"I have everything in my power to take you, Skyla." Marshall veils the threat with a thin smile. "The authority, the ability to bend your will to desire me. It would be stronger than anything you've felt for the Olivers combined, but I choose not to use it."

"Sounds perfectly criminal. The mercy is appreciated," I muse.

"It's freedom I give you," his features soften. Marshall glows serene, befittingly gorgeous. Nights like these were designed to showcase his beauty. That he should grace the common day, deprived of champagne and caviar, women in jewel tone dresses, those would be the true crimes here.

"Freedom to love anyone I wish," I nod, understanding full well what he really means—freedom to choose him. "Say, how would one get out of that weird mirror, back at Demetri's? You know, in the event one fell in." I'm quick to change the subject.

"The cranial ornaments weren't enough to deter you?" His eyes sharpen on mine. He knows damn well what I'm talking about.

"Chloe fell in the mirror, Emily pushed her. You promised me a beheading."

"I promised no such thing. I simply implied it to dismiss your eagerness to delve into mischief. In the event you've failed to make the observation, you, my dear, are prone to catastrophe." He gives an amicable smile. "Judging by the length of time Ms. Bishop has decided to indulge herself, she is very much enjoying her new world."

"Well, she can't stay there. People are starting to talk. The All State competition is coming up and she's falling behind in her classes."

"And for a minute there I thought you were rooting for the beheading," he gloats. "From this new line of debate I would gather you were trying to mother her. If you're so concerned, crawl in and extricate her yourself."

"No thanks. I prefer my head attached to the rest of me."

"Death won't find you there. As long as you're not the control subject, you're safe."

"And to get out?"

"Simply crawl back the way you came."

"What if it gets sealed over and I get stuck?"

He considers this a moment. "If I'm available, I'll oversee the situation."

My mother calls us over and we take our seats for dinner.

Marshall is going to supervise.

I think I just found myself a supervising spirit.

47

Table Talk

Tad has arranged for an elderly man with a shock of white hair and his much younger, stunningly beautiful—alarmingly pubescent wife to join our bawdy bunch. Turns out the geezer is Tad's Regional Supervisor, so I find it actually quite amusing to watch good old Taddy dearest bring kiss ass to an all new low. Plus, the fact Mrs. Regional Supervisor has two flesh covered cantaloupes held hostage in her dress trying to maneuver an Alcatraz worthy escape—it's going to make for a fantastically entertaining evening. I count four times her left nipple peeked out at us, and for the first time ever, I'm thankful Gage isn't around to witness the salacious event.

Ellis on the other hand, is soaking it in, memorizing it for the pornographic replays he'll indulge in later, openly staring down Mrs. Supervisor and her bizarre animatronic breasts. I totally swear it looks like someone is manipulating them by remote control from across the room just to mess with us. It's not natural the way they rise and fall, bob and whinny as they try to peer at the world outside the impenetrable blindfold she insists on keeping over them.

Mr. Regional Supervisor excuses himself from the table. Probably going to take his magic little pill in an effort to warm up the engine a good four hours in advance.

"So who's the new cutie?" Darla winks over at Ellis. "New boyfriend so soon?" She offers an approving nod.

"Sure it is," Tad swirls the wine in his glass. "Skyla changes boyfriends regularly. She has 'em all mapped out like a crop rotation."

Emily laughs.

I witnessed her knocking back a couple glasses of bubbly on the company's dime when she thought no one was looking. And, I have to say, she and Ethan make a way better looking couple than Chloe and Ethan ever did or will. Chloe and Ethan felt a lot more disingenuine, sort of like the aging supervisor and his augmented lady suitor. You know you're supposed to treat them like a couple, but deep down inside you're snickering at the financial implications of it all.

"Please refrain from making our guest uncomfortable," Mom chides over to Tad.

"Be comfortable," Tad offers an unconvincing nod at Ellis. "Dinner is on the house—loosen up your buckle son and open the hatch."

Figures. It's Ellis who receives Tad's backward blessing.

"So, Brielle," Mom is quick to relegate the topic, "please—share the baby names you've come up with thus far."

"Kaliope," Brielle widens her smile, examining each of us for our spontaneous reactions. "Lie for short, if it's a girl, and Beau-Geste if it's a boy."

The entire table takes a breath. It's not that there is anything wrong with those names—it's just that collectively, they're so non-ubiquitous. That, coupled with the fact she plans for her newborn to catch some dreamy Zz's in a casket, well, it all sort of spells out trouble with a touch of blasphemy. I'm betting Drake and Brielle won't be strangers to the Social Services Department.

"I'm not sure Lie works as a nickname," Ethan of all people pipes up as the voice of reason.

"It works for Skyla," Melissa is quick with the attack.

I scowl over at her a moment. Little does she know I've been cataloging the injustices that the Landons have been invoking on the Messenger arm of the family.

"We're gonna get matching tattoo's once we decide," Brielle continues. "The baby, too, as soon as it's safe."

"Count me in." Darla swipes up a dinner roll, breaks it in half and submerges it generously in her wine goblet. "You never need a good reason for a tat."

Demetri studies his date before clearing his throat. "I think having the name of someone you love permanently emblazoned upon your flesh is a monumental gesture," he nods into my mother as if he were speaking from experience. I half expect an unveiling of my mother's effigy across his hairy chest at any moment. Just the thought makes me gag.

I bet tomorrow he'll hypnotize her into embroidering his name onto her forehead. And oddly enough if he pays for it I really don't think Tad would mind. Have I mentioned, moron?

"Right," Darla holds up her glass and toasts without reason, "but you don't need some lifelong dedication to have some reckless fun at the, *Ink and Kink*," she nods. "We should go sometime, draw our names in a valentine right across our hearts." She leans into Demetri with all of the trappings of seduction but it comes off as fierce desperation instead.

The table grows quiet. Darla is a hard act to follow linguistically or otherwise.

"Can't believe that girl took off again," Mom balks.

Ha! I wasn't the only one that put desperation and Chloe together. Plus this twist in our conversation takes the edge off of Darla and Demetri's awkward exchange of needles and love, blood and the like.

"Her parents have launched a full investigation of what might have occurred that afternoon at the Estate." Demetri is quick to share.

"You get the case?" Mom mouths the word with pride as if Chloe's disappearance could be the crowning moment of his career. Oddly, this is probably true.

He nods. "So far I've no reason to suspect foul play."

"Emily saw her last," it speeds out of me for no good reason.

"Skyla was upstairs with her," she fires back. "I had to take off and the two of them were all alone." Emily spills the lie easy as oil.

"I thought you said she had to leave?" I know for a fact that's what she said. She might think she can pin me for this, but little does she know I can bear false witness with the best of them. Hell, someone should call Guinness because I'm about to break a fabrication record. "In fact, I thought I heard you two arguing right before you bolted for the door. You looked pretty shaken up about the whole thing." I dart a quick smile.

"Shut up, Skyla," Emily doesn't blink. "It was you who was arguing with her. Everyone here knows how much you hate her and why. No one could blame you for wanting to off Chloe. Not after that DVD she showed everybody—exposing you."

Shit!

Mr. Regional Supervisor returns without invoking the proper suck up greeting from Tad, inquiring on the amenities, was it one flush or two.

"What DVD?" Mom's voice is laden with concern.

"Judas Priest." Tad plucks the napkin from his neckline.

"This isn't X-rated material—is it, Skyla?" Mom's eyes expand the size of dinner dishes.

"Of course it is, Lizbeth," Tad is quick to inform. "Why else would it be a relevant topic of conversation?"

"Is that why Gage left you?" Mom leans in. "You made some bawdy movie of the two of you in secret? Oh God, it was with that old boyfriend—his brother, wasn't it? Tell me you're still a virgin, Skyla." The slight uptick in her voice is enough to halt conversations in a three-table radius.

I shake my head a little. I swore up and down I wasn't going to hammer home the topic anymore. I won't say it, even if she begs me.

My dear, love, you've landed yourself in quite the pickle, Marshall gleams a wicked smile. *Confess your lack of carnal knowledge, and put the fire of indignation out of both your mother's heart and mine.*

"Not on your life," I whisper.

"Knew it." Tad slaps the table so hard every bit of crystal dances to the left. "She admitted it." This pleases him to no end.

Demetri takes a tired breath. "Looks like I have a new lead in the investigation."

My mouth opens to correct them then closes again, and I land an awkward smile at Tad's supervisor who doesn't bother hiding the lascivious look in his eyes.

Shit. Shit. Shit.

My mother's face drips with disappointment.

I'm going to yank Chloe out of the realm of horrors long enough to take myself off the suspect list, then I'm going to behead her myself and push the rest of her right back in.

For damn sure I'm not going in there alone, but which one of these lovelies is going to come with me?

I pin Ellis with a look.

48

Dance the Night Away

Dinner ends with a bang—almost literally. The blond bombshell and Darla try to outdo one another by pawing all over their prospective dates. What with all the climbing and lap sitting, the moaning, the crying out of names, it certainly takes everyone's mind off of me starring in my own tawdry tale. With two live scenes playing out in real time, who cares about my post-production endeavors?

Unlike winter formal, the resort has extended its facilities to the outdoor gardens where a large dance floor is established under the night sky. Dancing has commenced under what theoretically might be a sky full of diamond-like stars but instead of gazing at their beauty a puff of milky air obscures our vision of the infinite expanse.

I watch in disappointment as Ellis slow dances with his favorite new tramp from East. I'd go over and join Mia and Melissa who are busy throwing pennies into a large brimmed fountain, really they should be throwing the Armistead kid in, but as much as I hate to admit it, he seems rather nice and has treated both of my sisters with an equal amount of platonic affection all evening.

My mind keeps rotating back to Gage. I envision us out there on the dance floor next to Ellis and the girl from East he abandoned me for. I can picture him holding me, caressing my back the way only a thoughtful man is capable of. Everything about him exudes nobility, loyalty—something I was fiercely lacking. Then as quickly as I picture him dancing with me, I envision his arms wrapped around some faceless girl. It hurts to imagine him with anybody else. I'm sure he felt the same way about me. My heart is still

expel

tender from the blades of his rejection. I can only imagine the pain I've caused him.

I'm completely unable to wrap my head around what's happened to us.

I take a brisk walk towards a long table filled with pastries. In the middle sits a seven-tiered cake fit for a wedding. I'm sure my mother is drooling over the logistics of such an architectural wonder of a confection.

"May I?" Marshall takes my hand and leads me to the distal end of the dance floor. My mother winks from over Tad's shoulder. She looks like she's busy rocking Tad to sleep so I just go with it. Dancing with my math teacher isn't the biggest sin. And it's Marshall, not my history teacher, the one with the face of a frying pan. I lean my head against his chest and his heart sings. Marshall is divine in every way. I should be eager to fall to his feet—any girl would. But I've already got two hearts I'm desperate to hold onto. Adding a third would be the worst idea possible.

"Nonsense," Marshall darts a mischievous look. "Jock Strap has removed himself, and *chance* removed the Pretty One. I'm fully available for your choosing, or perhaps you prefer the term, 'using'?"

I don't like the way he over annunciated the word chance.

"You did kill Logan." I'm astonished by this.

"No," he whispers. "By the time those bumbling wolves arrived at the scene, West Paragon's finest athletes were virtually drawn and quartered. Someone hungered justice far more efficiently than I that night."

"Remove the binding spirit so I can go back and see who it was." For the first time tonight my heart is racing.

"You know the rules."

"I need a supervising spirit. Be my supervising spirit Marshall," I take a breath and hold it.

"My apologies, love. That is one direction our relationship will not be headed."

279

"Why not? You agreed to supervise while I go in that mirror and yank out Chloe." I give his arms a squeeze. The vibrations that stream from him strangle me with their goodness.

"There's no supervising involved in that matter. Besides, I intend to play another role in your life—as suitor. I cannot do both."

"Tell me then, you already know. Who rammed the Mustang into my boyfriend's belly?"

"Perhaps there are forces at work you know nothing about," he suggests.

"Bullshit."

He looks beyond my shoulder into the bushes. I follow his gaze and see a frazzle of hair the color of fire.

"Ezrina," I hiss.

"Do excuse me, love. I have business to tend to." Marshall stalks off in that general direction.

A bird screams overhead. His cry breaks through the noise of the speakers.

It's Nev.

Something's happening.

The song ends, and another depressingly slow ballad howls into the atmosphere.

Ellis pops up by my side and takes up my hand before I can leave the dance floor.

A few feet away Drake and Brielle sway awkwardly. Brielle's belly protrudes between them like a small planet. From this vantage point it seems quite possible Brielle is having a litter. She'll have an entire row of miniature caskets lining the nursery, a real life Landon cemetery right there in the house. I can only image the howling—the barking at the moon that will take place nightly. I'm secretly hoping they'll shack up at Brielle's.

"Where's your newest acquisition?" I ask.

"Dancing with Daddy," Ellis ticks his head back annoyed. "Daddy likes me."

"Try not to sound so thrilled. The last time I checked that was a good thing. It means he won't chase you down the aisle with a shotgun when the time is right, or wrong."

"Mmm," he doesn't look convinced. "It makes me like her less," he shrugs into his admission.

"If it means something to you, I'm pretty sure Tad doesn't care for you."

"Now we're talking," he gives a twisted grin.

I laugh for the first time in a long while, shifting my gaze back to the bushes where Marshall went Ezrina hunting, only I don't see Marshall or Ezrina—I see...Gage?

I take a sharp breath and hold it.

The image evaporates into shadows and smoke. It must have been a hallucination. Either that or he's harnessed the power to cloak himself in the clouds. Then again Gage is a god—all things are possible. The fact we're living in this real life realm of possibilities together at the same juncture in time is nothing short of a miracle.

"I think I'll need you to help me get Chloe," I whisper, while finding a comfortable resting spot for my head.

"Knew it," he pushes back with surprise. "Where'd you hide the body?"

"Where I always hide the body." I blink a smile. "Nowhere."

"Uh—Skyla?" Ellis looks beyond me towards the ode to flour and sugar, and I turn expecting to see Brielle doing a faceplant in the cheesecake, or Emily emptying a tray of brownies into her purse, but I don't.

I really do see Gage.

"Oh my, God," the words exhaust from my lungs.

He came.

Gage dips into a sultry smile that only he can deliver. He's dressed immaculately in a sharp black suit, a tie the same color as his eyes. His dimples dart in and out as though they were calling me over.

"Sorry, Ellis, I have to go."

He gives a slight nudge, and I glide across the floor. Bodies swirl around me. They turn into a melting pot of color, making it impossible to bustle through the crowd. The music warps to something horrifically slow as though the entire universe were on hold for just a moment. Time elongates, stretches out for days.

So I run.

I push, and pull, and twist through the crowd never taking my eyes off him. I push past the last few stragglers, so close I can almost feel him. His perfect form stands there waiting. He lets me come to him. He waits for me with a knowing look that says so many wonderful things.

I leap up on his waist—wrap my legs around him secure and tight, victorious as an anaconda.

"Please, forgive me," I bleat.

Gage doesn't answer with words. He pulls me in by the neck and shows me exactly how much he forgives me with a scorching kiss that says so much more.

I climb Gage like a pole, send him stumbling backwards until he can't go any further and we fall flat onto the dessert table.

I let out a laugh.

Gage pulls me on top of him and moans into a sea of delicious kisses.

Dishes clatter, the table groans beneath the weight of our affection, a leg collapses, and we slide to the ground. Loud sharp gasps echo through the night.

Gage and I never open our eyes. Our lips never betray their unity.

The cold soft avalanche of a seven-tiered cake falls over us, cushioning us with its whipped vanilla goodness.

I give a gentle laugh at the sight of Gage with frosting dripping off his person, dig my finger into the icing on his cheek and put it in my mouth.

"I missed you terribly," he says it low, serious.

expel

"Oh Gage," my heart picks up again in fear. What if this were all some fluke, and he still wants out of our love?

"Let's go somewhere so we can talk," he presses in with another kiss.

And this time—I try to make it last forever.

49

Whiplash Love

"Skyla!" Judging by Mom's frantic expression, the venue in which Gage and I unwittingly decided to show our undying affection for one another should have probably been reconsidered.

Tad's face has lost all expression. Come to think of it every face staring back at us seems rather depleted of emotion.

Brielle helps me out of the slippery mess, as Gage bounces up by my side.

"Um," I'm dizzy from all of the unwanted attention. Not one person seems even slightly amused. "Sorry," I say, leading Gage by the hand around the congested mass of bodies and ditch into the parking lot by way of the side gate.

"You look amazing," he whispers, spinning me into him.

I take him in. I can't believe he's here—real and in person. His eyes glow, his dimples dance happy to see me.

"So," I sigh, "what brought you here tonight?"

"A very sweet handwritten invitation." Gage draws me in by the hips.

"Are you feeling OK? You're not sick anymore, right?" I ask, dusting cake off his shoulders.

Gage looks and sounds better than ever.

"I'm better now that I'm with you. Let's get out of here. I think we have a lot to talk about."

✺ ✼ ✺

We clean up at the resort and head over to Rockaway Point. My hair is full of frosting, and my dress blotched with

expel

dark stains, but I couldn't care less about what I look like. I'm walking along the black sandy shore of Paragon's most beautiful beach with the love of my life—*Gage* as the bedroom eye moon observes from above.

"I'm so sorry about everything," I whisper. "I don't know what to say or do—but I'd do anything for your forgiveness." I don't mean to knock us off the perch of our newfound happiness. But I owe it to him to grovel and beg forgiveness, now and forever more.

"Giselle stopped by." He wraps an arm around my waist, stills me beneath a stream of moonlight that baptizes us in its glory.

"She did? Did your Mom see her?"

"Not yet. She came to show me a few things. It really helped me understand what was happening." His spirit speaks to me in the quiet, fills in the void of silence as it rouses from its sorrow. "Why didn't you tell me what Dudley was up to?" His eyes try to cover the hurt, but they can't disguise the pain I've caused.

"I don't know. He was showing me things, and..." What do you say when you have no good excuses? "I swear I will never let Marshall touch me again. I don't care if the vision means the world might blow up." Not to mention mine sort of already did.

"I was visited by someone else who helped clear things." He nods into me as though I should confess to knowing who this might be.

"Ellis?" I ask, hopeful. "I swear on all that is holy that I was not doing what it looked like I was doing. I just got out of the Transfer and—"

Gage holds a finger to my lip.

"Giselle took me to the moment—saw the whole thing. Sorry about that," he rubs my open palm with the pad of his thumb.

"So, who helped clear things up for you?" If he says Chloe I'll run straight into the ocean. I'd rather succumb to hypothermia than to anymore of Chloe's dangerous half-truths.

"Logan." His head tilts just a bit as to allude to my guilt in the matter. "He told me why you were keeping his death from me."

I pull Gage in tight and collapse a sea of tears over his already damp shirt. Just hearing him say those words, knowing that they are in every way true, drills my bones with the grief.

"It's OK," he whispers. "Holden won't know what hit him. Logan will be all right. He'll come back to us, I promise."

"You don't hate him?" I say it lower than a whisper. My biggest fear was that I ruined their relationship. After all, I was the knife they plunged in one another's back, over and over.

"I could never hate Logan. And, I could never hate you." The words come out in a puff of smoke, encapsulating us like a cloud with their truths.

"You don't know how glad I am to hear that." I tuck my hands under his shirt and warm them over his skin. You could start a fire with the heat off his body.

"Come here, I want to show you something." Gage leads me over to the monstrous coral tree we've logged some spectacular hours beneath. Its long tangled branches give homage to the night with its delicate crescent blooms radiating overhead like a sea of salmon colored stars.

On the outset everything looks normal but the closer we get I note a hut erected out of branches and palm fronds.

"Oh my, God," I gasp. "Looks like someone's homesteading our land." I heard my father say that once back in L.A. when a film crew came to shoot a segment for a talk show at our neighbor's house. Turns out they secretly lived walled in by clutter for years. They looked so normal on the outside you would never know they were unable to contain the urge to purchase every single thing they laid

expel

eyes on—locked themselves in a sea of debt for stuff they never even took out of the packages.

"It's me," he pauses just shy of the four foot structure. "I've been homesteading our land." He gives a sheepish grin.

"You built this?" I'm fascinated as I duck down inside. It's warm in here, dark but safe from the harsh wind that sends biting sand flying against our skin.

Gage crawls in beside me and pulls me over to his lap.

"Skyla," it expresses from him, soft as a sigh. "I love you with everything in me." He looks down for a moment. "When I saw the DVD, I didn't know what to think. I was devastated."

I curl into him, stifling back tears. I could flood the tiny home with one good cry over the disaster I built with a sea of careless kisses.

"Gage," I look down unable to face him with my shame, "I'm so sorry I hurt you." Gage deserves so much more than words. "Do you think we can start all over?"

"Yes," he says it with a tender calm that assures me this is so. "Believe me, I know that you have a history with Logan. And I know things happen in the future that none of us can help," he gives a lengthy pause. "You don't ever need to feel guilty for having feelings for him. I promise you, there's a reason for them."

I'm dying to know what kinds of reasons, but right now if it doesn't involve me and Gage, I don't want to dig in that direction.

"But I think we need to be upfront with one another about a lot of things," he starts, "I need you to trust me enough to tell me Dudley's true intentions. I have things I want to share with you, too. And if we don't share the little things I don't know how we're ever going to share the big things."

There it is—the caveat to our future success or failure.

"I promise," I hold up a hand. "Everything, and anything you want to know."

"OK." He gives a quick nod. "Logan said you were desperate to see your mother but wouldn't say why."

My stomach lurches.

"I may have promised a certain someone a new trial with the Justice Alliance if she were to give Logan back his life." I hold my breath a second. "He was floating in Liquid Drano, for Pete's sake," I don't mean to come off as defensive, but at the moment that's exactly what I am.

"I would have done the same." His lips twist.

"And, besides, they were her terms not mine. I just wanted Logan back. I didn't for one second think she'd regenerate his body with the wrong soul."

"So what do you think happened?"

"Marshall," I wince. "I spit in his eye—right after accusing him of mowing the two of you down."

Gage shoots a look, sharp as a dagger, out at the raging sea. "How are we going to get Logan back?"

"We're going to have to kill him." My entire person quivers at the prospect of murdering Logan. You know you're in deep when the only way out is a felony-based resolution.

"OK," Gage acquiesces quickly to the morbid reality. "We'll get together this week with my dad and Logan, and figure it all out. Any clue if it was Chloe driving the Mustang?"

I wonder what Gage would do if he knew emphatically that Chloe were responsible—how he would react if he learned she brutally pinned him against a tree while relentlessly whacking into his body—that she killed Logan as a byproduct of her jealous rage.

"Nope."

"I tried moving out of the way," he says in a daze as though he were reliving it. "I tried lifting the hood off me—teleporting my way out of there but I wasn't able. If it was Chloe, she made sure we were left as helpless as possible," his eyes darken with hatred. "What did you do with her?"

"Nothing, I swear." I tell him all about Demetri's room of horrors, the magic mirror that swallowed Chloe and the fact this entire debacle navigated our least favorite detective in my direction. "Anyway, I just asked Ellis to come with me. We're going to pull her out as soon as possible."

"Skyla, do you really believe Marshall is going to play lookout while you dissolve into another realm that sits behind glass?"

"Yes, I totally do. He would never let me get hurt. I swear."

"When are you planning on doing this?"

"I have a key to the estate, so whenever he's off playing house with my mother I'm going to sneak in, or else I'll have to wait all the way until next Saturday."

"Why are we rescuing Chloe again?" Gage is more than disgusted with her, I can tell.

"So I don't get shipped off to prison when Demetri pins her disappearing act on yours truly." I relax into his chest. "Besides, I'm not finished with Chloe Bishop."

The ground beneath us wobbles. The air turns a strange arid blue as it slowly disintegrates the scenery of Rockaway Point to nothing.

I know exactly what this means.

Round two of the faction war.

50

Bay of Pigs

Earth recedes, and the ethereal plane opens up like a yawn. The sky stretches thin, almost luminescent as though it absorbed the beams from the bulbous lavender moon that hangs low enough to touch.

"This is it," I pant. "This is where I came the night of the accident." I pat myself down. "I don't have the disc." I examine the flat cracked ground. A forest beckons to our right, but other than that nothing but miles of weary wasteland.

"You won't need it," Gage assures. "I'd die before I let anything happen to you." He takes me by the hand and darts us into the woods. The clearing we evacuated explodes into a violent torrent of color as a cloud of fire incinerates the land.

"Shit!" I clutch onto him like a life raft.

"We need to keep moving." Gage jogs us deeper into the thicket.

A series of explosions follow us like a warning. Trees ignite one by one like birthday candles. They rain down soot and ashes, filling our lungs with toxic promises.

We land ourselves on a dark hillside as the land begins to tremble. The sound of thousands of hooves trampling in our direction riots through the atmosphere, vibrates over my skin with the intensity of a thousand tiny pinpricks.

Gage scoops me up, levitates us high off the ground just as a carpet of feral hogs, each the size of a small car, rush through the area. Their eyes are red as sirens. Each beast fixates upon me as it passes by. It's like they know I'm here—as if they were after me, specifically.

Gage holds me close to the beautiful dangling moon as the wild herd bruises the ground with its careless charge.

expel

It's humbling being suspended like this, arched between life and death. Strangely, it's in this moment that my love for Gage grows immeasurably. Gage is the eternal lover, rescuer, forgiver, savior. I lean my head into his chest and close my eyes until the sound from below dissipates to nothing.

Gage lands us both soft on the ground, presses a kiss into my forehead to let me know the danger has passed.

A masculine voice howls from behind.

Crawling along a proximal hillside, Ellis lies with his clothes torn, his body awash in blood.

Gage and I race over. His left arm looks dislocated in two places, creating an unnatural stair step with his skin still sheathed over it. My stomach cycles a hot bite of nausea, and I let out a groan at the sight.

I wobble to the ground.

Gage gently pushes my face between my knees and instructs me to take a few deep breaths before heading over to him. "You'll be alright," he says, taking off his shirt and wrapping it around Ellis's neck like a sling. "It's broken, just like that time you tried doing a wheelie on my dirt bike. Remember?" Gage places the disjointed forearm gently into a makeshift sling, eliciting a powerful groan.

"I'm not going to be much help to you," Ellis looks over at me with disappointment.

A series of loud popping sounds come from the other side of the hill. Gage speeds over to a shelf of boulders and looks down into the valley, inspects the other side of this mysterious world before coming back.

"They've got weapons, machetes, guns that I've never seen before with darts flying out of them. There's a mass of injured bodies. I saw two flat out evaporate."

"What does that mean?" I pant, scooting into Ellis. Clearly we're the weaker vessels.

"I think it means they're dead," Gage swallows hard at the thought. "Look, there's got to be some kind of instruction on what to do—how to get out of this place. Why don't you two get up over to that hedge, take cover in the bushes in case there's another stampede. I'll run down the hill and talk to somebody see if I can figure out what the hell is going on."

Ellis and I move like turtles. Every muscle aches, every step feels lethargic and heavy like walking underwater.

"Something's wrong," I say, ready to pass out by the time we hit the overgrown shrub Gage suggested we cower under.

Ellis pulls me in with his free hand, and we crawl into an alcove that faces the meadow below.

"Oh my, God," I can't breathe. Bodies in piles, faces masked in agony. A fresh black circle blooms across the vicinity as another explosion goes off.

Ellis and I are perched above the casualties like a bunch of first world spectators watching from the peanut gallery.

I feel horrible. I should be down there fighting with my people.

"There he is." Ellis tracks Gage with his finger. He's at least a mile away speaking with a man as tall as a telephone pole, his hair a burnished red that glows in the haze.

A loud clap detonates from behind.

Ellis pulls me to my feet and we race downhill towards Gage. A fire line erupts at our back, the shrub we were nestled in already reduced to cinders.

Gage sprints over at supernatural speeds. "We need to leave." He doesn't bother with an explanation, simply takes up my hand and leads us back over the hill from where we came.

"Skyla!" My name howls from a ridge in the distance. I try to stop but Gage doesn't let go or slow down. I try to tell him to pause for a moment, decrease his speed, but I can't catch my breath. My fingers dislodge from his grip, and I cease all movement as he and Ellis roll on ahead before trotting to a stop.

It's Logan—Holden actually, calling my name. He's on the outer-banks, furthest from the hillside reduced to ashes. He's holding a crossbow, waving at me with the other arm.

"This is for you!" His voice carries like a warped melody. He draws back the bow and fires a series of flaming arrows into a crowd of victims lying helpless on the ground. Each arrow combusts into a powder keg explosion, powerfully wild—destructive as dynamite.

"No," I whisper.

Gage clasps his fingers around mine and tugs me along.

"There's a lake on the other side of the forest," he pants. "We need to get through it to reach region three." His chest rises and falls spastic with each word.

"How do we know for sure?" I shout over the bombs going off in the distance. "What if it's a trap?"

"There's a man in charge. He says he's an orator. He knew my name and told me where to go."

We tread on for miles, exhausted, bone tired—the skin on my face slick from the strange atmosphere, thick as oil.

"I can't," I say, too tired to finish the sentence.

"You don't have to." Ellis nods in front of us.

The forest gives the illusion of dropping off to nothing. We trek over carefully. A steep narrow trail leads to a beautiful expanse filled with wild flowers that glow in the night, writhe in the breeze like cattails. The air is thinner here, the heavy scent of lavender perfuming the atmosphere. In the center of this fairylike garden lies a shimmering body of water with moonlight dancing across in a river of brilliance.

"Dammit," Gage stares out at the far end of the lake where four bodies dive into the water one by one.

"That was Nat," I say. I'd recognize those rusty curls anywhere. "Probably Pierce, and Holden—maybe the fourth was Chloe?"

Gage doesn't bother analyzing the situation. Instead, he leads us down to the base and shouts for us to jump in.

"Then what?" I scream, trying to keep pace with the two of them.

"Swim to the center," Gage instructs. "Swim to the bottom. It's the only way to secure the region."

We race into the icy waters. Gage takes up my hand as we struggle to swim down further and further. I open my eyes and try to make sense of this murky world bubbling by—try to make sense of the fact the bottom of the lake holds the key to winning anything.

Ellis tugs on my hand, slits his throat with his finger and floats back to the top.

I can't do this either.

My lungs burn from the effort. The urge to inhale a lungful of water is outweighing my desire to win the region.

Gage pulls me down deeper, faster. My Celestra strength—it's gone, fully diminished. Everything in me is weak as paper.

A thousand glowing eyes ignite the murky depths. The feral pigs, the sodden hogs that trampled Ellis, appear. They were here, waiting. This was a trap. Hooves on my back, my head, my legs pinned down heavy as stones.

Can't breathe.

Must take a breath.

Water fills my mouth.

This secretive underwater world loses its shape, all of its texture.

The color disappears—then so do I.

51

Get It on Like That

My chest explodes with the urge to cough, instead, a warm stream of water vomits from my mouth. Gage turns me over, gently pumps his fist into my stomach in an effort to drain more lake water out of my body. I cough and sputter until I'm able to sit up.

"We're back," I marvel. Back in the little hut Gage built for us right here on Rockaway Point. An icy breeze pushes overhead, rattles the dried fronds like skeletal remains. "Ellis," I say, gagging on his name.

Gage puts in a call, nods and says sporadic words that don't clue me in at all to his condition.

"He says he was dancing, the next thing he knew he fell off a table and broke his arm," Gage raises his brows.

"Nice move, Mother," I whisper. "So what happened? Did we win the region?"

"No." Gage shakes his head. "I left out a few facts."

"What?" I'm stunned Gage would omit an all-important detail.

"The orator said, once we touched the bottom we'd have to swim through to the other side."

"We couldn't have done it," I shake my head. "It was too deep. I lost my strength."

"I had mine," Gage examines me. "Do you think that's a part of your punishment? Having your powers revoked in the ethereal plane?"

"God, I hope not. If it weren't for you, I could never have gotten away from that stampede." I take a deep breath. "Come to think of it—my mother did say something about my punishment for going against the Faction Council would be doled out in phases during the war. I'll talk to Marshall and beg for a meeting with my mother." A thought occurs to me. "You know, when I was in the Transfer, Ezrina said the only way out was to run as fast as I could. I ran full speed into the side of a cliff and ended up the base of Devil's Peak."

He leans back onto his hands and considers this a moment.

"We could have done it, Skyla. Somebody did."

"You see anything when you were down there?"

"I saw the rocks, they were lit from the inside—glowing. The entire bottom of the lake looked like it was on fire," he shrugs. "Then we appeared here."

"Something tells me we have a lot to learn," I lament as a swirl of fog rolls in through the makeshift opening. "What about Chloe?"

"Tomorrow is Sunday," Gage nods. "Demetri never misses church. I'll pick you up at eight?"

"Sounds like a date."

A lustful gleam ignites in his eyes as he offers a seductive smile.

"But we're here now," he whispers it out husky.

"Alone," I add, tilting into him.

"God, I missed you, Skyla," he breathes out the words while pulling me in.

I reach over and unbutton his shirt, take it off his person and drink him in like this. Gage is perfectly sculpted, a testament to the glory of the human body.

He pulls me down, lays over me as we collapse in a pool of warm kisses. I run my fingers around the rim of his pants, slip my hands inside the back of his boxers. Gage carefully pulls my dress over my hips, crests my shoulders before tossing it aside in a heap. We roll in the sand with nothing but the sound of the ocean crashing to earth outside our makeshift door. It's heaven like this, with my skin pressed hot against his. We share fierce kisses that burn brighter than any star in the universe.

expel

I have my forever back, my beautiful gorgeous Gage, and there's not a thing that will ever keep us apart again.

When I finally arrive home, I find that Mom and Tad still aren't back from Althorpe's mandatory celebration.

I shower the sand off my body and put on my comfy clothes. As soon as I turn out the lights, Logan illuminates the room a beautiful cobalt blue that rejuvenates my energy just looking into his aura.

"Skyla," his teeth glow like a row of tiny suns. His flesh forms. He's wearing the same t-shirt and jeans over and over. I suppose laundry really isn't an issue once you've stopped existing on a material level. "I heard about the war—I'm still proud of you. You did good."

"I did lousy. Too bad you couldn't fight."

"I was there in body." He winces because we both know Holden was a liability.

"We lost." I head over and wrap my arms around him for an immeasurable span of time.

Sorrow pours from his spirit, nothing but walled-in dejection, overflowing grief.

We head up to the butterfly room and close the entry behind us. It's bliss like this, entombed within its solemn beauty, the paper wings flapping with our slightest movement.

"Thank you for talking to Gage." I pick up both his hands and warm them with mine. Logan feels real in every way, but his scent is gone, his essence is all that truly remains. "You helped him see everything."

"It was time." A depleted smile comes and goes. "He was better, and I couldn't bear seeing the two of you in so much pain."

"Logan." I scoot in until our knees are touching. "If there's supposed to be a purpose in all things, what do you think was the purpose of you dying?"

"There's not," he's quick to answer. "Some things play out because of Man's carnal desires—his foolishness. It wasn't my time. I can come back."

"Apparently, it's never Holden's time. It's clear he's going to ruin my life as long as I'm still sucking air on this planet."

"I don't know about that," Logan rumbles a soft laugh. "But I'm coming back," he assures. "That I can promise."

"It's because of what you saw in the future, isn't it? That's how you know." I offer an anemic smile. I hope he's right. Gage thought he and I would marry in a courthouse, and all that really happened was we found ourselves at the receiving end of an exasperated judge.

"Gage plays a role in your future, Skyla." Logan tugs at my hand.

To hear Logan say it, see the words form on his lips, sinks my heart like a stone on fire. Ironic, since Gage reassured me just hours before there was a reason I had feelings for Logan.

"And you?" I ask. Somehow he seems convinced of both.

Logan searches the outer reaches of the room, traces the walls with his eyes like a lion trapped in his own den.

"I was at the dance tonight," he sighs.

"Marshall was there. I thought you were on a supervised time out where he was concerned?"

"The vicinity," he acknowledges. "I watched from the sky. When they said the sky was the limit they were lying." He gives a passive attempt at a smile. "I saw everything," it comes out despondent. He soaks in my features, gives a slow blink as if he were savoring them. "I want what you and Gage have." He seals his gaze over me, galvanizing his love in this strange sentiment that would have seemed so crazy last summer when he had me completely. "I don't want it with anyone else but you, Skyla."

There are no words to comfort him with, not one simple phrase that will make it all go away.

Logan pulls me over and we sit there with his arms around me staring at the colored tissue wings freckling the walls.

"Remember when we sat here last summer? You asked what we had to do to be together." Logan tightens his embrace around my shoulder.

I nod. "I asked what we had to do, and you said take down the Counts."

"And you said, that's what we'll do," he whispers, sad, forlorn.

"Then you pledged your allegiance to them," I whisper. Our love proved nothing more than a tragic roadmap.

"I tried to save us," he sighs. "And I will. All we need is a little magic—and a miracle or two."

Logan holds out his hand and waves it like a magician before interlacing our fingers again.

The butterflies shiver and flutter. The room livens with the rumple, and one by one they exchange their waxed wings for real ones—each becomes their own unique creation as they fly around the room.

It's magic, a miracle—the exact two things Logan is counting on to save our relationship.

52

Deus Ex Machina

Sunday morning I force myself to shower and get dressed, still sapped of energy from the ethereal plane the night before.

Mom is already downstairs when I amble into the kitchen. She's fully dressed in a white silk pantsuit with enough gold bejeweling her body to arouse a Pharaoh right out of his tomb—hell *all* of them. But I'm well aware the only false deity she's trying to stimulate is Demetri.

"How did it go last night?" Her eyes widen with anticipation.

Tad steps up to the counter and plunks down his mug. "As long as a video camera wasn't rolling, I'd say it went more than well." He glares openly at me. "Are you aware of the fact that boy you brought to the party turned into a drunken mess and toppled off a table? He had to leave on a gurney, which, by the way was the second most peculiar exit of the evening. Do you realize no one ate cake?" His skin changes so many violent shades of purple it's alarming to watch.

"Gage talked with Ellis last night. He's going to be OK, no surgery or anything," I assure them. "He's getting it set in a cast later today, and sorry about the cake." It was French vanilla—the raspberry filling was to die for. I bring my fingers to my lips, still warm with the memory of eating cake off Gage's flesh. It's the only way to do it.

"So is everything OK with the two of you?" Her eyes swell with emotion for me. Mom wants Gage in our lives as much as I do.

"Everything went great." I flick my ring in the air advertising the fact our forever brand of love, lives on.

expel

"I'm so happy for you," she swoons. "When you find that perfect person, you should never let go. Fate could step in," her eyes darken a sodden shade of moss. "You could end up with the entirely wrong person due to time and chance, and miss out on an incredible love story that could have really taken you places." She loses herself, gazing out at the powder white fog pressed against the window.

Dear God, she means Demetri.

I'm horrified by this.

"That's right," Tad wraps an arm around her shoulder. "And in less than a month we're giving it all we've got, one more time."

"I'm taking the girls to the mall this week," Mom doesn't even acknowledge Tad's prideful boast. "Let me know when you're free. I'll help you shop for spring break."

"Thanks!" I hop up on the balls of my feet at the prospect of a new bikini. "So you guys are really OK with Cain River?"

"We're more than OK," Tad picks up his cup of coffee and salutes me. "We're going with you."

✺ ✼ ✺

I sulk to Gage all the way over to Demetri's. There is nothing more embarrassing to haul to spring break than your parents. In fact, they are the completely wrong accessories to lug just about anywhere.

Tad surprised Mom with the chaperoning gig as a gift—an early second honeymoon. There are so many things wrong about conducting a honeymoon in a camp laden with teenagers—me being one of them. I don't even know where to begin.

"You probably won't even run into each other." Gage gives the hint of a wicked smile. "I'm pretty sure on our honeymoon we won't be leaving the room."

A searing bite of lust rips through my abdomen at the thought of honeymooning with Gage.

"For like a month," I add, biting down a smile.

Gage raises his brows, flashes the lamplight of his teeth before continuing. "Besides, we hardly ever see staff, they specifically try to stay out of our way." Gage reaches over and squeezes my knee in an effort to comfort me. "And, yeah, a month sounds perfect. We should make it two just to be safe."

"We're going to have a lifetime," I bring his hand up to my mouth and kiss it, run my lips over the hills and valleys of his knuckles while taking in his clean scent. A bloom of sadness awakens in me for Logan. How does Logan squeeze into a lifetime of happiness with Gage? I try to shake the thought of him out of my head by changing the subject. "You know who never stays out of my way?" I ask. "Marshall. He specifically tries to *get* in my way. Speaking of which, he's hosting some island-wide garage sale."

"What gives?" Gage wraps the truck around the back of the estate. Demetri's mansion is daunting to look at from this angle. It rises from the ground like a monolithic skyscraper.

"No clue. Says he's going to give all the money raised to the Community Center."

"Is he planning on selling anything?" Gage squints into the idea.

"Don't know." Just the thought of him peddling his haunted trinkets sends a shiver through me. "Talked to Ellis this morning. He's pretty bummed he couldn't be here. He actually asked if I needed help hiding the body."

"When I heard Chloe was missing that was the first thing that ran through my mind," Gage gives a devious smile. "Figured you'd have it taken care of though." He leans over and presses in a supple kiss that sends a mean shiver through me. "I died everyday without you, Skyla."

expel

My stomach swims with the rhythm of his voice. I pull him in and share a deep kiss that has the power to ignite the two of us into a Molotov worthy explosion. There's something more profound than lust here, something stronger than puppy love, or infatuation. We sit for a small eternity fogging up the windows with the heat from our desire.

"We'd better go if we want to get out in time," Gage pants the words in a whisper.

Somewhere, Chloe is smiling for interrupting yet another exhilarating moment between Gage and me.

"It's time to unleash the witch back into the wild," I say, getting out of the truck.

One thing is for damn sure, if I were ever to make Chloe Bishop disappear for good, I wouldn't leave any tracks to follow. I would be the last person Demetri would want to investigate.

And that's exactly what I plan on doing one day soon.

✹ ✹ ✹

Demetri's grandfather's abode is more than a little freaky with no one around. Of course, Gage is with me, but even with the two of us, it seems isolative, exceptionally strange, like walking around in a museum after closing time.

I lead Gage upstairs to the entry that's now conveniently sealed over.

"I'm pretty sure this is it," I say, patting down the wall like a thief.

"How are we going to get in?" Gage takes pictures of the wall, the hallway. He documents our every footstep.

"There might be another way." I lead us down to the library.

The elongated rows of spines sit up at attention, all on good behavior in our honor. The opening at the far end still exists, but it's reduced to half its size. As it is, I'll barely be able to squeeze on through.

"I won't fit," Gage tries to push his shoulder in but his chest can't clear the opening. "There's a binding spirit I can't teleport."

I take in a breath and press myself to the other side. The narrow space irons out my stomach as I slide back out towards Gage.

"I'll go in by myself," I say it weak. The thought of hopping into an alternate universe all by my lonesome doesn't really appeal to me.

"Get Dudley," Gage is resigned to the fact this is going to happen.

I send a quick text to Marshall. At the Althorpe dinner, he did offer to play lookout while I crawled inside to get Chloe.

"What are you going to do?" I pull Gage in by the waist.

"I'll wait here—read a book," he pulls a wry smile. "I'm not taking my eyes off that mirror. I'll give you fifteen minutes before I tear down the walls and come in after you."

"I'll be quick." I land a kiss on his lips before squeezing into the Fem memorial. I decide to wait until Marshall shows before actually diving into an alternate dimension.

I pause at the gilded frames that encase pictures of unsuspecting victims right before a surprise Fem attack. An entire shelf dedicated to the candid eerie photos. I pick one up of some guy walking on the beach and shake it just the way I saw Chloe doing the day she disappeared.

"Oh my, God," I take a quick breath.

It moves—morphs into some kind of miniature television. I watch in horror as a boy around my age is attacked by three menacing creatures. One of the Fems has his entire face buried in an unnaturally full beard, the body of a bovine, arms like a man but far too long, cloven hoofed feet. The second is a panther-like creature with hind legs of a bear, and the third a bloodied clown. I turn away when the

expel

panther mauls the side of the poor victims head, his face peeling off like a mask. I place the picture back on the shelf in haste. The clown twists his neck abruptly and looks right at me. He gives an eerie grimace as though he knew who I was, as if he remembered me.

"Have you ever entertained the phrase, do not touch?" Marshall whispers from over my shoulder. He's transparent in nature, and I assume this is to keep Gage from ogling him as if he didn't already know who Marshall really was. "You've aroused an entirely new form of ill will upon yourself. Which one have you called," he muses, inspecting the frame I just set down. "Ah, yes, the clown, you must be loathing the fact you ever laid a finger on him. Do refrain from such pleasures in the future. Come, Love," he ushers me towards the mirror. "In and out, we've got a date this afternoon."

"We most certainly do not have a date this afternoon," I correct. "I'm back with Gage. I'm spending the day with him."

"Very well—Jock Strap, the Pretty One, even the Chemically Deluded one can join our reindeer games. It matters not, the faction war waits for no one."

"So you heard?"

"Two for two," he says with heated violence. "There's no getting around what I must do with you later. How can I make this anymore clear? My day job depends on it." He traps me with those copper eyes and holds me in a masterful gaze that both reprimands and beckons. "I have a meeting in a quarter of an hour."

"What if I'm not back by then?"

"You will be," and with that he gives me a powerful shove right through the oval framed mirror.

🦋 🦋 🦋

I land flat on my back in the trophy chamber of horrors—same one I came from with the exception everything here is in reverse order. I drift into the hall and the décor takes a drastic downturn in both quality and character. Gone is the gilt and stone, replaced with plaid carpeting, oak paneling with pictures of Chloe and her family lining the walls. I walk slow and steady from frame to frame. So freaking bizarre.

Downstairs it looks homier than the house in its original state, kitsch—something about it resonates ordinary people, or should I say humans.

A garish wall slaps me in the face with its questionable décor.

I take it all back. This is neither ordinary nor human.

Twin paintings—colossal in size—eat up half the living room wall, emitting their prideful effigies. The first one is of Chloe in a black strapless gown, a simple string of pearls bisect her neck. There's enough cleavage to warrant an R rating. The canvas stretched by its side is a picture of Brody donning his football uniform from West. A helmet and a face guard are planted square on his head, which I find almost unsettling. It's as if Chloe was allowing her brother into her fantasy but under her own terms.

So, I get it, I think. Chloe and her family live here now.

The scuttle of heels clip clop in my direction and a body crashes into me from around the corner.

"Skyla?" It's Brielle. She's thinner, obviously without child, but there's something off about her in addition to that.

"What are you doing here?" I take her in, she's wearing full French maids regalia, only it's not nearly as hot as the one Gage picked out for me at Halloween. It's more of a cross between a nurse and a nun.

"Working," she says, annoyed. "I was just getting ready to hand wash Chloe's cheer uniform. She's the best cheerleader that West has ever seen."

Honest to God, I half expected her to laugh or roll her eyes but she stands there solemn as though she had just spouted off the pledge of allegiance.

I'm a little miffed by the display of robotic attention. I'm not sure what the rules are, but it's obvious the 'best cheerleader ever' has the ability to manipulate them.

"Where's Chloe?"

"She's in the viewing room," she points down the hall. "But you can't disturb her, she's with Gage." Brielle gives a challenging look as if it should mean something.

"Gage?" Shit. "Oh, I won't disturb them," I assure, speeding down the hall. I plan on calmly collecting Chloe and getting the hell out of Dodge.

I open door after door until I come upon a small hallway with a giant framed picture on the wall of Chloe staring out at a pale fog of light, the word *Matinee* printed just beneath.

I don't hesitate opening the door. It's dark, and the air is stopped up with the heavy scent of popcorn. The carpeted walls clot the sound of my footsteps as I fast approach the end of the long dark corridor. A wall-sized screen blazes away with a flickering seizure of color. It's a freaking movie theatre, loud as one, too.

I peer around the dividing wall, stealth as a sniper, and to my horror I see Chloe sticking her tongue down some poor guys throat. They're indulging in one serious flesh-fest with an intense vigor that sets off a primal alarm in me. I recognize that glossy black hair, those strong arms stretched over her like a canopy.

Oh shit.

That's what she's doing with Gage?

I pluck her off his body so fast her wild-eyed expression clues me in on the fact, I'm the last person on the planet she expected in this fornicating fantasy.

Gage snatches my arm, and I pause, examining him. I marvel at the details, every last whisper of his being is in place. What an immaculate replica. This doppelganger is like Gage in every way, right down to his perfect lips, the woodsy scent of his cologne.

I smack him in the chest before dragging Chloe out. She bucks and writhes in an attempt to liberate herself from my vice-like grip. She claws and kicks all the way upstairs. It takes all of my Celestra strength to keep her from launching the two of us over the railing. Even if Chloe did manage to off herself in this delusional world, I'd totally drag her body back to Paragon, leave her to rot in Demetri's dungeon until the bumbling detective came upon her carcass.

"Let go." She pushes me off as we land in the library.

"You have to come back." I block the exit with my body.

"Did I miss All States?" She pants from the struggle. Funny, the only thing she asks about is some stupid competition, doesn't even bother inquiring about her mother, her frantic father who swore on television this ordeal was shaving ten years off the backend of his life—the friends she left behind, not that she has any.

"We leave in less than a week."

"Perfect." Chloe heads over to the mirror willingly and crawls on through.

The world around me disintegrates, evaporates into a blue expanse of nothing, arid like the sky on a perfect L.A. day.

I make a beeline over to the mirror before it completely disappears.

Something tells me I've just found a way to make Chloe do just that, forever.

53

I Do?

A staffing emergency arose at the bowling alley, and Gage had to fill the void. I offered to cancel our faction-centered play date with Marshall but he wouldn't hear of it.

"I promise to knee him in the balls if he tries to kiss me," I say, leaning over and pressing my lips into Gage like some silent impassioned plea for him to stay.

"I promise to do the same if he tries to kiss you." He looks through the windshield over at Marshall's sprawling estate. "I'll see if I can't get someone to cover the shift. Either way, call me when you're ready. I'll swing by and pick you up."

"Done." I get out and wave as Gage rounds his way out of the circular driveway—his black truck a perfect silhouette against the dull of afternoon.

Each day Paragon produces the same grey taffy world. It pulls out forever, entombs us in a cloudbank as if we had risen in the sky. I miss the sunshine back in L.A.—the dapples of light that burst unexpectedly into the house, the splash of warmth over the carpet where Mia's old dog would curl up and take his naps. I miss the stamp of nature's design over my back as I sat beneath a tree, lost in a book, robed in glorious light.

I ring the bell and wait for Marshall to show. He mentioned he had a meeting to attend, regarding the faction war. The last time he was there he spent his time defending me to the celestial higher-ups, which apparently included God himself. Marshall was totally in a foul mood when he returned, and I expect nothing less today.

The door flies open, a winded Marshall sweeps his hand for me to step inside.

"Skyla," he breathes my name in one lusty whisper. "Don't be hindered, please, come in," he gives an awkward smile, pants like a lapdog as he devours me with his eyes.

I can't figure out his heady grin, or the fact he's becoming more inebriated by my presence with each passing moment. Instead, I maneuver past him, ignoring his strange behavior.

"Please take a seat," he offers, as I'm about to plant myself on the couch. "May I offer you a drink? A meal perhaps? " His eyes widen. He's absorbing me, memorizing my nuances, the exact interpretation of my being, savoring it for later. He whisks his eyes over me as if I were royalty. "Would you be more comfortable with your feet up?" He retrieves a damask pillow from the corner and places it beside me.

"No, thank you." I try to assess the stupid grin blooming on his face but it's no use. "What the hell is wrong with you?" I say in the nicest way possible.

"I've just heard the words I've been longing to hear," his chest heaves, his eyes still magnetically locked over mine. "It's true. All I've ever wanted. It's been granted."

"Great," I shrug. I can't imagine what Marshall would possibly crave, hunger for so deeply that it could make him act like a five year old on Christmas morning. "A new longbow?" I take a stab at the subject matter.

He winces at the prospect of such absurdity. "No, love, material goods mean nothing." He falls to his knees before me and caresses my cheek. "It's you Skyla, you'll become my wife one day."

I try to convince Marshall there is no way his so-called *friend* got the prediction right as he leads me into the forest behind his house for the lesson in question.

"Delphinius is an orator," he says it with nod. "Makes my visions look like discernments from a Magic 8 Ball. He's an accurate source, I assure you."

This is probably going to play out like Gage's vision in the courthouse, leaving Marshall disappointed and me gloating because I was right. I can guarantee we will never marry. I'd say it out loud but I have a feeling it would kick off our ode to weaponry on the wrong foot.

Marshall plucks something up from behind a noble fir and carries it over to me, looks like a bow on steroids.

"Projectile weaponry at its finest—crossbow." He positions it over me and plucks an arrow from his quiver. "Far more practical for the terrain you'll be battling in."

"Lots of hills," I say, closing one eye trying to focus my arm on a target painted over a Red Alder not too far in the distance.

"Relax," he whispers. He stands behind me, nestling my body in his as he holds my arms in position. His lips touch my ear, and my skin quivers with the energy of a million tiny electrical impulses.

"No kissing," I puff the words into the fog. "I promised Gage I'd knee you in the balls if you tried."

"I believe the terms of your agreement were more in line with doling out a punishment—if I were successful." He touches his cheek to mine before dipping down to my neck and inhaling my scent.

"Marshall," I reprimand. I might have to knee him anyway for being so insolent.

"A stolen kiss might be worth the infliction," his lips curve with seduction. He takes my breath away without trying. "You realize I'm immune to pain."

Actually I forgot about that.

I look him over, his blessed by God features, his larger than life character that exudes an unearthly charisma. Being married to Marshall would be like falling into a supernova.

I'd be swallowed up and blinked out of existence before I knew what hit me.

"Not true." He doesn't bother hiding the fact he's reading my mind. "I will lift you up before me each day—our nights filled with such passion you'll ache in the interim for my touch to return." He squeezes his hand over mine before locking another arrow into position.

"Will there be chocolate?" I let go of the arrow and watch as it spirals through the air like a lame duck.

"Always," he pushes himself hard against my back as we launch an aggressive assault on the poor sapling we've set our sights on.

"You didn't happen to see your future mother-in-law at that meeting today, did you?" May as well milk the effort.

"Yes, the hormonal carp was present."

"Marshall!"

"She blew me a new one, as you would say."

"She *ripped* you a new one," I correct. "The word blow has an entirely different meaning. I suggest you remove it from your lexicon."

"Observed." He lifts the crossbow from off my shoulder and places it at his feet. "Skyla, you must be the victor of the next region and every one after that."

"I want to. It's not like I'm trying to fail," I look over at the plethora of arrows scattered just shy of the bulls eye and nary an arrow where it should be. The crimson blotch against the pale tree trunk mocks me with its unblemished stain.

"I mentioned your predicament with Ezrina."

"Thank you," I want to lunge at Marshall with a hug but restrain myself in fear Chloe has her demonic minions recording our every move.

"She's declined to see you," he gives a wistful smile.

"I suppose you'll offer to mediate in exchange for saliva."

"No such transaction is necessary." Marshall is cold as stone. "I would do anything for the mother of my child. But first, we have someone else to see."

54

Body Snatcher

The Transfer is tempered with cold sterile walls, the icy blue steel that glows off stainless counters. Each footstep produces a strange echo as we navigate the maze that comprises its corridors.

Marshall holds my hand, and I let him. We are, after all, in some viral version of hell, albeit free from suffering humans and devoid of fire—nevertheless, the demon that is Ezrina resides on the premises. This is her home, her throne, her lair.

"Can I see Logan after?" I bounce into my words like a child begging her father for a treat at the amusement park.

"Absolutely not."

"Why?"

"For one, he's dead. I believe it's time you let dead bygones be bygones, the operative word being gone. You have Jock Strap to fill the interim before we physically acquaint ourselves."

"So, I *will* be with Gage." A swell of relief fills me. "And, no Logan?" A spiral of grief rips through my insides. I thought for sure we had some kind of future.

"I'm not here to play fill in the blanks—see who'll warm my wife's bed in time and memoriam. Those are your affairs until we've sealed our union."

We step into a bulbous shaped room with a domed ceiling and light fracturing off the metallic furniture at strange apertures. I've never seen this room before. There's something spiritual, satanic perhaps about the sharp angles, the dome with a cutout window that bleeds in the dark of night.

expel

Ezrina sits patiently glossing over a book, her finger tracing out the lines as she reads them. Her hair is unruly, defying gravity with its wiry shag, her face deformed in horrific breaks with large pillow-like bags exploding beneath each eye. Poor Nev. This for sure isn't the shell of the woman he fell in love with. I wonder if what's inside is still the same? I can't imagine. I've never met anyone as abrasive as Ezrina, well, maybe Chloe.

"You come with news?" She slams the cover over her finger without extricating her hand.

"I come with Skyla, young lady," he says.

God, Marshall even flirts with Ezrina. His philandering knows no bounds. If he keeps this up he's going to make a lousy husband, and I refuse to believe it'll be to me.

Something about the gold relief work on the window frame reminds me of that haunted mirror. It has a similar pattern of long dripping leaves, acorns as accents.

"By the way," I say, briefly ignoring the fact Ezrina is in the room ready to disrobe my spirit. "You gave that magic mirror to Demetri as a gift?" I'm confounded by this.

"Indeed," he bows into me with pride.

"What kind of gift is that? It lets you go in and imagine yourself in the lap of luxury? To have desired people and places at your disposal?"

"Yes," he nods, shocked by my negative reaction. "He would have had the world at his feet as he always dreamed, thus it is referred to as the Realm of Possibilities."

I groan. "That's a cruel gift Marshall."

"Why in heaven's name is that?" He ticks his head back, genuinely perplexed.

"Because it lets you live a lie."

"It's nothing more than a fantasy, Skyla. It just so happens it contains flesh and bone and feeling. If I could mass market the device, your society would lose its every inhabitant. It's a novelty humans would gleefully trade their realities for."

"That may be so, but it's wrong. Chloe was *touching* Gage, and for your information, Gage doesn't want her anywhere near him."

"Skyla," he gives a long blink, holding back a laugh. "Men admire you from afar. They memorize your features while you patiently wait for your lattes, while you cheer with your limbs so freely exposed. They save the image for later with carnal intentions—nothing more than a fantasy. I can't say one is more wrong than the other. Even so, the mirror exists. I gave that incorrigible Fem more than a mind's eye view of what the universe would be like if he controlled it. He could have lived within the safety of its confines if he so wished. The only difference between the mirror and his decision to remain in reality was his own greed."

Ezrina comes over and touches my neck with the back of her gnarled hand. "Beauty," the word gurgles from her. "You failed, Skyla." She feigns a look of sadness.

"No," I shake my head backing up from her touch. "My mother, she's just difficult to get a hold of. I'm going to get you that new trial."

"Skyla," Marshall whispers in defeat.

"I will," I sharpen my tone. "I swear it!"

Ezrina comes to me, faster, more aggressive. I circle around Marshall before jumping spontaneously in his arms and burying my face in his chest.

"Logan lives," her bloodstained lips crack the words out. She grabs a fistful of my hair at the base of my neck, pulls my head back with a violent jerk. Ezrina hangs over me like a boulder. Her mouth opens, and a stream of white light pours out into mine before I can think to seal my lips. The room changes diameter, I'm falling, stretching. I land upright in front of Marshall staring down at a waif of a girl, long golden hair, encased in surreal beauty like that of a fairytale.

"No!" I scream.

My voice echoes for miles.

expel

"How in God's name do you justify this?" I ask Marshall as we stand outside the Transfer watching Ezrina, well, me, run as fast as she can into a sheer granite wall. A blue aura spasms around her body just before she disappears.

"This will quell her for now—buy you more time to remove yourself from the covenant you're embroiled in. Let this be a lesson, never cavort promises with celestial beings that you have no intention of keeping. I'm repeating myself in the event you're unaware."

"I had every intention of keeping that promise. It was my mother who was unwilling." Everything in me wants to cry but apparently Ezrina is hardwired not to—just speaking feels as though I've moved a boulder with my teeth. Ezrina's flesh is an iron cage two sizes too small.

"Then let me rephrase—refrain from entering into sacred pacts, when you have no authority. Your mother is anxious to see you, by the way."

"Now you tell me?" I resist the urge to hack him to pieces. "No," it stamps out of me.

"No?"

"That's right. My terms—my way. She wasn't there when I needed her and I plan on returning the favor."

"It's regarding the faction war."

"The war?" I gag on the thought. "You have to get Ezrina out of my body. She's beyond dangerous. She'll probably go on a hacking spree from the sheer bloodlust of it all and chop up all the wrong people. And what about Gage?" The thought of her touching his body, those lips, nauseates me.

"The war can't be fought without you, Skyla. You're the guest of honor. And I wouldn't worry too much about your precious Gage. I'm sure after a few romantic sessions he'll be quite aware."

"A *few*?" I gasp. "How long do I have to live like this?" I ask, walking through the cobbled streets of this strange underworld. Every step in Ezrina's flesh feels like rigor mortis is about to set it—like being stuck in a rusted suit of armor.

"Two weeks," he sidesteps in the event I should swing at him.

"Two *weeks*?" I knew he'd make a lousy husband. "She'll ruin my life in two weeks!"

"She knows your routine inside and out. Ezrina maintains she will be on her best behavior. Do you realize this is her only respite since her arrival over a century ago?"

"What am I? A day spa?! If you expect me to feel sorry for Ezrina, you are sadly mistaken. What Nev ever saw in her is beyond me," I wince as a trail of foreign sounds escape my lips—they echo in triplicate into the fields. Ironically, I do feel bad for Ezrina, only now I'm less apt to verbalize it since she hijacked my body. "Fix this Marshall. If I am ever going to be your wife, you will get me out of this situation far sooner than two week's time."

"You have her powers, Skyla. You can travel to Paragon, observe, become invisible, terrorize at random. Think of the entertaining possibilities."

An image of Gage burns through my mind. He could never love me like this. I wouldn't even make him try.

A black wrought iron fence catches my attention in the distance. The white mansion impresses itself into the dark expanse.

Logan.

I push past Marshall without so much of a goodbye.

Something tells me this is going to be the longest two weeks, ever.

55

Master Disaster

I ditch Marshall and speed over to the haunted mansion, the prize jewel of the Transfer, in search of my favorite dearly departed ex-boyfriend.

I'm surprised to find that the inside of the estate does, in fact, mirror Demetri's palatial replica. However, the color palette is in complete contrast, and the piano banging replaces the hollow sound of footsteps. Long strands of gossamer drape like curtains from the corners, the dust riddled chandeliers drip with melting wax. The cold dank air is dressed with a musty scent that reminds me of the pipes beneath the cabinetry in my bathroom, rife with enough black mold to secure the promise of lung cancer.

I head over toward the room Marshall housed me in while I, myself, was an unwilling resident here just before Christmas, then Gage after me. His incarceration was far more temporary, better classified as a visit.

The piano vomits out its nonstop ragtime clatter, violent and surging. It strums through the new twisted limbs I'm forced to reside in, makes my skin crawl with the unsteady rhythm.

I give a series of powerful blows to the heaving door. I watch as it bloats out as if it were filling its lungs, then exhales to a thinner version of itself.

Logan swings open the door proving my theory correct of where they might have stashed him.

Marshall is consistent. I'll give him that.

Logan attempts to slam it shut, but I manage to muscle my way inside.

"It's me," I rattle out. "Skyla." I hold my hands out for him to assess the damage.

"Holy shit," he pulls me in. "What the hell happened?" Logan is crazed by the turn of events. Finally, someone who matches my mood.

"I couldn't get her a trial," I howl in lieu of tears. "She just took, me. And Marshall just stood there and let her."

"Why?" His eyes saucer out.

"He said this was the only way to stave her off. She's locked in my body for two freaking weeks!" A glass pitcher sitting on the table shatters from the ferocity of my cry.

"Skyla," Logan doesn't hesitate to hold me. His wonderful arms wrap tight around this strange thick skeleton, this gnarled quilt of flesh pieced hideously over me. "We're going to fix this," he whispers, confident of this truth. Logan's reassurance seems the only thing I need. "I still love you, Skyla. I always will."

I find Logan's ability to love me in this putrid corporal state amazingly beautiful, just like him.

✾ ✾ ✾

Having Ezrina's body does have its advantages. For one, I'm able to transport Logan and I to the Landon house pronto to observe all of the wild shit Ezrina might be getting me into. Second, I have the power to knock things over at random and make Tad believe he's losing his mind, which brings me a mild sense of satisfaction.

We find the Landon clan downstairs where Mom is mutilating yet another perfectly good recipe in the name of procreation while Mia and Melissa finish up their weekend homework at the table.

I nudge Logan as Ezrina comes into the room, she looks well coifed with her hair spun in some old-fashioned up-do, makeup to a minimum with far too much sparkly blush applied all over her face at random.

expel

Sprinkles starts in on a mad barking spree, so violent and atrocious I'm half afraid the tiny mutt is going to bark himself right into an aneurism.

"Outside with that thing," Tad bellows over the noise.

"Come," Ezrina bends over and tries to quell the onslaught of non-affection but only entices a strange hissing noise to escape from the poor creature's throat.

"Geez, Skyla," Mia gets up and swoops him into her arms. "He hates you."

"That's because she kicks him when she thinks no one is looking," Melissa quips.

"I do not," I protest, but my words bounce around the room, hollow, impotent of yielding any results.

"Hey," Mia whispers over to Ezrina. "Can your friend Ellis hook Gabe up with more of that stuff?"

Ellis? I take a breath and hold it.

"Yes," Ezrina nods without fully understanding the implications.

"Will you drive us to the mall Tuesday? Gabe wants to catch a movie," Mia is on a roll.

"For you, anything, dear sister," Ezrina combs her hair back with my long slender fingers. "That's how sisters love each other best. They accommodate one another when they can."

Ezrina goes over and tastes the gruel right out of the bubbling pot Mom is hovering over.

"You like it?" Mom is hopeful her vomit-like concoction will please me.

"Tastes like heaven," Ezrina, pulls my mother in and holds her a very long time. "I miss touching," she whispers.

My heart seizes. Ezrina is hungry for love and affection. I find the possibilities more than a little paralyzing.

"Let's hope maternal love is all she's craving," Logan doesn't miss a beat.

"I have a feeling it's been one long hot century."

A knock erupts at the door and after a few minutes Tad calls out for me.

Logan and I shuffle after Ezrina.

Tad leans into her, "Why don't you invite the linebacker in. Maybe he'll vacuum up that slop your mother's brewing."

"Dutifully," Ezrina nods, "after, if it pleases my lord, I would very much enjoy a constitutional with my suitor."

"A what?" Tad snaps. "Listen smart ass, you're hanging by a thread. Whatever it is you're planning on constituting, it isn't happening on my watch. He leaves in an hour, and you stay put." Tad stomps off, validating the fact he's an asshole.

Gage comes in and gives a soft kiss before pulling away. "Everything go OK with Dudley? I swung by, but he said you left." Gage inspects my new spinster image and there's a rising level of concern in him far exceeding anything regarding Marshall.

Ezrina doesn't answer. She simply gazes up at him lovesick, spellbound by his magnificent beauty, the touch of his lips.

"Shit," I hiss at Logan as we follow them back to the dining room. The table is set, and Mom is coaxing Gage over to take a seat. "How can he be fooled?" I panic as Gage picks up her hand.

"She is you." Logan is quick to correct.

Gage takes a quick look at Ezrina. Her cheeks explode with color as he takes her in. Her entire person swells as if she might explode from the sheer fact she's holding his hand.

"Is something going on between the two of you?" Mom asks flushed with embarrassment.

Drake and Ethan file in as Tad doles out the Sunday gruel. And holy crap if it doesn't really look like bowls of steaming vomit.

expel

"If one person eats that I'm going to freaking hurl," I announce.

"Do it for me, too," Logan says, folding his arms. "I'm incapable of essential bodily functions at the moment."

Ezrina lets out a strange cry I've never heard myself produce before and lands in Gage's lap so fast you'd think her chair was on fire. She seals her lips over his and engages in an awkward pecking kiss that's not only hard to witness, it's hard to comprehend *my* body is in some way responsible for the carnage.

"She's going to get my kissing license revoked," I whisper.

"Unreal, Lizbeth," Tad says before darting a finger at Ethan. "Restrain her."

Ezrina rips off Gage's sweater and lands him bare-chested on the carpet. She pins his arms down like a prisoner and lashes her mouth over his neck as if slitting his throat.

"Do something!" Mom screams.

"I don't have a net big enough to hold her!" Tad hurdles over chairs and end tables, to get to Ezrina.

Gage rolls her over and exhausts her kicking tirade—looks right at her with a severe sense of doubt. "Skyla?" There's a question in his eyes that lingers a moment before he stands, dusts himself off like he's good and pissed. He knows.

"I've gotta run, thanks for the invite." Gage nods into my mother before heading for the door.

"Go—tell him it's not me," I push Logan in his direction.

"Can't," he says. "I've lost the ability to communicate or come back on my own. They're removing me from the planet one piece at a time."

Great. Just freaking great.

I have never been so completely screwed.

323

56

Love Shack

Life in the Transfer is slow. It's nefarious in nature as dictated by the odd spontaneous beheading, a random maiming. The screams of the victim fill the streets as he runs from the butcher with blood spurting out of his neck like water from a hose. Each act of dismemberment is met with applause from the strange old world audience. It's all a show. The victim takes a bow, initiates the chase once again.

"Why do they do it?" I ask, looking out from the window in Logan's room.

"No clue. Why do we watch horror movies or play violent video games?" He shrugs. "I guess it's entertaining."

"Mmm, something seems off. Something's wrong about the whole thing." I join him in the kitchen and help put the dishes away. Logan made dinner for me, homemade mac and cheese. He would have indulged, himself, but he's incapable of digestion at the moment.

Logan pulls me in. "You want to go back to Paragon, don't you?" He bumps his forehead to mine with a forlorn expression.

I nod holding back tears. In less than a week's time, I've managed to rewire Ezrina's brain to include heartbreak and longing, tears that roll like rivers.

"How can you look at me?" I'm stunned by Logan's ability to stomach me. He's a perfect creature in every way, a sharp contrast to the hideousness I've become.

"You're beautiful in every way, I promise." Logan plants a kiss on the top of my head, and we dissolve back to the island where it all began for the two of us.

expel

"There she is," Logan points over towards Ezrina as she walks the edge of the forest, right here on the Landon property.

Rarely have I gone out into the backyard. Once Tad and Mom lured me out here to gift me my father's bicycle they had restored.

Logan and I navigate through the outline of the woods as we approach her. Ezrina prances and laughs while nestled in my flesh.

"She's with him," I marvel. Nevermore sits perched on her shoulder, a noble creature of majestic stature. "You think he knows?"

Logan takes my hand as we tuck ourselves into an alcove carved out by a Juniper and dutifully spy on Ezrina and the love of her life, Heathcliff.

"Looks, like," Logan struggles to see. "I think they're..."

Ezrina touches her cheek to him, caresses his feathers with long impassioned strokes. It's love in bloom—ages of bottled up emotions unleashed with touch, and words, and endless secretive whispers.

"They're in love." I scoot into Logan trying to hide my bulky frame.

"You can pull people apart—remove them from the planet but you can't extinguish feelings. Love lives even in the face of death." He exhales a warm breath over my cheek. "I still love you, Skyla. Death can't stop what I feel for you, not by a long shot."

"Logan," I cover his hand with mine. It's a truth I'll know forever. "I love you, too." It comes out sad, genuine.

The forest fills with chatter. Ezrina, laughs—giggles like a schoolgirl.

"You hear that?" Logan leans in, puzzled. "I think she just said my name."

Ezrina gives a gentle chortle, mentions Cain River, Holden—something about an arresting spirit.

Logan and I exchange worried glances.

From the house, Tad shouts for me to get the hell back inside.

"Lizbeth?" He barks from the balcony. "Guess what I just caught our daughter doing? Experimenting with bestiality—with a bird! And you can probably guess which daughter."

"Shit," I hiss. "Let's get out of here."

Logan takes up my hand and we disappear.

※ ※ ※

Marshall finds me back at the Transfer sulking on the sofa while Logan whips up another gourmet meal. I do my best to give Marshall the cold shoulder, let him know how it feels to piss off his so-called wife-to-be—teach him a lesson on where flawed judgment gets you.

"She's doing spectacular with your schoolwork," he offers. "You've received an A on two pop quizzes I've given. Your English teacher shared a master essay she drafted on the works of Jane Austen with the entire faculty."

"Most impressive," my voice snarls for effect. Ezrina possesses the ability to make every word that breathes from these lungs sound like it's drowning in a nasty bout of phlegm.

"Come," Marshall beckons me off the couch. "Let's see what Ezrina is up to. Give your spirit some rest instead of holing up in misery with the Pretty One."

"Will I be back in time for dinner?" I look past him at Logan who has a wonderful aroma emanating from the kitchen. My mother could only wish she had half his culinary savvy. I'd offer to help, but I have an insane urge to slash Logan with a butcher knife each time I'm near one.

"Most certainly," Marshall assures.

I let Logan know I'm going to step out, and Marshall blips me away.

expel

✼ 🦋 ✼

We float hundreds of yards above the rich green football field of West Paragon High. Cheer practice is underway. Chloe barks instructions out with the tenacity of a drill sergeant while the rest of them kick and shout, in order to appease her agitated nature.

"Messenger," she goes over and screams into Ezrina's face. "I don't believe you're giving it your *effing* best. We're going to lose All State because you're too damn lazy to lift those tree trunks you call legs."

Ezrina pants from the effort she's just put in, her face is bright pink with duress as perspiration beads down her forehead. I don't ever remember getting that worked up during cheer. Obviously Ezrina is putting in a monster effort.

They fall into formation and Ezrina punches and kicks, shouts so loud, her mighty roar disrupts the clouds near our feet.

Chloe goes over and howls in her face again, reprimands her for not giving a hundred and ten percent.

"I'm not sure I like where this is going," I say to Marshall.

Ezrina lifts Chloe with ease, tosses her in the air like a ragdoll until she's inches from our feet.

Chloe flails, screams—the look of horror on her face is priceless—the flawless diamond of fear.

I laugh as she falls over the bitch squad in a heap.

Well, played Ezrina—well played.

✼ 🦋 ✼

Days drift by locked in this nightmare. A continual dull stream of grey afternoons, evenings that shift like shadows, just one long dismal existence.

Logan and I have decided to join the school on its adventure to Cain River. It's a nice break to be back on earth, back under the guise of daylight with Gage gracing the planet while a loon runs around in my body.

Tad asserts himself as the authority as they settle into camp, making everyone cringe and ask the all-important question of *who invited this idiot?*

I spy on Gage like a hunter, listening from afar as he hums a sad song in the shower, as he contemplates what's become of me while he lies under the branches of a hundred year old pine.

"Gage," I call to him in a broken whisper, the voice I produce replicates the sound of shattering glass but he doesn't answer.

The week presses on. With the All State competition breathing down our necks, Chloe has us, well, them, cheering from sunup till sundown but imposes a reprieve the day before the competition.

"Chloe has a heart?" I pose the question to Logan as we watch Ezrina bolt into the shower.

"She hurt her shoulder the day you tossed her sky high. I overheard her saying she needed to ice it." Logan gives a slight smile at Ezrina's effort.

"Perfect. Another thing she can blame me for."

Chloe sprints out of the woods and catches up to Gage on the walkway.

"No fair," I lament as they walk off towards the commons house together. "I hate this."

"You wanna see what she's up to?" Logan offers.

"I don't know," I trust Gage. Right now Ezrina feels like more of a loose cannon than Chloe.

Ezrina bolts from the shower facility, her hair still wet, her body wrapped tight in a white cloud of a robe. She speeds over to the forest and looks around in secret before heading in.

expel

"What the—" I take Logan by the hand and we race to keep up with her.

Off in the distance Holden is standing by the boathouse waving her over with one of Logan's killer smiles.

"Oh, no," I sigh.

Ezrina gives a brief curtsey. "I've waited—dreamed of this day." Her chest heaves as she says it, her hand falls flat against his chest, and she closes her eyes lost in the ecstasy of it all. "Heathcliff, I love you."

"She just called him Heathcliff," I say, stunned.

"Heathcliff?" Logan whispers as if they might hear.

"Nevermore—that's his name, and he hated me for saying it." I inspect the sky, the dark shadows of the branches in search for his ebony plumes, his sparkling onyx eyes looking down in disapproval, but he's not here. "Something's going on."

Ezrina and Holden—my body and Logan's, start in with soft impassioned kisses. He takes off his shirt, gazes down at my effigy with the look of true love in his eyes— nothing but longing and lust that have amassed from waiting, dreaming, wasting away in a prison of frail bones and feathers.

"Oh my, God," I whisper.

She takes him by the hand and leads him into the boathouse, the door slamming shut behind them. Logan and I appear in the tiny confined space without missing a blink.

She lies over him in a rusted out boat, her bathrobe open in the front, affording them an air of privacy. It's outright animal, love like a furnace—a blaze unfolding before us. A tangle of bare flesh with the robe she was wearing moments before disheveled over her bottom.

"Should we be watching this?" I stare in horror as the boat rocks to the rhythm of their affection.

"We should be living this." An approving smile slides along Logan's face as he places his finger to his nose with amusement.

"Oh stop," I push him. "Marshall!" I rattle the tiny cabin with the reverberation.

Ezrina begins in on a series of moans.

"No, no, no!" I shout. They're writhing and bucking and I'm about to vomit from the shock of it all. I can't lose my virginity to Logan slash Holden or Heathcliff, whoever the hell he is today. I'm going to nail Marshall upside down in the butterfly room. Pin a thousand angry butterflies over him to hide the body. He is going to pay in spades for letting this happen to me.

Through the tiny half moon window I spot Mom and Tad, threading in and out of the trees, giggling at one another, pausing every now and again to stop and make out. Eww. It's obvious they've decided to supplement their honeymoon with a tryst in the forest.

I fly out—right through the wood of the tiny log cabin, speed over to them with a vengeance. If ever they had my best interest at heart, if ever they were to save me from myself, the perfect opportunity was about to present itself. This was their moment. They could gloat for a decade for all I cared.

I flatten Ezrina's crooked hands over Tad's back and jog them along to the boathouse. I really don't understand why they can't see me, but it's for the best. If Tad saw Ezrina, he'd crap his pants.

"How about in here?" Tad raises his brows suggestively.

I so knew it! They were sneaking off to copulate.

They fall in backwards, buttoned together at the lips. My mother's eyes widen with horror as she spies the carnal catastrophe unfolding before her.

Mom and Tad, Logan and me, the four of us gape at the scene.

A breath gets trapped in my throat as I catch a glimpse of Logan's face lost in delirium, my neck rising beneath his. Our bodies connect in a frenzy—that's what we would look

expel

like, Logan loving me—me loving him back. As much as I hate to admit it, there is a beauty locked in this moment, a brilliant light shining in the nexus of something unimaginable, holy and right.

Marshall beams into the room, hovers by the ceiling in a half soluble state. *Petition your mother for a new trial, love. If not, this is the destiny that awaits you.* He points down over our bodies. *I'm afraid it's time to rise*, he calls to the two of them. Ezrina's eyes fly open, look right at Marshall with terror. She can see him, just like I could. *Heathcliff first*, he calls out. Logan's body snaps back as though he were electrocuted.

"Oh God," I whimper.

"Skyla," Marshall nods with the glimmer of an abominable grin.

"Skyla!" Logan shouts, pointing hard over at the body lying beneath mine. "Kill him!"

It's the last thing I hear as the room glides in a dizzying circle, and I blink back into my own earthy form.

57

Like A Lover's Voice

"Skyla Laurel Messenger!" My mother shatters the silence with her excavating howl.

I sit up, rolling Holden off in the process.

How in the hell do I talk my way out of this one?

Holden wrangles on his clothes, causing Tad to escort my mother out the door.

"You have five minutes to hit base camp, young lady—five minutes!" My mother roars.

Shit. She'll never buy that virgin routine now. Ezrina's gone and ruined everything. I am still a virgin, right? I pick up my robe and glance down at my naked body as though it might offer up a clue.

"What the hell happened?" Holden whines as he buttons his jeans. "Did we like just effing get it on?"

I look around the room for a weapon, an ax, a noose, hell I'd hack Holden up limb by limb with a machete if I could. I'm sure Dr. Oliver could pick up the pieces quite literally if he had to.

A long chain, thick and heavy, coiled in the corner peaceful as a snake garners my attention.

I secure my robe, rising to my feet.

"So you wanna do it again?" Holden tilts his head with a hint of pleading. "You know, real quick?"

"Sure," I say, hopping out of the aluminum vessel that only moments before had Logan and I comprising a duet with our flesh.

My feet wobble unsteady on this new light frame. I snatch the chain up from the floor and snap it to the ground, quick and violent. The metal cinches and crackles as a spark of lightning ignites from the bionic pull.

expel

"Shit," Holden hisses. "What the hell's that for?"

I thrash the metal leash with extravagant force—whip his left foot as it touches down on the floor.

"Crap!" He hops up.

"This is how I like it," I say, swinging the chain so fast it cuts the air with a whoosh.

"Calm down," he backs out the door, and I follow. Holden trips over a branch and rights himself immediately. "Get that thing away from me."

I don't like seeing Logan's face in pain, the look of confusion bubbling to the surface. I have to keep reminding myself that beneath it all it's Holden—that Logan's body is the last place he belongs.

Holden takes off, sprints in the direction of the creek and I take off after him. We traverse logs, avoid bushes, ditch in and out of the new spring grass that stands as tall as a man until finally trekking down towards the mouth of the swollen river.

Holden pauses at the tributary, looks at me one last time before jumping into the water.

I stop just shy of the river's edge and watch Holden as he struggles to swim across.

The faint call of voices emanate from downstream. I give a hard squint and make out a group of people lounging around on boulders—Brielle hopping up and down, waving like mad to get my attention.

I jump into the water and gasp as it hugs my waist with its icy bite. Holden bobs unsteady as if he doesn't know how to swim, fighting the current to cut through the middle. I pray Gage was on one of those boulders—that he saw me and he's coming to help me do the unthinkable.

"Skyla," Holden reaches for me as a rush of water cascades over his shoulders. He looks relived that I've abandoned my weaponry.

"Kiss me," I say, trying to smile through the pain. I let him reel me in as if this were all a wicked game, foreplay of a maniacal nature. He seals his lips over mine, and I pull us under gentle as a dream. If I didn't know prior to this that Logan's body was hijacked by an imposter, I would sure as hell know now. These may be Logan's lips but they are miles away from being his kisses. This is the bite of a python, the deadly infliction of some disease being dispensed with his wandering tongue. It reminds me powerfully of that night at the falls when I came across Holden in his proper form before digging my fingers into his neck, killing him the first time.

It takes all of my Celestra strength to wrestle Holden to the bottom of the river, pin him down with my body and lay over him like a stone. I remove my lips from his mouth, disgusted by the thought of Holden Kragger impaling me with his lust. Without meaning to I open my eyes, watch the bubbles blow out of Holden's mouth, his eyes ready to eject themselves from their sockets from the strain of holding his breath. He jerks and squirms, almost launches me off but I hone in my anger and render his muscular arms useless.

His face pinches in agony. And then he gives. Holden gulps down water, inhales long clean strokes like fresh spring air. I would have sold him for silver, done anything possible never to live this moment.

My lungs constrict. I choke trying to hold my breath another second. Holden goes limp beneath me. In the event he's bluffing I conduct my own reflex analysis by reaching down and wrenching his balls so tight Logan may never succeed at procreation. But Holden doesn't flinch. I pop to the surface unstoppable, take in a gasp of air so sharp it sears my lungs like fire.

Gage jumps in, dives down to the bottom without me having to say a word.

I pant and groan from the pain, as I make my way towards shore. I would never have been able to carry out that feat if Marshall hadn't taught me how to push past the pain, believe that I could linger just a little while longer. I guess in the end Marshall helped bring back Logan after all.

Gage tosses Logan up on the grass, limp and rubbery. He pushes him onto his side and Logan spills water from his lips like vomit.

"Shit," Gage rolls him on his back and pushes the palms of his hands under his diaphragm.

I crawl over and seal my mouth over Logan's, push in a series of steady deep breaths until I feel him jerk.

"Come back to me," I whisper. "It's over. He's gone. You and me, we're going to win this faction war, remember?" I try to coax him back into his body, wake him up so I can dislodge the idea that I may have inadvertently caused him brain damage.

Logan sits up and engages in the world's most violent coughing spree.

"You're back," I cry.

Logan nods, looks from me to Gage and pushes out a weak smile. "I'm back."

"Skyla?" Gage pulls me in, looks right into my eyes.

"It's me, I swear," I wrap my arms around Gage so tight I never want to let go. "We're both back and everything is the way it should be."

58

War Drums

My mother and I stare at one another in her cabin that reeks of Tad's grocery store patchouli cologne. Clearly, we are at an impasse.

"You were cheating on Gage," she rages.

"Not really." This is only slightly more awkward than it has to be since both Gage and Tad hover beside us.

"You were *kissing!*" She brings her hands up over her forehead in frustration. "For God's sake, I hope that's all you were doing."

"I bet she's finally managed to knock herself up," Tad announces. "Let the record show I'm not giving another damn dime to that clinic in Seattle," he saws through the room with his winded bellow.

"Fine," I say.

"Fine?" My mother balks. "Is that all you have to say for yourself? Fine?"

"She's probably *trying* to get pregnant," Tad snarks. "She's jealous over all the attention Drake has drummed up for himself."

"Not true." Let the record show I'd be thrilled with zero attention from either Mom or Tad. In fact, I'd be more than pleased if I wasn't realistically the only female in the room with any reproductive relevance. If Tad finally managed to knock up my mother, it would probably reduce the incidence of these kinds of conversations to nil.

"I think you owe everyone in the room an apology," Mom sags, fatigued from the confrontation all together.

"I apologize for my actions," I'm quick to admit. "It won't happen again, I swear." Like, ever, because I killed the bastard. Although technically it was Nev fondling my body,

expel

and speaking of which, I have one serious fucking bone to pick with him. "Um," I turn to face Gage. "I owe you the biggest apology of all," I really mean it. "Will you ever forgive me for the countless messes I've dragged us into?"

Gage raises his brows, amused. "Why don't we go for a walk?"

🦋 🦋 🦋

Gage. The ways he saves me are incalculable.

We walk into the woods—weave through ancient Hemlocks with trunks so fat you could park a car in them.

His left hand is heavily bandaged.

"What happened?" I pick it up gently and bring it to my cheek.

"Grazed myself with a nail gun renovating a cabin. And here I thought carpentry was going to be my thing." He pushes his shoulder into mine.

I notice one of the discs protruding from his side pocket, and I'm relieved to see it.

"Is that a disc in your pocket or are you just happy to see me?" I laugh because I screw it up and accidentally pronounce disc as *dick*.

"All of the above." He gives a sultry smile and pulls me down to the ground.

We lay side by side in a clearing, on a bed of fragrant pine needles, soft as a pillow.

Gage traces the outline of my jaw. His eyes never waver from mine.

"I missed you," he breathes. His finger traipses along the outer edge of my lips, dips into my mouth and he kisses the tip before dotting my nose with it. "Are you OK? Did he hurt you?"

I can read between the lines. I know what he's really asking. I had explained what had happened between Ezrina and Nev as brief as possible before my mother's detainment.

"I don't think so." I shake my head. Deep down inside I don't think that was Nevermore's intent. I can hardly blame Ezrina who was so parched, so thirsty. You could see Nev filling in the cracks of her existence, rehydrating her soul with his hands kneading over her hips. It would have been beautiful if it didn't involve my body—Logan of all people on the receiving end. It was a love song in the making just watching her shake her hair out for him.

"Skyla." Gage kisses me with my name still on his lips. "I am jealous for you."

His words swim through me. My spirit soars to hear that curious phrase.

I take him in with a sigh before he depresses over me, loves me with a quiet sadness. He sends his heated kisses rushing up and down my neck rabid and hungry.

I can hear the beating of our hearts, they escalate in sound, deafen my senses. The ground quakes beneath us.

I open my eyes just as the world fades to nothing.

ᴡ 𝐖 ᴡ

The scenery appears, a deep umber sky, a world dipped in sepia. The sound of a thousand helicopters flying overhead bombard our senses.

"We need to find the orator," Gage screams over the intense walloping that bullets through the atmosphere.

Ellis appears, covers his ears as he runs over.

"I got a lead," Ellis shouts. His eyes are lost in crimson tracks, glazed over with an oily haze.

"You're stoned," I say, disappointed.

"You were back with Gage," he shrugs.

expel

"Are you selling to Gabriel Armistead?" I forget about the war long enough to inject myself into Mia's wellbeing.

"No," he gives a hard look. "I wouldn't give it. He got it someplace else. I know that for a fact."

Great. Now I have Mia and Melissa's recreational drug use to police, not to mention the fact this Armistead kid has a standing date with the penitentiary at some point in the future. Obviously he's going to drag my sisters down. He's a lunatic, and once Mia and Melissa catch on, I'm sure there will be restraining orders involved. They'll be lucky if they get out of this three-way relationship without gunfire and homicide.

Speaking of gunfire, we follow Ellis over to a wheat-covered hillside, the blonde shafts move in a slow lethargic rhythm, cheering us on.

Ellis kicks at a mound of hay before reaching in and extracting a crossbow, same one Marshall taught me how to use.

My hair swirls wild as the wind stirs up in a violent rage.

"There he is," Gage points over to a group of men interlinked in a huddle, the orator stretches above them by three heads at least. "Stay here." Gage takes off in his direction.

Ellis retrieves a bow and quiver for each of us. The arrows spill—they rain over the splinters of hay, disheveled and impotent.

"Shit!" he cries out in anguish, his left arm still locked in a cast.

"Let me," I gather them quick as possible until we have a handful in each canister. I sling one over Ellis's shoulder just as something slaps his jaw in the opposite direction and sprays the air with blood from his mouth.

I turn in time to see Chloe brimming with pride, a wrist rocket dangling from her hand. She missed my temple by less than a centimeter.

Ellis drops his head to his knees before surging with a pissed off look on his face.

Chloe.

I can't recall if it was my mother or my father who told me that if you die in the ethereal plane you stay that way.

I swipe an arrow from over my shoulder, bend over and hoist up the crossbow.

An arrow. That's how Chloe Bishop will die. Not some mirror that fulfills psychotic wishes. I'll be damned if I ever let her crawl into her fantasy and have her way with Gage as a means to rid her from this world. Not on my fucking watch.

She pulls back her sling already loaded and ready to go. She heaves with a malevolent smile, shakes a shock of necrotic hair out of her eyes with laughter.

"Skyla!" Gage resonates through the incessant drumming.

It all happens so fast, two deadly weapons slicing through the air, whispering as they pass in the night. I drop to my knees only to find a stone staring me in the face.

The world quakes and trembles, reduces to nothing as the night is swallowed up in thunder.

Gage—he tossed the disc into the field and everything freezes.

Region three is over.

We lost.

59

Trip the Lights Fantastic

The next day, the All State competition is strange to say the least.

I look into the rows of endless faces set up on the bleachers. I scour the crowd with an intense scrutiny before our final routine and see Logan and Gage staring back at me, my mother next to them with blue and white pom poms in her hand cheering from the stands.

Chloe and I have chosen to ignore the fact we almost offed each other last night and join forces to initiate what just might have been one of the most kick ass performances of both our acrobatic, heel stomping careers.

Ellis isn't here—already I know that. Ellis might be suffering from a slight hairline fracture along his mandible, so Tad volunteered to escort him back to Paragon where his mother has a specialist flying in to assess whether or not they'll need to wire shut his jaw. I imagine that might temper the *pot runs* for a good long while.

The music cues up and Chloe and I jump and shout in unison in our final foray as inseparable cheer peers. We start in on the pair's section of the routine, smile our red painted grins at one another as if we were sisters. There's something haunting, almost erotic about the deception we're attempting to pass off on the judges. Chloe swings her hips in my direction, grabs my wrists and slides me down between her legs, and I pop right back up.

Don't wreck this, she says just before letting go.

It's the basket toss that has her riled up. Everything else in the routine is gingerbread.

The girls form a tight circle, Chloe, Nat, Emily, Lexy, and a crystalline-eyed Michelle. Here I am in the arms of my enemies. Each one might benefit in the event I suffer an unfortunate accident—watch with great interest as my head explodes like a melon against the bright yellow floor.

I hesitate just a moment, long enough to see my mother standing, roaring for my triumph. I growl in the face of my adversaries as I bounce hard onto their interlocked hands.

I fly—soar up so high that hitting the ceiling of the gymnasium feels like a very real possibility. I peak just shy of grazing an enormous wood beam that stretches across the structure, point my toes hard as I lean over and touch them in perfect formation. Gravity comes like a thief, pulls me down with its lead laden arms. I have to trust those who wait for me—trust them to spare me from certain death.

I zero in on Gage and Logan as I plummet through the air. I want their perfect faces to be the last thing I see if I never come to.

A hard wallop commences as I land hard in the hands of the bitch squad. Chloe helps me to my feet with the same hand she tried to kill me with in the ethereal plane just hours before.

"If I didn't hate you so much, I'd love you," she blows into my ear.

The crowd erupts in a violent storm of cheers.

I nod into Chloe's twisted line of thinking, acknowledging the fact this is the closest form of affection we could ever share.

We take our seats along the front row of the bleachers and wait for the judges to tally their final marks.

"You were freaking amazing!" Brielle pounces on me with a hug. "You're an acrobat, a bird or something!"

She plunks down next to me and takes up my hand. "You know, Skyla, since you risked your neck for West, I'm going to campaign like crazy to get you nominated for prom queen."

"I'm not a senior." I rock into her.

expel

"Junior prom." She rocks back. "But I think that performance was enough to justify the throne for two years. Speaking of performances..." She gives me that I-know-what-you-did-in-the-boathouse look.

"It was an accident—case of mistaken identity."

"I would say that I didn't believe you," she ticks her head to the side, "but I swear I've had that happen." She gives a quick glance over her shoulder before leaning in. "So, how was it?"

"I wouldn't know," like, really, I wouldn't know.

"Oh, so that's how you're going to play it? I get it. I mean you're back with Gage, right?"

"I'm *just* with Gage. I'll be with Gage forever."

The microphone at the front of the gym gives a high-pitched wail before adjusting.

Marshall comes over and sits by my side.

"Ms. Messenger," he says.

A representative from the judge's panel steps up to the podium. A skinny blonde who chooses to wear a visor when we are neither outside nor in the land of sunshine, clears her throat.

"The Best in Choreography Trophy goes to," she gives a dramatic pause. "West Paragon High!"

We exchange high fives, well, Brielle, Marshall and me. The only other team member who would offer me a high five is Ms. Richards and she's all the way on the other end.

"The best all-around routine goes to, again, West Paragon High!" Her voice takes a serious upturn into Carly Foster territory.

Another round of high fives, this time Emily makes an effort to slap some skin with me.

"The winner of the basket toss, is, no surprise here," she pauses to leer out into the crowd until she stumbles upon my face. "West Paragon High!"

Brielle and I jump up with excitement. From the top of the bleachers I can see Mom making her way down the stands, frantic and screaming like she's just been knifed. She lunges at me with tears as I take in her warm embrace.

"And the winner of the All State competition goes to, let's see if you can guess?" The judge teases. "West Paragon High. Come on down, girls!"

"Holy shit!" Chloe bounces up. "And we did all that with *Messenger* on our team?"

The rest of the girls run off to the front of the gym.

There's a look of hurt in Mom's eyes after Chloe fired off her latest and greatest barb.

"Don't worry," I assure her. "This is as good as her life gets. I have everything else." I look up at Gage and Logan and give a private smile.

"Go get your trophy, Skyla." Mom presses a kiss into my cheek. "You earned it."

Brielle and I walk up together.

The crowd rises to their feet and erupts in riotous applause. Chloe glitters like a fire under the limelight of her victory.

Well done, Ms. Messenger. Marshall nods in my direction. *Let's see if we can put any of those highflying skills to use in the faction war. The Fems have already requested I equip you with more discs. They've dubbed them, victory coins.*

I pull my lips into a bleak line. He knows full well I wouldn't be here if it wasn't for that last disc.

From the corner of my eye a pale swollen man catches my attention. A tuft of flaming hair shoots in the air a good six inches. His face is greased with thick pancake paste, and an apple red grin is painted over his flesh.

A clown.

He sits alone in the corner at the top of the bleachers, vacuums out all of the joy from this moment.

Yes, Skyla, Marshall tips his head into his chest. *You've managed to call him to you.*

"Shit," I hiss under my breath.

Worse yet? Marshall darts his gaze around the vicinity. *Rumor has it—he's brought friends.*

60

Home Visit

I see them everywhere.

There was one on the ferry on the way back to Paragon even though Gage swore up and down he couldn't see him. One at the edge of the parking lot at school today, and another in the woods behind my house that I spotted from the kitchen window. Clowns—tragically demonic jesters—horrific and scary, crying their silent bloody tears.

"What's gotten into you, Skyla?" Mom hands me a dry dish to put away.

"Nothing," I say, glancing over at Gage who sits at the table. He stayed over for dinner. Everything feels so wonderfully normal again with Gage.

He gives Drake pointers on his Algebra two assignment, looking back at me every now and again to flex a seductive smile. Gage is a genius, he could teach a pack of wild dogs to bark out the Pythagorean theorem to the tune of *Happy Birthday* if he wanted.

"You two mind picking up Mia and Melissa from their riding lessons?" Mom leans over the sink to get a better look up at the ever-darkening sky.

"Not at all," I say. Marshall made it a point to personally invite me over tonight. Tomorrow is the island-wide garage sale that he's instigated in which he singlehandedly transforms Paragon into a waste laden oasis of treasures and trinkets best forgotten. "You have your garbage ready?"

"Locked, loaded and ready to go," her teeth light up like lanterns. They hold a bluish tinge, so perfectly bleached they're almost translucent. I've never seen my mother so primped and polished. Ever since Demetri slithered onto the

expel

island, she's coifed and groomed herself to an exaggerated level of physical perfection usually reserved for the pageant circuit and transvestites alike. I bet Tad doesn't even notice how her hair shines, the extra bright smile, an entire bevy of low cut blouses that have accosted her wardrobe.

"Look who's here?" Tad comes in with Dr. Booth in tow.

"Time for another ambush visit, already?" I quip, following them into the living room. Gage shoulders up to me for moral support as we take seats opposite Mom and Tad. Team Oliver verses team Landon. I'm tagging myself as an honorary Oliver. It warms me to think of taking Gage's name.

"Skyla," Dr. Booth nods into me. "I suppose this is unexpected in nature," he gives a weary look in Tad's direction.

"She's jumpy and unpredictable," Tad counters. "Catching them off guard is the only useful tactic with these flighty types."

"It's a surprise to me, too." Mom gives an accusatory look.

Drake comes over and sits on the arm of the couch, a Landon family no-no. Figures. Drake can knock girls up, deform the furniture and no one says boo. What the hell did I ever do?

"Skyla," Dr. Booth's lips press white. "I hear there's been some hypersexual behavior occurring as of late."

Oh that.

"Dude—the night you tackled Gage during dinner was classic," Drake spews through a mouth full of garlic bread. "Or when you got it on with his brother during spring break?" He nearly chokes getting that one out.

"Any other *classics* you'd like to belch out before I nail you with your own prenatal misgivings?" I challenge.

Personally, I want a do-over as far as spring break is concerned. I so don't remember a damn thing Ezrina did—

although I did get to spend two weeks with the ex-dead love of my life. That was pretty amazing. Who knew Logan could cook?

"Sounds like a disturbing habit we should put an end to right away," Dr. Booth depresses his pen into his cheek. "One of the side effects of the medication we've started is spontaneous sexual outbursts." He nods with a sincerity so alarmingly believable I almost want to applaud the Oscar worthy performance.

"So you're saying," Mom grips her chest in horror, "all these strange acts of a sexual nature were caused by some chemical imbalance?"

Imagine that, a pill that would create a carnal beast out of a human being. And she herself was the acting Pez dispenser of the teen Viagra.

"Yes," Dr. Booth nods, "the trial is over. I'm pulling the medication immediately."

Mom zips over to the kitchen and charitably relinquishes the amber bottle.

"What about the strange behavior?" Tad protests. "She hasn't improved. She spent the last two weeks mocking me, curtsying whenever I walked into the room and calling me *my lord*. And, when I threatened to take away her liberties, she threw a butcher knife, that, by the way, I didn't even realize we had, right at me. Missed my neck by inches!"

Go Ezrina.

And she totally didn't miss. It was a warning.

Ezrina never misses.

"Skyla?" Mom's jaw drops at the homicidal implications.

I'm sure she's been busy the last couple weeks cavorting with Demetri. How could she possibly keep tabs on who was attempting to butcher who while she was out sacrificing wildlife with the man who murdered her husband? *And*, if I could have voted which of my mother's husbands Demetri was going to off, it for sure would not

expel

have been that one. God—I'm not even sure I would hate him if he had chosen Tad.

"I don't know what the heck he's talking about," I amp up my defenses. "But, I *have* been feeling really weird the past two weeks. Everything was sort of grey and fuzzy. It must have been the medication."

"I hate to be rude," Mom checks her watch. "But I've gotta run. I told Demetri I'd help him tag his items."

Tag his items? If that doesn't sound outright sexual in nature, I don't know what does.

"You should go with her," I shoot Tad a curt look for being such an imbecile.

"It's cold out." He crosses his arms and burrows deeper into the sofa. "I don't want to go."

Great.

"Gage and I have a half hour or so before we need to pick up the girls, we can help," I offer. The last place on the planet I want to be tonight is the Fem funhouse, but if it keeps my mother's visit chaste, it'll be well worth the effort.

Gage widens his eyes. He has a date planned for us tonight. A total surprise for me, and I love it in theory, but I'm pretty sure my mother is about to tag more than Demetri's miscellaneous clutter, so unfortunately, we might have to include the two of them in the grand design for the next few hours.

"Nope," I won't hear of it." Mom winks over at Gage as if she's in on his true intentions.

Perfect. Now I'm going to expect some secret engagement party, where Chloe does something freaky like pull all of our doppelgangers out of the Realm of Possibilities and confuses the hell out of the living and the dead.

Dr. Booth rises and says goodnight. Gage and I follow him to the door.

He waits until we're safely outside before turning to the two of us.

"There's an emergency faction meeting tonight at Nicholas Haver's home, ten o'clock sharp." He looks over at us with an insolence he's never exhibited before. "Heads up. The two of you are in a hell of a lot of trouble."

We watch as he stomps down the porch.

I can't think of a thing that Gage and I have done wrong—unless of course they're pissed about that whole faction war thing.

Like the fact we keep losing.

A lot.

61

Mommy Dearest

Marshall's home burns bright against the backdrop of a watercolor night. The night fog glows like paper, bleeds out its milky tendrils over the rim of the forest.

"Enter," he gives a slight bow as he holds the door open for both Gage and me.

I'm curious as to why he invited me over to begin with, but I didn't think he'd mind if I brought Gage.

"Mr. Oliver, I have a plethora of boxes in the barn, and I'd like them all placed on the front porch before morning. Might I trouble you to muscle them over?"

"Sure," Gage doesn't hide the fact he's not thrilled with the task.

"Do circle around to the side yard. I'd loathe for you to trail muddied footprints throughout the house."

Gage raises his brows in my direction before heading out back.

"Isn't this lovely, Skyla? We've our own personal lackey." Marshall's lips curve into a nefarious smile.

I shake my head at him. "You owe me," I say.

"Anything, Love." He picks up my hand and kisses it before I can snatch it back.

"You let Ezrina play skin tag with her boy toy, and now I'm questionably defiled."

"Nonsense. I'd pluck the wings off that ball of feathers myself if he mistreated my future bride in any way. There were rules—although vague—they were followed. You're pure as the driven snow you plowed that poor girl's head into. By the way, I was apprised of another near death you were party to inducing."

"That's right," I say, rather proud just thinking of the way I took down Holden. "I didn't need you after all." I nestle in the satisfaction of knowing I could kick some Count ass all by my lonesome if needed. And, boy, was it ever freaking needed.

Marshall pulls back, folds his arms across his chest, narrows his gaze into me. "You have no clue what you have or haven't done. You have an army of sniveling Fems ready to terrorize you out of your sanity, not to mention a war you've taken to losing right from the outset. You aren't even aware of who the enemy is."

"The enemy is Demetri," I say it simple.

"Who is his *Count*erpart?"

I take in a breath. "My mother?"

He gives a dismayed blink. "Skyla," he pulls my name out in a frustrated sigh. "Speaking of the mare, I've put in yet another request for you to speak with her—she's accepted."

"*Now*? Now that I'm out of the prison that is Ezrina's flesh and that Logan is alive and well and living in his own body—*now* she wants to see me?" I huff a laugh. "No way."

"You have to!" A female voice startles me from behind. It's Giselle, Gage's long dead sister. I go over and give her a hug. I'm relieved it's her and not me, well, the me from L.A. two years ago. I'm still a little freaked out about sharing my personal space with another version of myself. I was rather annoying at that stage of the game and, well, overall hard to get along with sometimes.

"Thanks, but no," I say. "I'm a little miffed at her at the moment."

"You have no choice, Skyla," Giselle takes my hand and the world begins to fade.

"No, wait! I need Gage," my voice thickens, echoes as if it were in a tunnel.

Marshall scoffs at the idea. "We won't be needing him. In fact, it would be awkward for all parties involved once I present you to the Justice Alliance as my future bride."

"No!" But it's too late to protest.

The world evaporates to nothing.

🦋 🦋 🦋

"Skyla." My mother rises to meet me.

We appear in Ahava over the lake with the twin falls off in the distance. A red glow illuminates from the lower tier where the sword of the Master is stowed. That's the culmination of this entire war. And here I am so close it hurts.

My mother takes her invisible seat next to three gentlemen, Rothello, who I'm not entirely convinced isn't something sinister, and two gorgeous men who could pass as Marshall's brothers.

"You've lost all three regions," it comes so benevolently from my mother's lips I'm alarmed at how comfortable she is with the idea.

"How about, congratulations on your All State win? Or, thank goodness you're in your right mind and oh, yeah, *body*!" I don't mean for it to sound as pissy as it does.

"You've come to grumble about my mothering skills?" Her eyes ignite crisp as lamplights.

"I haven't come at all—you dragged me."

"Skyla," Marshall's voice slashes like a whip. "There is a time for anger, and I assure you, this is far from it."

"I'm not angry," I'm quick to correct. "Anger would require me to care. I'm bothered by all of this." I throw my hands in the air. "My own mother wanted to send me out into a warzone with no protective disc should I need to get back to Paragon for oh, I don't know, the simple fact the two boys I love lay dying? But you knew about that didn't you? You started this war on the heels of a tragedy."

"You keep this up young lady and I'll be sure it ends with one," she snaps. Her hair glistens an iridescent gold, her face radiates a special aura all its own. Her entire being is lit up from the inside—reminds me of a firefly.

"Are you threatening me?" The words grate out of me, each their own sentence.

"Skyla," Giselle pulls me back onto the grassy blue hill. "Please don't infuriate the Justice Alliance."

"You mean my mother. Why are you afraid of her?"

"She has nothing to fear," Marshall takes me aside, "but you do."

"I've called you here, Skyla," my mother rises again, although this time she doesn't look so welcoming. "I was going to educate you on a few strategic principles that would sway victory in your favor." She gives a curt nod. "But I've decided against it."

Figures.

"Instead, I'm going to increase your level of punishment for going against the Faction Council for the duration of the war."

"I suppose you'd like a thank you," I say it low under my breath.

"I would most certainly like a thank you. I gave you life," she cuts a look that could carve a statue out of a tree trunk.

Funny, I didn't think they pulled the life card up here in the nether sphere where they cavort with angels and strum on harps all day. It's a tough job this Decision Council hobby she's got herself caught up in—boss around the universe, torment your only child.

"Enough," her voice erupts like a riot.

She hears everything, they all do, Marshall gives a wistful smile as if he were enjoying this on some small scale. *Proceed to thank her, Skyla, so we may be dismissed.*

expel

My mouth drops open at the thought.

"Thank you," I seethe. Giselle pats my back as if to say job well done. "For harvesting me," I continue, "like some able-bodied war machine you needed to *use* to fight your battles."

"Forgive her my fine people," Marshall bellows. "My future bride knows not of what she speaks," he cuts me a hard look.

I've just verbally spit in all of their faces and now there would be hell to pay. I don't need Marshall to spell it out for me.

We appear back in his kitchen abrupt and without warning.

"That was rude," I say, dusting off my arms as if there were intergalactic residue left from the trip. "She didn't even say goodbye."

"That, my love, is the equivalent of someone hanging up on you."

"I've had a mother or two mad at me before."

"Not this one," he doesn't waver his harsh stare.

"She'll get over it. It's not like she's going to kill me."

"She's on the Decision Council, Skyla." He lifts my chin, soft with his finger. "She can change everything."

62

Call to Arms

Once Gage and I drop Mia and Melissa off at home, we speed over to the faction meeting.

We park high on the property behind a long row of sports utility vehicles—glossy sedans that look fresh off the lot.

We're technically not allowed to attend these meetings because we're under three hundred, well thirty, same difference. But apparently our presence has been requested. I have a feeling I'm in for my second ass whipping of the night.

"Logan's here," Gage whispers. He takes my hand as we cut through the thick curtain of fog towards the barnlike structure in the back of the Haver's property.

"I'm surprised he hasn't painted his truck yet—impounded, tarped it in the least, anything to hide Holden's bombastic sense of self expression." Every time I see those crazy orange flames, it makes me want to smack someone.

"I mentioned it this morning, he said he was looking into buying a new one."

"I guess I forgot to let him in on the fact he owes Marshall 18K." Wait, I think I did.

Gage gives a little laugh. "That's what the bastard gets for pawing you." His dimples sink with the hint of a mischievous smile.

"I like this bad boy side of you."

"Oh yeah?" he sneaks a kiss just below my ear. "Wait till you see what I have planned for later."

"Is it bad?"

"It's corrupt, and vile, and most likely criminal in twelve different states," he growls, pecking my neck with a series of kisses.

We run into Emma and Dr. Oliver just shy of the entrance. It sort of puts a damper on the sexual banter—and just before we got to the good part—the heavy use of expletives peppered with sacrilegious overtones.

Emma pinches her lips at the sight of me. Dr. Oliver doesn't look too thrilled either.

"Something wrong?" Why do I get the feeling I've just stepped on a land mine?

"Let's get inside," Emma ushers us in quickly. "They've already begun."

"I saw Giselle tonight," I whisper, bribing her with the words I know she longs to hear in an effort to quell her hatred towards me.

"Bring me my daughter." She stops all movement and clutches onto me as if I've got her stowed away somewhere for ransom.

"OK, I'll bring it up next time she pops in." I give a circular nod as she glides me towards a row of empty seats near the front. I hate the front. It's the not-so-freaking-fun zone. People always get picked on for sitting up front, but something tells me this is reserved seating.

"Eighty-nine was the final count," Nicholas Haver says. He's a heavyset man with a triple chin whose broad chest and bright nose give the indication of an upcoming cardiac infarction. He grips his water bottle like a gavel. "In the event those who've just arrived missed the topic of conversation, eighty-nine was the number of Celestra souls sent to paradise during the last few weeks."

"Shit!" I say out loud.

All eyes cut over to me as I sit there stunned by the annihilation of my people.

"Yes, Ms. Messenger," Mr. Haver gives a cold steely look. "You should be appalled in every way," his voice escalates. "In fact, you should be downright outraged that the one who took his hand to God and sent those brothers and sisters home is seated in your midst."

He is? I do a quick survey for Demetri or Pierce or anyone who might remotely be capable of such bloodlust.

"Logan Oliver," Nicholas Haver darts his name out like a poison arrow. "Son, it has come to my attention that you have breeched trust with the Celestra people and given your pledge to the enemy."

A collective gasp circles the room.

"You may leave here tonight knowing full well you are no longer welcome at this or any other faction meeting that does not include your kind." He sharpens an eye in Logan's direction. "Boy, you see me coming your way, you had better cross the street if you know what's good for you. I have nothing kind to say."

"What about the war?" Someone shouts from the back of the room.

"A principality will be arriving to speak with us, in the near future. With the enemy among us I see no point in carrying on. Dismissed."

That's it?

The entire room booms with chatter as people gather their coats and head towards the exit. It's like the whole meeting was held to expose the fact that Logan, well, actually Holden was nothing but an ass. No one is more aware of that than me. I could have sent a mass email and spared everyone the trouble.

Dr. Booth catches my eye from across the room and motions me over.

"I'll be right back," I whisper to Gage and press against the flow of the crowd in an effort to get to him.

"Skyla, what's happened to Logan?" Dr. Booth glances over my shoulder at him, full with suspicion. "I thought you said his conversion was to gain ground on the enemy, not slaughter his own people."

expel

"It is—*was*. Look, it wasn't Logan. Logan was dead and now he's not. It was Holden Kragger's ghost. It was some bodily mix up when Ezrina tried to resurrect him back at the lab, only she couldn't get it right because I spit in a Sector's eye."

Dr. Booth indulges in a good long blink. "Sorry I asked."

I see Gage off in the distance talking to Logan. His blue eyes go off like high beams before retracting. His face sours at whatever it is Logan is telling him.

We make our way to the front where Dr. Booth exchanges niceties with the Olivers.

"Well, I suppose I'll see all of you tomorrow bright and early for our collateral exchange," Dr. Booth smiles over at them. "Logan," he shakes his hand. "I understand the pizza business is doing you no favors these days."

"It's a fair trade. I don't do it any favors either." Logan shrugs it off like it's no big deal.

"I have a luncheon next Thursday if you'd like the opportunity to cater the event."

I want to kiss Dr. Booth for being so nice to Logan after Nicholas Haver all but turned him into a social pariah. Logan will be lucky he can *afford* a pizza after the character assassination that took place here tonight.

"I'll pass," Logan pats him on the back before heading outside. Gage gives a puzzled look and follows him out the door.

"Thanks anyway," I offer.

Dr. Booth stares out curiously. "I gather he's pretty upset over the treatment he received tonight. Either that, or it's not Logan." He winks. "A good business man never turns down potential revenue. See you in the morning." He sails out the door.

Dear God—that better be Logan.

63

Face of an Angel

Long cascades of rain, wash the streets clean. It was dry as bones for three days straight. Clearly it had set some sort of climate record here on Paragon. Her roadways had become parched, singed from the prospect of another hour without a lingual embrace from the heavy clouds flirting above.

"So where we going?" I ask Gage as we turn down towards the coast after the faction meeting. "Rockaway?" Of course, we'll be sopping wet, but we'll be together, and I'm totally sure Gage and I could easily figure out how to have a good time in slippery clothes.

An image of Gage in a soaking wet t-shirt, clinging to his skin, his flesh illuminating from underneath brings the naughty curve of a smile to my lips.

"Nope, not Rockaway." All affect slides off his face as we turn towards Devil's Peak.

That horrible scene of me making out with Logan in the Mustang crops up in my mind. What if he's going to push me over the cliff because he's secretly been harboring all kinds of explosive anger? What if he's faked this whole let's get back together thing, so he can teach me a lesson?

I shake the thought away. What am I saying? This is *Gage*.

Instead of driving into the parking lot, he takes the long winding road down towards the base. The waves detonate over the rocky shore, powerful as grenades. The froth rushes forward, creating a magical white expanse before retracting—the ocean singing its refrain all over again.

expel

Gage backs the truck up in haste as far as the narrow strip of pavement will allow, revs his engine six times straight.

"What are you doing?" I'm not feeling so safe and cozy with Gage at the moment.

"See that cliff?" He points hard at the sheer granite wall set before us, tall as a building.

"Yes," I almost want to say no just to throw him off because there's something distinctly odd about his behavior, and I can't quite put my finger on it.

"I'm going to drive us right through it." There's an earnest intent in his voice I've never heard before.

"You can't drive us through it. All kinds of terrible things will happen—like for instance, *crashing* and *burning*." I shout in a panic. I'd love to educate him on all things paraplegic, but at the moment my heart is stopped up in my throat.

"I have a hunch we're going to be all right." He depresses the gas and the truck flies forward.

I throw my hands up over my face and scream myself right into another world.

✺ ✺ ✺

I'm not usually one to be particular of wherever Gage delights to take me. Nor do I make a practice of demanding where we'll go in advance, but after tonight, I'm reconsidering both of those elements of our relationship.

A low fat moon hangs overhead. A blue tinted fog burns bright through the windshield until Gage kills the headlights.

The all-familiar looking terrain of the Transfer fills in the landscape. An entire crowd of bodies flock to the oversized vehicle, and before we know it the trunk is festooned with men and women of eras past, laughing and romping around in the back.

"Let's get out of here," Gage kills the ignition.

"Exactly." I'll save the all-important question regarding where he may have left his sanity for later. Once we ditch this vile, soul-vermin infested place, I may have to revoke his driving privileges as well.

Gage slides out of the driver's door. In an instant he's replaced by a man with a handlebar mustache.

I race around to the front of the truck and smack into Gage.

"What the hell?" I scream over the noise of the crowd.

"I don't think we killed Holden," he says, bracing me gently by the shoulders. "I don't think that was Logan. But there's only one way to be sure. Take me to him."

I lead Gage through the wrought iron fence with the effigy of a screaming skull emblazoned at the crest. We hurry in through the gossamer-riddled doors of the haunted mansion and make a beeline for the suite reserved for Paragon bound transients. I give three brisk knocks and stand back as the door heaves itself into an asthma attack.

"Even Dr. Booth said he wasn't acting like himself," I point out. I should have grilled Logan once he came to. I should have known Holden is impossibly resilient like lice, or bed bugs, or intestinal parasites.

The door bursts open, and Logan in all of his rugged splendor stares back at us.

I lunge into him with a tight embrace. "I thought I killed you," I whisper trying to hold back tears. Something wasn't right about him after the drowning, and truth be told, I thought I gave him some mild form of brain defect.

"Come in," he offers Gage a knuckle bump before closing the door behind us. The living room smells like vanilla, and a plate of fresh baked cookies sit on the table. He motions for us to help ourselves.

expel

"Expecting company?" I swipe a warm chocolate chip cookie and let it melt in my mouth like the sublime confection it is.

"I miss eating," Logan laments. "I miss the scents—the way it could satisfy you." He gazes outside the window into the dark velvet night, void of any emotion, lost in the subtext of his words. "But I'm glad you're here. Don't let them go to waste."

"Holden is harder to kill than a cockroach," I say, biting into the heavenly delight. "You are rocking the kitchen!" I marvel.

"Thanks," it depresses out of him. "I can't tell you how glad I am to see you guys. I thought for sure he'd fake his way through the next fifty years."

"I'm shocked it lasted this long," Gage says, snapping up a handful. "Holden can't go two days without trouble. He told my parents that Skyla stole eighteen thousand dollars from the bowling alley, and now he wants a loan to help pay it back."

I take in a sharp breath.

That bastard. No wonder Barron and Emma were all uptight when I ran into them at the meeting.

"I *borrowed* twenty thousand from Marshall to give to the bowling alley because *he* bankrupt it," I correct, to Logan's horror.

"Skyla," his face bleaches out. I love how normal he looks and feels, even though he's appalled at what's going on. At least I can rely on the fact it's not going to kill him. "Please, give Dudley back the money. I'd rather borrow it from my uncle than have you owe that menace anything."

"Too late," I shake my head, "besides, there are no physical strings attached, no promises of me giving him anything of that nature."

"And what's appeasing him?" Logan is intent on squeezing out the truth.

"He," crap, I doubt this will go over well. "Marshall, might be under the false impression that he's going to marry me someday," I shrug it off like it's the stupidest thing in the world because, *hello*? It so is.

Logan and Gage exchange somber looks, don't say a word.

"He's not," I offer, but the mood remains the same.

"What makes him so sure?" Logan looks as though he's capable of cooking up a meal with Marshall's intestines.

"Some orator friend told him." I shrug. It's so ludicrous I hate spending my precious time even entertaining the idea.

"Skyla," Gage closes his eyes, hisses out my name like a steam engine just pulling into the station. "An orator?" His brows form a perfect letter V. "He mention his name?"

"I think he said, Delphinius—something like that."

"That's the guy from the faction war. He was the one giving me instruction." His gaze drifts past me. "Seems pretty accurate so far."

"Marshall's lying or being conned," I'm quick to point out. "Someone's obviously getting their wires crossed."

The room stops up with an uncomfortable silence. Both Logan and Gage let the weight of my words crash over their shoulders.

Gage gets up and pulls me with him as we start to make our way to the door. "Take care, man." He offers Logan a partial hug. "I still have to kick your ass when you get back. You know that, right?"

"Got it," Logan's face creases at the longitudinal cut I gifted him. "Looking forward to kicking some ass myself. Watch your back, bro." He socks him in the arm before pulling me into a hug.

Gage and I make our way out of the estate. We'll have to come up with some stellar plan on how to snuff the life out of Logan some other time because we've exhausted ourselves emotionally with the prospect of me marrying Dudley.

Apparently they believed him.

A lot.

Outside the main gate of the haunted mansion proper is a mass of congealed flesh, sporting the latest in petticoat fashion, odd suits that notch into butterfly bowties high at the collar.

"It's a zoo out here, we'll never get out," I say.

Gage pushes through the crowd and hits the unlock button on his key remote. The truck barks, and the lights blink twice, causing everyone to commission a reflexive gasp of admiration.

Gage helps me into the passenger's seat and climbs in over my lap to the other side. No teleportation here. I think the Transfer is where binding spirits actually go to die.

Gage starts up the engine and the whites of their haunted eyes enlarge as they freeze—petrified by the noise. He gives a few good revs, and the crowd scatters as the giant monster beneath us rouses from its slumber. He throws the truck into reverse, leans in and steals a kiss.

"Hold on," he instructs, as we bolt backwards at ninety miles an hour.

64

Treasures and Trinkets

After a long night of cataclysmic rain and hail, nothing more than a thin veil of fog puffs through our world this morning. Gage and I weren't able to partake in our mystery date last night since it was well after midnight when he finally dropped me off but he promised he'd more than make up for it. He would have stayed if it weren't for the fact he had Holden-sitting duty. I'm so pissed off at the aforementioned Kragger that if I could translate my feelings into action it might lead to a shotgun induced homicide, and even that couldn't kill him.

I open my bedroom window and take in a breath of fresh morning air, scented thick with pomade from the pines.

"Nev!" I shout, trying to sound like a bird myself in the event Tad should hear. God knows he's convinced of the torrid love affair I'm carrying on with a raven of all creatures—thank you very much, *Ezrina*.

A dark swirl descends through the atmosphere. The air parts as if it were honoring him as he lands with a gentle tap along the windowsill.

"*In*," I order. It doesn't come out half as hostile as I want it to.

He squeezes inside and hops nervously from the desk to the dresser before settling on the bed.

I place my hand on his back and warm his cool feathers.

An apology is comprised of simply words, Skyla. I cannot within good reason say that it would ever be enough, he says, adjusting his wings.

"Don't apologize," I sigh. "I know I should be crazy upset, and in a way I am, but if I were in your shoes and able to touch the person I loved just one more time, I would have done the same."

You are far too kind. I want you to know I've taken the liberty to arrange a special treat for you.

"Really?" I'm completely intrigued.

Since I'm unable to repay you in any manner for what you've given me I asked Ezrina to grant you one of your greatest desires.

"My greatest desire?" My heart gives an abnormal thump. "To get you another trial and ensure this farce doesn't repeat itself anytime soon?"

Time with your father, Nevermore cocks his head up at me.

"Oh, yes, totally my greatest desire." I don't mean to burst Nev's bubble but I could light drive back to him anytime I wanted, which by the way I'm completely in the mood for.

Ezrina has arranged a meeting in the near future. Since he's long departed to paradise he'll be visiting from the past. I surmise you appreciate the circumstances.

"Yes. Just let me know when and I'll get back there."

Oh, no, my dear girl. I'm afraid you've misunderstood. Nev twitches foot to foot. *I've made arrangement for him to come to you.*

There's a knock at the door. Mom shouts for me to get downstairs.

"I gotta go." It's the day of the not so great garage sale. "I'm not sure I know what you mean. Like *here*, here?"

Yes, here, *here. Paragon.*

"He'll need a supervising spirit then," I surmise.

Sector Marshall has volunteered as a temporary.

"Marshall?" I jump at the thought. "I'm totally going to kiss him when I see him. Not really, but you know," I say, escorting Nevermore back out the window.

I can't believe this!
My dream really is going to come true.
My father is finally coming to Paragon.

Drake and Ethan load up the Mustang with an army of junk that couldn't fit in the minivan just before I take off. It was bad enough driving without blind spots at every spare angle, but the fact I'm functioning with almost zero visibility at the moment actually explains why I've managed to receive twice as many honks and finger salutes than usual.

Gage and Holden both have their trucks parked along the side of the road so I sandwich between them. I just sit there thinking of the irony, when a dark shadow falls over the windshield. I look up to see Nev circling the vicinity. I almost wish I could've had Ezrina arrange for me to go back to the night of the accident. Even though I'm certain that Chloe took the wheel of the Mustang, I still feel like I need to see it for myself. Maybe Marshall would be willing to supervise *me* as a temp and circumvent that binding spirit? I think he owes me as much as Ezrina, probably more. If he doesn't want to lose his 'future wife' before he somehow miraculously acquires her, he should consider obeying my every whim—starting now.

A pale figure in the woods catches my eye. It disappears quick as it came, like a ray of hope when really there is none. Only this doesn't feel too hopeful, it feels evil with the patina of something sinister. It coats me from the inside, renews a fear in me only my darkest nightmares are able to produce.

I bolt out of the car and smack right into a body.

"Skyla," Gage backs up and smiles that infectious grin.

"I'm so glad it's you!" I stop short of letting him in on the fact I think I just saw a Fem. No point in ruining a perfectly good day with what might have just been a pale, frumpy, patron from the scrap and salvage having a seriously bad hair day.

Gage helps me drag most of the junk from the car and schlep it over to the table that Mom and Tad occupy with a strange assortment of material trappings from their past.

"Whose are these?" I place down a pair of clunky skis that had embedded themselves in my backseat.

"Those were your father's," Mom examines them before making a face.

"Dad used to ski?" How can I not know this about my own father?

"Long time ago—when you were little. We used to steal day trips to the mountains, but life got busy." She slaps a bright orange sticker on them that reads, $20.

"Excuse me," I say, indignant. "You can't just sell Dad's stuff." I pick the sticker off and shove the skis over to Gage.

"These skis are way too big for you," he kindly informs me. I gape up at the audacity that both he and his dimples have in siding with my mother.

"That's not the point," I say.

"Skyla, I'm getting rid of junk." My mother is nonplussed by my inherent sense of panic to preserve all things daddy. "Your father would have wanted me to get rid of them. Tad and I are keeping the important stuff and that's all that matters."

Dear God. Now would be a lousy time for my father to step onto Paragon. I can imagine his shock when he finds his personal belongings spread out unwanted with bright orange stickers advertising the fact he's been heavily discounted.

"I'm keeping the skis," I take them from Gage and lay them under the table.

"Fine," Tad doesn't bother looking up from aggregating his dead wife's belongings out into long neat rows. "Find another place to store them, would you? They're not welcome back at the house."

I look over to Mom horrified but she nods in agreement while arranging old picture frames and long stem wineglasses.

Gage pulls me in and pecks a quiet kiss on my cheek. "You can keep them at my house. I have a shed out back, but if you prefer them in my room I wouldn't mind that either." He suppresses a grin that veils the fact he thinks I'm sweetly insane.

I take him in under the bright illumination of a haze free day. Gage is impeccable—gorgeous both inside and out.

"Thank you," I say, pressing the ring he gave me to my lips then placing it over to his. Gage gives it a quick kiss before flashing his dimples at me. I love having Gage on my side—and, I plan on having him *by* my side every single day. Our forever has already started and it feels like heaven.

"My dad thought of a way," he nods back into the swelling crowd at Holden, "to take care of our little problem."

I look just in time to see him stretching his arms over some girl from East that I've never seen before.

"It can't come soon enough," I say. "What's the plan?"

"You're going to kill Logan at prom."

65

Silver and God

A wash of unfamiliar light trickles down from the atmosphere, enough to actually produce a glare in my eyes from the once-fabled orb otherwise known as the sun. I don't know how I stopped packing my sunglasses in my purse after doing so every single day in L.A., but on Paragon they are about as practical as a chariot on the freeway.

"I can't kill Logan again," I say to Gage as we hold hands, making our way through the endless tables of crap lining Marshall's expansive property. I refuse to entertain the idea of clobbering Logan into kingdom come at prom or any other venue for that matter. I've tried and failed at Cain River, and I don't have any plans of repeating the effort.

"It makes sense," he picks up an old leather catcher's mitt and tries it on before replacing it. "If me or my dad do it, Chloe might blackmail us, but she's already at a draw with you, so it won't change things too much."

"Apparently, I'm not really good at offing people," I shoot a look over at Holden who took the liberty to kill eighty-nine Celestra with Logan's own hand. That alone is reason enough for me to reverse my stance and want to succeed at the mission.

"This will be foolproof." Gage wraps his arms around my waist and slips a depleted smile. "I'll be there with you."

"Of course you will. You'll be my date." Just the thought of actually attending a formal event with Gage and not having to hide the fact we're together is thrilling. We could douse each other with passionate kisses right in the middle of the dance floor, and there's not a damn thing Chloe can do about it.

He shakes his head. "You need to get Holden to go with you. That's part of the plan."

"What?" I jump in disbelief. "Have I mentioned how much I hate this?"

Marshall's voice rises above the chatter in the crowd.

"Let's go see what he's pushing," I pull him along, hoping Marshall's trinkets will take my mind off bashing Holden's skull in with my high heel.

"Boxes of lead," Gage whispers. "I'm still sore from lugging whatever was in those cartons."

"I'll give you a massage later," I offer. "And bake you some cookies." I'll be the best girlfriend in the world if it kills me, not that it would ever kill me to cater to Gage.

"I'll hold you to that."

We break through the crowd that has amassed in front of Marshall's table and maneuver our way to the front. Hoards of people struggle to grab and ogle his questionable wares. Almost every person in the vicinity has migrated over. I bet in eagerness to discard his junk he's drastically underpriced everything, just like my mother.

I take in a sharp breath at the sight.

"Oh, my, God!" I whisper, looking to Gage for some sort of explanation.

Hundreds if not a thousand of gorgeous pewter trinkets lay strewn across the table. I watch in horror as dozens of foreign hands fondle and paw his haunted ironwork at a frenetic pace.

Gage and I make our way around to the other side to have a talk with our cagey Sector friend.

"Young Oliver," Marshall straightens in exhaustion, "I bid you to momentarily take over the reaping of finances so I may have a quick word with Ms. Messenger."

"A brief word," Gage glares into him. "Only words."

Marshall speeds me over to the periphery of the melee while keeping an eye on the treasures being haphazardly mined by the unsuspecting population.

"Did you make all those?" I have a feeling I totally know the answer.

"Every last bit," there's a touch of boastfulness in his tone. "I've also handcrafted an impressive pair of champagne flutes to toast our nuptials when the time arrives."

"Fascinating." In all honesty, I'm giving less and less thought to Marshall and his delusions of grandeur regarding our conjugal union. I'm totally convinced it's some celestial prank that his so-called prognosticating consort who goes by the frat-induced nickname of 'the orator' has decided to pull. "So what gives with the lustrous alloy arrangement? You've got a supervising spirit in each one?" Which is a nice segue to my next request.

"There's a vestige of wickedness cloaking the island." Marshall slits his eyes in either direction as if said vestige of wickedness was on the prowl for a flea market find. "This is merely a strategy to contain its ill effects."

"So—what? They're like vacuums?"

"They're a weaker version of a protective hedge. Place enough of these around the vicinity and the odds of the region becoming impregnated with evil ills decreases significantly. They're not to be worshiped or glorified, simply a spiritual air freshener if you will."

"In that case I'll take twenty."

"I'll have over thirty delivered to your room before tomorrow's witching hour," he purrs.

A white shadow moves along the border of the woods just north of the estate.

"Bright out today." I shield my hand over my eyes, trying to focus in on whatever seems to be vying for my attention. I have a feeling I'll be needing a little more than a spiritual air freshener.

Marshall waves his hand and without delay the sky darkens, inciting a shallow gasp from the crowd.

"You're powerful I'll give you that." I fatten up his ego for the kill. "Rumor has it you'll be acting as a supervising spirit for my father."

"Some rumors are true," he glares into the crowd. "Note and highlight the fact *I* am not the purveyor of this affliction. Ezrina and her featherheaded Romeo concocted the idea. Be warned—they are prone to bad ones."

"Are you kidding? My father coming to Paragon is a *dream*. I'd have to disagree with you, they're prone to great ideas—brilliant even."

"Very well." He flexes his cheek in disapproval. "You are aware Ezrina is growing most impatient for her trial," he takes in a breath, expands his chest the size of a wall, "And, knowing full well she won't get one, she's in the process of creating manuals to assist you once you take over her job in the gallows."

"Crap."

"You must implore your mother, Skyla. It's the only way."

"Help me," I plead. "Make this entire Ezrina situation go away and—"

"And what?" His eyes slit over me. He doesn't move a muscle in the event I renege the offer faster than I make it.

"Just help, please?" My chest heaves involuntarily—a serious warning bell for an onslaught of tears.

"When you decided to defile my vision with your lingual emissions," he pauses to frown, "I delicately removed myself from your dealings. I gave my word I would be of no assistance. Though, admittedly, my reaction was in haste, I cannot go against my word."

"How about getting Logan back in the right body? You have to help with that." In a fit of anger I've managed to ruin everything. This is impossible to rectify without Marshall and he knows it.

"I'll see what I can manage."

expel

"Thank you!" I swell with relief. I might get permanent duty as Ezrina's body double, but at least Logan will still have a chance at life.

"Allow me to relieve Jock Strap of his duties. Sales have slumped since I've stepped away, and I've no one to blame but him."

"Wait," I pull him back by the hand. "I was hoping you could do a little something for me." I bite down on my lower lip. "I want to go back to the night of the accident and see who was driving the car. I mean obviously it was Chloe, but I want to see it with my own two eyes."

"I can't be your supervising spirit, Skyla—conflict of interest and all those good legalities." He takes a step in the opposite direction. "Although, I will say this, a person only has access to one binding spirit. Devise a manner to fool Ms. Bishop into sending her binding spirit elsewhere. If it does belong to her, once she releases the spirit you'll be able to travel back and see the carnage unfold from the vantage point you're seeking."

"You are a genius!" I stagger the words out in awe.

"A phrase I'm looking forward to hearing you repeat many, many, times in the confines of our chamber." He gives a crooked smile before sifting back into the crowd.

Yeah, like that will ever happen.

It won't—will it?

66

Evil Incarnate

"Do you realize he just raked in an even grand while you two were talking?" Gage latches onto me with those intense eyes the same hue as the bottom of the ocean, and I systematically forget everything else. "So what did he want?" There's a marked irritation in his voice.

"He says," I pull Gage away from Marshall's table and the roving ears that surround it, "they're some kind of protective hedges. He says Paragon is being infiltrated with evil."

"Speaking of evil," Gage nods to the other end of the mass of humanity, "let's see what Demetri's doling out of his bag of tricks."

"And to think my mother helped him load up his possessions, emphasis on possess. I bet that's not all she was helping him do."

"I just don't think she's into him like that," Gage gives a dissatisfied blink. "She seems pretty devoted to Tad."

"I hope you're right. As far as I know the mock wedding is still on."

We head over to Demetri's table. I can hear his pretentious voice cackling through the crowd, cajoling the innocent patrons of Paragon right out of their last dollar.

"You guys selling?" Ellis pops up, blocking the path to our final destination.

"I wouldn't go around posing that question if I were you." Gage secures his hand over mine. *We should let Ellis in on our plan to off Holden. We might need all the help we can get.*

I gasp at the thought. Poor Logan. I know it's him we're trying to protect—bring back, but still, I can't help feel like we're ganging up on him. Holden does a magnificent job of screwing everything up.

"Sure," I acquiesce. " How's your jaw?" I ask Ellis, noting the fact he's moving it just fine and there's nary a sign of a wire.

"Lucky for Bishop, it's excellent." Ellis glowers, obviously still pissed at Chloe for the rock to the face.

Pierce and Nat stand off in the distance, talking to Demetri and a tall albino looking man with vacant eyes.

"Arson Kragger," Gage makes a face, "I'm not sure if he's aware of the fact he's got another son roaming around the island."

"We're going to need Marshall," I look up at Gage. There is no way I'm even risking another vagrant spirit jumping into Logan's skin.

"Who's Marshall?" Ellis says before doing a double take at Nat and the crowd of Counts.

"Dudley," I say, following Ellis's gaze to see what's harnessed his attention.

Another man, tall, with familiar looking features, steps over to Demetri, and they clasp hands. Demetri pulls him into a manly embrace before patting his back, speaking with him as if he hasn't seen him in ages. Demetri ignites the conversation with his moronic verbal rantings, and the crowd lights up with laughter.

"Who the hell is that guy?" I ask. I'm pretty sure anyone who's kindred spirits with Demetri and Arson Kragger is an enemy of mine.

Ellis hardens, freezes for a moment before relaxing into a sigh.

"Come on, I'll introduce you," his voice dips into its lower register, a dark place I've never heard him venture before. Gage and I follow in close as we head towards the unsuspecting group of adversaries. "Dad, this is Skyla. You know Gage."

I solidify. I can't even begin to comprehend that the Count still physically linked to Demetri is Ellis's father.

"Skyla," he extends his hand in my direction, says my name like a question.

A wickedness illuminates him from the inside. He looks remarkably like Ellis in every way just aged—harder.

I shake his rough, dry hand and quickly replace my arm by my side.

Demetri steps into me.

"Skyla, you must profusely thank your mother for me. If it weren't for her amazing organizational skills, none of this would have been possible." He wands his hand over the crowd huddled over his table.

I still haven't seen the merch he's pushing. For all I know it's headless Fems and haunted water globes or something equally as vindictive just to propagate his insatiable need to control the universe.

"I don't see any reason to thank her for you," I smirk. "I'm sure you'll find a way to do that yourself."

"Indeed," his lips curl into a black smile.

"Mr. Edinger?" Chloe crops up unexpected like most vermin do. "How much for the mirror?"

"Mirror?" I shoot a look in the direction of her crooked finger as she pulls Demetri aside.

Gah!

Holy freaking shit!

There is no way in hell I'm letting Chloe haul that thing into her bedroom. She'll have her way with Gage nightly. More often than *I* will.

"It was a gift," I hear him say. "I'm having second thoughts on parting with it," Demetri taps the side of his face.

"That's the mirror," I hiss to Gage.

"It's huge," Gage eyes it as innocent bystanders fondle its existence.

expel

"That's gonna look really F'ed up in your room," Ellis whispers. "I'd let Bishop score this one."

"No way," I head over to Demetri and Chloe where the haggling is well underway.

"How much?" I demand.

"Forty dollars," Demetri says. "I think that's a fair price. All funds go to the Community Center of course." He strokes Chloe's long dark hair in one fell swoop. "Would you like me to load it into the trunk of your vehicle?"

"Yes," Chloe is mesmerized by his touch. Her face lights up a slap cheek red—I do believe Chloe Bishop is blushing.

"No," I protest. "I'll give you eighty." I don't have eighty of anything but that's beside the point.

"One hundred," Chloe opens her purse and hands over a fist full of dollars.

I look to Gage and Ellis with cash strapped desperation.

"Two hundred," Gage pipes up. "For Skyla."

I give a passive smile over to Chloe.

Demetri cocks his head, amused. "You must care deeply for this young lady to want to give her the entire world. I assure you, it's the only way to love a woman." He digs into me with his dark eyes, accesses me with a newfound curiosity.

Surely he must realize that both Chloe and I have stumbled upon its magical curative properties where reality is concerned. Why else would I pay two hundred nonexistent dollars for something I already have in my room in triplicate?

"I really want this," I come just shy of touching him to prove my point. "Please," I lace my voice with sugar—an arsenic based sugar derivative.

"I was here first." Chloe's mouth falls open as the desperation oozes from her pores. Soon she'll offer up her body—her soul for the reflection collection. "I'll be sure to donate two hundred and *fifty* dollars to the Community Center first thing in the morning." She tries to pull him along by the sleeve, but Demetri doesn't budge.

"I've changed my mind," he narrows his wicked twin darts at me. "I'm giving it to Skyla. It's the least I could do to repay her mother for all the kindness she's endowed upon me since I've been back."

Your damn right it is, I want to say but don't.

"Ellis would you please help Gage load it into my car?" I ask with a relegated calm that's specifically reserved for pissing off Chloe.

They head over to the haunted looking glass and hoist it into the air.

Chloe pulls me aside. Too bad for her because negotiations are going to be a real bitch.

"What are you going to do with it?" She hisses.

"I'm going to crawl in every night and kill you over and over." I give a smug look of satisfaction. "No, wait," I huff a laugh. "I'm going to have Gage kill you over and over. He'd do it in real life but he's too damn nice." I give a short-lived smile.

She takes in a deep breath, looking over my shoulder as it disappears from sight.

"That was your last chance Chloe," I zero in on her with my hatred. "You will never have Gage now. You will never know his skin, his lips, what it's like to be wild with pleasure from his touch."

Her features glaze. Chloe's face smoothes over—turns to stone from the horror of it all. "I'm so damn sick of you," she seethes. "The Gagegasms, the Logangasms—the vaginal fireworks going off are totally sickening." Her chest heaves with loathing. "I want you to remember this day, Skyla." Her dark eyes penetrate me as they explode with hatred into mine. "This is the day you sealed your fate and that of your loser group of boyfriends."

"What are you going to do?" I taunt her slow and reserved, swill her panic around in my mouth like fine wine. "Run us over with my car? Oh, wait, you already did that, didn't you?"

She leans back, bites down on her lip, controlling a criminal smile. "I'm going to hit you all right, and you will never see it coming." She spins on her heels and disappears into the crowd swift as a demon.

The last time Chloe uttered those words it almost cost me Gage.

My insides loosen as I scan the crowd for him.

Please God don't let it be Gage.

67

It's Raining Caskets

Sunday, it rains all day.

The harsh precipitation unleashes all of the pent up fury it was forced to suppress the day before while Marshall donned his weather god hat. The sky is pissing all over Paragon after being forced to hold it a solid twenty-four.

An entire watershed has dumped off on us already this afternoon. It's violent needle-like protrusions against the infrastructure of the house feels heavy, as if it were pressing down on my shoulders instead.

The Landon house is playing host to a baby shower today.

Since teenage girls are often short on cash, and neither Brielle nor Drake have large extended families looming in the wings willing to glom together and purchase entire sections of Babies 'R Us, Mom decides to take on the responsibility herself. She opts to have a small quick shower consisting of presents purchased almost exclusively by her.

Of course, Gage, the Landon clan, and Brielle's frequently inebriated mother will be in attendance. Ethan's dysfunctional other half will be making a cameo, which, by the way, I'm still waiting for him to hang her by her long intestines or something along those lines as a means of revenge.

Crap. I just thought of something. Ethan is such a dumbass he probably doesn't comprehend the true meaning of the word revenge. He probably believes it has the *opposite* implications.

I try to put the thought out of my mind by tending to decorations.

expel

I set a buttery yellow tablecloth over the coffee table where my mother instructed me to arrange the presents in hopes to usher in a festive mood, as if teen pregnancies weren't festive enough. But all I can think about is the fact Gage is taking me out later this afternoon. Now that Ellis is aware Holden is using Logan's body as a hideout, he volunteered to Holden-sit so we can be alone.

"Skyla, blow up some balloons. They'll be home any minute." Mom shoves a fistful of blue and pink latex at me, ironic because if latex were employed about nine months ago, none of us would be subject to the layered cake molded in the shape of a fetus today. She spins me in the direction of a fat helium tank and takes off towards the kitchen.

Drake and Brielle took Mia and Melissa out for a quick mall crawl. The girls have been in 'bitch squad training mode' all week.

"Tell me why my presence is needed again?" Tad looks unreasonably burdened by the fact he needs to stay put the rest of the afternoon. He blows up a balloon by mouth and knots it off. Hot air is his specialty so it's no coincidence his balloon floats without the aid of chemically altered gases.

"Support," Mom bellows, clearly annoyed. "You're supporting your son during a milestone in his life."

"That's where I disagree," Tad contests. "You see—he *chose* to be flagrantly irresponsible. Therefore, if I stay, I'll only be supporting the fact he's immature and essentially immoral." He stares blankly at the wall. "And he's completely unaware of the fact condoms are more than just room décor."

Ethan and Chloe emerge from his bedroom. His hair is sticking up in the back and Chloe sports an undeniable post-coital glow.

I guess Tad is two for two when it comes to immature and irresponsible children. Let's hope this one knows the power prophylactics hold when it comes to warding off demonic spawn.

"Oh, hi Chloe," Mom shoots a nervous look to me. "You're more than welcome to join us. We're having a small baby shower for Brielle."

"I'd love to. How can I help?" Chloe is quick to bend and pucker in my mother's presence.

"Let's get these banners up in the front hall," Mom leads her out of the room.

"Guess what, Sis?" Ethan frowns into me.

"Don't call me that." It weirds me out because that's exactly what Holden used to call me when he was wearing Ethan's skin sweater.

"Chloe's making plans for you," he whispers.

"Yeah? No surprise there. I thought you said you had a little revenge plot of your own brewing?" I look him up and down.

"I do," he gives a quick nod.

"To be initiated—*never*?" Maybe sleeping with her is his revenge? He does have a severe case of desperate dick syndrome. Revenge always equals sex to a guy—come to think of it most things do.

"Prom," he deadpans.

"You taking her to prom is supposed to invoke fear into her?" Crap. Why do I get the feeling I've just been Landoned.

"Did I hear someone mention prom?" Tad floats over. "You know most teen fatalities occur on that glorified night of illegal festivities?"

"What's this about?" Mom and Chloe drift back in the room.

"Just discussing the inevitable side effects of indecent frolic and formal wear," Tad says, while stringing a balloon. He lets it float up to the ceiling and it pops with an obnoxious bang.

"Prom is a magical time of year," Mom shakes her head, "don't listen to him."

expel

"It *is* a magical time of year." Chloe initiates a smile from my mother with her 'bend over—me kiss you long time' routine. She clasps onto Ethan. "Will you be my prom date?"

"Anything for you," he cuts a quick secretive smile in my direction.

Why do I have the sneaking suspicion that Ethan is in bed with Chloe in more ways than one?

There's a brief knock on the door followed by a familiar hello.

Gage breezes into the room with an apple red ribbon tied around a miniature white casket.

"Aw," I say petting the smooth glossy wood. "It is *so* freaking adorable." It's from Gage and me to Drake and Brielle. I just know they're going to love it. Well, they should—after all, she was the one who requested it.

"Are you mentally challenged?" Tad stomps over. He looks sick like he might vomit over it *and* Gage. "Clearly you have voided the warranty on that micro encephalon. Get that bad omen out of the house. My grandchild is not sleeping in that sarcophagus."

A scuffle erupts off in the entry, screaming and shouting, and the sound of something thumping into the wall, then the very distinct crash of glass breaking.

"What in the hell?" Tad leads the way to the front hall.

Mia and Melissa scratch and claw—pull each other by the hair in every direction.

Gage and Ethan jump in, plucking the two of them apart like bouncers at some wild bar fight.

"Wouldn't it be great if we could settle our differences that easily?" Chloe purrs into my ear.

"I hate you!" Mia rattles the words into Melissa's face.

"I'm going to make sure you die a slow and painful death!" Melissa fires back. Coming from a Count that sounds like a promise more than a threat. Then again Mia is technically one, too.

"All things I'd like to say to you," I lean into Chloe and smile.

"Eat dirt!" Mia snaps.

Tad injects himself into the ruckus and claps his hands over his head. "Whatever the hell it is that has you girls up in arms, get over it. I won't have this infighting going on. My roof, my rules."

"You are an asshole!" Mia barks in his face before zooming upstairs.

"Get the hell out of my room!" Melissa speeds up after her.

"Lizbeth!" Tad spears a finger in their direction and they both shake their heads at the failed experiment that is our family.

"Come to think of it, I think this is an accurate portrayal of what life would be like if we were sisters," Chloe pulls a lock of her coal colored hair and slips it into her mouth like a slithering reptile.

"I thank God we're not genetically related," I seethe. "I think nature mutated you in everyway but physical."

"Thank you," she quips.

Gage steps in behind me, wraps both his arms around my waist and rests his head on my shoulder.

"I take that back," I seethe. "I think physically you should be in a casket. I'm sure Gage would be happy to supply one if needed."

Gage doesn't say anything, just suppresses a small laugh as if to attest to the fact he would indeed supplicate a pine box if such a glorious occasion arose.

Chloe gasps for air, lets her wild gaze stray from Gage to me before settling on him with her full throttle anger. "There will be a casket, Gage. Only it won't be my body in it."

68

Pink and Blue

Mia and Melissa put down the proverbial boxing gloves long enough to join us for the revelry or lack thereof. Darla dragged in Demetri, her latest, not so greatest main squeeze, and Mom keeps laughing and giggling into him like they're not so secretly getting it on in private.

Brielle thinks we should start the party off with cake so I man the dessert table while systematically destroying the overpriced rendition of a baby. Why, exactly, my mother deemed it acceptable to order a cake designed to look like a giant baby shrimp metamorphosing into a human, escapes me. Did she not know there would come a time when one of us would be forced to lop off its crustacean humanoid head? And that a baby's head on a platter, albeit a paper plate imprinted with tiny yellow booties, looks no less offensive than if it were real?

"Old habits die hard," Chloe snarks while I hack off an arm. She takes a piece and slinks back to Ethan without offering to help.

Tad pops up behind me and runs his finger over the decapitated pastry.

"So, I hear there's a wedding next week," I scoff, disgusted at his inability to keep my mother from falling right into the snake charmer's basket.

"Sure is," Tad snaps about half a dozen cookies off a tray.

"So, are you like the best man or something?" I continue to lacerate the hindquarter of the heavily frosted infant while Gage retrieves the ice cream from the freezer.

"What?" he hisses.

"You know, at Mom and Demetri's wedding? Are you playing the role of minister or greeter? Because you sure as hell are not going to be the groom." I nod over at Mom who lets out a full on sexual moan right in the middle of the room while Demetri straddles her from behind and indulges her in a shoulder rub.

"I bet you would like that wouldn't you?" His tiny eyes squint into nothing. "I bet you'd volunteer to be the photographer at that event just to encapsulate each precious moment your mother is with anyone but me." His face explodes with color.

"Not true," I interject.

"Let me tell you something, Missy. Your mother and I share a bond you know nothing about. We are closer than most couples who have been married for fifty years and I wouldn't normally say this as I realize I'll be crossing a serious line, but let the record show you drew first blood. Your mother and I are far more intimate than she ever was with her former husband who did nothing but keep the blinders on and shoulder her from the truth. I would never disrespect her that way, so that makes me miles better." He dumps the cookies back on the table and stomps off.

"What the heck was that about?" Gage steps in.

"He's insane," I shake my head. "He actually thinks he's better than my dad. Can you believe that? What a joke." I try to get my bearings before stabbing into the rock solid ice cream with an oversized spoon. "He accused my dad of keeping secrets from my mom." Which was sort of true.

"You think he knows?" Gage jabs each piece of cake with a fork. "You think she let him in on the fact she's a Count?"

I cut a heavy gaze over at her. Demetri is still going strong from behind and now Tad has her shoes off and is indulging her in some weird foot rub that looks both torturous and x-rated at the same time.

expel

"It's like they're attacking her." I lean into Gage for support while my mother endures a caustic assault that doubles as a morbid form of entertainment.

"Present time!" Darla spins in a circle while bolstering her Mimosa high in the air.

"Mine first!" Melissa insists.

"Gimme, gimme," Brielle squeezes her fingers as Melissa hands over a small yellow bag. She quickly tosses the tissue paper and plucks out a small rubber duck. "That's it?" Brielle dumps the bag upside down before tossing it aside.

"Yeah, but I bought it with my own money," Melissa glares over at Mia as if she received a loan from twelve different financial institutions to subsidize her gift.

Mia hands her a small velvet box. Something tells me Melissa's inclinations about Mia's gift might be factual. Or in the least, she's in serious debt to our mother.

Brielle lifts up a tiny ring with a circumference the size of a pencil.

"No freaking way!" She screams with delight. "I can't believe how awesome this is! This is so going to be on my baby the minute she's born. This baby is going to have some serious bling attached at all times." Brielle holds the tiny band of gold out for all to inspect.

"It's going to be a *he*," Drake corrects. "And he's going to look just like me."

"Hope not," Brielle cracks. "The last thing I want is for it to have that Count Dracula V coming down into its forehead like it's about to lose an eye to a sickle."

I look over at Gage. Those sounded an awful lot like fighting words. But, I *so* agree about that whole Count Dracula thing. Really, it's kind of creepy. We should mandate a prayer vigil in hopes it's recessive.

"If you really want something to be optimistic about," Drake starts in a little louder than necessary, "let's hope *she* doesn't inherit your mother's urge to get hammered every time there's a public gathering. *And*," he yanks the ring from Brielle's hand. "If you put this on the baby it's going to choke to death in the first five minutes."

Darla laughs. I don't think she quite understood that an insult was hurled in her honor, or the fact the death of her yet unborn grandchild was just broached as a topic.

"Give me that," Mia snatches it from him. "Contrary to what your stupid sister believes, I did pay for that with my own money."

"Enough," Mom howls, although it's unclear who she's shouting at, the scuffle unfolding or the scrimmage Demetri and Tad are waging over her body. Nevertheless, it all ceases. "You two are going to enter into one of life's most amazing privileges—becoming parents," her voice softens. "Brielle, you will love your child even if he or she is endowed with the Landon family mark of condemnation. And Drake, you will trust Brielle enough to know she would never allow that child to hurt itself. She is infused with God-given maternal instincts. She is going to be a fantastic mother. Mia and Melissa, you will learn to get along because you are both about to become aunts to a wonderful baby who the two of you will adore for the rest of your lives. And, I expect everyone here to get along next week when I marry the love of my life." She reaches down and picks up a hand without looking, presses Demetri's fingers to her lips and kisses them.

I give a gloating smile as Tad's jaw hits the floor.

But it just so happens this time, I hate being right.

69

Man in the Mirror

Soon after the abomination of desolation takes off, a.k.a. Demetri—he was the last freaking partygoer to leave, even Brielle took off long before he dragged his slithering tail out the door, but I digress—Tad drags Mom upstairs to progress to a full body rub. His words, not mine. The whole idea makes me vomit a little in the back of my mouth.

Of course, Gage doesn't leave. He's more family, less partygoer and we've yet to have some alone time. That date we keep trying to have continues to evaporate into a future that doesn't seem to have a place for it so we grab the bull by the horns and decide there's no time like the present. I pull him upstairs to my room to get *operation save the date* underway.

A foreign chessboard sits on my desk. Pewter cast chessmen each with their own unique effigy stare off blankly into one another.

"Looks like Marshall dropped off his spiritual air fresheners," I say fingering the glossy onyx board.

Gage picks up a piece and examines it before holding it out.

"It's you," he whispers. "You're the queen."

I bow into the board and heavily scrutinize the faces of the delicately carved creations. We're all there, Logan taking up the space next to me, Chloe on the opposing lineup with Ellis next to her on one side—Gage on the other and this puzzles me.

"Marshall has an interesting sense of humor," I gloss over the board one more time before pecking a quick kiss into Gage. "I'm going to hop in the closet and change," I give a seductive smile. Really I'm going to sneak up to the butterfly room and arrange the pillows and comforter I hauled up this afternoon after Gage planted the haunted mirror in my closet. God forbid anyone actually find the demented speculum and fall in.

It's been way too long since Gage and I had a magical moment together and what better place to make magic happen than the butterfly room? I've been fantasizing about this moment all day long. His arms wrapped around me, me peeling his shirt off all slow and seductive, a hot trail of kisses raining down my neck like fire, butterflies actually fluttering in our midst. There is no greater magic than Gage and his kisses.

I close the door behind me and turn on the light fully expecting to see my distorted effigy in that screwed up mirror of Demetri's, but I don't. Instead, a monstrosity so horrific stares back I jump out of the closet and scream until my lungs burn with fire.

"Shit!" Gage startles, his face bleaching out in an instant.

"Clown Fem!" I hiss.

Mom and Tad file in the room with differing levels of undress. Mom with her blouse unbuttoned and bra fully exposed, Tad in his boxer shorts and knee high socks that brand themselves against his pale flesh like twin black stains.

"Judas Iscariot!" Tad belts out.

"What the hell happened?" Mom looks me up and down, terrified.

Gage jumps over and wraps an arm around my shoulder. "I proposed." He grins at the two of them.

"And, I accepted," I say, still panicked by the not so nice man in the mirror.

"You did?" Gage's eyes sparkle with a laughter all their own.

expel

"Of course, I would accept," I soften into him, outlining a heart on his chest with my finger. "Yes, yes—*yes*!" I peck a kiss on his cheek.

Gage bears into me with a heavy gaze, never wavering with that look of joy in his eyes and suddenly we're having one of those memorable relationship moments right here in front of a partially dressed Mom and Tad.

"Congratulations!" Mom shouts, touching her hands to her ears. She lunges over and embraces the two of us before breaking down into deep heaving sobs.

I glance over at Gage, a little afraid of the fact we may have emotionally damaged my mother. There could be permanent psychological trauma for all parties involved if the truth be told at what the hell I was really screaming at.

"I'm just so happy," she sniffs back tears, recomposing herself just enough. Her face is awash with tears as she sweeps back her hair. "I'm going to throw you a party."

"No, you don't have to do that." The last thing I want is Tad bitching about how much he spent on our fake engagement dinner.

"Hear that, Lizbeth?" Tad muses. "We're off the hook. Lest you forget that we're still making monthly installments on that little welcome home party we threw Ethan after Christmas."

"I insist," she clutches onto me with her icy hands. "This means just as much to me as my own wedding. "Oh," her fingers speed to her lips as she reaches an epiphany, "why don't we celebrate right alongside our vow renewal, Saturday? I'm sure Demetri won't mind if we make the announcement. And as soon as I'm able, I'll throw you a real party. I just can't keep this good news contained. And the Olivers will already be there. It's perfect."

Gage and I appraise one another before nodding into Mom, who is still completely hopped up on her latest nuptial triumph.

"We'll leave you two alone, but don't stay late," Mom points a finger into Gage before pulling him into a tight embrace. "You're going to be my son-in-law," she whispers. "Welcome to the family! Tad get over here and welcome your new son."

"Don't you see what's happening here? They've rolled the dice, and now they gotta pay the price. This is your basic shotgun wedding playing out only they're voluntarily running down the aisle."

"What are you talking about?" Mom practically vomits out her disgust.

"Teen pregnancies are an epidemic. Skyla, here, sees all the attention the other two are getting, what with all the fancy cash and prizes, *caskets* no less, she wants in on the take."

This again?

"The take?" Gage drops the smile from his face. The only thing it looks like he wants to take on is Tad.

"That's right, the *take*," Tad comes over and shakes the words into Gage's face. "What better way to shack up with your girlfriend on my dime than to knock her up and marry her? Let me guess, just before summer break you two will have another little announcement to make." His fingers twitch in air quotes. "And mark my words, Lizbeth," he turns to my mother, "there will be two tiny caskets lining our bedroom in a few months time, when every one of these bozos figures out it's not so easy to stop an infant from wailing away at three in the morning. Oh, sure, they'll have excuses, they have school in the morning, a football game—they have to get ready for prom. We'll have two extra mouths to feed, and before you know it, they'll realize this arrangement of inconvenience no longer fits their lifestyles, what with Skyla's insatiable desire to rake against his brother whenever she has a scratch to itch."

expel

"It was a side effect from the medication." Mom barrels into him before reverting her attention back to me. "Tell him you're not interested in Logan."

I open my mouth but nothing comes out because technically that wasn't Logan or me in the boathouse back at Cain River.

"Ah-ha!" Tad dances a jig in his underwear. "She hesitated!"

"No," I shake my head at Gage. "I'm not interested in him. I swear."

Gage presses out a depleted smile.

"I was thinking about Holden," I whisper.

"Who's this Holden kid?" Tad straightens. "See, Lizbeth? Case in point. She's got a long list of suitors we've yet to discover."

"He is not a suitor. The only one for me is Gage," I say, fatigued by the whole Tad and Mom circus that erupted spontaneously. "Gage and I will be thrilled to share our news on Saturday. Thank you for extending the offer." Now get the hell out, I want to say, but opt for a manufactured smile instead.

Tad holds the door open for my mother while glaring over at the two of us.

"You had to open a can of worms and ruin everything," she scolds him on the way out.

"It's called the truth," he barks. "Something your girls don't seem to know too much about."

"My mother should lace his food with lighter fluid," I say, shutting the door and locking it.

"I volunteer to hide the body." Gage slides the dresser fully over the door.

"So I guess we're engaged." I bite down on my lower lip, trying to hide a smile.

Gage backs me gently into the wall, picks my hands up over my head and presses a light kiss on my lips.

"Would you marry me?" He winces when he says it.

395

"Is this a proposal?" I needle into him with the challenge.

He shakes his head. "This was just a preview. I have a proposal planned that you will never see coming."

It reminds me of Chloe's words, and my stomach lurches.

"Well, then, let me give you a preview of my answer," I pause, drinking down his anticipation, the rise and fall of his chest as it touches up against mine, "*yes*."

Gage and I fall into a kiss that has the map of our entire future emblazoned in it.

A vision emerges, awakens my senses to the scene unfolding before me. It's me in a white dress. I'm walking down a petal-strewn aisle. I watch as my satin shoes move in rhythm, the fabric runner moves beneath me, the blades of rich green grass on either side liven the world with color. Down at the end of the aisle a man dressed in a dark suit waits for me. I look up and see a familiar bright smile, anticipation and longing written all over his face—Logan.

I pull back and take a breath.

Gage drops his hands to my waist and lets out a sigh. "I saw it, too."

70

Vision Division

I help Gage hoist the mirror of terror into the bowels of the attic. Gage swore the image was gone, even knocked on the solidified glass to prove his point but I had him throw a sheet over it anyway.

He climbs back into the butterfly room just as I finish arranging the pillows, and I lure him over to me by way of a kiss.

"Tell me," he pauses to take a breath. "When Dudley shared his visions with you is that what it was like? You saw them at the same time?"

I feel horrible. I want the ground to open up and swallow me. I want to feel the earth press back together and crush my bones right out of my skin.

"I'm not trying to make you feel bad, I swear." He twirls his finger around a loose lock of my hair. "It felt intimate—beautiful sharing something like that with you. Not the actual image—that was quite possibly the worst vision I've had to date. But, strangely I feel closer to you now than ever before."

A swell of tears blur my vision, holds the tiny room hostage as they warp my lenses and make the butterflies pinned to the walls wobble for me.

"I never wanted Marshall's kisses. He is a master of manipulation. The visions—" I stumble in search of words.

"No," he places his finger to my lips. "It's OK."

"I swear I will severely injure him if he ever gets near me again." I press my lips together. "That vision we just shared—"

"I've seen it before," Gage whispers, gazing past my shoulder. He sounds tired, defenseless to the horrible truths that are unraveling around us.

I've seen it before, too, but I'm not in the mood to share that tidbit of information. I don't see the point in yanking his balls off and grinding my heel into them.

"Well," I pull him in close and slip my hand inside his shirt, give a light scratch at his chest, "the only person I'm going to spend the rest of my life with is right here in this room."

Gage gives a gentle kiss, pulls at my lips with his and lingers before letting go. "Nice save." His chest vibrates with the idea of a laugh. "But, I don't want you to feel like you're chained to me. Maybe Logan's right, we should finish out the faction war and then give you some breathing room, let you figure out who you want to be with."

"No," I pull him in by the back of the neck, "Logan is not right. Logan is hardly ever right. I know I want to be with you."

"Skyla," he compresses a sorrowful sigh, "please, don't deny you have feelings for him."

"Why does this night keep going there?" I sink my head back in frustration.

A tender trail of molten kisses trace up from my chest to my ear.

"Much better," I whisper, running my fingers through his hair and clenching on. "Less talking, more kissing." I find his lips and seal my mouth over his. I don't plan on letting Gage come up for air anymore. I plan on reminding him of how much it is I love him and plan on loving him every single day. I hope he sees our whole future unfold like a love letter.

It's going to happen.

I'm going to make sure it will.

expel

I spend most the week drifting in and out of a conversation about my own wedding with my mother. I swear it's like she's suffered a psychotic break and all she can focus on is marrying off her seventeen year-old daughter.

"Shouldn't you be fixated on uniting Drake and Brielle in holy matrimony?" I give a devious smile over to Brielle. In all honesty, I do prefer my mother's attention calibrated on me rather than Demetri.

We're shopping for bridesmaid dresses at the mall. Mom has delved further into her insanity by suggesting we each choose our own dress to wear this Saturday and opened up her wallet carte blanche.

"Oh," Mom tilts her head with curiosity, "I didn't think you were still together," she whispers into Brielle.

"You know how that goes." Bree shrugs.

"What?" Clearly this is news to me. An argument over the casket debacle does not a relationship break.

"He's already asked Emily to prom," she says nonchalant like it were insignificant on some level.

"*What?*" I shriek.

Brielle ignores me while sifting through a whole line of tents that she could easily hide that mountain of flesh erupting from her stomach. I swear, if I were her, I'd totally be expecting an alien to pop out at any moment—then again, if it were me, that might be a very real possibility.

"It's not that big a deal. I'll go stag," she says it like she means it. I appraise her for a quivering lip or flushed cheeks, but she doesn't look like she's about to cry or throw things or lop off Drake's balls.

"You will *not* go stag." I'm defiant about this. "You can go with Gage. He would *love* to take you." I don't feel bad one bit offering my boyfriend up to another girl, well, not this girl anyway.

"Who are *you* going to go with?" For the first time Brielle's voice breaks with emotion—finally a crack in the armor. I was beginning to wonder about her.

"I'm going with Logan."

"What?" My mother's mouth squares out in horror.

"It's a mercy thing," I'm quick to correct. "It was Gage's stupid idea." Actually Gage is impervious to stupid ideas. It was genius—every breath that boy takes is a work of art.

"Gage?" Brielle looks up as though she were envisioning it. "That's like going with my brother, you know, if I had one. I guess that'd be OK."

"Good—pick out two dresses," I encourage. "One for Saturday and one for prom."

Mom makes crazy eyes at me from behind Brielle. She's probably just envisioned Tad crapping his pants.

"And I'll do the same."

My cell goes off. It's a text from Marshall.

I have a dress for you.

A breath gets caught in my throat. I pan the vicinity for signs of his being, but something tells me his voyeuristic nature precludes logical bounds and limitations such as flesh and bones—time and space.

No thanx ~S

It has magical properties. He counters.

I'm sure it does. I'm sure it would bewitch me right into your arms. ~S

For that I'll wait until our union officially commences. This frock has the ability to absorb a floating spirit. In the event one had a spirit one needed to assign to a certain body. Just imagine a night with the Pretty One wrapped around you like a sheath.

The thought of Logan caressing me all night at prom makes me dizzy.

expel

My cell buzzes softly in my hand. **You're intrigued already I can tell by the color in your cheeks.**

I walk over to the mirror—startled to find my rosy flesh staring back at me.

I want a guarantee. ~S The last thing I need is another bodily mix up.

I can attest to the method myself. It's practically foolproof.

I twist my lips at the words *practically* and *foolproof*. In and of themselves they're dangerous—together they read like a bad omen.

"How's this for prom?" Mom holds up a dress reminiscent to the one Chloe wore the night she disappeared.

"I think I'll dig something out of my closet, save you some money," I offer.

"Thank you!" She mouths. "Now pick out something nice to wear to your engagement party. I have a little surprise cooked up for you." She winks before drifting off into a sea of pastel dresses.

I look over at Brielle with her swollen belly, no promise of forever from Drake who has all but pulled the plug on any kind of future they might have had outside of genetically engineering a child together. It makes me feel so amazingly lucky to have someone wanting to spend their forever with me—*three* someone's.

I squint out the window into the dull grey sky. I wonder what my celestial mother and her peeps at the destination station have up their sleeve as far as my love life is concerned?

On second thought, I'm pretty sure I don't want to know.

Not that she'd tell me.

Know it all bitch.

71

Power Surge

The sky over Paragon shifts and turns, changes every color the dark rainbow has to offer with the ease of a kaleidoscope. I study the veining that spiders through the clouds, the thick cords that snake through the sky like the roots of some infallible tree, a herculean Cedar of Lebanon erecting itself in a shadow that lurks up above.

In my mind I make flowers out of the smaller less aggressive clouds, the textured dark coils become exotic blooms that take a foreign shape, they have no name, no color. This is a dark Eden hovering above, drawing us in, engulfing us in its wicked garden.

Gage and I walk hand in hand to second period under the cloak of a threatening sky. The heavy underbellies of the precipitous brumes, full and fat, beg to rip apart and release their fury over the island.

"Hope your mom has good weather tomorrow," Gage looks up just as the sky fractures into tendrils of sizzling light.

"You mean, hope *we* have good weather tomorrow," I press a soft kiss into his lips. "You warn your parents?" I would ask about Logan slash Holden, but we both know Holden couldn't care less—hell, he couldn't care less if we reprised our performance from the Althorpe dinner and started rutting in the wedding cake. That might actually *amuse* Holden on some level—give him ideas.

"They've been sufficiently warned." His eyes widen.

"What?" I tug at his hand and cease all movement. "Tell me. I'll make sure we're severely late to second if you don't spill. What was that face? Your mom isn't coming? I knew she hated me."

"She doesn't hate you." He tries to control the wild grin waiting to explode onto his face.

"What?" I'm dying here.

"She thinks you may have manipulated the situation a bit, to get even with your mother for remarrying Tad." He hits the airbrakes with his free hand. "I set her straight."

"How pray tell? By way of the truth?" I totally didn't manipulate the situation but since the situation arose, I'm rather glad to detract from any farce that includes the glorification of Taddy dearest—especially since it involves yet another sacred union between him and my mother.

"Yes." Gage hypnotizes me with his ironclad gaze. "I told her I'm madly in love with you. And, if one day you would honor me by deciding to stand by my side for the rest of our lives, then, yes, we should very much celebrate that fact."

"Aw," I jump up on the balls of my feet and glide a wet kiss off his lips.

"That, and I told her about the Fem."

I smack him in the chest as we head into second.

❦

Marshall radiates a quiet repose. He bleeds most of the hour with a dry routine, espousing numbers, letters, and formulas as though he were reading a recipe from the back of a box, not his usual engaging demeanor. During the final ten minutes, he stares blank and wide in my direction as though he were looking through me, but the explosion of lust emanating from his being suggests he is rather focused on my person.

He hands a couple of students a stack of graded papers to pass out and takes a seat on the corner of his desk, openly pillaging me with a come hither look in his eye.

Chloe raises her hand, clears her throat to get his attention.

"Hands down." He doesn't bother breaking contact with me to reprimand her, doesn't blink, just takes me in, absorbs every nuance. I can feel something shifting, crackling down on a molecular level. He's calling me, encoding himself into my genetic design, grafting his soul onto mine. A strange pull takes over and I want to suction to him like a magnet. I seal my fingers over the rim of my desk and hang on, try to stop myself from doing something foolish like falling on my knees before him, begging him to take me in front of the entire class and Gage.

Ellis swivels in his seat. "I'm, like, really tripping out right now," he gives a low guttural laugh. His eyes shine glassy pink.

I try to revert my energy to Ellis, his perfectly straight nose, his small bowtie lips, but I snap back to Marshall and gasp. Marshall has become a full glorious breath in an oxygen-deprived world. This spell—this bondage he's placed me in is far too strong to ignore, and nothing in me wants to ignore anything about Marshall right now. Oddly, it doesn't feel like I'm being controlled, it feels genuine and right.

I can feel Gage shifting from behind—the tension rising like mercury in the desert. "You have five fucking seconds to knock this shit off." He booms over to Marshall.

The entire class takes in a collective gasp and turns towards Gage, but I can't pry my eyes off Marshall. I'm so close to giving in, going over and drinking down a warm pool of kisses straight from his mouth.

Marshall's lips curl into me. His chin dips into his chest while he molds my body with his eyes.

Gage spikes out of his seat, bullets to the front of the class. He picks up the metal stool Marshall usually lounges on and launches it out the back window at superhuman speeds—nearly decapitating the entire third row in the process.

expel

A growl of thunder rolls into the classroom, accompanied with a hurricane level wind.

Gage clocks Marshall onto the floor and the two of them roll around like tigers, nothing but fists, a tangle of legs moving so fast I can't tell which is which.

Ellis and a couple of other guys struggle to pull them apart.

Marshall pats his lip with the back of his hand and examines the crimson stain on his flesh before staggering to his feet.

"Your stay here," Marshall seethes into Gage, "has just been markedly reduced."

The bell rings.

"Take him directly to principal Rice. Inform her of the attack and let her know we'll need the windows boarded up at once." Marshall waves them off as they speed Gage out the door.

"He's going to kill Gage because he loves you," Chloe whispers the words in my ear like a necrotic poem. "The only thing better than me never having Gage is you never having him. All's well that ends well," she drips like a song.

I'm probably going to kill Chloe—and Logan is already dead.

Marshall and I will be the last ones standing.

Dear God.

What if that was the plan all along.

72

Oblivion Express

Marshall darts a look in my direction, and I find myself walking mechanically beside him down the hall.

"I demand an explanation," my voice hits a baritone that's unrecognizable, the walls wobble and quiver until they resize themselves, white and vacant.

I give a hard blink before realizing we're continuing our fervent gait while tucked neatly away in the Transfer.

"Holy crap!"

"Language," he barks, continuing his stride until we hit a corridor with a blue tint.

"What the hell just happened back there?"

"You mean the indescribable feelings of pleasure you just experienced for yours truly?" His lips curve with the hint of a maniacal smile.

"Yes," I grip him by the shirt and cease us in our tracks. "Did you put a spell on me?"

"I don't consort to witchcraft, it's the devil's way of dealing. I am a holy being, I assure you, through and through." He caresses my cheek with the back of his hand. "I merely called forth your feelings for me—demanded they surface and magnify themselves for us both to witness. It was a thing of beauty, Skyla," he says it breathless. "It was a roll call of your deepest desires and now I know there is a place in your heart for me no matter how insistent you are to deny it—no matter how hard you try to bury it."

He takes up my hand and walks us into the Count body containment facility brimming with human fishbowls as if the oral exchange never took place. I'm pretty sure I don't want to get into a debate with Marshall over my feelings for

expel

him, especially not while I'm at his mercy locked in the Transfer.

I try not to look at the floating limbs, the dead faces staring back at me from inside those tubes, the hands pressed against the glass as if begging for a way out.

He speeds us quickly towards the rear, where, hanging on a lone metal pole is a navy dress with what looks like upholstery tacks trimming the bottom and the top. It's a short dress—very short dress, as in you-will-share-your-underwear-super-short-hoochie-mama, run of the mill slut attire. I flip it around to reveal a giant bow which I surmise will sit squarely over my bottom. My fingers inspect the metal rivets, run over them in anticipation of what they might mean.

"You'll trap him in this?" I pet the gown that will inevitably hem Logan onto my person like a garment.

"Appealing to you—isn't it." It sounds almost accusatory.

"Yes, getting my friend back means everything to me."

"Friend?" Marshall balks. "It's me, Skyla. You never need to depreciate your true feelings about people around me."

"Can you appreciate how I'm feeling about you right now?" I seethe. "I didn't care for that stunt you pulled back in class and don't try to turn it around and say it had anything to do with my feelings. You know darn well it was a setup to piss off Gage."

"Infuriating Jock Strap was a perk." A simple smile adorns his face as he folds his hands before him.

"Are you going to kill Gage?" There it is, my biggest fear. He's already done it to Logan.

"Logan died at the hands of another. I assure you my payment for the spirit sword incident was usurped that night. I sent the wolves, Skyla, but it was too late."

"So you're not through with him." I finger the gown. "You want me to bring him back so you can kill him again."

"Nonsense. Why do for myself what I could have you do for me?"

"Very funny." If pissing me off is Marshall's goal he's achieving it masterfully.

"That's precisely what I was experiencing less than an hour ago." Marshall is making it clear he can read my mind down here. "Forty minutes straight, he copulated with you—nothing but a fornicating bonanza right there in my presence."

"Logan?"

"The genital support you harbor by your side at all times."

"Gage?" My mouth falls open. "You were listening in on his thoughts?"

"He was brutalizing me with fantasies of sexual savagery with my future wife!" He cuts the air with his tongue.

I grab a hold of Marshall by the shirt and pull him in. A fine pleasant wave washes through me, fulfils the longing I had when he was holding me steady in his unwavering trance.

"Maybe I *will* love you one day, but today you drifted us away from that horizon ever so slightly. Each time you're cruel to Gage—to Logan, you drive me further and further away from you. And maybe I will lose my mind and marry you but I will be Gage's wife before I ever will yours. You keep your threats and your bully-like ways the hell away from the people I love."

I speed out of the room and head out into the bowels of the Transfer.

I'm going to see Logan—tell him all systems are go.

I'm killing him next week at prom.

✶ ✶ ✶

expel

I walk the cobbled streets outside of the Transfer with all eyes roving over me as if I were a billboard. I manage to keep a safe distance from the long departed souls that descend in my direction, and I can't help but shake the feeling I'm about to be pounced from behind. Maybe leaving Marshall in such a huff wasn't the greatest idea. It never seems to be a stroke of brilliance to have Marshall pissed at me, even if I am perennially ticked off at him. He means well, he's just a brute beast when it comes to any hope of attaining my love.

I pause before taking another step and take in the majesty of the tall wrought iron fence stretching its arms out to heaven as if begging God for mercy.

Marshall loves me. It dawns on me for the very first time. I saw it in his ferocity when he induced Gage into a fit of wrath.

I take a breath at the thought. A vibration of laughter runs through me. All this time, I thought I was a pawn, a chess piece Marshall tinkered with to position at his leisure, to place in peril at his amusement, someone to exploit sexually if given the opportunity—but it's real. It's always been real.

A pale illumination dances on the periphery of the building. I turn quickly and gasp anticipating the worst, but there's nothing. The crowd continues to swell around me. I pick up speed and bolt to the oversized porch.

Skyla.

My name whispers from the outskirts of the ghostly assembly. A tuft of burnt coral hair rises from behind a group of women in ragged hoop skirts, their entire person clear as cellophane. From behind the fence he stares back at me, same bloodied clown that appeared in the mirror.

"Shit!" I struggle to open the door. The knobs twist loose but the door doesn't give. It's jammed or locked or broken.

The crowd filters onto the porch and bodies press against me every bit as real as anyone on Paragon pretends to be. Long dead hands prod my ribs, touch my hair, a strange electrical current surges through me as one of the women lays her cheek next to mine.

I let out a scream and kick into the door. It rumbles and creaks as I release my aggression over it. The crowd gasps. A woman sticks her nose to mine, and I bat her away, her skin a strange shade of grey as rows of papery wrinkles enwreathe her eyes.

The crowd parts swift as the Red Sea as the clown Fem moves between them.

"No," I whisper, rattling the handle, pressing and pulling, begging it to open.

"Excuse me?" His voice elongates unnaturally, eats away at my eardrums, corrosive as battery acid. I give a quick glance over my shoulder.

He's here.

My breathing grows erratic, pulsates out of control along with my racing heart.

He's going to touch me. I can't do this. I pound into the door—kick at it until the wood groans and cracks from under the pressure.

A hand glides over my shoulder, pale with dirty fingernails. The putrid stench of death spikes through my nostrils.

I crash into the seam of the door with my shoulder.

"I can set you free," it vocalizes in a strange manner, like an animal that was trained to mimic the words without fully understanding the meaning behind them.

"Marshall," I bleat out in a panic. The door gives beneath the weight of my body, and I burst into the cool unwelcoming arms of the dungeon-like mansion. I slam the door shut behind me like a reflex, yank over a cumbersome end table with carved cherubs at the base and use it to seal

expel

off the entry. A steady series of knocks erupt from the other side.

An echoing laughter, dark and sinister comes from the elongated hall before me. The flickering candles expose a pale shadow, the Fem appears locked in a death grimace as he staggers towards me.

"Logan!" I scream, running down the hall. The heavy rhythm of the piano strums through the walls. My feet vibrate with the hard ragtime music until I hit the bloated door just outside his room. "Logan!" It comes out like a cat on fire as I pound, and kick, and rattle the knob.

The clown Fem progresses in my direction. He strums his fingers against the wall, whispers something melodic in a language I don't recognize.

"Logan," I press my back to the door and watch frozen with fear as the clown reaches up to his forehead, runs his fingers down over his nose—his neck, causing his flesh to part like a zipper. His head splits in two, sags to the side like a Halloween costume revealing new flesh, the color of life underneath. A shock of inky dark hair, arrogant eyes reveal someone hauntingly familiar—Demetri.

The door opens up and I fall backwards into Logan's waiting arms.

He slams the door shut and locks it.

Logan wraps his arms around me, holds me for hours, days, weeks. I press my face into his chest and don't let go. Logan is a fortress. I can feel his affection washing over me in warm satisfying waves.

"He won't hurt you, Skyla," he gives it all in one hot whisper. "I will never let him."

"I wish there were a way to get rid of him, destroy him."

"There is," Logan cradles my cheeks in his hand and presses a kiss to my forehead. "And that's what we'll do."

73

Torment in the Transfer

Logan suggests we take a walk.

We head outside the same way I came in. Although this time it's uneventful in nature, no sign of Demetri the cowardly clown, and we draw no interest from the throngs of people walking arm in arm, rushing around like an army of hungry ants.

"My Mom thinks I'm engaged," I say, studying the fat low hanging moon. The purple night sky illuminates in pink and iridescent blues, so reminiscent of the Soulennium it must all be related somehow, but how and why?

"Are you engaged?" He asks, hushed, as if he were on the verge of making a grand discovery.

"Maybe," I shrug into it. I'd hate to deny anything about Gage, even if we're not at that point yet.

I tell him about the Fem that's been following me, the strange sight of it unzipping itself, revealing Demetri underneath.

"It's symbolic. They want you to fear him most."

"Who are *they*?"

"Fems, Sectors, your mother. It could be anybody." Logan wraps an arm around my waist as we head off the cobbled path. We take off towards a large lake, black as oil with a set of peaceful waterfalls that release into it at the far end. "Does this look familiar?" He tilts into me. The moon kisses him with its lavender beams, accentuates his perfectly carved features and blesses that hint of a smile Logan always saves for me. "Three falls. Marsh to the left."

"Oh my, God," I breathe. "It's a replica of the Falls of Virtue."

"That's right."

We sit on a mound of soft grass, blades as thick as fingers. Logan pulls me in and we watch the water shed into the thirsty mouth of the lake, steady as tears. The ground beneath us rises and falls as if the hill we were sitting on was the furry back of some mythological creature, ready to rouse from hibernation. "It's OK." Logan rubs his hand up and down my arm.

"I think Marshall's in love with me," I say it weak.

"You're just now figuring this out?" He pulls a wry smile.

"He's totally convinced we're going to marry. There's no doubt in him, he just accepts it like it were the truth."

Logan inches his head back at the thought.

"I had this dream," he shakes his head.

"I think I know."

"You too?"

"I had a vision with Gage," I take a breath. "And with Marshall."

"Of me?" His eyes glint in the light. He tucks his chin and tries to hide the smile that wants to erupt in victory. "You were so beautiful."

I had never seen the way I looked in any of those visions.

"You saw it through a different perspective," I whisper.

"I saw it through my eyes," he holds my gaze strong as steel. "You were walking towards me."

"You think it's a prophecy?"

"I know it."

"It's probably like the one Gage had." I stop shy of saying it was taken out of context. Saying those words out loud would be rebuking the idea of me ever marrying Gage and that's one idea I'll never shoot down. I don't care how many orators or prophetic visions try to get in my way. Gage and I are going to have our forever. It's coming. I can feel it.

Logan rattles my hand playfully, gives a halfhearted smile letting me know he heard everything.

"I'm going to get you back, Skyla." His chest expands with assurance. "I know something else, something that makes dying and living in this hellhole worth every painful minute."

I stop breathing in anticipation of what might come from his lips next— something wonderful, apocalyptic, a revelation of my future, all of the above. Anything seems possible.

"You love Gage," he expels softly with tears glistening, "but you love me, too. A powerful, hungry, unstoppable love that deep down, you can never deny. I can see it engraved inside your heart just as it is in mine." The revelation is just within reach but he won't give it. Instead, he expounds on the painful truth. I love Gage, and I love Logan.

I fill my lungs with a breath, until it becomes painful not to exhale.

"I do love you, Logan. I love you so much it hurts," it depresses from my lips like a secret mired in truth and agony. "I'm going to kill you at prom," it slips from my lips banal, as if death alone were the only way to steer us out of this conversation.

"That means I'm coming back to you."

"We need a codeword, so I know it's really you."

"Happily ever after. It will come." Logan wraps an arm around my waist.

It takes everything in me not to fall under the spell of this moment. Logan has convinced himself emphatically that we'll be together, and it's hard to refute something like that when I've had visions that back up his theory.

"Happily ever after?" It sounds loaded.

"It is loaded—with promise." He dots my cheek with a kiss. "Happily ever after."

expel

I blip back into my skin at West as if a single moment never went by. I bleed out the rest of the day—work a short shift alongside Gage at the bowling alley without mention of my dimensional jaunt with Marshall and Logan.

Thankfully, Gage was only reprimanded with detention for trying to rearrange Marshall's bone structure. It seems so lenient, makes me wonder if Marshall had something to do with it. Strange. But, then again, Marshall most likely has a far more severe form of punishment awaiting the love of my life.

A horrible sadness ebbs away at me from the inside until late in the night as I lie on my bed contemplating the absurdity of thinking I could ever know my future, that anyone else could for that matter.

A blue glow warbles next to the bed. A shimmer of light ignites bright as lightning before Giselle appears before me fully formed, warm, in a red cable sweater, jeans and boots.

"You look deep in thought." Her dimples go off, identical to Gage. "What's going on?" She hops on the edge of the bed, exploding her perennial good mood all over the place. I don't like it. It depreciates all of the melancholy I've invested in. It begs me to cheer up and match her enthusiasm, but I don't.

"Just busy," I shrug, "You know, plotting the revenge of my enemies." With prom just a week away that's really where my head needs to be—wrapped completely around Chloe's demise.

"So are you going traditional? Vat of pigs blood?" Her lips curve as she holds back a laugh.

"I'm thinking something less obvious yet equally as traumatizing. Nothing quick and dirty, that's too easy for Chloe."

"Just Chloe?" She raises her dark brows, amused. Giselle looks eerily like the female version of Gage. If Gage and I ever have a daughter I would love for her to look like Giselle in every way.

"I'm entertaining a few violent scenarios for Logan, too," I say.

"You mean Holden."

"Correct. Any ideas?"

"Let's see, you've already tried asphyxiation, how about poison? Or a hacksaw to the gut? You could pull his intestines out like unraveling a sweater." Giselle is rife with lousy ideas tonight.

"I'm thinking something a little less invasive, something without long lasting side effects."

"Like a heart attack," she gives a knowing nod.

"A heart attack," I say, envisioning Logan writhing on the ground gripping his left arm, wracked with excruciating pain.

"An electrical jolt to the ticker," she suggests. "It could kill instantly. Of course, you'd need another power surge to bring Logan back and lots of CPR. We can't afford the brain to be deprived of oxygen too long."

"This is great," I marvel. Who knew Giselle would be such a wealth of knowledge when it comes to celestial takedowns. "How do I jolt his heart?"

Giselle snaps at attention towards the closet as if she were suddenly distracted. Her face blanches out as she begins to disintegrate.

"I have to go," her voice melts as her flesh dissolves in a cloud of molecules.

Before I can protest, my mother appears in all of her illuminating glory, an emerald rainbow crowns her from above, casts a strange aura over her long glowing hair.

"Hey, Candy," I say, completely uninterested in the fact she's chosen to suddenly insert herself in my bedroom, right here on Paragon. "Aren't you breaking all eleven commandments by gracing me with your presence?" I salt the words with enough sarcastic inflection to let her know she's not wanted in these parts.

No wonder Giselle took off. I would too, if I could.

"You disrespect me." She offers a peaceable smile. It makes me want to trust her, give into the illusion that she might actually care about me.

"Welcome to the paren*t*hood. I think I hear violins in the background, and, oh wait, what's that?" I put my hand to my ear. "Oh, that's right, I don't give a rat's ass."

"Skyla," she bemoans with a smile. "I love you, dearly. I command you to lose this adolescent angst at once."

"Oh," I tilt my head amused. "You *command* me? You *so* understand how the teenage mind works." I give a mock salute.

"I understand how your mind works." She scoots into me and takes up my hand.

"Only because you can read my thoughts," I snatch my fingers free.

"It's because I care enough to know you," she corrects.

"What's my favorite color?"

"Purple."

"Blue." I lie. "Who's my favorite parent?"

"Your father."

"And never you." I fall back onto the pillow and close my eyes.

She lays the cool of her hand over my forehead, strums a peaceful harmony through my being with her simple touch. I can't imagine that being in paradise feels too different.

"Why don't you ever help me when I need you?" I don't open my eyes—just let the current of her affection run deep into my marrow.

"Each time you call out to me I'm by your side, Skyla. Anywhere you are, when you call me, I'll be there."

"Ezrina needs a new trial or I'm doomed to walk the netherworld forever wearing her head as a hat. Will you help me?"

"I will always help you."

"Why do I get the feeling we have a different idea of what that help might be."

She doesn't say a word, just curves her lips into a curious smile that lets me know I'm right.

74

White Wedding

The rain last night swept away the clouds, the debris from the air, dropped the scales from our eyes so we could see Paragon without its constant shroud of fog. The crystalline morning air exposes all of the island's secrets, not in whispers as the fog tried to do, but in loud clapping shouts. Our world is naked, the trees, the soil, every rock unimaginably real, distinct. The boldness of the lingering sunshine hardens the edges. It outlines the landscape with rigid lines, makes us aware of its unfriendly borders. It reveals the dirty roadways, the gaping holes between trees like missing teeth. It forces the island to expose itself with its skirt lifted high, bearing its shame for all to see.

Gage and I examine the back of Demetri's estate with awe and wonder at the transformation that's taken place. An archway of white roses, an entire army of ladder-back chairs, each adorned with a pink satin sash, tulle running wild in every direction. Long white tables are set out in the distance, complete with a uniformed staff tending to them, nervous as a beehive, as if royalty were expected.

"He really went all out," Gage pulls me in, buffers me with a quick kiss as Tad and Mom descend upon us.

This garish display of affluence, this embarrassment of riches—this is nothing more than a box trap on a stick. Demetri holds the string in wait, and my mother is the unwitting sparrow.

"You see the cake?" Mom picks up my hand, her fingers cold as an ice bath. Probably something akin to cold feet and hopefully she'll change her mind. We could pay Ellis' mother a quick visit once she realizes she could never make the same mistake twice.

"We were just on our way," Gage pushes gently into the small of my back, guiding me away from the two of them. He's still really pissed at Tad among other people, Sectors to be exact.

"Not that one," Mom spins me around to another table with an equally gargantuan confection springing up from the center. "I had the bakery make one up just for the two of you."

Tad steps in. "It's all getting a little too real, isn't it, son," he says, slapping Gage on the back.

Gage is resplendent in his formal black suit, matching ebony tie. I would much rather it were our wedding and rumors of engagement were swirling around Mom and Tad. I'd squash those like a bug, wash Tad off the windshield of our lives like bird crap.

"Let's go," Mom takes up my hand and scissors us over with the steady swish of her dress. It's a white sheath, luminescent in nature and has goddess topknots over her shoulders. A heavily plunged neckline accents the front and will double as entertainment the second she bends over. She looks more ready for a Toga party than a wedding, but to each his own.

I'm wearing a black dress with white polka dots, one size too small, my rear effectively hanging out the back. It's similar in size and stature to the soul catcher Marshall will strap me into, come prom. Actually, they didn't have this dress in my size, but it was so cute I don't mind the fact I can't completely inhale from the vice grip it has around my waist. Not that I'll need help passing out once the preacher reasserts the fact Tad is a permanent fixture in our lives.

"Wow," I say as we come upon the tower of icing erected like a statue in our honor.

Skyla and Gage is spelled out in blue gel that bleeds into the perfectly spackled frosting, smooth as glass.

"It's beautiful." I swipe my finger down near the bottom and stick an inch of heavenly cream into my mouth.

expel

Mom slaps my hand with her loose glove.

"What?" I say. "Let them eat *your* cake. This one's just for me and Gage," I give a devious smile up at him before relaxing into his warm chest.

"You do realize this mix of flour and sugar cost over seven grand," Tad espouses as if he squeezed every nickel out of his ass himself. "And in the event you're both unaware, it's meant to be eaten in a civil manner, not bathed in like some public fountain."

Gage widens his wicked grin. I dip my finger into the cake again and fill each of his dimples with a mound of sugar.

"Unbelievable," Tad gurgles.

"Leave them alone," Mom drags him off in the direction of the house. "They're in love."

"I *am* in love with you," I press my lips into his left dimple. "You're sweet, you know that?" I wish it really were our wedding. I couldn't care less if an entire army of Fems were in attendance. Starting our forever today would be amazing.

Gage swipes his finger alongside the edge of the cake and smoothes it along my lips.

"You're sweet, too," he says, sealing the sentiment with a most delicious kiss.

ᴡ 🦋 ᴡ

Guests fill in nearly every seat. I'm not sure who these people are or if in fact they are people, I just know bodies have arrived in formal attire, large brimmed hats as if it were race day at the Kentucky Derby.

"You see my mom?" Brielle hobbles towards me with her swollen belly shooting out, subtle as a projectile missile.

"Nope."

A dark shadow glides over the vicinity, offers a respite of shade to the over-bright sky if just for a moment. It's Nev. He circles the area above the floral archway as if he were offering his blessing, or placing a hex, either or.

Gage nods over in Nevermore's direction as if I should know what it means.

"Places everyone!" Brielle's mother flails her arms in hysterics as an entire string section starts in on a beautiful melody.

"Guess we'd better get ready," Gage presses a quick kiss on my cheek. *Something's happening.* He pulls back and examines me as if to assert his theory.

"We'd better get in line," I nod into the words.

Gage is going to walk down the aisle with me—then it will be Drake with Mia, then Ethan with Melissa. This is sort of our couple's announcement to Paragon high society. It's doubtful Mom will stay in their good graces. Once they get a whiff of Tad, her socialite days will be over before they've truly begun.

We walk across the soft fine lawn and my heels sink into the soil, still soggy from days of rain.

"Ms. Messenger," Marshall hastens from the sidelines.

Gage and I turn in unison with our arms intertwined.

"Mr. Oliver," Marshall gives a curt nod before taking a seat near the back.

You look irrepressibly beautiful. He gives a gentle smile. *It's unfortunate your stride down the aisle will be precluded with unforeseen events.*

"I'm pretty sure no one's going to stop me," I whisper.

"Skyla, Gage, you're up," Darla motions her finger down the long ivory runner.

"It's go time," Gage nudges into me.

Marshall turns to look at me, along with the dozens of people who've bothered to show up to this matrimonial mockery.

Hard left Skyla, emerging from the shrubbery. Marshall nods.

I snap my head over expecting to see Demetri wielding an ax, an assortment of disfigured Fems—but I don't.

Instead—I see my father.

75

The Visit

"Shit!" My heart thumps erratic at the sight of him.

My father steps out into the light of day, disoriented as if he just woke from an unsettling dream.

"Is that?" Gage stops short of finishing his thought.

I shove Drake in front of me and instruct him and Mia to go on ahead.

From inside the black hole of Demetri's estate, I see my mother adjusting herself against the reflection in the French door, oblivious to the fact her oldest child is about to vacate the premises.

I take Gage by the hand and speed over to my father, over by the box hedge.

"Daddy!" I muster all the fake enthusiasm possible.

Damn—Ezrina really *is* a wicked witch. How she and Nev could possibly ever think bringing my father to Paragon just in time to see his wife marry another man, is a good thing, boggles the mind.

Dad squints into me. "I was just about to take out the trash, and I walked out of those bushes. You have anything to do with this?" He gives a sly smile.

"You're here," I say, fanning my arms out. I haul us through the shrubbery, and we land in a rose garden that stretches out for miles with its labyrinth-like design.

"So this is Paragon." He looks around, taking it in. "It's beautiful. Am I interrupting something?"

"Just some stupid wedding," I shoot Gage a look that suggests I might be moved to slit a throat or two to keep the identity of the bride and groom a secret.

"Weddings are never stupid." His forehead wrinkles. "Are you sure you don't want to head back? I could steal a seat. No one would ever notice I was there."

"Oh, I think they'd notice," I whisper.

"Small town, everyone knows everyone," Gage adds.

"Skyla!" My mother's voice booms from behind the hedges.

A soft buzz emits from the other side.

Perfect.

Less than five minutes into the production, and we've managed to fuel enough island gossip for a decade. "Skyla?" Mom emerges from the bushes, pulling the veil up from over her face.

"Lizbeth?" Dad's eyes widen first with delight, then horror.

Nev circles above before darting into the evergreens for cover.

He'd better fly away—far, far away to be exact. I might pluck him clean, later just for fun.

"Nathan?" Mom drops her bouquet, christening the lawn with a shower of white petals.

The simple sad song of a violin, sirens through the air. Even its soothing rhythm can't quench the silence that has encapsulated the two of them like a membrane.

"Why don't I walk you back," Gage picks up the ball of pale roses and tries escorting my mother through the bushes.

"Did you do this?" She accuses me openly—doesn't bother hiding her irritation.

"No." How am I ever going to convince her it was a distorted apology from my evil friend the *bird*.

"Lizbeth, go ahead," Dad pleads. "You, too, Skyla, there must have been a mix up."

I can't stand the pain rising behind my father's eyes.

"No." My mother steps forward. "I'm not going through with it." She doesn't take her eyes off my father.

"Gage, please tell everyone I'm not feeling well, give my apologies." She links her arm into his, and they delve deeper into the flower garden together. A lanky bush of citrus colored petals engulfs the two of them. The sun washes them in a shower of gold, arresting them in the silhouette of a newly married couple. But it's all an illusion. It's nothing that could ever be.

The only thing that's real right now is the fact Tad is barreling in this direction.

"Crap," I whisper.

"I'll take care of it." Gage intercepts Tad off at the pass and walks him back through the shrubbery.

Just freaking great. It's up to me now to, of all things, convince my mother to go back and finish rehitching herself to Tad so that the people trapped in stadium seating can actually eat cake. But I don't. I have no intention of inciting such nonsense.

A violent crush of leaves sends me jumping to attention. Another loud crunch—this time closer, adjacent to the bushes my parents are standing near. My parents—how sweet the sound.

A large dark shadow swipes in and out of the hedges. It's nefarious, and scary, and definitely not human.

"Mom!" I bolt over. "Maybe you should wait in the house for us." Really, I don't think she's ready to graduate to flesh eating Fems. Besides, the last image I want to have of my mother does not include her being ripped to shreds in a wedding dress.

"Are you sure?" She sniffles into my father not paying attention to a single word I've said. Obviously, my father is just as enthralled with the conversation because he's not at all concerned that we might be jumped by a pack of rabid beasts.

"I'm sure," he walks her over to the opening in the hedges and escorts her through.

And, here, my mother was afraid there would be no one to give her away. I shake my head at the irony.

A set of heavy claws land on my shoulders and knock me to the ground.

"Skyla!" Dad races over just in time to have a dirty hyena-like creature barrel onto his chest. We lie flat on the moist dirt, the sky rotating above us as they drag us by our legs. Dad kicks at it with his free leg before spiking up and wrestling the beast off his person. He tries to lunge towards the Fem that has me captive, but it sails away with me scraping the flesh off my back in the process, grazing my scalp along the fine pointed rocks until it feels I might pass out from the pain.

"Skyla," Dad lands hard on the creature, gives it a bear hug from behind. My leg drops from its mouth as it turns to snap at my father. "Run, Skyla!"

I twist in the dirt, my left shoulder on fire from the effort. The trees shift position as I struggle to get my bearings. The earth rises to meet my feet. I overshoot the hedges and race around to the back of the house in an effort to avoid running the rabid beasts straight through the wedding.

I try to glance back at my father and a snapping jaw clamps shut just shy of my nose. The heft of its body forces me to do a faceplant in the dirt. It lays over me with the weight of a small car—its putrid breath, blowing in my face.

The world fades in and out as I claw my way over to the grass. I can see the bottom of the ladder-back chairs, men's dress shoes, women's heels.

Can't breathe.

A growling snout buries itself into my neck, hot saliva circles around to the front and swims down my chest. Knife-sharp teeth puncture my skin, locking up my muscles as the long canines skewer deep into my flesh.

A set of smooth brown legs with feet pressed into black stilettos move swift in my direction. The ebony shoes stop at the edge of the lawn, as their owner inspects my misery from above.

"Well, look what the Fem dragged in."

Chloe.

I don't need to look up to affirm that bitchy whine.

"Don't mind me," she purrs. "Feel free to bury her alive. That's what she hoped they'd do to me."

It takes a moment for it to register that she's talking to the Fem. Of course she wouldn't help. Why would she? I killed her when I had the chance.

My head grinds into the dirt, my mouth fills with pea gravel, and through the agony I can hear the very distinct sound of Chloe's laughter.

That's it. I hone all of my Chloe-based anger, zero in on every acrimonious inclination I've ever had and turn, dig my fingernails into its sides until I feel its flesh shred between my fingers. I give it a hard push and eject the creature off me like a rocket.

"Here," Chloe reaches down, "Let me give you a hand."

Foolishly I accept. Foolishly I'm flying through the air, hurdling over the bushes like a pole-vaulter. I land flat on my back on something soft, slipping down the slope of what appears to be my engagement cake before systematically taking down all seven layers. Gage swoops by my side wide-eyed and puzzled by my latest acrobatic feat.

Tad and Mom appear, both equally miffed and stymied.

"Knew it," Tad yells. "She was planning this stunt all along," he gives a dismissive laugh. "I've got news for you. The wedding went off without a hitch and *this* is the precise reason I insisted your mother get you your own damn cake," he turns to Mom. "I told you Lizbeth—cake diving is the new planking."

"Take her inside and clean her up," Mom pleads with Gage.

Tad speeds her off into the circulating crowd.

expel

Down towards the altar I see Mia and Melissa posing for pictures with, of all things, a clown. He looks right at me, drops the smile off his face, just glares.

Shit.

"What the hell happened?" Gage helps me up.

"My dad, he's still out there," I pant.

"I just saw him slip into the house."

"I need to find him. I need to make sure he's OK."

76

Icing on the Cake

I bolt up the marble stairs, slipping, clawing against Gage just to keep myself upright when I smack right into Marshall.

"Oh dear," he feigns concern looking down at himself. "You've made a mess of my shirt." *Your father's upstairs in the game room admiring the variety of creatures his soon-to-be assassin has on display.*

"Nice." Holy freaking shit.

I tap up the remainder of the stairs so fast it feels like I'm floating. I bolt down the hall and find an opening to the game room as wide as a wall. Gage and I walk in together.

"Look," I motion up at the horrors mounted near the ceiling.

"Fems." A voice comes from behind.

I turn to find my father staring back, perfect and unharmed.

"Daddy!" I jump into his arms and inhale his spiced cologne with an urgent greed. The scent alone acts as a bookmark to an entire era of my life. It takes everything in me not to find Mia and bring her to him.

"I saw her." Dad's eyes sparkle with tears. "Skyla, so much has changed in both your lives. I feel like I've missed a lifetime."

"It does feel like a lifetime." I bury my face in his neck.

"I don't mean to interrupt the family reunion," Gage pipes up, "but isn't that a replica of the mirror Demetri gave you?"

I walk over and touch the cool of the glass. My hand melts through to the other side and I'm quick to retract.

"You think he has two?" I wonder.

expel

"Skyla," my father gently pulls me back from the contraption, "if Demetri Edinger gave you anything, I want you getting rid of it immediately."

"You know he's a Fem, don't you." I appraise my father in this new light. I've yet to know more than him at any given time. Even in death his knowledge has increased, much like Logan.

"I do," he gives a sad nod. "I also know hanging around him too long is a sure guarantee to getting yourself removed from this planet."

"I'll get rid of it," I say without hesitating. "I saw this horrible clown in it, all it does is follow me around. It goes as far back as me touching these pictures." I walk Dad and Gage over to the haunted photomontage. I pluck out the frame that houses the picture of me at West and shake it, let them watch the entire scene unfold from an aerial perspective.

Dad takes it from me and places it back onto the shelf. He opens his mouth to say something before reaching to the back and pulling out another gilded frame, ornate with pressed roses lining the top and sides.

"This is me just now in the garden," Dad holds it out for us to see.

"But how?" I take it from him. The picture neatly trimmed, sealed behind glass, the scene less than fifteen minutes old.

"They don't incorporate time the way we do, Skyla. This earth is their playground." Dad glances beyond my shoulder. "I have to go." He pulls me in, touches the bruises on the back of my neck without meaning to. "Love you. Don't be such a stranger. Bring your mother, your sister when she's ready." He brushes the pad of his thumb along my cheek before patting Gage on the back. "Take care of my baby." He walks to the door and gives a forlorn look before disappearing into the hall.

"So that was it?" I collapse my arms around Gage and let loose a torrent of wild tears over his dress shirt.

"We'll visit. We'll do an L.A. date," Gage blinks his dimples on and off. "Let's get you cleaned up. I want my dad to look at these abrasions."

I give a gentle nod.

"It's also time to discuss how we're going to bring Logan back."

"Yes," I whisper.

Killing and reviving Logan are at the top of my to-do list.

Gage and I leave the reception early because, for one, I'm drenched in frosting, and second, I'm in no mood to celebrate the union of Tad and Mom, this day or any other.

Nevermore circles the Oliver house as Gage and I pull into the driveway. He fans out his plumage so brazenly it makes me wonder if Nev is even remotely aware of the infliction he caused earlier.

Fresh spring lilacs scent the air from Emma's border garden as Gage helps me down from the truck. He catches me in his waiting arms and spins me.

"I'm going to carry you over the threshold," he says, dipping his arms behind my knees, cinching a kiss up on my lips for good measure.

"So what did you think of our engagement party?" I bat my lashes with every intention of seducing him, forgetting that my hair is slicked with butter cream frosting, that I have a mashed candy rose stuck in my cleavage.

"I think we might need a do over, just me and you," he says it low and husky as though tonight were a real possibility for this to happen. "And perhaps a more romantic proposal—a ring would be nice." His brows arch over his pale eyes.

I wave my forever band in the air.

"I was thinking something with a little more sparkle," Gage inspects my finger for a moment and makes a face, as though it were a mere paltry offering of his affection.

"You're all the sparkle I need."

Gage gives a devious grin and melts a sea of kisses over me as he lets us into the house. He jockeys us upstairs. I can hear his bedroom door shut, the twist of the lock. I keep my eyes closed—enjoy the fruit of his mouth as he continues us over to the bathroom. The pipes twist, a light spray of water sprinkles over my arms, my chest, the left side of my face.

I kick off my heels, grab Gage by the collar and don't let go.

A rumble of laughter escapes soft from his chest. He pulls back and looks down at me.

"Skyla," he means for it to be admonishing in nature but he rasps it out with a whisper of desire.

"Gage," I try to equal his intensity. "Come on, you know you want to." I bring his finger to my mouth and press it against my lips.

Steam rises, fills my lungs with its sweet precipitation. Gage sets me down on the warm shower tiles, still in my dress, takes off his shoes and joins me. He picks up a bottle of shampoo and holds it out like a peace offering. I open his hand and watch the golden liquid drizzle into his palm.

Gage crashes in with soft kisses, lathers my hair as gentle as handling a newborn. It feels sacred, like a rite of passage to be cleansed by the hands of the one I love. The day melts off me. Gage runs one long hot kiss from my ear down to the base of my neck, examines me under the deluge of rain with a fierce intensity.

"You're so beautiful, Skyla," he whispers. His shirt glows, clinging to his skin beneath.

"I'm yours forever." The words resonate inside me long after they leave my lips.

His cheek rises on the side, never breaking our gaze. Gage is a censer filled with a pure golden fire. His desire emanates hot and proud as the steam wraps around us like a veil. His eyes shine like cisterns of deep water, his lips alive with lust for me.

"Forever," he whispers covering my mouth with his.

We let the water run over us, drench us in its rich eternal spring—raining over us like tears from every love story that ever had to come to an end.

We are forging our own love into the symbol of infinity, independent of time and space with no end and no beginning. We hover over the cusp of a beautiful horizon just within our reach.

This is forever.

Eternity within our grasp.

77

The Break Up

The heat in the shower rises to inconceivable levels, the steam soaks in our carnal desires and we manage to extinguish them before we end up on the floor mixing around in the debris of cake and frosting.

Gage leaves to change and I indulge in a real shower washing a sugary glaze from all sorts of interesting crevices. I think of Gage's fiery touch and I ignite all over again. Who knew cake could be so disturbingly erotic? Maybe Tad is right and cake diving will really take off. It was sort of fun even if it was Chloe flinging me into the multi-layered wall of icing.

I wrap a plush towel around myself, cobalt blue the exact color of Gage's eyes. It feels warm, safe, and makes me want to run out into his bedroom and latch onto him before getting dressed. It's not until I realize, the only outfit I have is lying in a sopping heap, that running and latching onto his person in this delicate state of undress is a very real possibility.

I knock on the bathroom door before entering his room.

"All clear," he says, clad in a t-shirt and navy colored sweats.

I love Gage with his hair slicked back. He's so freaking hot I just want to rip my towel off and attack him.

"You have any sweats for me?" I skip over, flaunting my clothing deficient status.

"Nope," he hides his smile behind a look of mischief. "You're holding them all hostage. I haven't had the chance to replenish my supply."

"I'll just hang out like this." I hold up my hands exposing my barely-there appearance.

"My dad wants to talk to us about," he nods over towards Logan's room.

"Regarding my thrill to kill?" I arch my brows, trying desperately to get him to remove my towel. I would moan like a dove for Gage.

"You know what I hate more than you having to kill Logan?"

"What?" I wince at the thought of actually having to kill Logan.

"Not going to prom with you."

"I'll be there." I run my fingers through the wet tendrils of his hair. "And you'll be there."

"We have to make it look real." Gage shakes his head. "Holden's going to wonder why you suddenly want to go to prom after not carrying out a single conversation with him for the past few months."

I lay my head over his chest and listen to the steady thump—let its rich soothing cadence reverberate through my skull.

"I hate this, too," I whisper. "I hate having to convince Holden of anything. Wish we could just flood his bed with water while he sleeps and throw in a toaster."

"How did you know there would be electrocution?" The corners of his lips hold a devilish smile.

"Your sister—who, by the way is working for my mother, who, by the way is the strangest being in the universe."

Gage presses his finger to my lips.

"You may not want to incite her," he whispers, dropping a kiss on my lips. "I have a feeling the last thing we need is your mother after us."

"I know, right?" I wrap my arms tight around his waist. "Hey," I jostle him from side to side. "It's kind of like we're dancing."

Gage picks up my right hand and holds it out, presses his hips against mine and moves in rhythm.

"We are dancing," he corrects.

"This is our prom."

"You look gorgeous tonight." He dips into me with a quiet grin. "Have I mentioned how much I love your dress?"

"And you look dashing in your attire as well. I especially love the way the color of your *suit* brings out the prince charming in your eyes."

Gage throws his head back with a slight laugh before taking on an ultra serious demeanor.

"Would you be my princess?" His dimples flare, no smile.

"I'm humbled to be considered for the honor." I hike up on the balls of my feet and sway into a blistering kiss that lets him know exactly how honored I am to be his anything.

We find Dr. Oliver downstairs in the back office. Turns out Gage did find a pair of sweats for me, so I don't have to face Barron, or worse, Tad later in a towel that hardly covers my bottom—was sort of a nice prom dress though.

I give Gage a secret smile. I so loved our private prom. I can't wait to do it over and over again.

Gage pats the couch beside him, and I sit a respectful arms length away.

"Skyla," Dr. Oliver folds his hands over a stack of papers on his desk, "Gage has implied that you're to distribute the fatal blow. How do you feel about this?" His glasses shift as he anticipates my answer.

"Um," I look over at Gage. "Yes. I want to. I mean, Chloe has me in a corner, and even though we're sort of at an impasse at the moment, if either you or Gage were to kill him, she might use it against me," I glance over at Gage, "us."

"Very well," he takes off his glasses and rubs his eyes momentarily before depositing the frail looking spectacles on his desk. He reaches below and lands a small box in front of him. A long erect needle sits attached to a tangle of blue wires that protrude from the device. "This," he holds up the unit, "has the capability to stop a man's heart with one quick jolt."

"God," I cover my lips. "I have to stick him in the heart with that thing?"

"You not only have to stick him—to do so properly, you'll have to penetrate the protective shield of his rib cage." Dr. Oliver looks from me to Gage. "Skyla, you must dig into the reserve of your strength. This won't be easy."

"What if I can't?" Usually thinking of Chloe or Michelle gets me riled up, but what if I miss the opportunity and am left to my own weakling devices?

"Regardless, whatever happens, make sure this isn't used against you." His face grows cold as stone. "This could just as easily multiply the tragedy we've already experienced."

"Nothing will go wrong," I say.

"Famous last words." Dr. Oliver pierces me with his heavy stare.

"I won't let it," Gage offers. "Come on, let's get out of here." He pats me on the knee. "It's time to break up."

✺ ✺ ✺

Totally, I think breaking up with Gage is going to be a ton of fun.

Emma has graciously invited us all into the kitchen where she's doling out her latest sweet treat, a steaming hot apple pie served over a bed of vanilla ice cream.

expel

Of course, she and Barron have been completely debriefed to the situation about to unfold, so I don't feel bad at all about wolfing down two whole slices before hacking into her son.

Holden slogs down three pieces before sticking the entire can of whip cream down his throat and indulging in one long squeeze. It comes out of his mouth like a tower before he collapses his lips over the creamy mess, and the reserve drips onto the floor. Charlie goes over and licks at his feet. Come to think of it, Charlie has made quite the habit of following Holden around these past few months and with good reason—Holden is a freaking pig.

"Are you just going to sit there staring?" Gage stirs the pie on his plate, good and miffed while mowing me down with a palpable hatred. "Why don't you just crawl over and sit on his lap." He cocks his head at me. "You know you want to."

My mouth falls open. My heart picks up pace because suddenly it doesn't feel so fun anymore.

"Maybe I will," I counter. "Maybe I'm sick of you talking to Chloe Bishop whenever you feel like it. I know for a fact she's been texting you."

"So you're checking my phone now?" He pushes his plate away.

"You're the one who planted the seed of doubt. You gave me no choice."

"Whatever," Gage huffs a laugh and gets up. He heads towards the counter and scoops more vanilla ice cream onto his plate, never wavering from his annoyed expression.

Holden gapes at the two of us, he's buying this bull by the crap-load.

I follow him over, abandoning the pie, which is truthfully the best homemade anything I've ever eaten. I miss the days Mom would make edible meals for us. With her ovaries on the line, it's all zucchini and entrails from here on out.

"I'm really getting sick of you telling me I can't talk to Logan," I hiss, "that you want me to quit my job because you're so insanely jealous every time I'm within ten feet of him. I'm not gonna stand around and let you tell me who I can and can't see!" I shout the last few words in his face.

"Everyone calm down," Dr. Oliver says it low for added effect.

"I'm really getting tired of this, Skyla." Gage looks bored, his aggression boiling just beneath the surface as though it were real. "I never signed up to be anybody's second anything." He tosses his spoon into the sink a good five feet away in a fit of rage. "I'm sure there are a lot of girls out there that would treat me with enough respect to cut their ex-boyfriends out of their lives." The copper kettle on the stove vibrates as his voice blasts across the room.

"Is that what you want?" I howl back. "For me to ignore Logan at school? Treat him like he's dead to me because you can't freaking trust me?"

"Everybody knows I can't trust you," his voice booms off the walls, reverberates within my skull long after it leaves his lips. Gage spears me with a look. The hurt in his eyes tells me this isn't entirely a fabrication, that he's seen proof, and so has everyone else.

The moment seems to stretch out an inordinate amount of time, just Gage and I lost in a tunnel of horrible truths. It cuts through me, rips me apart from the inside like a thousand rusted hooks.

I take a breath before going on. "Maybe it's you nobody can trust. Weren't you the one following me around like a puppy just waiting to find a crack in my relationship with Logan, so you could inject yourself? *You* broke us up!" I accuse. "You had me convinced Logan was some monster who did nothing but womanize, and you were so self righteous. Ha!" I laugh in his face. "As soon as Chloe came back into town you glued yourself to her side like she was macaroni and you were cheese." OK, that last part was

expel

insanely stupid and unnecessary. Thinking on my feet is not my strong suit. "Face it," I go on, "you cannot stand the thought of me and Logan together because secretly you know that it's him I really belong with. Logan and I could start a fire with the electricity we produce from across the room, and it kills you that no matter how hard you want to make me yours—deep inside you know it's going to be me and him in the end." I point hard over at Holden. "That is my forever Gage—the one you could only dream of."

The room quiets to an unnatural hush.

Gage ticks his head back a notch as if I had physically slapped him. The undeniable look of hurt in his eyes lets me know I've gone too far. It was believable enough with the first few barbs. This is *Holden* we're talking about. He won't be considering a career in rocket science anytime soon. I should have stopped before I carved Logan loves Skyla all over Gage and his tender heart.

"Get your shit out of my room," he seethes before speeding away and picking up his keys off the counter. "I'm sure you can find a ride home." He glares over at Holden.

"Fine!" I follow him out to the entry. *I'm sorry!* I mouth.

Gage holds up his hand, and I give a high five before he takes off into the driveway.

"I hope I never see your sorry face again!" I shout into the virginal night, with thoughts of Holden behind every word.

78

Fake Love to Me

A frigid wind blows through the open front door, sending the newspaper sitting by the entry into a violent shiver. I gaze out at the empty void in the driveway where Gage's truck sat only moments before. Lavender shadows ascend from in between the trees—tint each blade of grass, soft like a wash of snow. From this angle the driveway hold the curves of a well-endowed woman, the shadow of an evergreen caresses her at the hips like a lover.

I watch the red glow of taillights long after Gage leaves before slamming shut the door and stomping my way upstairs.

It's been an eternity since I've been in Logan's room. The door sits ajar, so I let myself in. Laundry lies about unsettled, drawers left half open with clothes vomiting out, a trail of papers slough off the desk and onto the floor. The entire room has a ransacked appeal.

On the wall above his desk, splayed out in a neat and organized fashion, are pictures of my faux-tattooed body. Emily had inked me up during ski week at the Pine Pole Lodge. It was supposed to mean something, each image some significant marker that told another chapter of my life. It looks erotic like some kind of gangster girl porn, sans the actual naked body parts necessary for it to qualify. Another row of pictures line the left of his bookshelf, the drawings from Emily's house that depict the faction war. We were going to pour over these together. This was the Logan I knew—the analytical thinker, the student launched headlong in the worship of this strange girl who isn't even human—and that inhuman girl just happens to be me.

I head over to the closet and dig into the deep recesses that maybe Holden hasn't infected with his poor sense of fashion. I retrieve an untouched sweater still neatly folded on the highest shelf in the back. It holds the geometric configuration of something freshly laundered, or never worn. It's clear that once Holden jumped on the douchebag bandwagon, he evicted all of Logan's plain white tees and jeans. I would have accepted them by the bagful.

I flatten the sweater out over the bed and lay over it as if it were Logan himself. It holds a clean scent, the slight hint of cedar, but sadly, it does nothing to remind me of Logan at all.

A thin film of tears lines my lashes. I can't believe I said those horrible things to Gage, nothing but a string of hateful indiscretions. I'll move heaven and earth to grovel an apology on my knees before sunrise. I didn't mean any of it, but I know if I'm going to kill Logan—*Holden*, I needed for him to believe every single word. If ever there was a time for Gage and I to slash each other to pieces with the shards of our tongues, it was tonight.

"Knock, knock," Holden comes in, holds his hands out with a bewildered look on his face as if he were about to surrender. I wish.

I bury my face in the sweater—try to conjure Logan out of it by pressing in a quick kiss against the sleeve.

"Hey," he rubs my back, snakes his hand down to my bottom so fast I jump up towards the headboard like a reflex. "I guess you guys really had it out."

"Yeah, I'm done with him." I crawl over on my knees and pat Logan's perfect cheek with the back of my hand. I miss Logan with a terrible ache. "I'm not going to let him keep us apart anymore." My stomach sours. Gage would never do that. He would bless me if I ever wanted to go back to Logan because he loves me more than himself.

"You and me?" This bewilders him.

"I know, it's about time, right?"

"I guess you had it pretty bad for him," his eyes round out, "me, I mean Gage," he shakes his head trying to play off the oversight.

Holden is such an impossible dolt he can't keep his identity straight.

"So," he pulls me in by the hand, "where did we leave off?" He burrows his face in my neck.

"You know," I push away. "It's been a while. Maybe we should take it slow."

His features harden. "I don't like slow. I'm sick of slow. If I don't get some action soon I'm going to explode."

"I know, me too." Crap! "Let's take it slow this week. We can pick things up later."

"Later?" His brows furrow exposing the fact this is going to be a serious challenge for him. "Like when, later?"

Like never, I want to say. "Like after prom." My lips twist holding back a devious smile.

"Like prom *night*?" He digs those dark amber eyes into me, and my insides melt.

I nod my head trying to orient myself to the situation.

"That's right. Prom night," I whisper. "You and me. Bring protection, you're going to need it." A bulletproof vest couldn't save him from my wrath.

"Cool, I'll get a hotel room."

"Totally!" I muster all the fake enthusiasm possible. It's a miracle I haven't slapped him by now. And, who knows, maybe Gage and I can put it to good use?

"But one thing needs to happen before I give you some of this," he grabs a hold of his crotch. If Logan ever did that I'd kill him on the spot for being a moron. "I want all that Celestra magic infused right back into my blood. Do whatever witchcraft necessary to make it happen. Because without that," he lifts my chin hard with his finger, "there is no this." He points to the bulge in his pants.

Nice.

Killing Holden will be a pleasure.

expel

🦋 🦋 🦋

Once I arrive home, I have the distinct feeling if I don't shower soon my skin will melt off from the toxic slime Holden drooled over me.

I make my way upstairs silent as a mouse. I'm not in the mood for the Mom and Tad show. Mom, because she'd want to talk about Dad, and Tad because, well, he's just an ass. Plus, he got away with remarrying my mother once again, and that, in and of itself is an unforgiveable offense.

Drake slinks out of the upstairs bathroom. He has a commode of his own, why he insists on destroying the girls' toilet is beyond me.

"Hey," I yank him to the corner, "why on freaking earth are you not taking Brielle to prom?" I should hit him over the head with the spiked heels dangling from my fingers.

"None of your business. But, since you make everything your business, it's because I already asked Emily. Why isn't Gage taking you? I hear he's suddenly got a fetish for knocked up teens." His brows pitch.

"Because," I take in a gulp of air, "Logan already asked me." I don't wait around for Drake to gloat. Instead, I bolt into my bedroom and shut the door before he espouses something profanely reflective on how we're both doing the same things for the same reasons—because it would *so not* be true.

The walls tremble with laughter—a boy and a girl. I move closer to the closet. Sounds like their coming from the butterfly room. I open the closet a crack and listen—more buzzing.

Sounds like Mia. But what if it's not? What if it's a pair of clown Fems getting it on just waiting for me to go up there so they can take turns strangling me?

I pick up one of Dad's skis that I rescued from Mom's 'discard my ex-husband pile'. I never planned on letting

Gage store them for me. Contrary to what Tad believes, my father's things do belong in this house.

I give a good shove and knock the transom to the butterfly room off its base.

"Crap!" I hear Mia's worried voice clear as a bell.

A familiar face pops in and out of the opening, boyish, about fourteen.

A surge of adrenaline gives me just the right amount of courage to climb up after them. I pull myself up into the butterfly room to find the two of them cowering in the corner.

"Out!" I point hard at the exit. It's Gabriel, I recognize him from the Althorpe dinner, then today at the wedding. He's got a dodgy look about him, same beady eyes as his untrustworthy sister, sharp handsome features that would make any two girls turn their backs on one another.

"Do you want me to go?" He turns to Mia for support.

My jaw goes slack at the audacity.

"Yes, she wants you to go," I answer for her, throwing a pillow over at him, "and she wants you to never come back. Get the hell out. If I ever see you messing with my sisters again, I'm going to make it my personal mission in life to humiliate you on a grand scale."

"On a grand scale?" He mocks on his way towards the exit.

"I'll make sure the entire island knows you have balls the size of chestnuts and that you sleep in diapers." He's obviously some male version of a home-wrecker, honing his skills right here on my sister.

His features loosen as though I hit a nerve. Obviously I was spot on about the diaper, probably the microscopic nuts, too.

"I'll catch you later," he says, climbing into the dark oblivion, which reminds me—that twisted gift from Demetri is still lurking up there.

"Call me!" Mia shouts after him.

"*Call me?* Are you insane being alone with him in here?" I scold.

"Me? You're the one who keeps it stocked with pillows and bedding. I was afraid to sit down. I had to turn the covers over not to get grossed out by the bodily fluids you've probably littered them with."

"I haven't done anything up here." Not worthy of disgust, anyway. Of course, if Holden gets his way we will, but not until after prom, and for sure not here—but he'll be dead by then, so it totally won't matter.

"I think he likes me," she bites down a guilty smile.

"What? He doesn't *like* you—he's using you. I saw him pawing all over Melissa today at the wedding."

"He's getting ready to break it off with her."

Dear God. He's drafted Mia into the home-wrecker training program.

"That's what they all say. I promise you, any guy who's willing to two time is no good." Gage and Logan flash through my mind. That is technically how Gage and I started out, with him pretending to be my boyfriend. I still remember the day he gave me his class ring. My stomach does a soft roll as I soak in the sweet innocence of it all. But anyway, Gage and I are different. "You need to find someone else." If only Gage had a little brother, hell I'd take a Harrison offspring at this point.

"I don't want anyone else. There's only one person for me and that's, Gabriel." She knocks me back on her way out. "And Skyla?"

I recognize that satisfied smirk on her face. It's usually followed up by a threat so big you can drive a truck through it.

"I know," I start, "if I don't enable your secret relationship you're going to run to Mom and Tad and rat out the butterfly room."

"I was going to say," she drills into me with venom, "thank you for caring about me enough to share your opinion." She shrugs. "But you're right." She sinks down into the closet, landing hard on the floor with a thump. "He's coming over tomorrow at ten. Consider yourself warned." She shouts before scampering out of the room.

I fall back onto the pillow. I hate this. Who knows what they were doing—about to do. I'm going to have to burn the butterfly room just to sanitize it from the carnal offenses they might have committed. I'm going to have to keep it stocked with condoms to stave off Mia going the way of Brielle. Just thinking of Mia and condoms sends a shiver down my spine. There has to be a way to keep Mia out of the butterfly room once and for all.

Gage blips into the room, startling me back to reality.

"Gage!" I get up on my knees. "I'm so sorry! I didn't mean any of those things. Please forgive me." I pick up both his hands, pull him down to me and offer a kiss.

"There's nothing to forgive," he whispers. "Holden just came in and told me you two were back on—that prom night is going to end with a bang." He flexes a half-smile.

I exhale in disgust. "He's a real poet," I say, wrapping my arms around his neck. "The only person I plan on sharing my life and my body with is right here in this room."

"Well then," Gage pecks in a quick kiss, "I look forward to both." Our eyes lock, radiating the gravity and joy presented by those two prospects.

He leans in and offers softer more melodic kisses that span a stretch of time immeasurable. Gage writes a poem over me with his tongue, his teeth, his lips. He absolves all of the fleshly offenses that Mia and her boy toy may have violated the butterfly room with. Gage could cleanse the world with the breath from his lungs.

We continue to wash it clean until the sun comes up.

Secret Love

I'm not thrilled about faking feelings for Holden all week. I'm not thrilled with the fact Gage is busy giving me the cold shoulder whenever we happen to glance at one another in the halls, and I'm *beyond* not thrilled when Brielle does the very outlandish thing of nominating Logan and me for prom king and queen.

"I love this," Chloe coos after cheer practice. "You continue to turn your life into such a craptastic mess, I can't help but admire the ferocity in which you choose to destroy it. In fact, in honor of your pristine ability to botch things up royally, I came up with a new cheer," she pauses as Michelle, Lexy and Emily gather like sheep. "Two, four, six, eight, who can we decapitate?" She throws her head back, cackling into the pale dense fog. It billows from her nostrils thick as smoke.

"That's sick," I say, turning around. Figures, the one single shit Chloe gives about me happens to center around the botched bag of goodies I've smashed my life into.

"You know what's sick?" Michelle pops up beside me. "The way you keep toying with Logan and Gage. I think us island girls need to teach you a little lesson. You don't come here and mess with our boys on our turf."

Turf? I want to laugh in her face. It's obvious I never should have suggested she take off the rose of horrors from around her neck. A drugged and sleepy Miller was definitely an asset more than she was a liability.

"Yeah, well," I step into Michelle—too bad for her because I've been a power bitch on overdrive all week. Between all the Holden bullshit, and Mia camping out in the butterfly room utilizing it as a seventh grade love shack, Tad and Mom *practicing* for their honeymoon as they choose to label their marathon fornicating—I'm more than a little bit stabby. "If you *island* girls knew what the hell you were doing, I wouldn't have half the male population trying to figure out the combination to the padlock on my chastity belt." Wait—did I want to say that? Don't I want Chloe to believe Gage and I have already done the deed and thus drive her insane with the illicit implications—not to mention mind-boggling images?

I try to head towards the gym but she grabs a hold of my arm.

"Why don't we show, Skyla, what we think of her chastity belt?" Michelle glares into me. "As if you didn't already sleep with Dudley."

"I think you've just been voted off the island," Chloe says it low as she steps over.

A tangle of arms and legs latch onto me. My head is stuffed into someone's shirt and I'm blindly jostled and pounced. A sharp pain explodes over my back, knocks the wind out of me as they drag me to some unknown location.

I should break all of their bones for jumping me right here on West's soil, under the watchful eye of Cerberus.

My face meets up with the dirt. I look up in time to witness Chloe climbing down from an evergreen quick as a spider monkey.

Lexy wrestles with my feet. I glance down to see a thick-cabled rope looped in triplicate around my ankles.

"Goodbye, Messenger. See you at prom, if you make it," Michelle gives me the finger.

"Oh, she'll make it," Chloe quips. "One of her many suitors are likely to rescue her. Besides, I would never want her to miss out on all the fun." She holds back a laugh ensuring me of the torment to come. Little does she know I have high hopes to return the favor.

Emily drops something behind me.

expel

The rope cinches around my feet so tight I'm convinced I'll lose them both at the ankle.

I sail into the air, my toes pointed towards the sky.

The bitch squad cackles below like herd of rabid hyenas as I sway back and forth like a pendulum, twenty feet off the ground—my cell phone sailing to earth without me.

"I'm afraid of heights!" I scream as they descend into the parking lot.

"Oh *are* you?" Chloe exaggerates a frown. "Oh dear, skanky, skanky, Skyla. I do plan on making all of your nightmares come true." She sinks into the driver's side of her car and speeds away. One by one they all take off.

I'm left alone, dangling, with my cheer skirt wrapped around my waist like a closed up flower.

Dank sallow light dispenses through the thicket of clouds, recedes—leaves me lounging in the murky shadows.

Blood pools to my temples, bloats my lips as my teeth begin to chatter.

We let out from practice far later than usual. Any other day, the football team would be heading out to their cars right about now. Any other day, Gage would be here and not tending to a Holden inspired emergency at the bowling alley. Something tells me this is more than a coincidence.

A soft rumble emits from the bowels of the forest. A series of trotting footsteps press out, approaching in this direction. One by one large overgrown wolves emerge from the woods, congregating around me like a pack of wild denizens. Their pink tongues light up the dark like flames.

"Crap," I hiss. "Mom?" She did mention she was always around. This seems as good a time as any to put that theory to the test. "Um, hello? Unearthly Mother who insists she is available twenty-four seven?"

The mangy mess stirs frantic, one of the rabid beasts picks up my cell and chews on the casing.

Oh good! He's going to butt dial somebody. With my luck it'll probably be useless Holden, or worse, Kate because she just so happens to be dead.

His jaw lights up an electric blue, before he spits the phone out, and another one comes over and gnaws on it with a frenzied determination.

"No! Bad dog!" Shit. "Mother?" I pull up and try to reach my feet, causing the rope to oscillate like an earthquake. My left foot slips through the noose, bulleting my knee into my face. Figures. It's not bad enough I was the subject of a group beating—my own body has decided to join in on the fun.

The rope cinches around my right ankle cutting into my bones with a vice-like grip.

The wild mutts leap into the air in turn. They catch my hair in their snapping red mouths—yank my head in twelve directions at once.

"This is your last chance Mother!" She said she was here—that she could hear me, see me, be with me if I called out to her. "If you don't get me out of this right freaking now, I'm going to seriously believe you are a fucking liar."

The wolves look up in unison—cease all of their frenetic movements, nothing but a group of twin ruby eyes glowing back at me.

Certainly I've crossed some sort of imaginary line that not even Fems in their right minds would consider crossing.

The sky ignites like a crackling orb as a clap of thunder explodes overhead.

"Exactly the person I was looking for," a male voice floats up from the dark.

Marshall appears, causing the wolves to disperse back into the forest. He holds out his hand unleashing a bolt of lightning so fierce it triggers a fire line melting the rope just above my ankle.

I sail towards the ground and land safe in Marshall's waiting arms.

expel

Looks like Chloe was right after all. One of my favorite suitors did save the day.

"Received an upgrade, did I? I'm glad to know I'm a favorite, Ms. Messenger because I'm taking you home with me."

And with that we disappear.

※ ❦ ※

The scenery around me unfolds like a mural—large black windows gape at me like soulless bodies, a familiar couch, the glitter of an ornate chandelier. We land in the center of Marshall's living room where he promptly lands me to my feet and hands over my cell phone still wet with Fem slobber.

"Tis' the season for catching souls." He walks over to the staircase where the prom dress hangs from a wrought iron prong like a superstitious amulet. I'm sure it would make any sorceress fashionista proud to don the haunted frock—except me. I'm neither a sorceress nor a fashionista, and for once, I'd like to invest US dollars and purchase something made from humble human hands that doesn't hold a single supernatural promise.

"I'm rather hoping the next dress I bequeath you, is to be worn at our wedding." Marshall's eyes are fueled with lust and wonder, a daring combination that amplifies his sharp gorgeous features.

"Yes, well, I hope so, too." Like that will ever happen.

"It will," he corrects without realizing. "Though our love linger, wait for it."

I break away from his strangulating gaze. The last thing I want to do is piss off Marshall. He, unlike other celestial beings, actually shows up when I need him to.

"Our wedding will have to be a spectacular event," I say, taking the dress from him, petting the soft navy velvet."

Gah! I push it back at him. "That's the stuff lining the walls of the haunted mansion."

"Hot off the bolt," he presses it into me until I take up the hanger once again. "And, in regards to our wedding, the sky is the limit."

"You mean the *Skyla*," I wink, playing off the words he said to me a while back. "I want to make sure we set all the celestial socialites aflutter." I play along to satisfy his itch. "I assume all of the Sector *upper crust* will be in attendance."

Marshall scoffs, "You, love, are marrying into the upper crust. No need to look any higher than yours truly. Proceed to the minute details because I assure you, no request will go ungranted."

"Excellent," I sing. I'll ply him with such outrages requests that he'll seriously reconsider this celestial love connection. "Of course there will need to be lots of bling—I'm talking diamond studded toilets, fountains with real cherubs peeing into the pool, that sort of thing." It takes everything in me not to break out into a fit of laughter. "And, the menu totally has to rock. People will expect a lot from us since we'll be loaded, as in mountains of currency welcomed worldwide. You might want to get some pyramid scheme in the works, rob a few banks because I plan on being extravagantly high maintenance in my old age."

"That's the glory of unifying yourself with someone of my stature," he strokes the underbelly of my neck, creating a sharp sizzle. "I can promise you the face you have now until your dying breath as an aged woman of a hundred and twenty. You will defy gravity in every way," his eyes dip. "Your mind will be ripe and sharp from one life to the next."

"Great." I find the way he interchangeably talks about life and death a bit unnerving.

"And the guests?" Marshall leans in clearly placating me now. "What shall they feast upon?"

"You can wow the crowd with five fish and two loaves of bread, or we can go the conventional route and let them eat cake."

"Spoken like true royalty." His cheek slides into a half-smile.

"Actually," I stride past him, heading towards the kitchen. All this talk about food is only heightening the fact my stomach is growling like a prehistoric land mammal. "We should have a memorable menu, you know—whale sushi, barbequed zebra, tiger," I pause taking him in, the look of amusement mingling with seduction radiates from his being. Clearly he's taken with this nuptial sized banter. "None of that Bengal shit either. I'm talking white exotic."

Marshall explodes with a laugh. "So what you'd really like are protestors littering the compound. I'll up your facetious requests and make sure to have a live animal sacrifice right after the ceremony. A dolphin, perhaps?"

"You're disgusting." I swat him in the stomach.

"I'm simply following the leader." He opens the oven and pulls out two plates brimming with fried chicken, mashed potatoes and gravy, biscuits and coleslaw. I promptly travel behind him as we make our way to the table.

"Mmm, the Colonel's finest offerings." I take in the popcorn-esque aroma. "I approve."

"I thought you might."

The table is set with tall amber goblets, the exact shade of Logan's eyes, stiff cloth napkins with a twisted coil of metal gathering them in the center like the waist of a shapely woman, a fork and knife protruding from the top. I assume the flatware is a part of Marshall's enchanted cutlery collection. I pull my fork free to observe whose effigy I might be dining with.

Logan.

"I like this one." I wave it in front of him. The light glints off the silver as if Logan himself were fighting for my attention.

"Do you?" He adjusts his napkin over his lap before darting his crimson colored eyes into mine. "Do you desire him enough to follow him into death?"

"I can't die—I mean I won't."

"My dear," he leans in fracturing the peace with a look of repugnance, "if you haven't learned by now that anything is possible—perhaps you never will."

80

Dress You Up in My Love

The Saturday morning of prom stretches out slow and lethargic like some ethereal dream in a quiet parade of glittering fog. I inspect the area outside my bedroom window for signs of Nevermore, but nary a shadow exists in our world on this fine morn. I press my hand to the glass, and a gentle aura of perspiration warms around it.

This is the day of possibilities, both fatal and life giving. Nothing like the thrill of ridding the world of Holden Kragger on prom night.

I glance back at the tiny velvet wonder Marshall has generously supplied me with. I have his assurance that as soon as the zipper hits the top I'll be sporting Logan's soul like a pair of painted on jeans. Just the thought of his skin over mine sounds disturbingly beautiful. I pet the soft velvet, run my fingers over the upholstery tacks that line the ridge before heading downstairs for breakfast.

A mountain of duffle bags line the entry. A long vinyl sack with duck tape adhered across the top marked *tent* spills into the hall.

If Mom and Tad are planning some ambush household retreat right smack in the middle of prom, they can forget it. Aside from executing Holden, I very much plan on spending a romantic evening with Gage. A hotel room may or may not be involved.

I head into the family room and open my mouth to say good morning, but a quick high-pitched scream sails out from my vocal cords instead.

"What's that?" I shriek.

The mirror of terror has floated down from the attic and managed to plant itself successfully in the living room, complete with a thick red ribbon crossing over it like a pageant contestant.

"What the heck are you screaming bloody murder for?" Mom rushes out from the kitchen.

Chloe comes up, clad in her see-thru shirt and a pair of men's boxers. "Looks like you've had a glimpse of what the rest of us have to put up with when we look at you."

I don't know what's scarier, Chloe taking up residence, or the mirror of horrors mysteriously showing up in the living room.

"Isn't it to die for?" Mom wrinkles her nose inspecting the thick ornate frame. "Tad gave it to me as a wedding gift."

"A wedding what?" I gasp as he pops up behind me in the reflection.

"That's right. I've been hunting everywhere for that perfect treasure," he pats his hair down before stepping out of view.

"And where did you find this amazing work of art?" I already know the truth.

"Let's just call it one of those lucky attic finds. Fixed the leaky roof above the entry, too."

Just great. Now we'll never be rid of it.

"So where will you keep it?" Chloe is quick to nail down the new locale of her jaunt to Gage's arms. I'm sure she'll be sweeping in and out of it, racking up some serious frequent flyer miles to the land where she can rut with Gage freely.

"I was thinking right here or out in the front hall." Tad returns, clutching his coffee.

"I was thinking, next to my dresser." Mom taps a finger beside her cheek. "I don't have a single decent full-length mirror, and I'd love to have this up in the room. Besides, it has special meaning," Mom reaches up and strokes Tad's neck.

expel

I suppose it's the right place to sequester it since that will severely limit Chloe's ability to storm in there whenever the hell she feels like it.

"So when will you be coming back from your trip?" Chloe doesn't let up with her selfish inquisition. I bet she has a half a dozen fantasies lined up in the queue.

"Monday," Mom beams. "We're camping near the falls," she nods into me. "Second honeymoon," she mouths.

"Sounds fantastic." Chloe drips a malevolent smile.

Chloe will be molesting Gage by midnight. There's a good chance she's already had more action with my boyfriend than I have from her last hallucinatory sprint. Shit, shit, shit.

"This isn't fair," I say just under my breath.

"What's not fair?" Mom wraps her arm around me with curiosity.

"Oh, um..." Great. "You won't get to see me in my prom dress. You know—take pictures."

"Oh, but I will! I have a meeting with a client this evening. Tad and I won't be heading out to the falls until later. You're leaving at five, right? I'll be around to take plenty of pictures. Although I'm still not pleased that you and Gage are in the business of doling out mercy dates." She gives a harsh look of disapproval.

"I'm glad you'll be here." I'm not too thrilled with the mercy dates *she's* been doling out either. "What kind of meeting are you having on a Saturday night?" I can probably guess who'll be in attendance.

She shakes her head slightly, darting her eyes over to Tad.

I make my way to the calendar hanging over by the kitchen window, run my finger down the short list of Saturday's until I hit this one. New Moon.

I turn back around to find both Mom and Chloe admiring the mirror.

Yes. I know exactly where my mother will be tonight.

Since Gage and I are faking this acrimonious leg of our relationship, he's opted out of the limo ride, as arranged per Holden, and has already picked Brielle up in his truck.

I've hidden the contraption Dr. O developed to zap Holden out of existence, into a small sequined purse Mom bought me the Christmas I was twelve. It was sort of out of place in my life back then, but now it's found its true purpose as a covert killing machine.

I pluck the navy dress off the hanger, gaze into it as if it were Logan himself. The depth and richness of the texture and hue hypnotize me into wanting to stare at it all night long. It holds the grandeur of the night sky, the rivets reflect like stars. It will barely cover my top and hardly reach my bottom, but I deeply appreciate the fact Logan will swim around my torso—touching me so brazenly—so intimately all night long.

But, it's not fair to Gage, and, for sure I don't think I'll be reminding him that his cousin slash uncle is straddled securely over my hips. It's bad enough I'm technically going to prom with Logan, the last thing I need to do is rub his face in the fact Logan gets to fondle me freely for the next seven or eight hours.

I slip into the velvet dress. The cool of the ironwork singes my skin as it shimmies over my curves.

"Here goes nothing," I whisper.

I reach back and take the zipper up as far as my fingers will allow, missing the top by at least four inches.

Perfect.

I head into the hall and call for Mia. Melissa emerges from their bedroom instead, and I point over my shoulder.

"Can you?"

"Sure." She lays her ice-cold hand over my arm and secures the zipper. "So how late do you think you'll be out?"

She's so stupid. I'll probably have to reword the question three times before she gets it right.

I turn around to gape at her but she drives up the zipper so hard it makes me jump.

A warm tingling feeling wraps itself around my waist. It shimmers through the dress from the top to the bottom in a continuous spiral of warm affection. "Logan. He's here," I whisper.

"He's been downstairs for like half an hour." She averts her eyes. "So, again, how late will you be out?"

"Oh, right. Midnight?" Probably more like a half past never, or quarter till afternoon, but I'll never fess up to that one.

She crimps a tiny smile.

"You're having a party, aren't you?" Figures. Evidently you can't turn your back on the tween scene for one hormonal second.

"Just a few friends. We're watching a movie, and don't worry—it's not the one you starred in. Oh, and thanks for the nickname—*Loose Landon*—in the event your little sis forgot to mention all the love we've been fielding from our growing list of frenemies. And, don't worry, no one will be allowed in your precious little room."

Somehow I find this doubtful. And, technically, I'm not a Landon. Besides, they probably acquired that nickname all on their own trying to outdo one another in the boyfriend tug of war.

"OK," I shrug. "Look," I soften into her still absorbing the warm comfortable feeling of having Logan seeped around the circumference of my body. "I don't know what exactly is going on between you and Mia, but it's my suggestion that you both dump that loser Armistead kid and each get yourself a good guy of your own. If anyone is calling you Loose Landon, it's because you're both putting out—to the same freaking guy." That breeds disgust in acres.

She takes in a sharp breath. "I knew it!" She staggers. "She is seeing him behind my back!"

"No!" I clap my hand over my mouth in horror, but it's too late she's already locked herself in the bathroom. "Melissa, wait!" I pound on the door.

"I'm never coming out!" She screams.

The loud shrill whoop of a siren explodes from downstairs. I snap my purse off the dresser and head down.

"It's you and me Logan," I whisper holding myself at the waist as I descend the stairs.

A warm burst cycles through the dress.

I hear the words *I love you* echo through every fiber of my being.

81

Promenade

"What the hell happened?" I scream.

Everyone is gathered outside the gaping mouth of a waiting ambulance, pulled up high on the driveway. Its red pulsating beams send a seizure of light hacking through the ever-darkening sky.

"Look at you!" Mom shouts with surprise. "Oh, Hon, you look fantastic! I don't remember that dress."

"I sort of accidentally stumbled upon it. Its vintage." More so than she or I will ever know. "What's with the show and tell?" I ask, pointing at the monument to medicine flaring for attention. No one appears to be injured—yet.

"That's your date's chosen mode of transportation." Tad nods acceptingly.

"What?" I collide into Holden.

I take a breath and forget to exhale. Holden—*Logan* is gorgeous beyond belief, sublime in every way. I open my mouth to say something, and there are simply no words.

"Tonight's your lucky night." He holds his arms out and slips a greasy grin in my direction. "How you arrive to prom defines you," he thrusts his hands at the waiting ambulance as if he miraculously made it appear.

"How does this define us? By saying we're sick and feeble?"

"It says we're better than everybody else," Holden drops his chin. "We're special—different. When we show up at the party, people are going to hear about it. They're going to come out in droves just to see what the hell is going on."

"Oh, they're going to wonder what in the hell is going on alright," *with you*, I want to add but don't.

Going to prom in an ambulance is perhaps the biggest irony of all because, most likely, Holden will be leaving in one.

I give him a dirty look before panning the crowd. Mom and Tad, Drake, Emily, Chloe and Ethan. I take in Chloe and Emily, both adorned in a different version of a red glittering dress that makes my short accouterment look like proper attire for afternoon tea.

"Stand together so I can take pictures!" Mom bursts. She smacks Tad in the chest until he produces a camera, and she happily snaps away. "So we'll be back Monday morning. No monkey business." She glances down at her watch. God forbid she miss out on her own version of monkey business. I'm sure Demetri would be happy to morph into a chimp if she wanted. Oddly, he seems more than willing to oblige my mother's slightest whim.

"This is effing insane!" Drake hops inside and starts slapping down switches and knobs alike. I feel sorry for the poor suffering soul who actually requires its services once he's through damaging the equipment.

"I think *he's* effing insane," I whisper to Mom. "He should be going with Bree."

"I think you're insane for not going with Gage," she's quick to fire back. "I don't get your relationship—one minute you're engaged and the next you're going to prom with your ex-boyfriend. It's not right."

"You know what else isn't right?" I whisper. "The fact I know you're going to pull a quickie with Demetri before taking off on your second honeymoon with your so-called husband."

Her back straightens involuntarily. Everything in her freezes.

OK, perhaps waiting in line to file into an ambulance on prom night isn't the appropriate time to bring up my mother's infidelity but she started this war. And, it just so happens that my tongue is the most committed soldier in my

expel

self-defense army. Speaking of war, I pat my thigh just above my dress where I have a garter belt that rivals the abilities of duct tape. I tucked away the last disc Marshall gave me should the faction war decide to break out while I'm busy exterminating Holden. I feel very Russian spy at the moment, and apparently that makes me believe I can take on my mother and her roving marital eye.

I trot over to Mia while Tad helps Chloe into the garishly lit hospital wagon.

"I may have accidentally mentioned that you were seeing that Armistead kid," I whisper.

"To Melissa?" Her face contorts in horror.

"It was an accident," I duck an inch.

"You are such a bitch, Skyla! I *hate* you!" She stomps off towards the house in a fury.

"What was that about?" Mom comes at me, snapping off a few more group shots in the process.

"She's sort of seeing Melissa's boyfriend."

"Melissa doesn't have a boyfriend." Tad steps in from behind.

Mom grabs a hold of my wrist and gently pulls me in. "When I get back, we'll talk," she nods into her whisper.

I know full well it's in regards to Demetri.

"Right." I step over to Holden's waiting hand. "I'd better get going. You two kids have a great time sleeping under the stars." I would add, *look out for rabid wolves*, but I'm not that lucky.

I hop into the stainless interior of the medicinal looking transport. There are probably a million different microorganisms crawling all over us right now. I'm betting Holden doesn't put too much weight on things like hygiene and super bacteria that can crawl into your nostril and eat your brain, especially given the fact I've readily supplied him with a new body each time he's needed one.

The truck starts down the road with an aggressive wobble.

"Skyla and I got a room at the Sunrise Motel," Holden is quick to proclaim.

"The Sunrise Motel?" I gape. "Isn't that a never-ending convention center for cockroaches? Where they proliferate freely while planning a hostile takeover of our people and government?"

"Nothing but the best for my angel," he scowls into me as though I were an ungrateful bitch.

"You know," Chloe starts in with a devious smile. Her lips painted a bright arrogant shade of crimson that bounces off her face like a warning. "I always thought you two were better suited for each other." She gleams with delight, digging her steely gaze from me to Holden. "You both lie, you both cheat, and you would kill your own mothers to get what you really wanted."

"That's where you're wrong, Chloe." I glance out the tiny back window. "I would never kill my mother." Before the sentence can sail from my lips, I see my mother's car take a turn toward the estates. She *is* going to see Demetri. I freaking knew it.

My heart starts to race at the prospect of what exactly they might be doing to together.

A vision of Demetri taking off my mother's dress sears through my mind. She shakes her hair out with laughter.

Dear God.

I am going to kill my mother.

✤ ✤ ✤

The siren on top of this rescue transport saws and wails all the way over to the Paragon Palms Luxury Resort that backs into the white sandy beaches on the south end of the island. This is a way nicer venue than the one we had for winter formal.

It's killing me that Gage and I have to pretend we can't stand one another, at least the first part of the night. Once I kill Holden and land Logan back in his body, we can resume our love fest right there at prom if we wanted. And, of course, the Sunrise Motel will have an empty roach-filled room waiting on Logan's dime, but I might concede the offer. I'm sure whatever hotel room I end up in with Gage one day, won't have a crime scene cutout of its last patron emblazoned on the carpet.

A crowd amasses outside the long awning of the resort, nothing but startled faces for miles as we scream our way to the entrance. I spot Ellis loosely holding some girl from East. Ellis has the slight look of alarm on his face, as he should because he's normal, unlike Holden, whose idea of a good time consists of medical supplies and heart stopping sirens. But, lucky for me, there won't be a single medic around to help when I stop Holden's heart tonight.

The EMT on escort duty opens the twin doors and lets in the cool of the evening. Emily and Chloe bolt out so fast you'd think they came to their senses and realized who they were with, but in contrast to that lucid thought they wait acrimoniously outside the blinking vehicle for their respective dates, mortified as they should be.

"Shit," I hiss for no good reason as Holden yanks me down to the asphalt.

"I gotta piss like a racehorse," he hitches his thumb towards the facility. "I'll catch you inside."

"Sure," I tug down my dress. Glad to know Logan's bladder is still functioning, although his liver might be another issue—Holden reeks of booze.

Brielle gives a wild wave in my direction, and I head on over.

"Where's your date?" I pan the vicinity for the sharpest man around and find no one that even comes close to the perfection that is Gage.

"Said he needed to talk to Logan," she dips into me. "I totally know what's going on."

"You do?" I'm stunned Gage would trust Brielle with our delicate state of felonious affairs, especially since said state of affairs could involve manslaughter charges if I don't execute them properly—execute *him* to be exact.

"Totally, I mean why else would you fake being with Logan? He's been nothing but a turd the last few months. It's because you really care about me." She wraps her arm around my waist, and her stomach extends like a mixing bowl.

I take in the cinnamon scent of her hairspray, her arms and neck glitter under the lights from the awning.

"You've totally figured us out." I still don't know if I can trust Brielle one hundred percent, but for sure I'll never forget that after Chloe aired that sleezy DVD, it was Brielle who peeled me off the ground in the middle of a downpour.

I tighten my embrace.

I'll always love her for that.

We start making our way towards the entry, arm and arm. From the corner of my eye I see something white vanish into the woods across the street, subtle as lightning. It backtracks, stares me right in the face with its blood-soaked smile.

My heart seizes.

I pull Brielle quickly into the resort.

Looks like Holden and my mother aren't the only ones I might have to kill tonight.

82

Promtastic

The Madison Lights Ballroom dwarfs any other grand location we've managed to assemble in style. A plethora of twinkle lights wrap around nearly a dozen miniature trees lining the periphery of the room. A blue glow tints the ceiling, illuminates from the stage just beyond the dance floor. West and East are present, although it's a smaller student body count considering it's the junior, senior prom, and by the end of this evening, I'm hoping to subtract one more from the guest list.

Gage nods into me from across the room. His dark hair is slicked back, his dimples pressed in, offering their secret smile. I set my shoulders back—straighten as I drink him in. He looks magnificent, an aristocrat, a man of nobility. I keep inhaling until my lungs hurt from the effort. His eyes laser into mine a cool glacial blue that relaxes me under their watchful supervision. I feel safe just knowing Gage is in the vicinity, that my voice could carry through the crowd and touch him even if I'm unable.

A glittering parade of hostile sequins quickly covers his person. Chloe shags out her dark hair and laughs as she attempts to strike up a conversation with him. She looks horrid in that band-aid of an outfit, like a siren from hell—hound to be precise.

"You are a stunning creature, Ms. Messenger," Marshall stands tall beside me, resplendent and majestic.

"Thank you—and you clean up nicely yourself." I try to sound casual. Truthfully, if someone were to lay eyes on him for the first time tonight, they'd risk having the breath knocked out of them.

"These mediocre humans," he continues, "will one day realize the flagrant error of refusing to appreciate your eminence," he purrs. "They would bow to your royalty if they knew the presence they were in."

"It's doubtful anyone will ever bow to me. Maybe if I drop a dollar to my feet."

The bitch squad, sans its fearless leader, ogles me from a short distance.

"Miller at three o'clock," I whisper. "You could get very lucky tonight. She's lucid and dangerous. I'd like to volunteer her services once again for Fem training—Fem training in nocturne," I hold back a laugh. "Sounds downright poetic."

"You should never have coerced her into removing the necklace in the first place. How soon you had forgotten her wicked ways. Your forgiving nature is a magnificent flaw."

"Too forgiving? Isn't that the basic premise of the people from which you spawn?"

"Correction—created. No spawning or involuntary indwelling involved whatsoever. As for acquitting trespasses, what you suggest is true. However, your nature to forgive has resulted in your enemies flawed precept that you condone their aggressive behavior. It could prove deadly. I'm not sure you see this."

"You know what I can see? One of those freaky mirrors you gifted Demetri is now a permanent fixture in the Landon residence."

"Impossible." He nods at a group of girls who strut by admiring him, sending all sorts of lewd invites with the lowering of their eyelids.

"No really, I convinced Demetri to give it to me after Chloe tried to buy it at the garbage sale. It's in my mother's bedroom as we speak."

He gives a clear look of concern before pushing in close.

"Skyla, it's impossible for Demetri to have gifted you the mirror. Once the mirror is gifted, it can no longer transfer ownership under any circumstance."

"There's still another one back at his estate."

"There's just one Realm of Possibilities in existence."

"Are you sure you didn't give him two? It was probably centuries ago and you forgot. There can't be just one."

"One, and one alone."

"The one he gave me had a Fem inside. I saw it—scared the living crap out of me. You think the mirror in my mother's bedroom is capable of the same kind of trickery as the one you gave him?"

"I can assure you, whatever mirror he dispensed cannot replicate the beauty and wonder of living in the fool's paradise I had reserved for him. Do not under any circumstance go near that thing. I'll be by in the morning to pick it up. I'll have to find solid reasoning before removing it from the premises." Marshall creases his forehead with irritation. Color rises to his cheeks, amplifies his anger. Very few things move him to the point of excitability, let alone anger.

"My parents are camping." I catch a breath at the thought of referring to both Mom and Tad collectively as my parents but I let it slide since the music just hiked up ten decibels and brevity was necessary.

He gives a curt nod. *I'll have it hauled out in the A.M. Please extend my condolences as it will meet with an unfortunate demise. I'll have to destroy the mirror—above all things I am not a liar. And neither is your celestial mother. Watch carefully the words you let escape from those kissable lips. She has a zero tolerance policy when it comes to attitude. Do stray from provoking her to anger.*

Chloe begins to make her way in this direction, a giant Fem eating grin plastered across her face.

"Help me get her to remove that binding spirit," I say. "I want her arrested for making Gage and Logan kiss my grill."

She bypasses us and begins cackling away with Michelle and Lexy, regarding her one on one with Gage.

Follow my lead, Marshall turns a little in their direction. "So this mirror must be protected," he shouts the words like a fire and brimstone preacher. "We can't have anyone using it. It's an absolute danger in the wrong person's hands."

"So, when can you get me that binding spirit?" I make a face at Marshall not sure if I had overstepped the line. The next thing you know I'll be announcing the fact he's a Sector and turning myself into the Counts.

"In the morning." His eyes slit to nothing, letting me know exactly how far I pushed it. *She'll need to disappear and retrieve the binding spirit herself. If Chloe leaves for any given amount of time you'll know she's releasing it from its duty and delegating its services elsewhere. If you'll excuse me,* Marshall tilts his head in curiosity at something towards the back of the ballroom, *I need to tend to something myself.*

Marshall stalks off at a frenetic pace. I'm tempted to follow him, but sure enough, I catch Chloe darting out the main entrance with a spark in her ass.

I shoot out after her, making sure to keep a respectable distance in the event she should turn around and gouge my eyes out with those three-inch cat claws she's pressed onto her fingernails. But she doesn't. Chloe moves with heightened determination. The opportunity to fornicate with Gage has presented itself, and she's not one to pass up an offer when the right penis is involved.

While the rest of the student body rallies in the frivolity of prom, Chloe secures her lot in life. She opens the door to the ladies room and nearly mows down a group of

expel

seniors making their way out. I watch as they gawk at her overtly rude behavior.

From the corner of my eye I spot Ellis with his hands hidden beneath the skirt of his date.

I slip into the restroom and walk stall to stall in search of a familiar pair of sequined heels. Instead, I meet up with a pair of legs far too pale to belong to a cinnamon skinned Chloe, and the other pair have pink-laced hose pooling at the ankle, a crime in fashion that might have Chloe offing herself voluntarily for ever committing.

The door on the end is locked, no legs. I climb on the toilet of the neighboring stall and peer inside.

Empty with the exception of a heart-shaped purse hanging from the hook.

Time to witness Chloe, trying to kill Gage and Logan, first hand.

Light Drive

I snatch Ellis away before he completely does a disappearing act beneath that hussies dress and whisk him off into the narrow service hall just shy of the entry.

"Wanna go on a quick light drive?" I'm not really giving him a choice.

"Code?" He takes up a defiant stance as though I am in fact a Fem.

"Love honeys," I say, annoyed. "I need you to get Gage for me and meet me back here. Don't let Logan see you."

"Why can't Logan see me?"

"Because *Holden* isn't going to be too impressed with me going anywhere with Gage," I hiss, scooting him back out into circulation.

"Why did you break up with Gage?" He leans in with concern.

"Never mind just hurry. We don't have a lot of time. I having a stabbing I need to tend to by midnight."

"As long as I'm not on the receiving end," he mutters, taking off down the hall.

Nat and Pierce stroll by hand in hand. Pierce does a double take in my direction and heads on over.

"Got word from your lawyer you're not dropping the charges." His face is lost in shadows. Pierce has a menacing way about him when he's not mad, let alone pissed.

"What?" Clearly I need to rein in Ellis's mother. I specifically told her I wanted all this to go away. And isn't she supposed to consult me when making big decisions? Especially asinine decisions like these? Obviously, it's impossible to keep a Count in check.

expel

"I'm staring down a three month stint in juvy, a sixty-five thousand dollar fine for intent to harm while under the influence." He butts his shoulder into mine as Nat keeps watch from behind. His breath is soured. His cloud of cologne engulfs me thick as smoke.

"Wow, you said that well," I gasp for breath. "You should consider a career in law."

"Maybe I will. Persecute people like you who commit crimes and place the blame on others."

"I believe you mean prosecute. And you can go to hell, Pierce. You're no angel." So what if he's a Count? There seems to be a long road between being a Count and behaving like an angelic being. It's a questionable relationship at best.

"Maybe I will," he whispers. "Maybe I'll take you with me," the words ferment on his lips. "Or, maybe I'll just take you someplace else." He snatches a hold of Nat's hand and her wiry curls spring wild as they race out of the narrow hall.

Shit. Talking to Ellis's mother is on the top of my to-do list tomorrow unless of course I'll need to use her as my one phone call from the precinct later tonight. But that's not going to happen. Nothing is going to go wrong.

I try to shake off all the bad juju vibes as I shoo away Pierce's nasty cologne like an unwanted ghost.

All kinds of insane thoughts run through my mind as I wait around for Ellis. What if Chloe is in my mother's bedroom right this minute crawling into that twisted mirror of Demetri's? What if she's able to pull Gage's look alike out of the mirror and there's two of him running around the island? Knowing Chloe, she'd keep one prisoner in her bedroom and have her way with him nightly. What if she pulls another *me* out of the mirror and has me running around committing all sorts of felonies? Not that it would be such a stretch.

Gage and Ellis duck into the hallway. Gage looks amazing in his pressed inky suit. I pull him in and offer up a brazen kiss, let the warmth of his mouth comfort me. Gage is a man above gods. He groans into me before dislodging.

"Are you sure you want to do this?" He nuzzles a kiss into my neck as he says it.

"It may be our only opportunity. The mirror will be gone by morning." I grab a hold of Ellis and think about that horrible ill-fated night back in January.

"It's time, Skyla," my name trembles from the walls in a series of horrific echoes.

"Is that?" Gage cocks his head to get a better listen.

"Ezrina," I pant. I'd recognize that twisted voice anywhere.

The world melts beneath our feet. Time splinters until as we slip through its stringent confines.

※ ❦ ※

We land in the dirt field just outside the bowling alley, a light rain pelting us from above. The pungent scent of fresh mud mixed with the thick bouquet from the forest, ignites my senses. I hadn't remembered the spice in the air, the cold feeling of the wind as it lights each raindrop on fire over my flesh. Then again, I was in shock. It's a wonder I remember anything from that night at all.

"There," I point over to Logan, Gage, and me, standing in the distance.

The Mustang pulls in slow, rolls to a stop before flicking on its headlights.

"I'll go check it out," Gage darts across the field, ducks just shy of the driver's door.

"Who do you think it is?" Ellis looks suspiciously at the Mustang as it revs its engine.

"Do you even have to ask?" I hesitate adding Marshall into the equation. "Bishop."

"Chloe?" His Nordic features looks unimpressed with my theory.

Gage runs back, squatting low to the ground.

"Well?" A hot spike of adrenaline surges through me. This is it. I'm going to hang Chloe upside down by her toenails once I have proof she and her claws were behind the wheel that night.

"Nobody's in there," the whites of his eyes glint like bicycle reflectors. "The seat's empty."

"No." The thought of Marshall inflicting this horrible crime upon the two people I love most is unimaginable—unforgiveable.

The engine revs over and over, the Mustang accelerates, slamming into Logan and Gage. Logan slips down beneath the vehicle while Gage is struck over and over, pinned up against the trunk of a weathering pine. That tree should be hacked to pieces for involuntarily participating in the heinous crime—for not reaching down with its branches and snatching Gage up out of the line of fire. But I guess the same could be said for me, I froze like a coward—died a thousand deaths just watching.

"Let's go back," I grab a hold of Ellis and Gage.

My own cries fill the night as I scream in the background. They sound foreign, primal. Marshall inflicted this punishment on me.

Looks like I've just added another victim to my kill list tonight.

The Madison Lights Ballroom has dimmed considerably. Bodies slash around on the dance floor in and out of rhythm, a sea of arms and legs intertwine as they struggle to move to the impossibly loud music.

I see Holden over by a group of girls, seniors I don't really know. He's talking to a tall blonde and has his hand placed strategically over her thigh. Ordinarily, I would make a beeline over and slap him silly, but my hostility towards Marshall has eclipsed any anger I might have felt for Holden who was simply a spirit lying in wait for a new home. But it's Marshall I'm interested in sending back to the Soulennium, the transport, the Transfer. I want him anywhere but here on planet Earth where he can hurt the ones I love.

Logan warms the sheath around me, ignites the dress in waves of approval regarding my newfound vendetta.

I spot Marshall towards the back with arms folded across his chest, staring stone cold into the crowd like an FBI agent officiating over the scene.

I push my way through the jostling bodies—split up Drake and Emily from a serious lip-lock on the way over, before finally landing square in front of him.

"You, are coming with me," I roar, leading him towards the exit.

I'm startled to see we've landed ourselves outside. The concrete bleeds into sand.

"Romantic walk on the beach?" Marshall purrs, proud of his teleportation feat. "I was hoping you'd acclimate to me quickly, but this is a dream come true." He gives the slight curve of a smile.

"The car was *empty*," I mean for it to come out aggressive, but it comes out a sob as though I were ready to grieve my relationship with Marshall instead of kill it. A part of me still doesn't believe he was capable. There's no way I can surrender to hatred unless he asserts to the fact he spearheaded this tragedy. Then he'll be dead to me, leaving a void he had filled so beautifully.

"Correction, love, the car *appeared* empty," he takes me by the hand and leads us over to a row of pigmy palms. "You were able to go back."

I nod.

expel

"I trust she's already secured the mirror. Once she realizes it's not the same pleasure cruise she'll have the spirit back within the hour. Come," he takes up my other hand gently by the fingers, "I'll return to the scene of the crime with you just this once."

Marshall speeds us to the exact location I was standing in earlier with Ellis and Gage—only we're not standing, we're hovering near the Mustang. The rain pours through me as if I were a shadow.

I watch as the door opens, the engine turns before the car rolls forward—not a soul in sight.

"That's where you're wrong, Skyla," Marshall corrects. "There *is* a soul in sight—tucked secure behind the wheel."

"I don't see anyone."

"Open your spiritual eyes." Marshall wands his hand over my face and I see a body, plain as day, sitting in the driver's seat, reaching down and flicking on the lights.

"Oh my God," I pant the words. "I should have known."

84

Confusion is Nothing New

The twinkle lights gleam overhead like intoxicating beacons from some far off unknowable city. I blink into the ceiling several times before I realize I'm once again standing in the ballroom. Logan warms over me like a dream, and I stroke my abdomen as though I were carrying his child.

I know who is responsible for this terrible act of injury that took his life.

Gage sits at a table off in the corner with Brielle by his side. He's got one leg kicked up on a chair and he's checking his phone intermittently while carrying on a conversation with her.

This isn't the best time to go over and share personal space with Gage especially since Holden is on red alert for any suspicious activity on my part but, at the moment, I don't really give a shit.

"Are you OK?" I shout into Brielle, posturing myself so that I look like I'm still putting the freeze on Gage in the event Holden should decide to make use of Logan's brain cells.

"I'm thinking about ditching out early. Like after they crown you," she winks.

I laugh, pretending to drop my purse on the floor between the two of them. Gage bows to meet me.

"You look gorgeous," he rasps, pressing a searing kiss on my cheek as we stoop near the carpet.

"Thank you. You look amazing, yourself." I dot his lips with mine. "And, by the way, it was Holden in the car that night," I latch onto his gaze. "He wanted a body and he arranged to get one himself."

expel

"Shit," Gage is indignant. "After the ceremony get him outside, alone, by the water. I'll meet you there. Do *not* attempt to do this by yourself, Skyla." I've never heard Gage take such a demanding tone before.

"OK," I rise to my feet and stride out the Madison Lights Ballroom.

I open the door to the ladies room just as Chloe grapples her way out. Her face is pale, and she startles at the sight of me.

"What's the matter?" I ask, trying to sound nonchalant like I didn't suspect for a minute she was in my mother's bedroom trying to start a fake forever with Gage.

"The mirror," the words tumble from her lips.

"What about the mirror?" I pull her back inside as a mob pushes their way through. Chloe must have had the clown Fem scare of a lifetime. I try to hide a wicked grin.

"I went...and," she shakes her head like an apology. "Never mind." She marches out of the restroom chin up and stoic as if she had just come to her senses.

Whatever Chloe saw in that mirror, jolted her, bled the color from her face and sent her packing for prom. The last time she went in Demetri's mirror she lingered for weeks, I had to extricate her like dragging a child out of an amusement park. Something tells me this was no wonderland where she ruled the roost.

I still find it hard to believe Chloe wasn't responsible for the accident. I guess everything that's wrong in this world is not directly related to Chloe Bishop.

It just feels like it.

I watch Chloe and Holden's every move. Not exactly how I envisioned spending prom. I try to watch Gage, too, but he's pretty much in the seat next to Brielle, and they're switching back and forth between a lazy conversation and staring into their cell phones. I don't know who will call either of them. I'm the primary person in both their lives, and I'm standing right here.

Is everyone rightfully full of hatred and loathing? Marshall appears by my side.

I touch my bare thigh to his dangling fingers. I doubt anyone will notice because it's so freaking crowded in here. There are so many damn people sardined inside this place, I swear we've broken the fire code three times over. And where in the hell are all these people coming from? There seems to be way more than when we first started out.

I'm full of loathing and hatred, I offer. *Gage is downright pissed.* I give a depleted smile. *Lucky for us, we're killing Holden before the night is through.*

Why do you insist on trusting Gage? Marshall is clearly miffed by the concept. *How do you know he won't botch the resurrection at the last moment because just perhaps, he really does prefer the Pretty One dead?*

Gage? He doesn't want Logan dead and he's totally trustworthy. I glance over at him patting Brielle on the stomach, and suppress the joy surging within me. *Gage would give his life to save Logan—and me. He's an altruistic being in everyway. He might even do something foolish to save yours if it came right down to it. He's a lover in every capacity,* I say.

Do Tell. Marshall gives a long blink of disgust.

His head turns abruptly.

Marshall's full attention has been waylaid by something on the other side of the room. *You must pardon the intrusion. I'll speak with you soon.* He speeds off towards a door that leads to the back, dissipates from view quick as smoke.

expel

Something is happening.

I turn to find both Holden and Pierce headed in this direction.

Shit! Why would Holden so obviously be hanging out with his late not so great brother? And heading towards *me* of all people?

I duck out in the same direction Marshall took off in and run smack into Ethan.

"Hey, you seen Chloe?" He looks over my shoulder as if I were harboring her like a fugitive.

"Nope. Speaking of the witch—when is that great act of revenge you've plotted out against her going to unfold? And by the way, I totally don't believe you."

"It will, and you should. I've put some serious effort jerry-rigging one unforgettable show." He pushes past me deep into the crowd.

I can only hope he's right. There's nothing I like more than letting someone else do my dirty work.

"Skyla," Holden calls, waving at me. Pierce and Nat straggle behind.

Drake and Emily float by, and I slink on over to the two of them.

"Hi!" I say, watching Holden on his last night disguised as Logan from a safe distance. "So how's it going?" I pan over the two of them. Really I'd love nothing more than to hit Drake over the head with my shoe.

Emily gives a grunt before excusing herself. Emily always looks like she wants to puke in my face, and I can never figure this out. I would totally be Em's friend if she would let me. She's the most normal person I know, and considering I'm aware of the fact she can put the future to paper, it's a pretty bold statement.

"I have a terrible feeling of foreboding," Drake holds his stomach like he might be sick.

"Don't say that," I reprimand. "The last time you said that all kinds of freaky shit happened."

Marshall pulses by in the opposite direction. "Whatever you've got planned, cancel it." He continues on as if it were an order I should obey.

The music changes speed, bodies churn on the dance floor quick and neurotic. A strong scarf of perfume ties itself around the room in a rainbow of floral scents, vanilla and grapefruit.

I run and catch up with him as fast as my four-inch stilettos will allow.

"What do you mean *cancel* it? I can't cancel. It has to happen." I pull Marshall to a stop just shy of the exit.

"I forbid it." He slits his eyes around the room not bothering to slow his agitation long enough to pay attention to me properly.

"You forbid it?" I straighten, not sure whether to laugh or slap him. "Let me tell you something *buddy*—that falls under the short list of things to never say to your future bride. In fact, it's the easiest and most assured way of landing yourself an ex Mrs. Dudley."

His eyes lock onto mine for one brief moment, and he gives a quick nod. "I forbid it." He marches off in pursuit of something or someone towards the front of the dance floor.

I give a little laugh at the thought of Marshall forbidding me to do anything.

One thing is for damn sure, there's not a soul on this planet that can stop me from killing Holden tonight.

If they try—*I'll* forbid it.

85

Safety Dance

A puff of white fog, thick as buttermilk, spills in through the open exit door of the Madison Lights Ballroom. It seeps in with its long frosted tendrils, observing the dew of youth as it floats around the dance floor.

A sad song belts out a steady rhythm that wanes, each note pulls out soft as cotton.

I undergo a major analysis of the exits, the structure of the room, the entire framework of the building, in the event Holden should try to escape. Luring him out towards the beach with raunchy promises will be easy. In fact, I'm sure he'll come up with his own long running list of carnal titillations he'd like to introduce me to but Holden will be long gone before his fantasies take flight.

Ellis comes over and butts his shoulder against mine. "Come on," he nods towards the dance floor.

"Where's the future stripper?" I scan the area for his scantily clad date, not that I'm one to talk, or Chloe, or Emily. Oh, hell, we're all wearing some sort of ass enhancing apparatus, especially Chloe who sparkles like a hazmat signaling device—as she should.

"She passed out. Her friends rolled her under a table for safekeeping."

"Nice." Those girls from East have an amazing code of ethics.

"Last chance," he invokes the offer once again.

"Sure," I take Ellis's soft warm hand and let him lead me through a maze of swaying bodies. We land behind Ethan and Chloe. She glitters under the faded house lights with the prowess of fire in a dim-lit forest. Chloe is a blaze all her own.

I rest my head on Ellis's chest—try to ignore the fact that his cologne is overpowered with the scent of something far more illegal. I wonder what a life with Ellis would be like? I'm sure we'd live close to the beach, well, probably on it—homeless. Our children would run around barefoot all the time because we couldn't afford shoes. I can see them clearly, two little girls with cotton candy hair, dirty faces scalded from the sun, parched cracked lips. I shake the thought away, imagine children with Gage instead—dark haired boys with bright blue eyes, dimples you could ladle soup out of.

The dress warms around my body unreasonably. Either Logan is getting antsy, or he wants a demonstration of what *our* children would look like. I envision a blonde goddess of a girl who could rule the universe with her looks alone. Logan can rule an empire with his smile. The dress tingles, ignites a happy vibration of joy in the same vein as Marshall.

The music comes to an end. The houselights brighten before dimming to pitch again. A spotlight covers the stage and Marshall chokes the life out of a microphone before releasing it from the stand.

"Ladies and Gentlemen of Paragon's finest esteemed schools," he hums into the mic. "I would like to draw your attention to the candidates of the royal court. Would the junior nobility of the evening please step up and take your places as we announce the victors of tonight's festivities."

"I guess that's me," I pat Ellis on the chest before heading towards the stage.

Holden flies at me like a magnet, drips a kiss off the side of my face as if that might somehow secure a win. The polls are over I want to tell him, but refrain since he's in a good mood.

"Time to end the drought." He slithers his hand up and down my back before reaching underneath my dress, landing open palmed on my behind.

expel

I jump out of reach and give a tempered smile. I'd slit his throat if he weren't wearing Logan like a jacket.

"I'm still trying to get my mother to grant you your powers back," I shrug. "So I guess I lose in the interim."

He twists his lips. "I'll let it slide just this once. No use in letting a perfectly good hotel room go to waste. But get on that tomorrow. It sucks not being Celestra."

"I'll get right on that." As if.

He takes my hand, and we make our way onto the stage. I squint into the crowd for Gage and Brielle. It's so close now. It's almost time to bring back Logan. Nothing can go wrong. My chest heaves in anticipation until I spot them standing near the front. I press out a nervous smile before focusing back on Marshall.

Skyla. My name rattles through the crowd.

Ezrina.

Shit! She must know I've got a life that depends upon me, a soul literally wrapped around my person.

Now. Her voice echoes, louder coming from my left. And there she is.

Double shit!

Ezrina is covered in a black velvet cloak, nothing but a shag of wild hair spraying out from under her hood like a tumbleweed locked in flames.

"I need my mother," I speed the words into Marshall so fast I don't realize my lips are level with the microphone until I hear my voice boom across the facility.

The crowd ignites in laughter.

Again—*shit*.

In due time. Marshall assures.

"You're etting embarrassing me," Holden pulls me back. "Stop being such a baby."

A drum roll purrs over the speakers. Marshall reads off a list of names from East before crowning their junior king and queen. A pretty girl with a familiar face and a tall boy with broad shoulders share a brazen kiss, their crowns hang precariously from their person.

"We should totally do that," Holden whispers.

"Do what?"

"Kiss like that."

Gah! That was a nasty kiss. It looked like she was trying to suck a snake out of his mouth just to save him. No thanks.

"I prefer a peck on the cheek in public," I'm quick to relay. "You know, save the good stuff for later."

"So you're a good girl." He leans in seductively with Logan's immaculate features. "I'll have you on your knees in less than an hour."

"Can't wait." I'm going to use my knees all right. Something in me reverts, and I bite down on my lip trying to return the seductive favor. "I won't have time to get on my knees, I'll be too busy bending over." *Mother F!* I don't even know what the hell that implies.

He pulls a single gold key out of his pocket, dive bombs it into my cleavage before shoving his face in and kissing it.

Everything in me freezes.

I shoot a quick look to Gage. His eyes are swollen with anger, his mouth gapes, and for a second I think Gage might jump on stage and kill Holden himself.

"The nobility of West Paragon reads as follows," Marshall booms. "Skyla Messenger and Logan Oliver."

Holden rights himself just after the spotlight catches him with his face in the Messenger cookie jar.

Marshall clears his throat before continuing, "Chloe Bishop and Ethan Landon, Emily Morgan and Drake Landon. " Marshall's smooth voice is a comfort, a strange shelter from the storm that is hurricane Holden. "The junior gentry—your new king and queen of the junior class are..." he bows slightly into the announcement, "Skyla Messenger and Logan Oliver." A polite applause erupts. I look over at Chloe and Ethan, Emily and Drake almost apologetically.

expel

I'm not sure how anyone in their right mind could vote for Logan and me since we weren't together almost all year long, unless, of course, it was their way of thanking me for providing endless hours of entertainment via Chloe's generous DVD distribution. I hear they play it on a loop during chess club.

A pair of freshman girls come at us with glittering headdresses, before I can properly observe my tiara, Holden does a faceplant over my lips. I press my hands to his chest to push him away and the dress electrifies, a personified hum emits as it vibrates like an engine. Logan is ready. I carefully unzip the purse and bring the needle to Holden's chest.

I slit my eyes open just enough and catch Gage taking off through the main entrance with Brielle.

What the heck?

Where is he going? After the crowning we were supposed to lure him outside. We were going to kill Holden together. Didn't he instruct me under no circumstance was I to pull this off on my own?

My face fills with heat as I finger the needle.

What am I doing? I take a breath as Holden continues to take free roam of my mouth with Logan's tongue.

Gage is wrong. I can do this on my own.

The lights go out. The music stops. A series of gasps circle the room.

I press the needle into Holden's chest and give a hard shove.

Holden jerks, lets out a sharp cry right into my ear. The houselights go on all the way before dimming down to nothing. The music picks up and the crowd gurgles back to life.

"What the hell was that?" He pats his chest in horror.

I replace the needle back in my purse and slip it behind my back.

Shit. One more second and I could have zapped him off the planet.

I wave a hand in front of him. "Just got my claws sharpened. I'm totally afraid of the dark."

"Shit," his eyes widen. Holden doesn't look amused by my professed fear of all things nocturnal.

"Let's dance," I nod towards the beach. "You know, in private."

"Let's." He whips us through the crowd at lightning speed.

A shadow moves outside the door, an orange blaze of hair gives the Fem away.

"In here's fine!" I pull him back inside so quick it looks like we're doing the Tango. I place his hands over my hips and begin to sway to the music.

"This is a good start." His eyes shine a familiar look of desire, and at this moment he looks and feels most like Logan—but he's not. He's a far cry from the boy I love.

The dress warms around me like an L.A. afternoon.

I scan the room for signs of Gage, but neither he nor Brielle have returned. Perfect. Why can't things go right when I need them to? Why does everything have to fall to crap the second I put my hand to anything? I'll be *lucky* if Gage and I get our forever. Hell—I'll be lucky if forever *exists* by the time I get through with it.

I reach down and pluck the needle out of my purse, and the small electrical box tumbles right out. I catch it between my elbow and thigh before capturing it safe in my hand.

"What's that?" Holden backs up and takes a good look at it.

"Speaker," I hiss. "New speaker I got for Christmas. I don't go anywhere without it." I'm quick to shove the heart stopper back inside the sequin satchel before he sees the needle.

expel

The lights cut in and out again, the music fizzles before recapturing its rhythm.

"Let's get out of here—start our own party," his hot breath lights a fire across my cheek. "I've got the room till ten in the morning."

"Sure." I dart around looking for Gage, or Ellis—hell, I'd take Marshall at this point.

My phone goes off. It's a text from Melissa.

I can't find Mia. She went in Mom and Dad's room and never came out.

Crap. Mia must have went into the mirror before Chloe sicked her binding spirit on it.

A surge of bodies push in. Young women and men with an odd sense of style descend upon us, dancing and swirling to a frenetic rhythm all their own.

"Dear God," I whisper. I recognize those full bustled dresses, those pantaloon knickers peering out from underneath. Handlebar mustaches adorn men who happen to be much too old to attend prom.

The Transfer.

"Something's happening," I pant.

"I know." Holden rubs the growing bulge in his pants abruptly against my thigh. "Let's get out of here."

A sharp scream emits from the center of the room.

I turn in time to see a body flying up towards the mirrored sphere hanging above the center of the dance floor. A pair of long brown legs kick up a violent tantrum. It's not until I take a step forward that I see its Chloe. She spins and clutches at her neck. Her red dress goes off like shimmering fireworks on the Fourth of July.

It looks as if the protective hedge has caught on something, a wire that dangles from the disco ball.

Holy crap.

Could this be Ethan's late, great, final act of revenge? Could Ethan Landon really be this big of a genius to hang

Chloe Bishop in front of God and country right here at the East meets West glorified dance-a-thon?

Chloe is showing us up in the moves department with her determined spin, sway, swing—the way she bucks into her own departure is glorious.

Screams erupt like a choir of hellish angels. All eyes are focused upwards at Chloe as if we were sharing in some mass hallucination—a heavenly vision that will christen our flesh with a radioactive glow for days to come. This is a blessed event, songs should be written about this moment, poetry to recite to our grandchildren.

I step forward, dazed—in love with the idea of watching Chloe meet her most timely demise.

It is a thing of beauty. I wish my father could have been here to witness the grand finale of all her wicked schemes. It comes down to this. Chloe Bishop dies as a spectacle, dangling fifty feet off the floor, glittering proud as a brushfire.

She bucks and writhes, clawing at her neck with sharpened fingernails. Her flesh erupts in a series of long blood-soaked lines.

I want her blood to flow—my blood. I want to open my mouth, drink down her pain. There's something orgasmic about this—sensual. I've achieved nirvana by the sheer prospect of watching her life expire.

Chloe lets out a horrid, gurgled cry. Ironic how the protective hedge is actually in the process of doing Chloe in. It must be a nice night for assholes to die. Unfortunately, if Chloe doesn't survive, Mia may not either.

I grab a hold of Emily and drag her over to Michelle and Lexy.

"Get me up there," I instruct. The bitch squad gets into basket toss formation. I conjure all of the angst and hostility I can muster towards Chloe in an attempt to leap to her rescue. "One, two, three!" I rocket up towards the ceiling easy and light as a butterfly. I pull down the metal hook that's adhered to the chain around Chloe's neck, hard and fast.

We fall in tandem. Her face, pale as plaster, lips as blue as a summer sky. The bitch squad cradles their limbs around Chloe, and I land with a gentle swish in Marshall's waiting arms. A quick bite of sadness twists through me. I was half expecting him to be Gage. I pan the facility as Marshall props me up on my feet.

"She needs a jump start, Skyla, or she'll be dead before help arrives." Marshall hands me my purse.

"This has a one-time use only," I scold, making sure he understands the dire implications of it all. "Besides, she's still wearing that protective hedge."

"Yes, Skyla," he leans in, "But if death is ordained in the near future for Ms. Bishop—the Decision Council might just let the tragedy slide."

He gives a quick nod towards the crowd amassed around her.

I look over to Chloe lying on the ground, limp as kelp, a most beautiful cadaver in the making.

My lips curve into the promise of a smile, my chest still panting wild from the effort.

I go over and touch my hand to her forehead.

I must choose.

Save Chloe and get Mia, or risk getting Mia out of the realm of Demetri's horrors all on my own.

I stroke Chloe's long dark tendrils arranged like snakes around her beautiful dead face and whisper, "Oh my sweet little bitch, how I hope you rest in peace."

86

If You Don't Know Me by Now

Gage appears, panting, bloodied from the elbows down, his shirt stained with a strange viscous fluid. He snatches my purse and removes the device, shrouding his body over Chloe.

Good God, he's going to zap her back into existence.

Her entire person jumps chest first off the ground an entire foot. Gage places his lips over hers, blows in breath after breath until she coughs and sputters. He spits out the residue behind his shoulder and wipes his lips down on the lapel of his jacket.

"What did you do that for?" It's more rhetorical at this point.

He offers a depleted smile. "Because I knew you wouldn't." He pulls out his phone and texts so fast the phone pops in his hands, wild and spastic. "Brielle had her baby," he pants glancing up at me briefly. "Baby Beau. She's on her way to the hospital."

"A boy! Is that why you're covered in—did you?" I slap my hand over my mouth as he nods.

"Shit," he barks down at his phone.

"What?" I push the device back in my purse as the EMTs settle in around Chloe.

"My dad says there's no way we'll get the charge we need for Holden."

That's because he wasted it on Chloe. I badly want to say that but don't.

She gets up on her elbows and bats the medics away citing she's more than OK.

Of course she is, she just had some real action from Gage—their first kiss right here at prom.

Ms. Messenger, I bid you to evacuate the premises, Marshall says, helping me up off the floor. "Immediately," he snaps. His jaw is distended, his eyes cut into the crowd with a look of vengeance.

I grab Gage by the hand and pull him along.

"Holden hard left," Gage whispers before dramatically plucking his arm free from mine. "Just because I helped your friend out doesn't mean I want anything to do with *you*!" He roars it so loud, the entire crowd reduces to a low rumble.

I glint over towards Holden. He's all eyes and all ears. Gage and I have the floor. One last opportunity to squelch the life out of him tonight and I'd better not blow it.

"I hate you Gage Oliver! I *hate* you!" It shrills out of me like a fire alarm. I make a beeline over to Holden and grab him by the wrist. "Get me the hell out of here. I need someone in my life who knows how to have a good time."

Holden huffs a laugh, takes me in with those serious Logan eyes—the dimple I gave him, by way of broken glass, pulsates in and out. He knows. He's probably got Pierce and Nat waiting in that hotel room ready to hide my body once they beat me to a bloody pulp, drink down my blood like a brood of thirsty bats.

He leads me out the side exit towards the ocean. A wash of powder fresh fog baptizes us as we rush into the night.

I pray Gage is hot on our heels. That he hasn't truly lost his sanity and isn't sabotaging the altruistic purpose of this charade just to keep Logan out of our lives for good. I have a feeling this humanitarian effort, a.k.a, *operation zap Holden out of existence,* is going to take a little more than his cooperation.

Holden runs us down to the beach. He holds my fingers in a vice grip, sprinting us to the waterline so fast I can barely keep up in this mini-dress and heels. He knocks me down to the chilled sand, runs his hot hands up the bottom of my dress without waiting for an invitation. We jostle and roll further to the shore, with him assaulting me and me wondering how far I should let it go before I try to save myself from his ever-wandering appendages. The sand grows damp beneath me. An unexpected wall of water slaps over our shoulders, crushes us in a bath of icy brine.

Holden forces a series of greedy kisses upon me, roves his tongue in and out of my mouth in quick convulsive spasms. His teeth chatter against mine, his fingers dig into my arms so tight I can feel the circulation cutting off.

A conversation I had with Dr. Oliver comes back to me. I distinctly remember him mentioning that hypothermia would be the best way to preserve Logan's tissue.

Waves topple us one after another until we're floating with the natural ebb and flow of the sea.

I latch a leg around Holden's waist, hook my elbow under his arm and paddle us out while offering up mouthwatering kisses. I spill kisses like lies, promises that will go unfulfilled as I sail us deeper into the dark expanse. I speed us out to sea like a dolphin, swimming hard and fast just the way Marshall taught me, like a marine animal trained for war.

My Celestra blood boils, keeps my body temperature comfortable and stable. I can feel Holden writhing in agony, teeth clattering like castanets. His chest heaves with convulsions from the icy waters.

I let go of him in the black calm of the ocean.

The sparkling resort is nothing but a simple dot glittering in the distance. I can make out the ridge of the island, the entire mass of granite a richer shade of ebony than the sky above it could ever afford.

The dress sizzles to life around me. Logan warms me. Leaves me secure in knowing that I'm not alone.

"Sh-sh-shit!" Holden seizes and thrashes before falling still to his waiting destiny.

expel

I don't say anything, simply pull him in by the fingers watch him slip peaceful into his final slumber.

Marshall appears glowing a translucent shade of gold as he floats above the surface. "This, my love, is death." A colorful spiral of light encompasses Holden as it suctions his soul up into its vacuum.

"Now what?" I shout in a panic.

"Breathe life into him." He floats up into the sky revealing an expanse of large feathered wings wide as a house. "The dress will do the rest."

"Logan," I cry, pulling him over to me—so still, so frighteningly still. I seal my mouth over his cold lips and give three lungfuls of air. "Logan!" I shake him, but nothing happens. He's not moving or breathing. "Marshall!" I dive down on Logan's mouth in a panic, pulling us under in the process. I blow in a deep lungful of air as my tears mingle with the ocean and wrap my body around him to warm him. My heart aches for Logan. I want him back, alive and with me, so we can watch the future unfold together, see where it might take us, see how far the path that destiny carved out for us leads. I give another gentle puff before pulling us to the surface. His lips twitch beneath mine. He returns a beautiful breath, consummates it with the impression of a kiss that I will remember for ages.

"Logan!" I scream jumping over him, submerging him under without meaning to.

He pulls us back to the surface. "Skyla," he laughs into the night.

He's back.

Logan is back—my Logan.

87

Fallen Angel

The navy sky hides beneath a veil of feathery fog as Logan and I wash high up on the shore, still glossy and wet from our adventure at sea. He pulls me in, rests his arm over my waist with his chest panting into mine.

"You saved me," he gasps for breath as he says it, pulling me in nose to nose. He grazes his teeth against mine still laughing, gasping.

"How do I know it's really you?" I can tell by the way his eyes dance over my face, the delight radiating from his being. There's something sweet and wholly unique to Logan that shines from deep inside his soul.

"Happily ever after," he whispers, pushing his forehead to mine. *There will be one, I promise.*

I get up on my elbows and offer a gentle smile. "It's already here."

A couple walking hand in hand along the beach captures my attention.

"Gage?" I scramble up to my feet and Logan follows. Chloe is gazing into him and they share a secret smile. "What the hell?" I run over.

"Skyla!" Gage races towards me and spins me in his arms, presses a kiss upon my forehead, my nose, my lips. He whips off his jacket and pulls it around me still warm from his body before looking up at Logan. "Hey, man, is it really you?" He pulls Logan into a half hug, ruffles his wet hair.

"It's me." Logan nods over towards Chloe who's already halfway back to the resort. "What's going on?"

To put it mildly that's exactly what the hell I'd like to know.

He takes a deep breath. "She was thanking me. I knew you were fine, Skyla. I saw Dudley take off toward the water and disappear like a bat in flight. Besides, I don't want to rock the boat with her, she knows Mia's in the mirror."

This catches me off guard.

Did I tell Gage, Mia was in the mirror?

"I was wondering," I pause trying to take in this entire crazy night. "Why do you think Chloe had a binding spirit around the night of the accident if she wasn't the one driving the car?" I search Gage like he might have the answer, hoping he does because I'm going to abandon my sanity if I meditate on the subject any longer. "It was Holden, by the way," I tell Logan, bringing him up to speed.

Gage squints out into the black of the ocean as a thin coat of fog puffs between us.

"Maybe you didn't go back far enough," he suggests.

"OK then," I lay my hand out, Gage covers mine, and Logan his. I close my eyes and think of that terrible night last winter that erected itself like a blade through the heart of our existence, and the world washes blank around us.

We appear behind the bowling alley as a light rain begins to pelt us. The three of us stand locked in an argument off in the distance. I can hear the rage in my voice—feel the tension between the three of us, distrustful as a pack of thieves.

The Mustang is still parked back where I left it. Chloe emerges from the service door clutching at her chest, choking back tears.

"She's dying at the thought of losing Gage," I say. "We had just showed her the movie where she slaughtered Ethan and Emerson." I sneak a quick look to Logan.

"It's no surprise she chose the same mode of torment to take you down," Gage says, pulling me in and offering a warm kiss. *I love you, Skyla. There is nothing I wouldn't do for you. You know that?*

Seems like an odd time for Gage to be professing his love to me. I give a short-lived smile.

"I know," I whisper.

"Look," Logan points over to Chloe.

She bats at the air, yelling at someone or something to get away.

"I bet that's Holden," I whisper.

She looks over at the three of us arguing under the evergreen and seethes.

"The keys are in the car," Chloe nods as if she could see him. "I want him gone. If he wants me out of his life so badly I'll gladly show him the way."

"She was after *me*," Gage breathes in disbelief.

"Chloe wanted you dead." I shake my head at the impossibility of it all. She'd want the entire human race wiped off the map soon thereafter, once she realized the egregious error she's committed. Life would be impossible without Gage. I especially know that.

"She didn't want him necessarily dead," Logan says it sober. "She wanted Holden to take over, and I'm willing to bet she'd spend the rest of her life with him."

The Mustang rolls forward, the lights flick on and off like a warning.

"Let's get out here," Logan takes up both our hands.

"Let's," I say.

And we do.

※ ※ ※

I retrieve my phone from the sand and put in a text to Melissa. **Did you find Mia? ~S**

expel

Less than a minute later. She got pissed and locked herself in Mom and Dad's room. She was bawling then it got quiet. I busted through the door and she's just gone. Everything was shut, the doors, the windows. I don't know where she could have disappeared to. I'm scared.

I know exactly where she might have disappeared to. And so does Chloe.

88

Body Language

The Madison Lights Ballroom is bathed in billows of precipitous baby's breath. A blue tinted fog aligns itself with the fact tonight is a new moon.

"Your people have entranced my mother," I say sarcastically to Logan as we enter the establishment. "She's been going to the meet and greets with Demetri, often and willing."

"I'll find out what's going on. If she's at the meetings I'll see her there for sure. I missed tonight's, but there's a follow-up three days later called the Slaughter of Plenty. It concludes the New Moon Festival."

I don't know whether to be frightened or impressed that Logan knows so much about the Counts. And the simple fact the phrase he just uttered contained the words *slaughter* and *plenty*, both frightens and unnaturally arouses me.

"There she is," he nods behind me.

"Let me," Gage offers.

"I'll go with you."

Gage wraps an arm around my waist as we head on over. Chloe pretends not to see us coming and continues to listen thoughtfully to whatever Michelle is filling her ears with.

A giant black rose lays flat against Michelle's swollen chest. I pull a bleak smile at the thought of Marshall actually taking my advice and gifting her a new one—bigger and better at that.

"There's a good chance Mia is stuck in the mirror." Gage lets into her with a tone that clues her in on the fact he's not shitting around.

expel

"What's it to you?" She snarls at the two of us as if she never did love him, as if she hated us equally.

"My sister is missing," I hiss. "Remove that stupid binding spirit you placed around it so she can get out in one piece."

"What the hell kind of hallucinatory drugs are you on?" Michelle pulls at a lock of her hair as Marshall whistles for her in the distance. She gives a sultry smile before trotting off dutifully like a well-trained dog.

"The mirror, dear Skyla, and everything in it is mine." Chloe cuts a scathing look to Gage. "Why did you bring me back?" She hacks into him accusingly.

His eyes widen. He looks from me to her. "I got a text saying her sister was missing, and all roads to trouble always lead to you, Chloe." He effortlessly slashes her with the blade of his tongue. "Do the right thing for once and let her go, she's just a kid."

"At the beach," her eyes gloss over, "you said you cared about me, that you had feelings for me. You were faking it all for that stupid brat. You've been faking everything, haven't you?"

Gage doesn't say anything. He lets his muted silence speak volumes about how much he loathes her.

I'm no expert, but I'm guessing that while bargaining for my sister's wellbeing, it's a lousy time to clue Chloe in on how much he hates her.

"I'll give Mia back," she doesn't look at me when she says it. She never takes her eyes off Gage. "But I want to speak with *you*, alone."

✺ ✺ ✺

I wander outside and find Logan leaning against the corrugated trunk of a palm, gazing out into a pale sapphire curtain of fog with a dismal expression.

I strum my fingers lightly over his arm. "Everything OK?"

"It is now." He pulls me in, doesn't hesitate wrapping his arms around my waist.

"Have I told you how dapper you look tonight?" Every Greek god should bow to his feet, but I don't tell him that.

"Where's Gage?" He sears my cheek with the question.

"Chloe—she's probably telling him off, or vice versa. I didn't feel like sticking around for the show." A strangled silence crops up. Now that I've got Logan back, there is so much to talk about it's impossible to know where to begin. "Hey," I jump. "I thought of a way you might be able to save the bowling alley."

"Please, share," he gives a little laugh.

"You could tie in the pizza kitchen to every school lunch program on the island." I leave out the part of me accusing Chloe of coming up with it. Technically it was me who had the stroke of brilliance.

"You, Skyla Messenger, are a genius."

I relax my head back and laugh. "I've been called many things, genius is not one of them."

Logan offers a quiet smile. He draws me in with his steely gaze, makes my heart skip a beat.

"You wanna take a walk?" He nods down a path that leads into the woods.

I take up his hand and we head into the forest, the thicket entombs us with a quiet calm, a stark contrast to the bad eighties music that's hijacked the speakers inside.

The moon glows above the mist, soft as a lamplight.

"God, that feels good," Logan takes in a full breath.

"What feels good?" I stroke his hand with my thumb. It's so nice to have him back inside his beautiful body.

"Air in my lungs," he presses the back of my hand to his lips, "but now you've eclipsed that." Logan sears into me with his ironclad gaze. He galvanizes himself around my soul, fills me from the inside with all of his formidable splendor. I know damn well it could be dangerous heading into the woods—heading anywhere with Logan on a night like tonight, when I have him back, when I want him so bad.

The wind picks up, brushes against us as we move through the forest. An entire herd of Transfer transplants whir past us, frenetic, chatting a mile a minute.

"What the...?" Logan turns and watches them head towards the resort.

"They're everywhere. There were a million at prom," I shrug. "Marshall's got it under control." I don't know that I really believe it, but I'm determined to let him work his black magic, and I'm going to stay the hell out of the situation.

We head further into the shadowed woods. Even the thin veil of moonlight is defused by the dark expanse. Each towering evergreen stands at attention, the blade-like tips of their branches extend, sharp as bayonets.

We stray hand in hand, make our way through a maze of tree trunks until the noise dissipates completely from the ballroom, all that's left is the sound of our breathing.

Logan takes my hand and places it over his chest. I can feel his heart thump wild and erratic from underneath his shirt.

"It beats for you, Skyla," his voice dips into its lower register.

He didn't need to go there. His presence alone seduced me.

"I need to get back." I try to turn my head towards the resort but I can't look away. It's like a car accident waiting to happen with Logan. I know I should run—Chloe loves the wreckage.

Logan steps in, backs me into a tree—grazes his face against my cheek, takes in the scent of my neck.

"I couldn't feel you," he whispers. "You weren't real to me," it comes out almost inaudible as though it were never meant for my ears.

"I'm here," I whisper soft as a lullaby and pull him in. It feels good holding Logan like this. Reassuring him everything is going to be all right because Holden isn't wearing him like a coat anymore.

"Being apart from you made me realize what hell it would be to live without you," he shakes his head when he says it. "I'm going to fight for you, Skyla."

I glance back at the Madison Lights Ballroom, which has become a mere orb of light smothered in a thicket of fog.

"Gage," I whisper. Gage is my life raft—my forever. A horrible sadness comes over me, thick as lead, knowing that I can't have Logan if I have Gage and vice versa.

Obviously the Decision Council knows nothing about love and everything about rotten timing or they never would have put two wonderful people in my life at once.

"You know," I whisper, "sometimes, I really hate my mother."

The whites of his eyes glint. Logan shakes his head as if I should never have gone there.

A dull sound whips through the air, cuts through the wind as it fast approaches. A horrific thud erupts in the trunk of the tree just inches above our heads.

"Shit!" I hiss, jumping away from ground zero. "What the hell was that?"

Logan nods up at a silver hatchet artfully lodged in the timber.

"*Mine*," a frazzled voice echoes from behind.

"We have to go," I pull Logan by the arm and run blindly in the other direction.

Ezrina appears like a crimson stain, blocks our path at every turn—her image splinters in each direction like a funhouse mirror.

"What does she want?" Logan pants, holding me as she stalks us from afar.

"She wants, me."

expel

A bird screams in the night. The rustle of wings brings Nevermore straight to my shoulder. He lets out a series of aggressive cries before settling in, sinks his talons through the fabric of Gage's jacket until he hits my flesh with a sharp bite.

"Trial?" Ezrina pounces forward. Her girth alone produces a solid thump.

"My mother's working on it." Even I know that's bullshit. The one time I asked for help she outright evaded the answer.

"Your mother?" Ezrina steps forward, the dowager hump on her back pronounces itself like a stone laid under her cloak.

There it is—I take her all in. The gnarled fingers, the spasms of endless wrinkles that encase her eyes, her lips—hair like twisted wire hangers. My future is laid out before me, and it appears my mother couldn't care less. I bet she's already seen it, read it like a book—the Ezrina years. My forever will be spent wrapped in a curse that was never intended for me.

"My mom wants to talk to you herself," I say, backing up with Logan. I'd gladly sic Ezrina on my mother. Now there's a showdown I'd love to watch—lightning bolts and hatchets flying every which way.

"Liar," she reaches up and snatches a branch right off the tree, thick as a leg.

"Shit," I hiss.

"Time," she takes a bold step forward, holds out a crooked hand and inspires Nev to scream out at her.

"Get Marshall," I whisper to Logan in a panic.

"I'm not leaving." He tightens the grip around my waist, annunciating the fact.

"I have Nev, just go," my chest heaves wild with alarm. The last thing in the world I want is for Logan to take off, but I need some celestial tap dancing and he just isn't going to cut it. "Please, I'm begging you. I brought you back—now I'm begging you to help *me* stay."

"No," he whispers it so low I barely make out the word.

"He's behind us in the ballroom, grab him and drag him back out here. Just go—*run!*" I shout, pushing him away.

"I'll be back in less than ten seconds. Don't move," he fixes his eyes on me with determined aggression. "You can count to ten. I will be back." His voice strangulates tight as a wire as he darts his anger towards Ezrina.

Logan melts into the anemic teal fog, disappears like a dream—leaves me swimming in a nightmare.

Ezrina, lunges forward, snatches a fistful of hair from the back of my head and breathes her putrid stench over me.

"Nev!" I cry out, my voice trails through the forest like a siren.

Nevermore flutters into the air, dive-bombs Ezrina with peck after peck.

"You're going to judge me?" She shouts into him. "You never had a day of labor! You know not strife—I will not allow you to judge me!" She swats him full force as he continues his aggressive assault.

Maybe this is Nevermore's plan to save me, or maybe they really are having the argument of a lifetime.

I don't really care.

Instead, I disappear.

89

Eye Hate You

I don't stick around to evaluate the situation. I take off running, hitting tree after tree, trying to navigate my way through the disorienting maze of the forest.

Ezrina's voice dissipates to a whisper. Nev's high-pitched cries melt into the vaporous night.

I clasp onto the smooth trunk of a Birchwood tree and try to control my erratic breathing. A gurgle of laughter bubbles up from the ground.

"Fuck off, Messenger," a female voice snipes from behind.

I turn abruptly to find Nat and Pierce intertwined. Her dress is severely twisted and his shirt is unbuttoned halfway.

"Maybe she'd like to join in?" Pierce hops to his feet with a crooked grin on his face. It's obvious he's drunk or high or simply hopped up on the fact he's a Kragger.

"No, really I wouldn't." I push my way past him, but he snatches me back by the wrist. "Let go," I squeal, trying to free myself from his grasp.

"I'm not letting go," he grits it out through his teeth. Pierce pulls me in with a bionic force as he runs his tongue up the side of my cheek.

"Gross," I squirm in his arms, "Nat? Are you going to just sit there?"

"Hey, let go of her. Don't be an asshole," Nat bleats, still firmly planted on the ground.

"You heard her, asshole," I hiss in his face.

"Did you know I have less than twelve hours before I have to turn myself in to authorities?" The unmistakable stench of alcohol sears across my face. "I'm not walking the stage at graduation—instead, I'm going to be locked up on some legal timeout all because of your sorry ass." He slips a hand underneath my dress and glides it over my thigh.

"Don't touch me!" I swat him away and manage to wrangle free a moment, only to have him pin my hands behind my back—my chest pushed hard into the trunk of a serrated pine.

"Nat?" I drill it through my lungs but she's nowhere to be found.

I twist around and try to wrangle free. Pierce knocks my head back by way of an intrusive kiss—thrusts his tongue down my throat so far I retch into his mouth.

He's all hands. His hot mouth emits a grotesque odor and I just want to kill him.

My blood boils. For the first time in a long while my anger builds on its own reserves, ratchets up my strength without relying on Chloe to kick-start the motor.

I give a viral shove into his chest and he takes me to the ground with him.

"Skyla?" It's Logan. My name reverberates from somewhere far off in the woods.

Pierce pegs me underneath him, lands hard on my chest and dives into me again with his unwanted affections.

"Skyla?" Logan's voice trails to nothing as he veers in the wrong direction.

Pierce burrows into me. I twist my head away from his disgusting mouth and let out the beginnings of a scream before he slaps a hand over my lips. I clamp my teeth down over his fingers, give one powerhouse bite that tears through tendons, sends a salty taste into my mouth.

"You bitch!"

My hands fly up over my head. Pierce locks me down with his arms and legs, pins me so efficiently with his own otherworldly strength, I'm no match against him.

A flash of pain ignites at the base of my neck as he grazes along my skin with his knife-sharp teeth.

I can feel the puncture—feel the suction as he draws out my blood in smooth even pulls. His Adam's apple rises and falls against my skin, his arousal made evident by the bulge pressed against my thigh. His fingers begin to loosen their grip on me.

The soft flutter of wings gets my attention. Nev procures a spot on a branch, high up above me.

I need Nev more than ever before.

Pierce groans with pleasure, his defenses weakened if only for a moment, and I slip my hands out of his grasp and wrap an arm around his head. I coil myself over his face like a serpent. It was his neck I was going for but he flinched.

"Shit!" He snatches for my hand but I pinch into his cheek, claw my nails like digging into a chalkboard. It's a morbid slow pull as he tries to remove my death grip. I may never outrun or out muscle his Countenance abilities, but I'm sure as hell not letting go of the only stronghold I have.

Pierce groans in agony as he summons the strength to break my hold. I land my fingers over his eyelid—dig into his socket until I can feel his eye push back.

"Let go!" he shouts. The command vibrates off my chest.

I can't. I'm too far-gone, too lost in all of this bullshit, boiling mad, so ready for revenge against the miserable Kraggers and their asshole relations.

My fingers push into the soft round tissue. Instinctively I retract my hand and his eyeball comes out with me.

"Shit!" I sit up in horror. "Oh my, God! Oh my, God!"

Pierce slumps over, groaning—smacks the ground a few good times before passing out.

"I'm so sorry," I pant staring at the mass of bloodied flesh.

Nev swoops down and bobs his head into the palm of my hand, feasts on the eye, gobbling it down in three swift bites.

"You ate it!" I scream, wiping my bloody hand in a bed of pine needles. "That's so freaking disgusting!"

"Skyla?"

My name expels from the woods in a strange groan, as if an animal were trying to mimic the sound. I've heard it that way before in the Transfer only then it was a—

A small army of mutilated Fems appear—every one of them dressed to impress as Demetri the clown. Pale white faces, hair sizzling into the night, each of them equipped with a long shining blade.

This is probably Ezrina's way of getting me back to the chop shop—in pieces.

I back up on my heels until I right myself.

"This isn't happening," I whisper. "This isn't real." If I believe this, accept it on any level I'll die, only I won't, really die, and that's not fair.

"Skyla?" My name echoes into the night.

It's either Logan or Gage it's too frantic to tell. And where the hell is Marshall? Herding the lost souls of the Transfer around Paragon like some demonic shepherd?

I reach down to grab a stick, a rock, anything, and touch down on Pierce's hairy leg instead. I don't overanalyze, or create a roster full of strategies. I simply give one hearty roar as I pick Pierce Kragger up by the ankles and spin him Mach 5 like a helicopter blade. I knock the clown Fems on their unsuspecting asses, easy as knocking back bowling pins. Pierce doesn't make a sound, simply falls limp—pliable to my every whim.

They come after me one by one, and I shoot them down, swinging Pierce Kragger around like my own private baseball bat.

One of them grabs me by the ankles and lands me hard on my side. I pull Pierce over me as a shield in time to see the carbon blade of a knife plant itself into his back.

"Shit!" I cower beneath him as warm blood pools over my dress. "Mother!"

expel

If there were no Marshall, no Logan, no Gage, no earthly savior, then my last breath would go to her. She witnessed the first gasp that filled my lungs—it's only fair she hears the last.

A strangled silence fills the woods.

A slow applause builds in rhythm as it emanates from above. I squint past Pierce's broad shoulders to see exactly who is applauding my efforts.

I give a depleted smile. "It's you."

90

Borrowed Time

A bloom of fog lifts from around her feet. Her dark cloak hangs loose over her hunched shoulders—Ezrina.

"Expecting someone else?" She says it low, without the echo that peppers her speech.

I dart a quick look around to find the forest void of Fems in any shape or size. Pirece gurgles as the final reserve expires from his lungs. I roll him off in haste and pant into the carnage I'm suddenly responsible for.

"Dead as a doornail," she laments. "You have much blood on your hands. Remedy your ills, come to me child." She takes a careful step in my direction.

Everything in me sags. I'm heavy laden on the inside from the blood Pierce managed to purge from me before I plucked his eyeball right out of his skull.

I pull myself to my knees—bow my head in retreat.

There is no greater sorrow than that of surrender.

Ezrina was right, who else would come for me? Logan? Gage? Even so, what could they possibly do to rectify the situation?

Her hand falls over my neck, lays over my flesh cold as a blade.

"Pulchra mulier," Ezrina sings the words, slow—morbid as a eulogy.

"I failed," a puff of velum escapes my lips. "I couldn't get you a trial. I have nothing." No mother to help me, no earthly father who could pull a few heavenly strings.

"Come," she helps me up. The night mist enrobes me, cleanses me like only the truth can do.

Ezrina pulls back my hair, extends my neck so taut the fresh wound Pierce inflicted stings like a sunburn.

My neck releases, I open my eyes to find Ezrina gone. I loathe to look down and confirm that the transformation has already taken place. My arms rise—far lighter than the last time I donned her like a bad Halloween costume.

"It's me," I whisper disbelieving. "I'm still here."

"And here you will remain." My mother glows ethereal, illuminating an aura of iridescent light. A pink haze surrounds her, lays over her skin like a bruise.

"You came!" I run over and wrap my arms around her tight. Perfect love emanates off her being, vibrates through me, pleasant, welcome as water to this thirsty soul. "So Ezrina gets her trial?" Maybe it's already happened?

"Yes, and no it hasn't. I've scheduled a hearing post faction war. There is much to be considered."

"Oh, thank you!" I jump up and down, taking her with me for the ride. It feels so good like this I never want to let go.

"You've killed another," she sighs, wrapping an arm around my waist as we step over to Pierce.

"Oops?" Not quite sure what to say to that.

"And his eye," she tisks at the sight.

"I'm sorry." It hits me hard like an unexpected wave. My personal death toll rises—Chloe—Kate, Holden, and now his brother, too.

"An apology won't be necessary. This was ordained."

Pierce groans, his body twitches before he fully rolls over, vomits onto the ground.

I jump and scream, ducking behind my mother for cover.

"I thought you said he was dead!" I disrupt the silence for miles.

"He is—the world won't miss him." She steps in further. "Holden, however, gets to live out the rest of his days as his twin. He shouldn't be a bother to you anymore." She waves her hand and he evaporates, still gyrating from the severe case of upchuck.

515

"Where'd he go?" I take in a quick breath not sure whether to panic or cheer.

"He's turning himself into the detention facility. The infirmary just had a bed open up."

"Can you help Mia?" I plead, squeezing her hands.

"Mia is safe."

"Safe as in?" I'm pretty sure she thought I was safe while I was held captive in the Transfer.

"Why, yes, I did believe you to be safe in Sector Marshall's care."

Sector Marshall.

"Nice." I take in all of her immortal beauty. "So you're here to right all the wrongs in the world? I can get used to this." I see my own face radiating back at me like a reflection. She is neither human nor Nephilim, but a perfect Caelestis. "Would you do one more thing for me? Well, not really for me, for Logan?" Already she's done enough, but I'd hate myself if I didn't ask.

"What would that be?" Her eyes soften over my features. They sparkle a brilliant shade of violet before returning to their natural cellophane state.

"Give him back all of his Celestra powers. Please, I beg of you."

"Reinstated." She blinks a benevolent smile.

"Just like that?"

"Just like that." Her demeanor changes, her mood polarizes and there's a darkness that coats her, dims the light she radiates like covering a lamp. "I must go. Do you remember what I told you a few months back about trust?"

I consider this a moment. "You said, trust is a word humans dangle in front of one another as a threat to get what they want."

She gives an approving nod. "And after that?"

"Trust only your heart."

"Words from your own lips, Skyla. Believe them."

expel

I run into Logan just shy of the resort.

"Skyla," he wraps his arms around me, gives a searing kiss just above my temple.

"Where's Marshall?" I look past his shoulder for a moving herd of Transfer transplants.

"Couldn't find him." His eyes rove over me pensive. "I swear I looked everywhere. I wasn't giving up."

"I was with my mother." I glance up at him.

"Everything OK?" He runs his hands up and down my arms making sure it's still me.

"Ezrina gets her trial."

"Yes!" Logan spins me through the air, lands me soft on the ground before taking me in, his grin melting into a gentle sorrowful smile. "And we'll win the war."

"We're not doing so good," I remind him.

"We'll do better." He wraps an arm around my waist. "Rumor has it you're my queen."

"I am."

"Music's still going. I think we should honor the long standing tradition of first dance." Logan looks into me full of hope—hope that far exceeds anything a dance could ever offer.

I don't tell him that I technically already danced with him as Holden tonight, that Chloe stole the show by hanging from the ceiling.

"I definitely think a dance is in order," I say. "And, Logan?" I step in still holding his hands. *I asked my mother to reinstate your powers.*

His ears peak back, his lips part as he takes a breath.

"I heard you," he whispers. *Skyla.* His cheek curls on the side as he takes me in. *I don't know how to thank you. I would have never asked you to do that.*

I know, I say. *I'm sorry I had them taken away to begin with. Will you forgive me?*
There's nothing to forgive.
Gage calls my name in the distance.
"We'd better get back," the words puff out, each their own cloud. "It's time to get Mia."

91

Know the Enemy

The face of the moon is stained with a blood-soaked fingerprint. It is openly red-faced, embarrassed to witness and know the things it does. It winks in and out of the fog like some lunar alarm trying to let us in on the magnitude of its intimate knowledge, but we can't hear. It whispers to us all of its secrets but our ears are stopped up. The ocean drowns out the sound, drenches the night with its own private lullaby. *Trust only your heart,* the ocean sings. It vibrates through the trees, creates a choir with the leaves, strums through the dips and valleys of the island until even the wind is lashed into submission, bleating out my mother's verse.

Logan and I emerge from the forest hand in hand, with Logan happy to have his Celestra abilities back and me just happy to have Logan.

"Gage!" I shout as I catch him in a thicket of miniature palms still sweating out a conversation with Chloe. Dear God, had I known he was far too nice to abandon the effort, I would have made it a point to rescue him earlier.

I jump up over to him and plant a kiss right on his lips.

Chloe shoots him a look, her lips curved in a malevolent smile.

"Did you remove the binding spirit?" As far as I'm concerned there's only one right answer. If Chloe refuses, I'll gladly feed Nevermore a couple more occipital photoreceptors for dinner.

"She can't get out Skyla," Chloe steps forward. "The only one who can help is Mr. Edinger," she lays it on thick as frosting. One false inflection and she would break—die laughing at my sister's dilemma. "You have to do something.

Go to him and beg him to get her out. It's hell in there, Skyla. I saw it myself."

I take in a breath and turn to Gage.

"We need to find Demetri," I pant. The world is closing in on me. I can feel the sky collapsing, the ground rising to meet it. I can't take another Messenger family tragedy, another bear trap we've stepped into because of the Counts, the Fems—Demetri. I can feel the lure, see the trail of breadcrumbs Chloe has set out for me, plain as day, but for Mia I'd walk blindfolded into the witch's oven—hell, I would run.

"I know where he is," Logan injects. "The elders are required to keep watch at the stone of sacrifice until midnight."

"It's midnight now," Chloe is quick to offer.

"Gage," I latch onto his hand and take up Logan with the other. Chloe slaps her hand over his shoulder as the world explodes into a black ball of dust.

Gage teleports us to a field just shy of the stone of sacrifice under the trace of a sanguine moon. It knew we would come, that evil would call us into its presence—require our attendance at this late hour.

"There he is," Gage wraps his arm around my waist, secures me in the comfort of his being. I could face Chloe and the Counts, every Fem on the planet with Gage by my side.

"There he is, Skyla," Chloe's voice emits like a demonic echo.

"Come on," Logan pats me on the back and leads us through a well-beaten trail. Logan knows the way. Logan always knows.

Three figures, still clad in their ritual cloaks, stand not too far from the sacrificial stone that gleams with pride, wings wide open under the powder white breath of God.

This all brings back memories of last winter. *We are the immortals*—that's how their boastful chant begins. I have never forgotten those words that the Counts sung in unison as they circled around my body. Logan's voice and Chloe's both in concert with the rest of the Counts. I remember that night like it was only moments before. Fear will do that to you—tattoo an unwanted memory right over the fabric of your soul, make you recall it at your weakest moment.

The Countenance believe they rule the world, this one, and the next. It's laughable, but if the faction war keeps going in the direction that it is, they just might have it all.

The three of them turn—stop their conversation midflight. I'm not surprised to see Demetri, Arson Kragger, and Ellis's dad.

"The congregation has arrived," Demetri holds back a laugh. His eyes never surrender their nefarious smile. "To what do we owe the assembly?"

I'm speechless—suddenly all too aware of where I am, where I may have inadvertently led, Logan and Gage.

"Marshall? Mom?" I whisper, inaudible, even to my own ears.

"Neither can help you here," Ellis' father steps out from Demetri's shadow and approaches me. "Morley," he extends his hand. "I'm afraid my son doesn't understand the merit of a proper introduction. He doesn't understand the merit of a myriad of things, but that's neither here nor there." He twitches his cheek and looks decidedly like Ellis in the process. "He is a traitor," he hisses. "My own son has turned against me—fights for the band of wickedness that is Celestra."

Wickedness that is Celestra? The idea alone disorients me. And I would expect nothing less than a binding spirit from this brood of vipers. I'm just surprised there's one strong enough to hold Marshall at bay.

"Mia's in the mirror," my chest heaves as I dart the words to Demetri.

Arson Kragger raises his pale brows, somber, as if this were startling news even to him.

Demetri glides a knowing smile in Chloe's direction.

"That's right," Chloe sings.

"Well done." Demetri doesn't sound impressed, in fact he sounds downright pissed. He turns towards Arson. "How are the supplies?"

"Low," he emits the same husky rasp as Pierce. "People are thirsty. The blood of a pure would more than replenish the reserve." He swallows down a laugh before blinking over at me. "You took my son."

"Pierce," I spit his name out, "Holden, he's back." My heart races, pulsates through my ears. It disables any capability in me to carry out a full sentence.

"Never mind those fools," Demetri growls, "we need blood and you need Mia." He bends over and picks up a long rapier off the edge of the stone. Its blade illuminates a bold electric blue before retracting, gleaming in this dim light.

"Spirit sword," I say under my breath. It's three times as long as Marshall's, half as thick. It gives a darker, more seasoned hue than I've ever seen the spirit sword produce.

"Up, Skyla," Demetri taps the tip of the blade against the stone, igniting a crackle of lightning throughout the rock. The landscape glows with a brilliant shock from the disarming display of power.

"No," Logan jumps onto the granite, "take me. My powers have been restored. I'm stronger than ever."

"You're a Count." Arson looks bored by the performance.

"Doesn't matter"—he pants—"take my blood. I pledged my allegiance to the Countenance, and that's where it'll remain." His chest expands and retracts, as he seethes the words. "Drain me. Keep me alive for a lifetime—two lifetimes." Logan redirects his attention to me. "Leave Skyla alone," he swallows hard, washing the stone with his heavy gaze.

"As you wish." Demetri flickers a disgruntled smile.

"No," I say, trying to push Gage off my waist, but he clamps down strong as a vice.

"Let him do this." Gage scorches my ear with his breath.

"Yes, Skyla." Chloe settles herself between Arson Kragger and Morley Harrison. She shoulders up, shakes out her long dark tendrils victoriously. "Let Logan die in your place like the coward you are."

My heart sinks at the idea of Logan suffering, spending the length of his days locked as a prisoner, kept alive for the commodity of his blood. I would have never restored his powers, never begged my mother to do a damn thing in his favor if I had known where it would have gotten him. I bet she's laughing her Caelestis ass off.

If she's so all knowing—if she's responsible even remotely for leading me down this misguided path, I'll declare war on the Justice Alliance and overthrow the whole council if I have to, in order to bring her down.

"What's the matter, Skyla?" Chloe takes a step forward. "Captures' got your tongue?"

Demetri steps onto the stone, prods Logan in the back with the tip of his blade.

"Lay your eyes on her one last time," Demetri instructs. "Memorize the look of fear in her eyes. When you're writhing in agony, you can recall how it was all worth the effort. And who knows?" He takes a careful step in towards Logan. "You might find comfort in the fact that Skyla will be spending her days and nights in the arms of the one you thought a brother."

It's OK, Gage brushes a kiss over my cheek. *Logan wants to do this. He wants you to be safe. I'll keep you safe.*

Chloe gives a hard sigh. "You don't need to be a mind reader to know he's filling your head with empty promises," she bristles.

"Enough," Demetri wields his sword in her direction. "I've had it with your self glorification." His features sharpen, his entire person glowers at her. "I will have her life in my time, in the manner in which I choose. I need no assistance from an underling whose moral victories rely solely on treason." The long sword gleams pridefully into the night, spirit sword blue.

"I laid her at your feet," Chloe has the balls to spout off.

"Your best maneuvers were mine," Demetri snaps. "I brought her to the island, I gifted you her blood. Your victories are shallow at best, blinded by your undying affection for the one who holds her now."

Chloe winces as if he'd slapped her for all to see. "I've got Gage," her voice trails, unrelenting. "*I* brought Skyla to the island, *I* robbed her of her blood from the grave." She steps in closer, glares into me with an intimate level of hate that I have never experienced before. "I set in her life, one well-placed boyfriend." She presses out a black smile.

"Looks like your secret is out," Demetri nods into Gage, his eyes wild with pleasure.

Gage gives into a long blink, his dimples go on and off like an alarm.

I shake my head. "Say it's not true."

Gage takes a breath and holds it a second too long. He sets his gaze in the forest just past my shoulder before locking me in on a nonverbal apology.

"Oh, Gage," it comes out barely audible. I close my eyes a moment and draw a black curtain over this newfound misery. "Damn it," I push him off, full with disappointment. I leap up onto the stone and shield myself over Logan.

"Can't move my arms or legs," Logan shivers out the words in a whisper.

expel

My body seizes, useless as tree limbs.

"Skyla don't!" Gage shouts. "It's a trap." The rock electrifies on the outer rim, forming a crackling barrier as a ring of lightning pens me in.

He did this. Let the record show, Gage punctured our relationship with a knife-sharpened blade the day he made a pact with Chloe Bishop to be my well-placed anything. The mortal blow being he conveniently forgot to cite any of the aforementioned bullshit, this entire past year.

"You lied to me." I can't believe the words as they sail from my lips.

"No, I swear, I didn't. I never lied."

"He just avoided the subject, Skyla," Chloe is quick to inject. "You of all people should understand how complex the truth can be."

I can't look at Gage. My heart breaks at the thought of him working with Chloe on any level. There was no way she could have blackmailed him right from the beginning. But, even still, I can feel his love for me—the soothing balm that tries to penetrate this newfound ache.

"I love you forever, Skyla," his voice hums through the night as if he had released a whisper that swam right into my ear.

"Skyla," Demetri prods me with the metal saber, motions for me to turn around and face Logan, and I spin involuntarily. "Ms. Bishop," he points the blade in her direction and Chloe is quick to appear by my side, spirit sword in hand. Figures—Chloe has no problem walking through a wall of raging electricity.

The wind picks up. A blue mist covers us, thick as oil.

"Why don't you leave this world with a kiss," Chloe pushes into Logan's head with the sword until he brushes his lips against mine.

We'll be OK, Logan assures. Although at the moment it doesn't feel so convincing with both our bodies in lockdown—a nest of lightning separating me from Gage.

"What's the codeword?" Demetri twirls his hand in the air, enjoying his taunt.

He was there in the Transfer.

Of course, he was. I saw him there myself.

"Oh, I'm dying to hear this," Chloe laughs. "Aren't *you*, Gage? Aren't you dying to hear what the procreators have been saying to each other? Don't you think that's a great idea, Mr. Edinger? You could have the two perfect Celestra mate. You can drink the blood of their children."

"Always thinking, Ms. Bishop." He cuts a dark smile over at me.

"The code?" Chloe digs the spear into Logan's back.

"Happily ever after," Logan expels with a sigh.

Gage steps into my line of vision, gives a slow blink when Logan says it. He eyes Demetri and Chloe like a predator waiting for just the right moment to pounce.

I look away not wanting to try and decipher whether or not he's in pain, not wanting him to see mine. It was Gage who saved Chloe tonight, it was Gage who held her hand, partook in a rather lengthy conversation with her while I was in the forest—Gage who was revealed to be the well-placed boyfriend. What does it mean? He was my forever, and none of this was real.

My mother's words come back to me—*trust only your heart*. She knew. She could see the deception from the throne room. This secret was only well guarded from me.

"Take me to Mia," I blink back tears and inhale my resolve. This isn't about me, or my wayward love life. It's about saving my sister.

"I'll give you one last chance, Skyla," Demetri lowers his head. "Assure the young man his chivalry was well worth the effort—go home."

"No," I swallow hard. "It's me who gets taken. If anyone gets to go home its Logan."

"He stays," Demetri is quick to answer.

"Then I stay with him."

expel

"That's right, proclaim your love for Logan," Chloe chides. "See Gage? You were right. She will never get over him. Oh, and, Skyla?" She digs something out of her heart-shaped purse, "I seem to have stumbled upon Melissa's phone." She tosses it over to my feet. "Can you make sure she gets it?"

Shit.

I look up at Logan in horror. She did this to us. She hooked us and reeled us in, shot us down like fish in a barrel.

"Skyla," Gage wastes no time.

"Save it." I might crack. I might lose my mind and bawl like a baby right here on this rock—I just pray to God it opens up and swallows me like a bad dream.

Gage jumps onto the stone, and a jolt of electricity crackles through him. It illuminates him from the inside as if he were his own universe, his body broken with bolts of lightning. He lets out a groan and struggles his way over, takes a breath as his body is restored, resplendent and new.

"There's something you need to know." He takes me up by the waist without permission, looks into me with those sacred blue eyes before touching my hand. *Those people who came from the Transfer were here for a reason. Chloe brought them.*

I try to wrangle my hand loose from his grasp, but he latches on tighter.

There's a bloodbath coming for Celestra. Chloe gave them the walking tour of your home, the school. She made sure they saw you crowned as prom queen. Come home with me.

"Go home, Skyla," Logan pleads.

A searing pain shoots through my stomach and exits my back.

"Too late," Chloe growls.

Logan and I look down, take a breath and hold it simultaneously.

"Skyla," Gage breathes my name as if he were grieving me.

The blade protrudes from Logan and skewers right through me. Logan's white shirt blooms with color, my dress is quick to gloss over around the newfound incision.

She's done this—Chloe holds the blade into Logan's back and pushes it in, moves it around until he cries out from the pain.

Gage knocks Chloe down with his shoulder and wraps his fingers around the handle of the rapier. A storming seizure electrifies his body, as the sword ignites a velvet blue.

Chloe jumps to her feet, wastes no time in relaxing her arms over Gage, causing his body to stop seizing from the electric shock. He removes his hands from the sword and exhales in exhaustion.

Logan and I illuminate from the inside a perfect sterile blue. My body trembles, a warm buzz vibrates throughout my veins, carbonates my blood. I look past Logan's shoulder at my beautiful Gage, my helper, my everything, my deceiver and mouth the words, *help me—my forever.*

Chloe lights up the fog between us with her anxious breath. "Here's to happily ever after."

The stone opens up, swallows Logan and me—the blade still skewering us together, holding us secure.

"*Skyla!*" Gage's voice goes off like a gong, reverberates through this timeless tunnel of embers in one desperate cry.

Logan wraps his arms around me, pulls me in until his lips crash against mine.

We fall forever.

We search for happily ever after, but it never comes.

Thank you for reading, **Expel (Celestra Series Book 6).** If you enjoyed this book, please consider leaving a review at your point of purchase.

*Look for the next book in the Celestra Series, **Toxic Part One (Celestra Series Book 7).**

About The Author

Addison Moore is a *New York Times*, *USA Today*, and *Wall Street Journal* bestselling author who writes contemporary and paranormal romance. Her work has been featured in *Cosmopolitan* Magazine. Previously she worked as a therapist on a locked psychiatric unit for nearly a decade. She resides on the West Coast with her husband, four wonderful children, and two dogs where she eats too much chocolate and stays up way too late. When she's not writing, she's reading.

Feel free to visit her at:

http://addisonmoorewrites.blogspot.com
Facebook: Addison Moore Author
Twitter: @AddisonMoore
Instagram: @authorAddisonMoore

Printed in Great Britain
by Amazon